GEMINI WITCHING

ELEMENTS 101

ROBERTA J GORDON

Gemini Witching
Elements 101

Roberta J Gordon

ISBN:
978-0-615-73435-4

Version 2- Re-Edited 2019

Dedication and Acknowledgements:

IT GOES WITHOUT SAYING THAT IT TAKES A VILLAGE. I DEDICATE THIS BOOK TO ALL THE STRONG FEMALE INFLUENCES I HAVE HAD IN THE COURSE OF MY LIFE THUS FAR, THOSE LIVING AND THOSE PASSED ON, FROM MY MOTHER AND HER SISTERS TO THE LIFETIME FRIENDSHIPS I HAVE MADE, ESPECIALLY TONYA, SUZAN, JOANN, SHELLI, LISA, CYNDI, AND JR.

IN THE PROCESS OF PREPARING THIS BOOK A NUMBER OF PEOPLE HAVE LOANED ME THEIR SKILLS AS CREATIVE INFLUENCES, EXPERTS AND READERS. THANK YOU ALL FOR YOUR HELP AND SUPPORT: KENDRA FOSTER, LINDA DEPRIEST, MICHELE LAX, DONALD & MALINDA SANDLIN, CASEY MYERS, LORI REHN, AND TERESA MASON.

FINALLY A HUGE THANK YOU TO MY FAMILY WHOM WITHOUT THE SUPPORT OVER THE PAST YEARS I COULD NOT HAVE MADE THIS HAPPENS.

CONTENTS

Sam 101	1
Sam 102	9
Sam 103	16
Sam 104	40
Sam 105	56
Sam 106	73
Emily 101	93
Emily 102	98
Emily 103	105
Emily 104	126
Emily 105	143
Sam 107	156
Emily 106	161
Sam 108	163
Emily 107	165
Sam 109	173
Emily 108	175
Sam 110	179
Emily 109	189
Sam 111	203
Emily 110	207
Emily 111	220
Sam 112	229
Emily 112	235
Sam 113	238
Emily 113	241
Sam 114	251
Emily 114	257
Sam 115	262
Emily 115	265
Emily 116	270
Sam 116	275

Sam 117   279
Emily 117   283
Sam 118   285
Sam 119   290
Emily 118   295
Sam 120   306
Emily 119   311
Sam 121   326
Emily 120   333
Emily 121   340

Realm of Lights   345

SAM 101

"*S*am, wake up."

I know I heard it, but man, I didn't really want to wake up. I squeezed myself into a tighter ball, becoming more aware of the cold concrete floor, in a place where I didn't want to be. I wanted to roll over and for this all to be a bad dream. I wanted to burrow under my favorite blanket and hide from the world, hide from what I knew I was about to face...again.

"Come on, Sam, Vicki will be coming in that door any minute. You know she's not going to be happy to see you here again."

Thank God it was Beth who found me this time, I thought as I rubbed my face with both hands, trying to wake up. Stretching, I couldn't tell how long I'd been here this time. If hours, then how many? I remember sitting on my couch last night watching a late movie, and then nothing. I sat up, leaning against the display counter that held all the food items the store carried, and then rubbed my face some more.

"Did you just get here?" I asked, stifling a yawn.

"No, we've been here about twenty minutes." Beth's

voice was more distant this time. I could tell without looking she was at the drive-through window, with her back to me.

"And you just left me here?" I raised my head, feeling the stiffness in my neck.

"Listen, we both know you've not been sleeping well, so I told Dale we'd let you sleep a little longer. Vicki's on early shift this morning too, so you'll want to get up before she comes through the door."

Trust Beth to be looking out for me, I thought, shaking my head to myself. I dropped my head again, arms wrapped around my knees. I figured I could at least take a peek at what clothes I was wearing this time. When I caught a glimpse of denim, I let out a sigh. Oh, my lucky stars. At least I was dressed.

That has been one of my main concerns since I started waking up in odd locations. The most embarrassing one to date was waking up in the student lounge on campus in my pajamas, compounded by the fact that I then had to walk home. Luckily, it had been early enough that traffic was light, and only the early commuters were entertained by my walking the streets ready for bed.

Since that happened, I tried to at least be aware of what I was wearing before I fell asleep. The only downfall today was I didn't have on my shoes. I was mentally giving myself a forehead slap when the bell to the front door dinged. Out of the corner of my eye, I saw Beth stiffen, but she continued with her work.

"Good morning, Vicki," she and Dale called at the same time.

Dale was coming out of the storeroom and stepped wide around me on the floor. His movement drew Vicki's attention straight to where I sat. "What's on the floor, Dale?" she asked.

I could hear her footsteps coming in our direction.

"Oh, not much," he replied.

You could always count on him to downplay any major activity. He could calm down the most irate customers, thus Vicki always wanted him working the morning shifts.

Commuter traffic in the City of Colleges was always heaviest from 6 a.m. until 10 a.m. Starbucks had multiple locations strategically located near the on-ramps for the interstate. Our location, on Highway 65 North, was probably the busiest.

I sat there, dreading Vicki walking around the counter, and I know I tensed my shoulders, thinking I should go ahead and get this over with. "Good morning, Vicki," I said with my head still hanging.

"Sam? Are you here again?" she asked, and her tone was light.

Huh? "Yes ma'am. I guess I am," I replied.

She came into view then, with both hands on her hips. That's all I could see, not wanting to look up and meet her eyes.

"Well, come on. I'll take you home," she said.

Glancing up, I found she was checking the time on her watch.

"Beth, do you think you can handle opening until I get back? I'll take Sam home and be right back."

"Sure. Dale and I have it all under control," Beth said, coming to stand by Vicki.

Dale joined the duo and leaned down to offer me a hand up. I took it along with a deep breath. I knew this was too good to be true. She was too calm.

Vicki didn't say anything until she put the car into park in front of my apartment. "Sam, I don't know what's going on, but we can't let this keep happening. This is the third time this week we've found you asleep in the store," her voice was stern but concerned.

I nodded, looking straight ahead at my front door. I just wanted to get inside.

"Vicki, I'm real sorry. I don't know how I got there either. I know I'm treading on thin ice, so I'll start looking for another job." I really didn't want to lose my job. I loved working at Starbucks. Working there helped me with my caffeine fix as well as earning a paycheck.

"No, Sam, we're not there yet, but it won't be long before I won't be able to help you out anymore. It's time to get help. You need to see a doctor and get help with your sleepwalking," she said, in a lower voice this time.

I glanced up at her, wondering how I was going to pull that off. This was finals week, and I still had a couple of big tests left, not to mention my evening shift at the store. I started to enumerate the reasons why that wouldn't work, but she placed her hand on my shoulder before the words could tumble out.

"Sam, no buts. I know money is tight and time is precious this week. If you want to still have a job, you have to do this. I want you to take the day off," she said, holding up both hands as if to tell me to hush before I could sputter "no," then continued. "Find a doctor. You bring me a note that says you've seen a doctor, and I'll see about letting you come back to work tomorrow. You've been sleeping on that floor too much, so I know you've not had a good night's sleep. This is not a request, Sam," she finished, dropping her hands to grip the steering wheel.

I looked at her for a long time, thinking of how to say what I really felt. She was being decent, but I needed to work. My rent would be due in a few days, and I needed that income.

"Vicki I've never been sick before, that I know of, so I don't know any doctors here except for those I've met in the ER."

"Well, the ER won't see you over this, Sam. You've got to see a GP."

A what? I frowned at the dashboard then. I guess I could dig through the phone book and see if I could find anyone.

"Listen, Sam, my family uses Dr. Hardin. He's an older man, real nice. Look him up when you get inside and call to get an appointment after they open." She was glancing at me sideways now.

I nodded and reached for the door handle, dreading the draw on my bank account. "Thanks, Vicki. I mean it. You've been great about this, and I really appreciate it."

Appreciate being made to spend my dwindling funds to go see a doctor so I could keep my job. Yeah, this was going to be a great day.

Several hours later I sat in the doctor's office, wearing the paper gown. You know the drill. After the nurse had done her triage duties, I was left hanging in the breeze. At least that's what it always feels like to me when you're kept there waiting. I wasn't even sure there was anything the doctor could prescribe for sleepwalking. Hell, I'm not sure why I had to wear the paper gown for the interview, exam, or whatever they want to call it. I'm not happy to be here, but I didn't have a choice. My job was in jeopardy if I didn't keep this appointment, so I was paying dearly for this visit.

College is a financial drain on most students I know. So, while I didn't have the money for this, I couldn't afford to be out of work. Thankfully, it's spring finals week, and I know I can pick up more hours at work next week, which would help me rebound from this healthcare crisis, at least monetarily.

I was nervous, partially nude, and sitting in a paper gown.

Definitely not a happy camper. But, like Vicki said, I had to endure this or be without a job. So, I was stuck. Finally, there was a light tap on the door, followed by the doctor's entrance.

"Samantha, how are you?"

Dr. Hardin was an older man, not overly tall and slightly slack skinned. He looked like a kindly grandfather, one you would see on a Saturday afternoon taking the grandkids to a movie. He extended his hand to shake, which felt clammy and puffy. *Yuck!* I was instantly wincing, wondering why I'd picked this man. Oh, yeah, my boss recommended him.

After greeting me, he sat on his little swivel stool and inquired about the reason for my visit. Some thirty minutes later, he was shaking his head. I, Samantha Carpenter, have the doctor baffled. I'm five foot five inches tall, thin, but not too much so. Let's just say I have curves. I had never been sick in my life, that I knew of. I have, however, had lots of accidents and have been to the ER several times with sprained ankles, cuts from accidental slips with a paring knife, and bicycle wrecks. Those were my normal klutzy misadventures. Other than waking up in some very odd locations, I had no symptoms for my ailment.

Dr. Hardin quizzed me about my sleeping habits. He asked if I was rested when I wake each day, and I always am. Being the health care player that he clearly is, he first suggested I see a specialist and go in for a sleep study. I explained my financial difficulties just paying for his services this fine day, and he took pity on me. He decided to go old school: He told me to keep a diary. He wanted me to write down everything that happened during the day before I go to bed, and where I am when I wake up. I received all this advice for only one hundred eighty dollars. Well, at least I had my note so I could stay employed.

I started my diary that day, or I guess that evening.

Writing down my daily happenings as part of my pre-bed ritual had a surprisingly calming effect on me. Of course, the fact that finals were almost over might have contributed to it also. The hardest tests had been taken, and I was feeling a little less tense. I started writing in my diary while sitting on the couch that night, and the next thing I knew I woke up in my bed the next morning. Maybe that was a good indicator.

The next night, with another test behind me and feeling less stressed, I turned back to my new diary. I reflected on how much I thought the previous night's rehashing of the day may have helped me to at least stay in my own apartment. I started out writing and kind of thinking how this might really help. Laying the notebook—my cheap version of a diary—on my lap, I started to reflect.

This semester was wrapping up quickly, and yet I had another year of school left before finishing my degree. I'd be able to teach junior high history when I finished. The next year would be spent with fewer classes and student teaching in a local school. Man, would I have my work cut out for me.

This summer, I'd have to start developing lesson plans and rubrics for each learning level. Just thinking about planning for the fall made me tense all over. But considering the changes I'd had over the past year, hormonal junior high students might just be a walk in the park.

Suddenly, I thought of Jeff. I missed and hated him all at the same time. How had things gotten so twisted? With the notebook still in my lap, I realized I'd been absentmindedly scribbling on the page I'd just started. I turned to a clean page and started to write while my recall of the events of the past year was still crystal clear.

I poured my heart out to the pages. I must've lost track of time as one blink led to an even greater pause between opening my cycs again. As my eyes started the eerie process of not being able to focus, I sighed and laid my head on the couch, too tired to walk to my bed. *History plays such a large role in shaping our lives:* my last thought before I could no longer open my eyes.

I woke up lying on the couch, with the notebook clutched to my chest. My neck and back were stiff, but I'd stayed in the same location! I didn't sleepwalk at all. Well, if I did, there was no one there to tell me any different. Finals were over, and so was my sleep walking—at least, I prayed so.

I guess there's a lot to be said for stress, I thought as I closed my diary and headed to the kitchen. I needed coffee!

SAM 102

*W*eeks later and still cured of sleepwalking, new worries grew. I was going to have to do something soon about my lack of funds, but I didn't want to think about moving just yet. My apartment was meager at best, and I've never been a decorating diva. I had the basics, and that was it in my one-bedroom, one-bath, ground-level apartment. My part-time job at Starbucks didn't give me enough hours to maintain my apartment, not really, but it fed my addiction to caffeine. I'd leave worrying about moving until the end of the summer, which was only weeks away.

My love of reading was a whole other addiction. Since I'm a poor college kid, I don't have a car. I have a bike, a helmet, and several wrecks under my belt. I've kept the sidewalk busy between the county library, my favorite bookstore, and work. When classes were in session, the route to the campus was added to that path.

On this overcast day, I headed to Hashtags Bookstore, one of my favorite hangouts. It was Monday, the 4th of July, and public buildings were closed for the holiday, so the library wasn't an option. I'd worked the early shift and was now free to waste my holiday. It wasn't too hot outside yet, but I could tell that the mild afternoons we were enjoying wouldn't last much longer.

I parked my bike and envisioned the inside of the bookstore. With a free coffee in hand, I would proceed to stroll the aisles—from romance to sci-fi, it didn't matter; I loved it all. I could find a used book and settle in. Given the book was already used, I'd feel little guilt.

There weren't many people in the store on this holiday, but it felt different as soon as I walked in. It felt crowded, but obviously wasn't as I wandered around mentally ticking off my favorites: Hamilton, Harris, Gabaldon, Kenyon, and Ward.

The hair on the back of my neck started prickling. I glanced around and noticed I had a stalker.

I'd first noticed the attractive lady in the first aisle I ventured down. She was around 5'7" and not super skinny but not as rounded as many women her age.

Of course, the first glance you make when someone enters your personal space (in this instance, my aisle), you smile, nod, and go back to your own business. But this was different. As I went back to my perusal of the books, I felt as if she were still watching me with sideways glances. Now the hair on my arms prickled as well, but how stupid was that? Yeah, I got weird vibes like that occasionally, but didn't everyone?

Today, I decided on Adrian. Ward had commented on the book, so you couldn't go wrong, right? I strolled back to the empty chairs and chose the one closest to the free coffee.

Not totally to my surprise now, my shadow peeked around the end of the aisle. She stood with her back straight and openly surveyed all she could see of the store. Having decided that the coast was clear (if that was her intent), she exhaled loudly, dropped her shoulders, and started walking toward me.

The armchairs in this section were casually arranged for easy conversation, like you'd find in someone's home. When I realized she was walking my way, I ducked my head back into my book. She stopped in front of the other chair and cleared her throat. It's always irritating when you don't want to be disturbed, but southern manners were something I couldn't avoid showing. I glanced up.

"May I?" she asked, indicating the chair.

"Sure," I replied, noticing she wasn't carrying any books. I pasted on the smile I used when greeting customers at work and turned back to my book. "*This is so not right*," was the thought running through my head.

She crossed her legs and arranged her long, billowing gypsy skirt. I was now a little more than irritated and slightly curious where this was going to lead. It didn't take her long to break the silence.

"So, do you come here often?" she asked, placing her elbows on each padded arm of the chair and folding her hands over her stomach.

Mental eye roll. *Great, a chatty Kathy!* "As much as I can," I replied, trying not to look like I was bothered, but I kept my head bent.

She took another long breath, sighed, and then plunged in. "I know you don't know me from Adam, but can we talk?"

It was my turn to sigh now. I closed my eyes briefly and opened them as I raised my head. I leaned back in the chair and forced my smile back in place. "How can I help you?"

I looked up and met her eyes: dark brown with flecks of gold. I took in her loose, wavy, shoulder-length brown hair. She had a kind smile and a twinkle in her eye. She must've been stunning in her younger days.

As I raised an eyebrow and returned to her eyes, I felt captivated. She smiled wider as she took me in as well. My appearance is always lacking. My clothes are clean, but wrinkles don't bother me much. I'm sure others find it off-putting. My hair has always been an unruly, slightly wavy mess. I've never been able to work with it and developed the habit of just tying it back in a ponytail.

A frown slightly creased her forehead, showing more concern than displeasure in what she saw. I really couldn't blame her. She took a deep breath, and the frown which was only present for a moment was replaced by her wide smile, showing her perfect, white teeth.

"You really do look just like her," she started out saying.

"Pardon?" Now it was my turn to glare.

She just shook her head, glancing at her hands. "Never mind, there's plenty of time to discuss that later. My name is Ruth. Ruth White-Oaks."

As she extended her hand out to me, I glanced at her hand then back to her face.

"Sam," I said as I slowly placed my hand in hers.

I'd only meant to make the briefest of contact, but as soon as my hand touched hers, she brought the other on top of mine. She leaned in while clasping my hand, smiling deeply, and I thought I caught the briefest glimpse of a tear in her eyes.

I glanced around to see if anyone else was witnessing this interaction, as the handholding was taking a little longer than needed, especially for introductions.

When I looked back, she was frowning again but looking at our hands. She turned my hand over and slowly withdrew hers, which was on top now. Not that it was unpleasant. When she continued to draw a finger across my palm is when I realized I really couldn't move. Not my hand or my sudden attention, which was now on the way she was taking in the features of my palm. Suddenly, she raised her head and let go of my hand.

"I'm sorry. That was so rude. I don't mean to frighten you." The sadness was replaced by a motherly concern on her features. "It's short for Samantha, is that right?"

"Yeah, it's short for Samantha. Have we met before?" I frowned as her features brightened again.

"Yes, but you were much too young to remember it."

While she was smiling again, a part of me wanted to say she was holding back a certain amount of sadness.

"Really? We've met? Do you mind telling me where?"

I suddenly felt trapped. I'd been raised in foster homes for most of my life. I'd been told that my mother had died during childbirth, and I'd been adopted immediately. The family who had taken me in had a series of accidents and illness that again left me in the foster care system when I was twelve. Not many want to adopt preteens, so I spent the rest of my public-school life moving from one family to the next.

At eighteen the state emancipated me, which had been just a few weeks before high school graduation. The family I'd been staying with allowed me to stay through the summer before I entered college.

Ruth, becoming solemn again, glanced away, dropping her head. "Sam, this may sound odd, but can we go some-place else to talk?" She finished the last of her sentence almost on an exhaled whisper.

"Why do you want to talk to me?" I could feel my irritation starting to show. "I don't know you from Adam, but I get the feeling you've been following me all over this store. How do you know me?"

To say she was nervous now was an understatement. She moved to the edge of her chair, like she'd just decided to leave, but she made no move to stand. She started looking around again, like she was being followed or didn't want our conversation overheard.

"Granted, you don't know me, Sam, but I know you. I was there when you were born. I was also the one to select your adoptive family. I really don't want to go into this here and now. I know that's unnerving for you, but this conversation cannot wait any longer."

I knew the whites of my eyes and the whiplash jerk of my head would have caught the attention of anyone passing by, but as far as I could tell, we were the only ones in the area.

I moved my mouth wordlessly, trying to find which question to start with, because my surprise was monumental. I'd checked the records of my birth and tracked as far as I could to closed adoption records. My fleeting need to find my true family had passed when I turned twenty, realizing I was making my own way in the world.

"Who are you?" was all that I could finally say on an exhaled whisper.

Smiling sweetly, she tilted her head while looking at me. The kind of tilt that asks, *"Which way do I approach this?"*

Finally, she said, "Sam, your mother was my sister."

Certain life lessons teach you how to respond to certain situations. Unfortunately, none of my life lessons had taught me how to respond to this. When you're in and out of foster care, you often dream of being rescued by long-lost relatives. I was dumbfounded. *Here sat my aunt!*

"Not to be rude, and forgive me for being a Doubting Thomas, but how do I know that what you're telling me is the truth?" I thought this was the best way to start: getting the facts.

Again, she came to the edge of her seat, leaning in toward my chair and lowering her voice. "Sam, I really didn't intend for this to unfold this way, but I need for you to trust me. We really do need to talk."

She started glancing around again but kept speaking. "I don't want to continue this discussion here. I know you rode your bike, but maybe I can give you a ride back to your apartment and we can talk there?"

"I don't think so!" Fact finding was over. I was astounded and decided to start voicing that opinion. "Apparently you've been following me for some time if you know I rode my bike here and that I live in an apartment. You wander in here and expect me to walk out with you?"

I rose to my feet, quickly gathering my purse, coffee cup, and book. No need to leave my mess for some store clerk to have to clean. She rose at the same time, possibly sensing my outrage. As I turned to give her a few more of my opinions, she reached out her hand toward my arm. The moment she touched me, the world went dark.

❡

SAM 103

I was having the weirdest dream. I was walking in a field under a scorching summer sky. Funny, I hated the great outdoors. The sky turned black, and lightning started striking all the trees around me. I instantly grew cold. My face was damp, but I'd been sweating, hadn't I? The skies opened to a light rain. How could the weather change so fast?

As I felt the rain on my face, I decided I liked the sunny afternoon better. The thunder and lightning were terrifying, and the hair on my arms was standing up. I heard someone close by murmuring, but I couldn't get away from it. I was turning circles trying to see who was talking so low, but regardless of where I turned, I saw nothing.

I decided I really didn't like this dream. If I just put my hand out, I'd come back from my nap. Moving my hand to my face, I felt a cold wet cloth covering my forehead. This was odd. The last thing I remembered was being at Hashtags, trying to find a book to read. Now I had a compress and I was lying down?

I hate embarrassing situations. Like when you walk out of a restroom and toilet paper is stuck to your shoe. How was I going to open my eyes and deal with everyone at Hashtags standing over me? It was the start of summer and a hot day ahead, but hell, it wasn't even noon. How could I have had a heat stroke this early in the day?

Not wanting to open my eyes, I tried to focus on the sounds around me. Better to know how embarrassed I was going to be. I decided that it was too quiet where I was lying. If I was in Hashtags, where were all the store noises? Then the murmuring started again. Someone gently placed their hand on mine, and my eyes opened immediately.

The voice became clearer as it registered that the stranger from the store was with me, talking. I adjusted my eyes and realized I was in my apartment. *In my apartment with a stalker!* I rose to a seated position too fast, and my head swam. Ruth was sitting on the coffee table in front of me, watching me struggle.

"It's going to be okay, Sam," she stated. "You need to trust me. I couldn't let you leave without trying to explain things to you."

My head was clearer, and I decided I needed distance. Jumping to my feet, I firmly said, "Lady, I don't know who you are, but you need to get the hell out of my house."

I started easing backwards toward my front door. I didn't know how we got to my house, but based on the fact we were here, I now knew she'd been following me. She kept her seat while her eyes tracked my movements.

Not wanting to make any sudden movements, I made sure I took small steps. My apartment is small, so the distance from the couch to the door wouldn't take long. When I was three feet from the door, she started shaking her head and pursed her lips.

"Sam, I know you're upset, but really, this was the only

way. I had to make sure we talked, so I helped you get home."

"You helped me get home? *Right*," I said, still easing toward the door.

When my hand touched the cool metal of the door, I knew I could dash out, but then I realized this was too easy. She just kept sitting and watching me. I could get out and go to the police. Then I'd rush out and find a new apartment. That sounded like a good plan.

I poised myself for the mad dash and turned the knob, but the door wouldn't open. I jerked it as hard as I could, and it wouldn't budge. I whipped around to find her still seated on the coffee table. She'd lowered her head and was filing her nails.

Without looking up, she started again. "Sam, honestly, I didn't want our relationship to start like this. But you can't leave. You can try that door and the back door or any of the windows. You're not going anywhere, so please sit down and let's try this again."

I glanced from her to around my living room. Everything looked the same. I didn't have many furnishings, but they looked just as I remembered. I realized if what she was saying was true, I was trapped. I took a deep breath and stood up straight. Giving a slow nod, I casually strolled around my living room.

"Right," I said as I made my way toward the front window. It was covered with plain mini-blinds she'd apparently closed while I was out of it. And speaking of 'out of it,' how did she knock me out and get me home? I leaned against the wall and crossed my arms over my chest, watching her as she continued with her nails.

"You can watch me, or you can sit back down so we can continue our discussion, but that window isn't going to help you," she said, still not glancing up.

I reached out to move the blinds and met an electrical current that jarred me to reality. Jerking back my hand, I took a step back at the same time.

"What the hell!" That was all I could utter while I rubbed my injured appendage. The sting was still roving up my fingers and lower arm when I turned back to her.

She'd put her file away and crossed her legs. Her eyes were twinkling as if she was amused. Reaching over, she patted the seat cushion of my couch. It was the only piece of furniture you could sit on, but I wasn't willing to give up yet.

"Sam, you have to trust me. I didn't want to use force, but you gave me little choice. That little jolt was just to get your attention. I had to make you believe me, without you getting hurt in the process. Trust me, honey, that was nothing."

"Ruth, I don't know what's going on, but I'd appreciate it if you'd make your point and get the hell out of my house." I was trying for bravery, but I knew my words meant little if she had me trapped in my own house.

The hair on my entire body was standing erect now. *That little jolt was "nothing?"* What the hell was the rest of what I was feeling in the air?

Keeping my back to the wall, where I could watch her, I started side-stepping my way to the kitchen. The whole time, she was shaking her head and *tsk*-ing me.

When I was almost to my tiled kitchen, she said, "I'm warning you, you're not going to enjoy the next surprise when you reach that tile."

That was a threat if I ever heard one. I glanced to the tile of my kitchen floor then back to her. She was watching my every move. The electricity in the air was palpable. I glanced back toward the kitchen, and the doorway *shimmered*; it reminded me of heat rising off the asphalt on a hot summer day.

I decided to take the threat seriously. I glanced back, and Ruth once again patted the seat cushion. Resigned, I took a deep breath. Exhaling with a loud sigh and dropping my shoulders, I edged back to the couch, watching her as I went along.

"Okay, Ruth. How did we get here? You want to start there?"

She turned on the coffee table to face me, using her hands to flatten her jeans on her lap. *Jeans?* She had on a skirt in the store. My stomach started to knot.

"Well, my car was parked outside the store, and I drove us over here," she replied with a side tilt to her head.

Of course, I thought. *Not!* "Well, why don't I remember leaving the store or getting here?"

"Sam, there's so much I have to explain to you, but if it helps, you walked out of the store after we purchased your book. We got in my car, I drove us here, then you walked in," she stated all this like it was an everyday occurrence.

I looked on the table next to her, and there was the book I'd held in my hands when she had introduced herself.

"Okay. To say I'm just a little freaked out would be an understatement." I was running ideas through my head, and none of them I liked. "How about the wardrobe transformation?" I decided to keep throwing out questions, pointing toward her jeans.

"I changed."

"When exactly did you do that?"

"Well, to tell the truth, it was while you were napping." She continued with her pleasant replies as if they were of no consequence to her.

"Why did you think it was necessary to track me down,

kidnap me, and change clothes? You hoping it will throw the police off when they start looking for me?"

She shook her head. "You've not been kidnapped. I know it appears that way to you right now, but no one saw any abduction. They saw two women chatting in a bookstore, make a purchase, and leave the store like old friends." She looked me dead in the eye and continued. "The jolts you've encountered are merely minor, and again, you have not been kidnapped."

Minor? I thought as I raised both eyebrows.

"You were napping for a while, and we missed lunch. Would you like a sandwich? Something to drink?" she asked while glancing over her shoulder toward the kitchen.

My kitchen. She was playing hostess to me in my own house! "Honestly, I don't think I could eat right now, Ruth, so no thanks."

"Suit yourself," she said, and rose from her seat.

Ruth collected her oversized handbag and headed to the kitchen. I heard a cabinet open then close. The drawer for silverware opened likewise. Moments later, she carried out a sandwich that looked like it came from an upscale deli—roast beef and fresh vegetables on a deli-style hoagie roll.

She sat down on the couch next to me, this time using the coffee table as her lunch tray. She had a glass of tea, but I never heard the fridge or freezer open. Not to mention the fact that I didn't have any tea made. Nor did I have any of her sandwich items in my refrigerator. I was lucky if there was a TV dinner in my freezer!

Ruth dove into her food, rolling her eyes after the first bite, then glanced back over her shoulder toward me. "Are you sure you don't want something? This sandwich is fabulous!"

"I'm good," was all I could say as I watched her eat.

When she was almost finished with her sandwich, I asked her, "Um, could I go to the kitchen and get some water without getting zapped?"

"Sure. Just remember you can't leave the apartment unless I let you. The shields I set are still on the doors and windows," she said without looking at me.

I rose slowly and eased my way to the kitchen. I didn't want to upset her with sudden movements and get shocked again. Who knew what items she had rigged to shoot volts as soon as you touched it?

Once out of her line of sight, I surveyed my counters. No mess. I checked the fridge. No extras from her meal. I stood there, frowning, trying to take it all in. How did she make a sandwich like that and not have anything else left? Where did it come from?

I leaned over the end of the counter and glanced at her. She was sitting back, sipping her tea. When she saw me, she gave me her sparkling smile. I ducked back into the kitchen and rolled my eyes. Maybe it was her stellar oversized hand-bag. Maybe she had it in there and just used my dishes. That had to be it.

I got my ice water and made my way slowly back to the couch. She again patted the seat. Like there were any other seats here. Maybe the coffee table, but that would put me face to face with her again. I didn't think I really wanted any more face-to-face or eye-to-eye with Ruth right now, but something was going to have to give.

"I know you're confused and concerned right now, but there's no need to be," she began, after she turned and wedged herself against the arm of the couch so she could watch me while she talked. "Not yet anyway," she finished.

Now, there was something to think about.

"So, you're my mother's sister?" No time like the present to get it all out.

"I was your mother's sister, yes," she replied.

I wasn't sure she was going to elaborate, until she sat up a little straighter and took a deep breath, which I'd come to appreciate as her jumping-off point in conversation.

"Your mother, Susan, was my little sister. You look a great deal like her, by the way." She slowly nodded her head as if confirming the matter to herself. "She loved you dearly." She paused only a second. "Susan wanted to save the world. Any cause to volunteer, and she was right there. She'd gone on a trip with a group of missionary workers to provide aid to some European villages. When she came home, she was pregnant. She never wanted to talk about who she'd met and would become visibly upset, refusing to talk about what had happened, so we left her alone. We thought there'd be plenty of time for her to tell us who he was, but things didn't turn out the way she'd hoped." Ruth's eyes lowered to her hands in her lap.

We sat in silence. I assumed Ruth was pondering what could have been, since I was deep in thought about what might have been.

"Please, go on with your, um, story," I quietly prompted, now wanting to hear what else she had to say.

"I arranged your adoption in Texas. But we're all originally from here. Arkansas is our home." She reached for her tea and took another sip, staring at her hands as if trying to decide where to go with her story now. "Whatever happened overseas is why your mother insisted on moving away from her family. She moved to Texas just before you were born. We felt she'd lived through a tragedy and wanted a clean start for the both of you. I think she worried about your safety if she stayed in

Arkansas. It was almost as if she was afraid she'd be found. But, if that was the case, it wasn't clear if it was your father or someone else who caused her to worry about your safety. It's the only reason I agreed to let you be adopted in Texas."

She paused only momentarily. "She knew she was dying in that last hour after your birth. We were in denial and kept trying to reassure her that everything was okay." She shrugged, and I could see her struggle. "Many women think they're dying during childbirth, and we lied to ourselves that was the only thing going on, but it all happened so quickly. She kept insisting that you had to stay in Texas, regardless of what happened to her. Susan said it was safer for you."

She took a second to glance to me a second before she continued. "A friend of mine helped with your adoption. Two stipulations she worked out were that you'd be able to keep your first name, and that we'd be kept updated on what was happing in your life. We agreed to not make direct contact unless it was absolutely necessary. I received notes occasionally over the first few years, but I didn't know until it was too late that your adoptive parents had moved to Arkansas and then passed away. By the time you were in foster care, we had no idea you were this close to us." She paused for another sip of her drink.

I was having trouble digesting all of this. Of course, all foster kids wanted a real family and dreamed of being rescued. My rescue never came, and I'd passed many of life's milestones alone. Year after year, without being rescued, I added another layer of ice around my heart. The thickness of that iceberg now would take years to thaw if ever given a chance. But, right now, that crystallization was the only thing that gave me strength. I'd told myself for years that nothing could touch me. I was stronger than any bumps in the road that I'd already experienced. That strength made me sit straighter in my seat. I knew I could handle just about anything she was about to reveal. Well, almost.

As she went on, I learned that my mother had been her much-younger sister, and Ruth also had a brother who she wasn't that close to. From the way she described his interactions with the family, he didn't come around that often. Ruth wasn't even sure where he was currently living. There had been another sibling, but the child had died young. Both of Ruth's parents had passed on, and per her description, it appeared she was the head of the family.

"That's how we've always lived. The oldest daughter becomes the head of the family," she explained.

I frowned in concentration as she laid out all of this. "But what does that mean, 'head of the family?'" I used air quotes because I'm one of those people who talk with their hands.

Ruth ducked her chin down slightly and turned her head to an angle that usually meant someone was thinking. "We're not like other families, or at least our bloodline isn't," she stated simply. "My mother, her mother before her, and so on, have passed down our history to the next matriarch."

The look on my face probably spoke volumes, because she paused in her story and raised her eyebrows as if asking if I had a question. I just shook my head so she'd continue.

She took one of her now-infamous deep breaths and then continued. "I had that same look when my mother described all of this to me," she started.

Ruth went on to explain that her mother and grandmother believed that we were more in tune with the earth than most people. They tried to live in harmony with nature and the elements, conserve, and the like and, when necessary, step in to help.

"Help? Do you mean like bagging sand for flooded areas?" I couldn't help it. I always have questions.

"No, more like healing the injured, putting out fires, or stopping floods," she said without batting an eye.

Riiight. Fire fighters! I thought. "Ruth, cut the crap. What are you trying to tell me?" I asked, shaking my head. "Are you telling me that you're a nurse or a doctor? That the women in our family have been fire fighters and aid workers like with the National Guard?"

"No, I mean stopping the rain before it can become a flood," she said matter-of-factly. "I mean making the flood take another route when needed or forcing a tornado to sweep toward more open areas. But we're not always lucky; things still do happen. Some natural disasters would've been and could've been worse if we hadn't stepped in."

Okay, we'd just entered Weirdsville, population one. The hair on my arms started rising again, along with goosebumps down my body. My spine started tingling, and I didn't know why. Oh yeah, now I remembered, a lunatic was sitting here with me.

She marched on. "If it helps, I think the closest you can come to understanding our family heritage would be to say we are witches, but not like the stereotypes you see in the media."

I'm sure she paused here only to let me grasp what she was saying. "Potter and Grainger? Is that what you are trying to make me believe?" I started to giggle. *Witches!*

"No, more like Darrin and Samantha. Your mother always liked that show." She was shaking her head. "No doubt she wanted to pay tribute by naming you after the main character. I'm sure she thought it would be funny one day," she said, half smiling. "I know you have your doubts right now. I assure you I had all the same thoughts. Heck, when my mother told me, I was so shocked I ran out of the house, but I didn't get far. She found me before I even knew where I was going. That's why I locked you in here with me. When we're in a city, it's harder to keep everyone from knowing what we are. If you'd run, and you would have, then I would've had to catch you, and that would have been too risky." She paused, leaned forward, and placed her hand on my forearm.

I wanted to jerk it away and bolt from my seat, but I'd already seen what she could do with electricity. To my shock, a sense of calm radiated out from her hand and went through me. My giggles, which were leaning toward hysterical, ceased. I didn't know what she was doing which caused my heart to race a little, but the calming peace I felt steadied that beat. I might've been calmer, but the ludicrous questions started stacking up in my head. If Ruth wanted me to believe that she was a witch and that I was because we shared blood, I had a few other ideas. I opened my mouth to start with my own ideas, but a question fell out all on its own.

"If you are telling me that witches are real, then I guess the boogeyman is real, too?" My giggles started to bubble again.

"Well,"—she took a deep breath and turned her steady brown eyes to mine—"that depends on what your idea of what the boogeyman is."

I laughed so hard my ribs started to hurt. *The boogeyman!* Then I quickly sobered. What was the boogeyman? What about ghosts, Bigfoot, vampires, werewolves, the tax collector, and things that go bump in the night? She saw the change immediately and realized that I was about to become panicked again. She reached over and put her hand on my forearm again. Calmness flooded me.

"We're attuned to the elements. If we practice our abilities enough, we can specialize in controlling certain elements and some emotions. I know you want to run right now, but I need you calm and focused. I have a lot of information to share with you and not a lot of time to do it."

I nodded my head very slightly and leaned back to my side of the couch. Ruth snapped her fingers, and the lamp beside her flashed on all by itself. I thought maybe my wiring was short circuiting, but she snapped again, and it went off, making me jump backwards. All I could do was stare at the lamp.

"You turned the light on?"

"I had to concentrate, but it wasn't difficult. I can turn on lights and some small appliances. Those types of things," she said, shrugging her shoulders. "There are larger things we can do as well. Some of us have the ability to influence fire, water, and wind. You know, the elements," she went on.

"You keep saying 'we.' Are you meaning others like you?" I was ignoring my fight-or-flight instincts to get the hell out of there.

"When I say 'we,' I mean you and me," she finished. Then she flashed that brilliant smile again.

I was shaking my head no, slightly at first as she was finishing her statement, but it grew to the point I feared I'd have whiplash. My own hysterical giggle wasn't far away. I wasn't hearing what she was saying. Well, I guess I was hearing it. I just couldn't swallow it. The harder I shook my head in the negative, the more she was nodding hers in the affirmative.

"It's the truth, honey. You can't accept it right now, but it is the truth, and it won't go away just because you don't want to think about it." She'd now taken the tone of a mother reassuring an injured child.

My brain hurt. I dropped my head into my hands, still shaking my head and trying to rub my temples. I couldn't think. I started to feel like I couldn't breathe. My chest was constricting so fast I was starting to gasp.

Again, she leaned toward me, and this time placed both of her hands on my shoulders. My heart slowed, and the throbbing eased. I might not want to accept what she was feeding me, but I couldn't ignore the fact that what she was doing made me calmer.

I slowly raised my head and felt tears start to form as I looked into her deep-brown, kind, caring eyes. My stomach unclenched, and the breath I didn't realize I was holding came out in a quick exhale.

"I know. It's a lot to take in. More so for you than it was for me. I knew my family, so I didn't get the double dose that you're getting. But you possess skills and talents that don't begin to emerge until you turn twenty-one."

She was still leaning in with her hands on my shoulders. A tear started a path down my check. She raised her hand and brushed it away, then held my face in her hand.

"I have no daughters to carry on behind me. My sister is dead, Sam. You are the next in line," she finished, with tears misting her vision, too.

I didn't want to feel close to her, but it was an emotion I was having a hard time fighting. She leaned in closer and hugged me tightly. Within a few seconds, I returned the hug and didn't know why. Not only did I have a family, but the boogeyman was real too! I felt more lost than I had in a long time. Lost and found at the same time. How did that happen?

We sat there for what seemed like a lifetime, then returned to our own corners of the couch. I leaned back into my corner and picked up a throw pillow, pulling it onto my lap and hugging it. I'd felt safe and protected when she hugged me. I hadn't felt that in years. Not since before my adoptive parents had passed away. It felt good. The child in me wanted to be protected, but what she was telling me would certainly change my life. I didn't know how, I just knew in my gut that things were about to be different. Hell, they already were.

"I just turned twenty-two, so how is it that you're just now coming to deliver this little news flash?" I asked.

She smiled. "Like I said, after you were adopted, I kept tabs on you through your adoptive parents. But they didn't advise us they were moving. When I went to check on you and couldn't find you, I started searching Texas. I searched for years, but my mother finally convinced me that when it was your time, I would find you. You must've been having a very hard time these last two semesters," she said.

"Well, yeah, these past two semesters have been trying, but what does that have to do with anything?" I was puzzled at the change of direction.

"And did you have any arguments with anyone during those two semesters? Maybe one this last semester that was an uglier argument than the others?" she asked, with one eyebrow raised.

"Well, there was this guy I was kind of seeing. We did have a few arguments. Then there was a class where I got pissed off at the professor, but that was it. No bloodshed, no police called," I explained.

I hadn't realized I'd done it, but I'd crossed my arms over my chest. What about it, I thought? People can get ticked off, can't they? It wasn't often that I had anyone I wanted to call a boyfriend. Jeff just happened to be a jerk that I found out about all too late.

"So, what do my tiffs have to do with anything?" I asked, on the verge of getting miffed again.

Ruth's calming smile came back, along with a pat on my

arm. I realized the calming effects immediately. "That's how I found you."

"Excuse me?"

"You got upset. That's how I found you," she explained.

"How did my getting upset lead you to me?"

"Well, as I explained earlier, we have influence or control over the elements."

I knew I had that look on my face again, because she gently smiled before she continued.

"Have you heard of or felt any of the recent earthquakes in the area?" she asked, with a serious, almost accusatory look.

"Yeah, what about it? The news said it was because of all the drilling in the area. Fayetteville Shale and all that."

Heck, who hadn't felt the last big one? It was a 4.7 quake and wasn't something our state experienced on a regular basis. I had friends sending me Facebook messages from far north and south Arkansas saying they felt it.

I'll never forget it. I heard it long before I felt it. Or maybe it was a combination of both. It would start as the sound of distant thunder, but the weather was clear, and that was my first clue. As the sound grew in intensity, as if coming nearer, subtle vibrations would increase to a jaw-banging jolt and then *boom!* It would sound and feel as if a bomb had just gone off right where you sat. Then it was over for the moment. Smaller tremors and aftershocks would roll around later, but they were always less intense. Still, they all came the same way.

Ruth started shaking her head with a forced grin. "Did you ever wonder why those quakes always hit on the day you had those arguments? Almost within an hour of those incidents is my guess." She was cocking her head again and grinning at me fully.

I froze. "What are you trying to say? That I caused that?" I thought she'd really gone too far now.

"I am not *trying* to say you caused it, dear. I *am* saying you caused it."

"Bullshit!"

"Why do you think I've been making an effort to keep you calm now?" she asked.

"Because you didn't want me upset? Hell, I don't know, maybe you get your jollies from it."

"It's well known within our circle that these kinds of events may happen before you can control your talent. You've had a lot to digest today, and I don't think letting your emotions get out of control will help." She shrugged. "Sam, I have a degree in geology, and I work off and on as a consultant. I've spent a lot of time the last few months supplying information that some of the drilling practices have caused lasting damages in other states and that it could be a factor here, too. So far, the environmentalist and geologists have bought it. Drilling has eased up in the area now, and there haven't been that many quakes, so I don't think your lack of control right now will help them buy what I'm selling."

She stood and walked to the window. She touched the shade and looked out. She touched the shade, and nothing happened. No zingers! *What the—*

"So, you say I caused the tremors, and you just showed up here now? Those two things aren't close enough together to draw a straight line, you know what I mean? You knew where I lived. You knew I was at the bookstore. How did you find me, really?"

"Well, it pays to know people. I knew you weren't far from the quakes, given your age. So, I started with the larger cities and the utility companies. It didn't take long after that. I've watched you for several weeks. I wanted you to finish with your classes before I introduced myself. Something came up that required me to be out of state, and I'm just now getting back. I'm sorry I missed your birthday." She even sounded a little sad about it.

"I've spent many birthdays by myself. This wasn't any different."

"Sam, I know that, in your mind, your life is spiraling out of control right now. But there are still many things I need to tell you, the least of which is that I need your help." She checked her watch, crossed her arms over her chest, and started pacing.

"Is there something else going on?" I got the impression she'd suddenly become unsettled.

"I don't think I'm the only one that's been looking for you," was all she said as she continued pacing. She pulled her cell phone out of her pocket and started checking text or emails; I couldn't tell which. She laughed once and put her phone back in her pocket.

"That's it? You drop several bombs in my lap, and now you just decide to wait on the rest?" I was feeling indignant now, and I still wanted answers. It seemed like for every question she answered, I had fifteen new questions based on that answer.

"Sam, I need you to take a short road trip with me, but we need to leave when it's closer to dark. It will be safer then."

"Safer for whom?"

"Both of us." She stared me down for a few seconds then did a 180 and broke out in a smile. "I don't want to give you the wrong impression, Sam. You are safe with me. Safer than you are without me. Can you trust me?" she asked, still smiling.

"Can I trust you? You mean after this whole day, now you're asking for trust?"

"I asked you to trust me from the start, Sam, and you need to reach the point of actually believing you can. Before, we were just strangers. Now you know a little about where you came from, and we've moved beyond being strangers. You have to ask yourself if you can put your life in my hands. The perspective has changed." She finished with her arms crossed.

Well, hell! She was right. A total stranger asking you for trust generally means a flash of a smile and they're out of your life as soon as they get what they need from you. Now I have someone who is a blood relation giving me answers to many of the questions I've longed to have answered. I felt safe and protected with her, and she was asking me to trust my life to her. Did I have a choice?

Not only do I have a family, I've also learned I'm from a line of witches. She'd demonstrated enough of her talent that I didn't question her abilities. I just seriously doubted that I was in any way similarly gifted. Sure, there were oddities about my life that I couldn't really explain, but didn't everyone have that? Couldn't most people sense when something peculiar was going to happen before it did? Not that I knew exactly what was going to happen, just that something strange was going to pop up or occur. Surely, that little oddity couldn't be what she'd meant.

Given the history lesson she'd just given me, whoever would take over the head of the family would have at least the skill level she'd demonstrated. Shit, she could touch you and make your world go black. I could touch you—well more like stumble into you—and make you drop your coffee. Not much comparison.

Her phone rang in her pocket, and it brought me back from the conversation in my head. She looked at the number, held up a finger to me as if to tell me not to talk, and then hit the front door to go outside.

When the door was closed, I shot to my feet to see where she'd gone, but I stopped short of touching the blinds. I stood there, looking at them, my hand halfway to the side, wondering if I'd get shocked again. I paused and squinted my eyes to see if I could see any shimmering effects like I'd seen earlier near my kitchen. Squinting didn't help. I eased to one side of the window, back to the other, and then squatted down to look at the bottom of the shades. Nope, nothing was attached to them anywhere other than the brackets that held them to the wall.

I slowly stretched one finger forward, hunching my shoulders, already in fear of what the shock would be like. Closing my eyes, I shoved my finger to make contact, and nothing happened. No shock. Just my plain old mini-blinds.

I released the breath I'd been holding and lifted one louver, trying to peer through the window to see where Ruth had vanished. She was standing at the open driver's- side door of a black Land Rover. She'd frown, then talk into the phone, raise her eyebrows, and listen, frown again, then start the process all over.

After a few minutes, she elevated her eyes to the window, and I dropped the shade, stepping back quickly. I was suddenly mad at myself. Why did I care if she saw me watching her? I felt guilty in a way, but then I remembered this was my home.

I stepped back to the window, and this time just raised the whole damn shade. To hell with being sneaky. Ruth glanced back to the window, saw me, and smiled. She was nodding as she was listening to her caller. Her face went blank, and she turned to the inside of her car. I assume it was her car. I knew most vehicles in my complex's parking lot, and the Land Rover definitely didn't live here.

After a few minutes, she came out of the car with a briefcase and opened it on the hood of the car. She held the phone on her shoulder to her ear as she took out a folder and pen and started making notes. *Hmm.* Was she really a consultant, or did she just play one? I suppose geologists needed to consult.

I lowered the shade and went to my bedroom. I had a wave of guilt over the mess in my room and didn't want her to see it. But she'd likely already been through my entire home while I'd been knocked out. I needed to keep myself busy, so I locked myself in the bedroom and started tidying up.

Damn, I'm a slob.

I must've been in the bathroom scouring the shower when she came back in, because I never knew she'd returned. When I came out of the bedroom, she was sitting on my couch, with her briefcase open on the coffee table. Papers were put in neat stacks. Every inch of the table was utilized, and she was reading from a folder on her lap that was at least an inch thick. It looked like she'd already read through half of it. One stack of papers was topped with what looked like an antique envelope. It looked really old; not the kind of envelope you see every day.

I walked over to the coffee table and surveyed the stacks. Other than the stack with the old envelope, the others were just ordinary stacks of business correspondence, but none of them were in English. I glanced at Ruth and frowned. She kept her head bent over her reading material. I wondered just how much other information she was going to throw at me. She obviously must know how to read all these languages. Even what she was reading in her lap wasn't in English.

Suddenly I was regretting not having taken any second language classes. I had no idea what language she was reading, but it looked different than the other stacks on the table.

I stood there glancing back and forth between what she was reading and the stacks on the table, comparing as quickly as I could to see if they were the same language. But that envelope lying face down on the top of one stack kept drawing my attention. It was different enough that I wanted to touch it. It just looked like it would feel heavier than normal paper.

Glancing at Ruth, still absorbed in her reading, I placed a finger on the envelope. It felt smooth, almost like fine leather. Oh, to hell with it. I picked it up and turned it over. In the middle, in Old English-style calligraphy was the word *Prime*. That was all. The lettering was in a dark color, and I got the impression it wasn't in any ink I'd ever seen. Before I could lift the flap on the back, Ruth seemed to realize what I was doing and reached out to me.

"Sorry, Sam, I can't let you do that just yet," she said, snatching the envelope out of my fingers. She folded up her reading material and started loading everything back into her briefcase.

I stood there frowning as she packed. "What do you mean 'just yet?'" I asked.

Coming to her feet and raising her arms above her head to stretch, she replied, "There are just some things you're going to have to wait to discover."

And that was it.

She looked at her watch while flexing her shoulders. She was still apparently stiff. "I got busy reading and lost track of time. Let's run by Sonic then take a little road trip," she said. "You must've been busy in there. I didn't think you'd leave me to myself for so long. Is that a little bit of trust you're sending my way?" She finished that by placing her hands on her hips and cocking her head to the side with that small amount of gleam to her eyes.

I knew she was enjoying herself all of a sudden. I tried hard not to blush, but to hell with that, too.

"I, uh…well, I guess you probably already figured it out for yourself, but I don't usually have many guests over, and I'm definitely not Suzie Homemaker. I kind of just let things fall where they may," I said with a sigh. "I was embarrassed to realize I'd been living like a pig, and I was trying to do a little damage control."

"Don't bother, Sam. You don't have to try to impress me, and you really have no need to explain yourself. I was just teasing. You need to lighten up a little. Come on. Let's grab some grub on our way out of town."

She gathered up her purse and the briefcase and motioned me toward the door.

I liked her car. *Expensive* was all I could think as we rode to the Sonic closest to my apartment. It was all dark leather and even had heated seats. I was so busy inspecting the interior that I didn't realize she was already parking the car. We placed our order, but she never killed the motor. It had warmed up this afternoon, and I think killing the motor would've made the car too hot. I was still wearing my shorts and sandals, and I really didn't want to stick to her impressive upholstery.

Classical music was playing softly, and we didn't talk much as our order came and we ate. I always feel better with some food in my stomach. When I finished my cheeseburger and tots, she put the Rover in gear, and we hit the highway. We were heading north, and there was no traffic, which I thought was strange.

Ruth glanced at me quickly, reached over, and laid her

hand on the console, palm up. Strange, I got the impression she wanted to hold my hand. *Huh?* Trust, remember? Trust is what she was asking with another quick glance. So, I exhaled and placed my hand on hers. She entwined our fingers, peeked at me again quickly with a smile, and the world went black again.

Well, shit!

SAM 104

J awoke—if it can be called waking up—sitting in a parking lot. It was dusk, and the canopy of trees made it much darker. Ruth was nowhere to be seen. I moved and realized I wasn't stiff, so maybe we hadn't been in the car that long. I didn't remember falling asleep. Well, not at first. Looking down at the console, I discovered my soda from Sonic. Crap! Now I remember.

Glancing around the lot I saw a national park sign. How long had we been driving? The closest national park from my apartment was Hot Springs or Blanchard Springs, and neither were short trips. But we'd only left my apartment, what, forty-five minutes ago?

I searched the car for my backpack to find my phone. Sure enough, the clock only showed an hour had passed, and as most forests in Arkansas go, I didn't have a cell phone signal.

I looked up to see a dim figure emerging from the walking trail. It was Ruth. Dang, she knocks me out then parks to go for a walk? *WTF?*

As she drew closer, she saw me watching her and flashed

a smile. Instead of getting into the car, she came to my side, motioning me to exit the vehicle. I opened the door slowly and gingerly slid out, still hanging on to my backpack. Exiting any vehicle larger than a car is very unladylike when you're not super tall, and I fall into that category. I learned a long time ago to take it slow or live with the embarrassment of an unplanned exhibition on the ground—namely me, accidentally flashing my panties or sprawled out with scraped knees.

Ruth gestured toward the walking trail she'd just come from. "It's not far from here now. Let's get started while we still have a little light left."

"Just exactly where is here?" I asked, turning in a circle to get my bearings. I got the impression we weren't just in the forest but also close to water.

Ruth, not letting up on her smile, looked at me and said, "Blanchard Springs. Have you been here before?"

"No, not to this location, I don't think."

I was puzzled. Why were we in the middle of a national park? I guess it really captured my fuzzy brain, because before I realized it, I'd followed Ruth back toward the trail head. I guessed she wanted me to see the springs.

While there was minimal day light left in the parking lot, the trail wasn't as fortunate. The trail had new wooden bridges crossing over the running water of the creek and hard-packed dirt in between. The trail was handicap accessible but treacherous none the less. I learned both of those facts when I tripped coming off the bridge and landed on all fours on the hard-scape. Now I was dirty and had scraped knees and hands, with an added touch of embarrassment. Ruth helped me up and dusted me off as if I were a toddler.

"I think it's only fair to warn you that I'm a natural klutz, and I'm terrified of snakes and bugs." I told her, trying hard to look around to see things that go bump in the night. At least until today, those had been the only things I worried about in the dark. Now I had new fears. We were going to have to talk about the Boogeymen.

"Soon you won't even worry about those. The more time you spend outdoors, you just get used to your environment."

Gee, she sounded confident. Me, not so much.

We slowly made our way along the path. I say *slowly* because now I was hesitant about taking a step without knowing for sure where my foot was going to land. The scent of pine trees was fresh around me. Ruth frequently sighed heavily along the way. I was beginning to think she might believe she indeed did have the wrong woman. Surely, if I was a member of this family, I'd have a lot more courage.

When I began to hear sounds of splashing water, it dawned on me to ask why we were here. I couldn't understand why I hadn't started asking questions as soon as I left the Rover. I'd gotten out and played follow the leader. This was so not me.

"Um, Ruth, why exactly are we here? And just for shits and giggles, how the hell did we get here so fast?"

"You'll see," was all she would say as she kept walking.

It was now pitch dark, and I was constantly scanning the area while trying to keep up. I was afraid of the dark while she apparently wasn't. I definitely didn't want to get separated or fall again.

The farther along the trail we got, the louder the splashing grew. The trail ended in a kind of cul-de-sac type of finish. *"Ta-da! You are here!"* was what it felt they'd been saying when they ended the trail.

And here we were. The splashing I heard was no doubt from the waterfall we were now looking at. The mist from the falls had cooled the temperature drastically. If we stayed standing long enough, I could see we'd eventually be soaked. The illumination emanating from the moon and stars made the water gleam silver in the night.

"Beautiful, isn't it?" Ruth asked.

She only stopped for a few seconds before she took a deep breath and headed around one of the larger boulders. The boulder sat on the edge of the creek head that began under the fall. I just stood watching her.

"Ruth, all these signs around here, I'm pretty they sure warn you not to go past these boulders and boundaries. You got a death wish or something?"

"Just watch where I step and follow me. We're almost there. I know you don't like the dark or the creatures you could meet, so I suggest you stay close." She'd had to raise her voice above the sound of the falls for me to hear.

Crap! She was already ahead of me, and by the time she'd finished her sentence, I couldn't see her anymore. I thought, but only for a second, that maybe she'd come back to get me. Then I realized the longer I waited, the farther ahead she'd get. Damn!

I took the route she'd taken and started stumbling past the boulder to catch her. I wished like hell she'd mentioned hiking in the program before we'd left my apartment. Dressing appropriately would've been a plus! Hiking in the dark wasn't a good thing to do with sandals and shorts. I bet the Boy Scout handbook even advised against it.

I didn't want to know about the various creatures she was referring to. I decided to sing a song to myself as I carefully pushed limbs of the nearest bushes away from my face while I tried to catch up. Maybe trying to remember words to songs would keep my mind off the fact that the small pings I felt against my arms, legs, and face were anything other than small insects. Did it work? Not much. The Yellow Submarine wasn't helpful in this situation. I had my shoulders drawn up around my ears by the time I caught up with her.

She'd walked about fifty yards past the actual head of the pool, where the water continued to spill out of the mountain, stopping suddenly. My last steps had me stumbling again, coming to rest by knocking into her. She recovered, exhaling again as she turned to me. I know agitated when I hear it, and she was definitely starting to think she'd found the wrong foster kid.

"All the women in our family have been coming here since the beginning. Or so my mother and grandmother told me. It's a treasure. Our family treasure that's kept us alive, as a source of income as well as our source of strength and protection."

The path in front of us was overgrown, but you could faintly make out that it was a trail. Some of the boulders, which undoubtedly had slid from the side of the mountain, were as large as Ruth's Land Rover.

Ruth reached for my hand and started guiding me across the trail. We were practically doubling back toward the falls, but closer to the base of the mountain. I doubt she was trying for the effect of calming me, as she appeared to be concentrating on walking this gauntlet in the dark, but that was exactly the effect her hand linked to mine created. Calm. It no longer worried me what critters were scurrying about. I knew I was safe.

One of the larger oblong boulders stood (if you can say a rock stands) like a sentinel. You could see and hear the falling water behind it. It was taller than Ruth and me combined, and wide enough that we could both hide behind it and no one know we were there. A smaller, flat boulder sat at the base of the sentinel stone, and Ruth stopped there.

Releasing my hand, she turned and sat upon the flat rock

while pulling up her purse, which I just realized she'd brought along. I think that purse must be possessed. I was reflecting on her lunch and change of clothes in my apartment, wondering if that purse could have really held all those things, when she started rummaging through it. From it she produced a flashlight and a pen knife.

"*Now* she finds a flashlight?" I murmured under my breath, but she heard me anyway.

"Well, rangers do patrol the park. If they'd seen a flashlight on the trail, they'd be coming to investigate the source and would've followed us in. While many people do venture off the trail back in this direction, none of them know of this entrance. It's sealed," she explained. "The national park system has invaded our space, and we try to let them think they own it. Have you ever been on the tour?"

I raised my chin looking up the side of the mountain. "Yeah, one of my high school science teachers brought us up here. It was a long, boring trip, but it was interesting once we got inside. They said the caverns are alive. Which reminds me, how did we get here so fast?" I was facing her with my hands on my hips while she remained seated on the rock.

"I'll get to the trip later. Give me a hand," she said, reaching out.

Without thinking, I extended my hand. I'd thought she needed help to get up. I wasn't watching her and was shocked when I was stung on the end of a finger. I snatched my hand back. There was blood welling at the tip of my index finger. Not a sting or a bite, she'd cut me!

She'd apparently opened her pen knife while I was yammering about that field trip. I could see it in her hand now with the blade glinting in the moonlight. She wiped the blade, nicked her own finger, folded the blade, and then dropped it back in her purse. She flipped the flashlight on and shined it up into my face. I placed the wounded flesh in my mouth, sucking on the cut. It was copper tasting, and the flavor floated to the back of my throat, into my sinuses. I knew it wasn't a huge wound, but the sucking did make it feel better. It also kept me from letting a few choice words flow out of my mouth. While I knew I wasn't in imminent danger, I didn't want to press my luck by pissing her off.

Before I had myself under control enough to speak, she stood quickly, jerked my finger out of my mouth, and said, "We don't need to let the flow stop."

Without missing a beat, she forcefully dragged me toward the stones. Ruth put one arm around my waist to keep me close, while holding my hand with the other. It was her right hand on my right hand. She leaned into me and, extending both of our arms, wiped our fingers on the standing stone. When she loosened her grip, I jerked out of her hold and backed off a few feet, just staring at her. As if this day could get any stranger…

Within minutes of whatever ritual she'd just performed, the flow of the water started slacking and within five minutes had completely shut off. Just like someone had closed the dam or stuck their finger in the dike. There was a little trickle that continued down the face of the rock, but behind, where the water had fallen, in the solid rock was an entrance.

I was dumbfounded again. How was I ever going to get used to all of this? She flashed her light toward the opening then turned it back toward me.

"I'm sorry about your finger, but the passage had to know you. It's the only way to get in," she said, shrugging her shoulders as if to explain this freak party. Reaching back to me, she grabbed my wrist and started pulling me along toward the opening.

"If I ever come back, will I have to do that again?" I asked.

"Yes. It only opens for a blood member of our family who has the gift that we do."

"So, this hole isn't always here?"

"No, it will close back when we leave. The magic of what it is, and what it means to us, will keep it shielded from anyone else, even when we're inside. Anyone looking this way from the trail will still see and hear the water falling."

Beads of water were still dancing down to hit us on the head as we passed through the entrance. Ruth was shining her light along the floor so we could see where we were stepping. It was smooth stone, not dirt. The passage was only large enough for single file, but Ruth kept my wrist held close to her. I guess she was afraid I'd run back out. While I was a little intimidated by walking into a hole that hadn't been here ten minutes ago, I was growing curious as to our destination. It wasn't the damp smell that I knew from the upper caverns, but it did remind me of a fresh linen smell. How odd was that? The floor sloped away from us, but not enough that we had to lean backwards to keep our pace. You knew it was leading down, deeper into the mountain.

We walked for what seemed like an hour. The tunnel had taken some turns but kept leading downward. I started to wonder if we were heading to China, when the tunnel finally started to fan out on either side. Ruth, having never released my hand, gave it a quick squeeze then let me go. She glanced back to me, still smiling, and announced, "We're here."

She kept the flashlight pointed straight down now, like she wanted to see her shoes. She took several more steps, then turned towards me, sweeping the flashlight up into my eyes. I was blinded instantly and started staggering. I felt the sudden sting of tears you get when blinded like that. Raising my hands to my eyes, I stopped and swayed.

"Oops, I forgot what I was doing. Here, take my hand again."

I did as I was told and started waving my hand in front of me to make contact with her hand while rubbing my eyes with the other. She lowered the flashlight to the floor. When I was able to see again, she smiled practically from ear to ear and turned off the light. Ruth must have felt me tense, because she squeezed my hand again quickly.

"It's alright. Just wait a second."

It was my turn to take the deep breath. Maybe it ran in the family. When I thought my eyes had become accustomed to the dark, a slight glow started all around us. It started faintly, and I'd at first thought it was like the pin pricks of light your mind tells you exist when you find yourself in the pitch dark, especially when you get up in the middle of the night to go to the bathroom, but it slowly started getting lighter. It was the walls, or maybe it was just more magic. I'd been standing there holding her hand, slowly turning my head around so I could see where we were.

It wasn't a large cavern. It seemed to be a good twenty-five feet in depth and completely round. While the walls glowed, it was the smaller iridescent glowing that looked like crystals in the wall. I released her hand and walked to my left. I was mesmerized by the glowing rocks. When I got close enough, I could see they were of all different sizes set in the walls.

I reached my hand out and laid my fingertips lightly across one rock. As soon as contact was made, that rock glowed brighter, and I could feel a hum. Yes, *feel* below my fingertips. I jerked my hand away, the light dimmed, and the humming vibration stopped. I put my hand back, touched it again, and the process repeated. I glanced back at Ruth. She was watching me with a knowing smile on her face. I placed my palm against the stone again, and it became so bright I could see the whole room in crystal clarity.

"What is this place?"

"This is our treasure I was telling you about. It's our heritage. You do realize you're touching a diamond, right?" she asked with a nod back toward the wall.

"Diamonds! Really? All of these rocks glowing in the wall are diamonds?" I was a little amazed. I took my hand back while I was asking it. I'm not sure why. Just a little overwhelmed, I supposed. While the light dimmed a little, it didn't go as dark as it had been when they'd first started glowing.

"How is it they glowed brighter when I touched it?" Again with all the questions.

"All we know is they seem to draw energy from us." She walked over and placed her hand on the opposite wall—if there is an opposite wall in a round room—and again the room was as bright as if we were in the full sun.

"I know there's the diamond mine south of Hot Springs, but I thought that's near an old crater, you know, an old volcano." I said glancing back to her. I couldn't keep my eyes off the glowing stones. I had to keep in constant motion to see which ones would glow brighter as I let my fingertips glide over the wall.

"Well, I am a geologist, remember? And, yes, that deposit is supposedly the site of an old crater. The waters that make Hot Springs so famous are reportedly heated by that same vein."

I was frowning as I thought. I was turning back to start with more questions when she laughed and kept going. "Have you been anywhere around Heber Springs? It's closer than

Hot Springs, but the water isn't quite as welcoming as those to the south. It smells like straight sulfur. I've heard that smell is equated with brimstone. It only stands to reason there has to be another inactive crater close by as well."

"Okay, so now, how does all of this," I said, spreading my arms to encompass the room, "help our family?"

"We take some stones from the wall when we're in need. I've sold my share of these gems over the years, just as everyone that came before us. This room also heals us when we need it. I know it sounds far-fetched, but this room is full of healing energy. The diamonds soak up our energy, but they also return it tenfold. Look at your fingertip where I cut you."

I'd forgotten about the cut, but when I looked at my finger, I couldn't find where I'd been cut. I placed my left hand against a cluster of stones, making the room ultra bright so that I could see better. Still, even with practically a spotlight, I couldn't find the nick. I looked back to Ruth. She was leaning against the wall now, with her arms folded across her chest, eyes closed. I just continued to watch her. She really was amazing, my aunt, my mother's sister. I felt connected suddenly, connected to something larger than myself. Safe; I also felt safe.

Ruth took a deep breath and held it for a few seconds before she let it go as she pushed herself away from the wall. She took a few steps toward the center of the cavern, motioning me over to her like a child, but she wasn't looking at me. She'd been looking toward the floor. The next moment there were two stones. No, not stones, boulders. They just appeared there, making me jump at their appearance. I think I might've squeaked at the same time. Ruth glanced at me, motioning to the boulders.

"Sit with me," she said, striding over to rest on one of the boulders.

Trying to stay in the moment and not let on how unnerved I was, again, I walked as calmly as I could and sat on the other rock. Ruth leaned forward, placing her head in her hands, with elbows on her knees. I wasn't sure what was going on, but this wasn't helping me to calm down. I could feel my heart pounding as blood rushed through my veins. Without lifting her head, Ruth reached out one hand and placed it on mine.

"I can hear your heart pounding too, Sam. It's okay, I was just trying to gather my thoughts."

"Well, by all means, please continue. I'll just sit here and wait. Heck, I might even take a nap. But, then again, I think I've had a few of those today. Are you going to explain how we got here so fast? I don't mean here, this exact spot. But how did we get from my apartment to that parking lot out there in what appears to be little under an hour?"

Ruth took another of her signature deep breaths and started laughing. "Damn, you do ask questions, don't you?"

"Inquiring minds want to know."

She straightened herself and turned to face me. She'd stopped laughing, and a serious look was coming over her. "Sam, you will learn these things the older you get, and how to concentrate on what you want or need. When we left your apartment, I placed you under. I didn't want to overwhelm you again, and I needed some time to think. When I got on an open stretch of road, and there were no other cars around, I just wished for us to be in that parking lot where my car now sits. That's it. That's all I did."

Her look didn't match her statement. I'm sure mine didn't either. I squinted with one eye to look at her and again started with my doubts, but suddenly she wasn't there. I jumped to my feet and started swinging around wildly. Ruth was standing at the part of the wall where she'd stood minutes before the boulders showed up. She had that mischievous look again, standing there smiling. She nodded once toward me and was again gone. I hardly had a chance to jump before she was sitting beside me, back on her boulder, which caused another squeak to jump out of my throat.

"See? I just had to concentrate. No spells, no wands." She leaned toward me, hands outstretched with palms down. "Look at my rings and bracelets," she instructed, impatiently thrusting her hands toward me.

I reached out and held her hand, the way you do with a girlfriend showing off their engagement ring. I leaned closer to her hands, squinting. The lighting had faded some since we weren't touching the walls. Her perfectly manicured hand had four rings. She had an engagement ring and wedding band on her left ring finger and a completely diamond-encrusted ring on her thumb. On her right she wore a fashionable index-finger ring with a stone similar to her engagement ring. She also had another diamond-encrusted band on her pinky. She wore bracelets on each wrist, one tight on her left and a loose chain on her right, both loaded with smaller diamonds.

I nodded when I had completed my inspection. "Very nice," I said looking up.

She'd tucked her hair behind her ears before she'd presented her hands for inspection. Now I could also see her diamond earrings.

"So, now what?" I asked.

"Now we gather some rocks to take with us. A few we'll have cut for your rings, and the rest we'll sell. You'll need to wear them to increase the range of your abilities. Remember, we draw strength from them."

She placed her hands back on her knees, looked down for a minute, and then stood, nodding her head as if she'd just made a decision.

"How are you with air travel?"

"Like airplanes or the travel like we did to get here?"

I wasn't going to lie; my air travel had been limited. One trip up around the city airport then back on the ground. That had been a Girl Scout trip in Texas before my parents moved us to Arkansas. Things were good then, and my adopted mom had really wanted me to be social and spend more time outdoors. I'd hated the outdoor experiences, but the plane ride, donated to the troop, had been fun. Luckily, she only made me do that one year.

"Airplane. We're going to have to take a trip." She paused, "I'm sorry, but you'll have to quit your job."

"Excuse me? Quit my job? That's my only income. How do you think I'm going to live?" I was aghast and felt my anger start to rise quickly.

She held her arms wide and turned a slow circle. "What do you think this is, a costume jewelry store?"

I stared at her. When I finally realized what she was saying, my mouth dropped open. I really didn't realize it until she walked up, put her index finger under my chin, and lifted it shut.

"This can't be really happening. My brain keeps screaming that this is an elaborate dream and I'll wake up. I'll wake up penniless in my apartment and be late for work."

"Sweetie, except for keeping up appearances of a real job, you'll never have to work again or worry about an income. Well, not career work at least. There are still many jobs that I do, but they're not things you'd put on a resume."

I just continued to stare.

"You'll need to call in the morning and quit, then pack some clothes. I hope we won't be gone longer than a week, but you never know. We'll need to arrange a flight. Do you have a computer and internet connection at home? It'll make this a lot quicker."

"Yeah, I've got Wi-Fi and a laptop. Where exactly are we going, and why?"

"We better sit down again," she said, indicating our rock seats.

Somehow, I felt like maybe this was going to be the boogeyman discussion.

"Sam, I want to show you something and then tell you a few more things before we leave here."

At that, she grabbed her purse and started fishing through it again. She came out with a contact lens case and some lens solution. Taking the solution, she rinsed her fingers, then opened the case to leave it resting on her knees. She reached up and removed a contact lens from her right eye, bent, then placed it in the case. When she looked up, I nearly fell off my seat. Her right eye was a dark jade green. She smiled at the look on my face, almost nearly to the point of laughing.

"I told you that there'd been a sibling we lost when I was younger. That sibling was my twin sister," she said, shaking her head sadly. "Genetics are a weird thing. My sister had the same condition with her eyes, except her eye coloring was the opposite of mine. We lost her in a car accident when we were nine, and it took me a long time to get over losing her. Losing your mom was just as hard, because we lost you, too…until now. Now we get to put everything back together."

My eyebrows drew together, trying to take it all in.

"Sam, I know you're wearing one contact, too," she said raising both eyebrows.

Yeah, I had a colored contact lens in to make my eyes match. *Heterochromia iridium,* or simply iridis; I remember hearing those terms very early on. My natural colors of blue and green had made me a freak show when I was in grade school. My mother had watched me suffer from being picked on until she was sure I could handle contacts. I didn't need them to see; my eyesight was perfect. Still is. She bought my first pair when I was nine.

"So, this is hereditary?" I asked cautiously.

"Yes, it's hereditary. But it only shows up with twin births," she said, compressing her shapely lips into a stern line. Ruth looked like she was waiting for me to absorb the meaning.

"You're saying, what, that I had a twin?" I asked, the truth beginning to set in.

"No, not *had*. Have."

I fainted.

૨

SAM 105

I awoke in my own bed to find the sun peeking through the blinds and my brain slowly coming online. I listened to the street noise outside and the sound of the air conditioning units kicking on. The cool air just made me want to curl up under my quilt and go back to sleep. What a night. I couldn't believe the dreams I'd had. Where the hell did all that come from, anyway?

I rolled over and started to stretch, when I smelled coffee. I froze. Someone was in my kitchen making coffee. Reality set in. I hadn't been dreaming. I rose up on my elbows and glanced around the room. The clothes I'd been wearing were in a pile by my closet door. I was wearing my sleep shirt, and my ponytail was gone. Slipping out of bed, I pulled on my day-old dirty shorts and cautiously made my way to the kitchen.

Ruth was sitting on my couch drinking coffee. She'd showered and was wearing a whole new outfit. She smiled when she saw me. "I hope you slept well. We have a big day ahead of us."

Shit! Of course she was a morning person! I gave her the

talk-to-the-hand sign and kept it in her direction as I walked around the couch to the kitchen. I didn't want to start thinking without coffee first.

I found my favorite cup, poured the coffee, loaded it with cream and sugar, then stood sipping it with my eyes closed. *Ahh. Heaven.* I leaned against the counter and kept sipping.

I was barely halfway through my first cup when Ruth came into the kitchen. She refreshed her coffee and offered to top mine off as well. I allowed her to fill mine, then I doctored the consistency all over again. She didn't say a word, just poured then left. When I'd lightened the color of the coffee to my satisfaction, I went back to the living room and sat on the opposite end of the couch. I stretched my legs in front of me, resting my feet on the coffee table. Miss Sunshine could barely contain herself.

"I found your laptop. I hope you don't mind. We're booked on the 4:55 to Salt Lake City this afternoon. So, we have some time to sort through a few things before we have to leave. Are you hungry? I can find us something to eat." She was already rising from her seat.

"Yeah, sure, whatever is fine." I just wasn't a morning person, and until I finished at least two cups, I wasn't interested in detailed decision making.

She went to the kitchen, and I heard the cabinet doors open and close. Plates and utensils clattered, and within seconds, I could smell food. Not pop-in-the-microwave food either, but a full-blown meal. How does she keep doing this?

Since I was close to the end of my second cup of coffee, I had enough energy to rush to the kitchen as she was turning toward me, carrying two plates. Eggs, toast, and bacon were heaped on both plates. I looked from the plates in her hands, to her face, and then back. I leaned into the kitchen and looked over at the stove. Again, nothing appeared to have been used, and there was nothing left on the counters either. I looked back to meet her gaze.

"How do you do that?"

"Ancient Chinese secret," she said while rolling her eyes. "Let's eat."

After I was re-energized with food and two more cups of coffee, I hopped in the shower. I left Ruth alone to handle the breakfast post-game party. I was sure that her strange ability to whip up a meal meant she could handle the cleanup in the same way.

Last night she said I'd need clothes for at least a week, and I still needed to call my job. They weren't going to be happy about my early retirement, but hey, it's a college town, and staff turnover was always high. I knew they'd be able to fill my position quickly.

As I realized I was really going to meet my sister, I suddenly had goose bumps running up my spine. My sister. My *twin* sister. Holy shit, Batman! My twin sister who has eyes the opposite color of mine. This was just too crazy. I mean, how were we going to find her? I wondered what led Ruth to believe she was in or near Salt Lake City.

While I dressed in shorts, t-shirt, and running shoes, I could hear Ruth on the phone in the other room. I got my duffle bag and packed as many clothes as I could. I left the duffle on my bed and went into the living room. Ruth was wrapping up her conversation, pacing between the kitchen and living room. Ending the call, she turned to me.

"We have an appointment with the jewelers down the street. I've used them a few times in the past, and they're very happy to try and get these cut down and fitted on you before we get in the air." She was beaming.

"Okay. Are you going to let me know how you know where my sister is? And don't forget, there are still a few things I need clarified. Like your mention that there were others looking for me." Yeah, I'd been keeping a list.

"Well, your sister's name is Emily. You are identical twins except, like me and my twin, your eyes are opposite colors. Emily was placed with an adoptive family in Texas, just like you were. She graduated high school early and attended Baylor University for a year before dropping out. The last contact her adoptive parents had with her was two years ago when she was in Las Vegas working for the police department. We've been tracking unusual seismic activity. There are networks within our own culture, I guess you could call it. Some networks you try to avoid, and some you depend heavily upon."

She walked back into the kitchen and started washing her coffee cup. I followed, and she kept talking.

"So, we put out the word to a trusted network in Utah that we were looking for her. They have contacts in the police departments there. When we found your location, I started looking at earthquake patterns around the Las Vegas area as well. I found patterns that matched our quake patterns, not necessarily the same dates, but in intensity and frequency. I came here to find you, and my friend Aurora went to Salt Lake City."

She dried the cup, placed it in the cabinet, hung up my dishtowel, turned, and leaned one hip against the counter while crossing her arms over her stomach. "I'm sure you've noticed my phone activity," she said. It was a statement, not a question. "Aurora and I've been in touch constantly. She's pretty sure she's located Emily." She smiled, flashing her brilliant white teeth.

"Am I related to Aurora, too?" I asked.

"Um, no, not a direct relative, but she is my oldest and dearest friend. She's the only other living person who knows the truth of your existence. She helped me make the arrangements for your adoptions."

I didn't realize I was scowling. I guess because I was thinking too hard about the information she'd just given me. She reached out and chucked me under the chin with her knuckle.

"Lighten up and lose the frown. Things are just going to get better from here," she said.

Turning, she walked into the living room, and I again followed her. Ruth grabbed her purse—or whatever it is.

"Let's head to the jewelers, and I'll continue this story. The quicker they get started, the sooner you'll have greater protection."

Protection? *Right.* But she hadn't lied to me yet, so I decided to go with it. For now. If she feels diamonds protect her, I'll play along.

We made the trip to the jewelers without my blacking out. A vast improvement, from my perspective. However, deciding what I needed at the jewelers was more difficult than I'd expected.

Ruth's style of accessories fit her, but the size and number of items didn't suit me. I'm not outlandish on my likes, but I'm not frou-frou either. She attempted to persuade me to order earrings to go with one of the rings, but I nixed that quickly. I'd pierced my ears in high school, but never liked the feel. So, after I stopped wearing them, the holes grew back together, and I really didn't want to repeat that process.

One of the associates had a watch they suggested could be adapted quickly for the stones on the band, and I agreed. We'd return to the jewelers on our way to the airport to pick up the items. Ruth made arrangements for the jewelers to keep the remainder of the diamonds to sell and pay for our purchases. We then headed to some clothing stores in the area. Ruth wanted to find additional items to take on our trip.

I felt I needed a reality check. It was only yesterday that I went to the bookstore to find a good read and ended up with a family. We had a family outing to visit a cave hidden in a remote mountain in the middle of nowhere, picked up a few "rocks," and were presently shopping to go on a trip. Toto, I don't think we're in Kansas anymore.

Ruth had a lot of text messages while we were shopping, I guessed from Aurora, but she never commented on those. She told me more about my sister and how her adoption had been so different from mine. While she never spent any time with Emily, she'd received photos and letters from her adoptive parents until Emily graduated and left home.

"You see, we all go through those periods where we need to be away from what we know. We want to experience something new. At least, that's what Emily's adoptive parents thought. They believed that she'd have some kind of life experience and then come home. But she stopped calling. Not long after that, her cell phone was found in a bus terminal in Kansas City. Then she went for months before she'd send them postcards, none of which had any postmarks that could be read, but they had postage."

Ruth sat across from me, with her hands on the table, one hand absently playing with the ring on her forefinger as she talked. She looked different to me now than she had some twenty-four hours ago. I thought she was more sophisticated than what I'd originally thought. She really wasn't a stalker. She even seemed taller somehow. The brown of her eyes was almost chocolate in color, with flecks of gold thrown in. Well, at least the real eye color of one of her eyes. She'd shown me the other eye, green, but not long enough that I could study it.

Her shoulder-length, wavy hair was a deep chestnut color and shined with a high luster.

Then it hit me. She was wearing a wedding ring. How could I have overlooked that detail?

I pointed to her hands. "So, you're married? I never thought to ask."

Her interest flicked back to her hand as she stretched it flat on the table.

"Many years," she stated, and she seemed to sit a little straighter. Her eyes crinkled with her smile. "We have three boys. Well, I say boys," she said, glancing back up to meet my eyes. "They're grown men who chide me when they hear me referring to them as boys."

For someone who had three grown children, she didn't seem to look old enough, and I was shocked she hadn't mentioned them before now.

There weren't many people left in the café where we'd decided to eat. It had been the late lunch crowd when we arrived, but now there were only a few other tables occupied. The noise level had started out as a constant buzz, making it hard to even hear ourselves think. Now I felt almost like I needed to whisper so the rest of the room wouldn't hear our discussion.

"Ruth, why can't one of your sons take over as the head of the family?" To my way of thinking, if she had children, then she really didn't need us, did she?

Leaning in on the table, Ruth glanced around the room. "Despite popular myth, men cannot be witches," she started explaining, then held up a hand quickly when I opened my mouth. "I'm not saying men can't do magic. I'm saying in blood lines, you're either one or the other. Our bloodline is of witches," she said on a whisper. "While wizards are a whole other bloodline. For witches, it will only be females that inherit the trait, while in a wizard family, it will only be males."

I was frowning in concentration because, like she'd said, this went so against popular belief. Why was I talking about popular belief? They're myths, for heaven sake! Then I froze. We were so not talking about fiction anymore. This is real, I reminded myself, and I suddenly felt the need to rub my temples.

"Okay," I sighed. "How do you think we're going to find her?" I asked, and just kept the questions flying. "How do you think she's going to take this? We're just going to show up like you did to me? What if she doesn't want to talk to us?" I placed my hands in my lap and lowered my chin to examine my jagged, bitten nails, a nervous habit I developed after my parents passed away. Sure, I'd gained a family since yesterday, and Ruth was extremely happy to have me around her, but if Emily had experienced a wonderful childhood, she might be more comfortable and not want any more family, regardless that we're twins. I felt like I was on an emotional roller coaster.

"Well, as I said, Aurora is pretty sure she's located her. She's a police officer, Sam. I know we—I mean, you—will be a shock. But I'm sure, once we make contact, she'll not want to be separated." She smiled back at me. The smile brought the tiny lines around the outside of her eyes into focus, giving a small hint that maybe she'd had some experience in life. Hell, if everything else she wants me to believe was true, she must've seen events no one else had.

"You've not been in close enough proximity since you were born to have developed that link that makes your bond stronger." She paused, giving me a serious look with brows slightly drawn. "I'm sorry we weren't able to keep you together. There was no way to keep you truly safe unless we made sure you were unknown, even to each other. My mother used to tell me stories of the other twins that came before us —in our bloodline, that is. She said the link forged makes a Gemini Witch a stronger power than those not born twins. That power, even before you become of age, attracts those who can sense our powers."

She ended that statement and sat up straight like she'd been hit with a jolt of electricity. She started looking around the room, then eased back into her seat, exhaling. The look of fear that had sparked in her face relaxed as well. "I forgot where we were. These aren't topics that we need to discuss in the open, if you know what I mean." She winked at me as she started to rise from her chair.

She paid our bill, and we headed back to the jeweler's. We didn't talk much on the short trip back across town. Traffic had picked up, and while the distance wasn't far from the café, the volume of traffic kept us longer than usual. Shoppers in this small town always made my skin crawl. I stared out the side window, watching all the traffic going nowhere fast.

I thought about the coffee shop where I was no longer employed. Vicki had been ticked off but understanding that family business had come up. She said she appreciated the call, even if it was short notice and I couldn't give a two-week notice. By the time I'd gotten off the phone, she was asking me to get in touch if I wanted the job back when I returned to town. Would I need a job when we got back? Could I live like Ruth has lived? Lost in my own thoughts, I wasn't aware we'd parked until Ruth was already standing outside of her door, reaching in for her purse. That purse had to be magical. There was no other way of describing it.

Inside the jeweler's, Ruth was beaming. You could tell she'd spent a lot of time here. They treated her like she was royalty, but if she'd been bringing them diamonds and ordering her accessories here since she was my age, why wouldn't they? I was only mildly surprised that Ruth wouldn't let me see what we'd ordered as soon as they brought out the boxes.

The owner made an appearance, and the deep hand-shaking and smiles began. He picked up the boxes then herded us behind the counter and down a hall. I was thinking we were headed to a storage area, but it turned out to be his office. Nothing says Arkansas more than a man's office decorated with Duck Hunter's Paradise accessories.

Ducks were mounted and pinned to the wall to make them look as if they were in flight. He had an old-fashioned roll-top desk pushed against the wall, with two armchairs in dark hunter green to the right of his desk. Nothing between him and his customers, or that's what the setup would have you believe. You could tell he liked to play touchy-feely with his valued customers.

He stood smiling, just to the side of the door, as he motioned us in. As Ruth passed, he ran his hand down her back in a fatherly manner. I was afraid he'd touch me too, but he only nodded as I passed then closed the door and left us in his office.

The owner had handed Ruth the boxes before she entered the office, and she in turn sat at his desk. The desk was open and cluttered but had space enough to place the boxes. She was still smiling.

"Do you always get the royal treatment when you come in here?"

"I've been doing business here a long time. It's benefitted Mr. Hill, and it's benefitted me, too. It will definitely make a big change in your life also, dear."

She opened each box and left it where it sat. She stood

and turned to me where I'd taken my seat in one of the armchairs. She reached out to me with both hands, and I placed mine in hers.

"Now, I have to tell you that when you put these on, you'll be slightly overwhelmed. That's why I've always acquainted myself with my jewelry back here in Mr. Hill's office."

Was she kidding me? "Okay, Ruth, its jewelry. Granted, its diamonds, but are you telling me it's going to glow like it did in the cave?" I hesitated as she was drawing me to my feet, and I resisted slightly as she pulled me up. The look on her face had me wondering if I really wanted to do this now.

She led me to the desk, and I quickly glanced at the boxes then back to her face. She had a completely blank look on her face, and I wasn't exactly sure what that meant, having only been around her since yesterday. Expressionology with Ruth wasn't a science yet.

I looked back inside the boxes, slower this time. They were perfect. Not that I liked a lot of jewelry, but heck, I'd never really been able to afford any. Maybe I'd learn to like a little bling.

I reached down and carefully touched the largest stone in all of the pieces. A slight glow emitted out of the box, making me draw my finger back as quickly as I could. I just wasn't used to this type of mystical crap happening. I'm not sure I'd ever get used to it, but it seemed this was probably less frightening than the time travel that Ruth could pull off.

Ruth picked up the anklet and pinky toe ring. "Sit down and let's get started. We're going to have to finish here, grab our luggage, then head to the airport."

I sat back in the chair and slipped off one tennis shoe. I'd decided after our trip last night in the woods that travel with Ruth would require sturdy clothes and footwear. She knelt and placed the anklet around my right ankle. I was waiting for her to put the pinky ring on, but she looked up at me and frowned.

"Now the other foot," she commanded.

I slipped off my other shoe, and she slipped the ring onto my smallest toe. I wasn't sure how I was going to like this. I wasn't one to have things stuck between my toes. Even my sandals had to be those that didn't fit like a flip flop. I just could never stand it, and now to wear a toe ring? I stood up and looked down at my feet.

Ruth stepped back to the desk, looked down at the other boxes, and then raised her hand out to me, wanting me to join her. She handed me the watch, and I placed it on my left wrist. I was surprised to see no glow. I glanced from the watch down to both feet, not feeling any different. I was puzzled at what she'd been going on about.

She lifted the last piece out of the box. A gold band with small diamonds encrusted all the way around it. She ran her fingers over it lovingly, then turned to me with a huge grin as she handed it to me. I took the ring from her, looked at her grin, and placed the ring on my right hand while I was watching her face.

I felt it immediately. There was a tingle at the base of my spine that spread outward down my legs and up the back of my arms at the same time. The look of shock on my face only made Ruth's grin wider. I held my arms out away from my body, looking at each one in turn. I was wearing a short-sleeved t-shirt, but all I could see was chainmail, like knights had worn. Still tingling, I shook my head quickly, like a dog shedding water, and looked back to see my bare arms. I was panicking, and I looked to Ruth quickly, only to see her looking at me with a raised eyebrow.

"What just happened?"

"What did you see?" She stood there with her arms crossed around herself now and a slight upturn to one side of her mouth.

"I guess it looked like a knight's armor, the chainmail type. What was it? Did you see it?"

"No, I didn't see it on you, but I saw it on myself the first day I put on my stones. It's just part of the package. You are officially protected now."

"What does that mean exactly?"

"Remember the glow in the cave? This is part of the stone's glow, except you're the only one able to see it now. It will help defend you against other witches. Not everyone one is as—how shall I put this?—socially adept as we are."

I was looking at her like she'd grown two heads. "I still have questions for you regarding all those *others* you mentioned earlier. Don't think I've forgotten them."

I'd started running my fingers over the watch band while I was watching her. I didn't think I felt any different, but that tingle that had started in my lower back returned to my extremities and just stayed there now. Odd.

"Yes, I know you still have questions, and I am pretty sure we have lots of time. If you think you can walk out of here normally, we can get on our way. I'm sure Mr. Hill would like his office back."

Could I walk out of here normally? I put on some jewelry; I didn't break my leg. I frowned at her, narrowing my eyes, and shook my head. When I turned on my heel to head for the door, I spun all the way around. I would've made another spin if Ruth hadn't put her hand out to grab my arm.

"What the hell was that!" I gasped.

"Maybe you're not as ready as you think. It affects us all differently. My grandmother would tell about her Aunt Exie, who levitated when she put on her jewels. How about walking slowly from wall to wall first?"

She still had her hand on my arm and turned to guide me. Just think slowly, I repeatedly told myself. I finally got the hang of it, and she soon let me walk on my own. Who would've thought that these stones would've made a difference in how I walked! Then it hit me.

"This is how you move from one location to another. The time travel, right?" I asked in my best accusatory voice.

"Something like that, but you're nowhere near moving at the speed of light yet. Let's just make it to the airport first," she said, gesturing to the door again so we could leave. This time, I made it just fine.

We checked in at the airport an hour before takeoff. I was a little lost, not being an expert on air travel, and so I just followed Ruth. She pointed things out that I wouldn't have known to do, like take your shoes off to go through security. Hurry, hurry, hurry—and for what? Just to sit and wait in some uncomfortable chairs. Ruth would frown at me when I'd complain or let out a long sigh.

A family walked up to our gate and started to sit close to us. Four kids on a plane. I could tell how this trip was going to turn out. I've seen movies. Two of the kids looked to be under the age of five. One of those was in diapers. Ruth closed her eyes as if in silent prayer. Before the family could camp their rears in the seats near us, the father decided to move closer to the gate, and he said something about it being quicker as they moved away. Ruth opened her eyes, sighed, and grinned at me.

Ruth handed me my ticket, so I studied it as best I could. It read "one-way ticket" to Salt Lake City. I turned it over. Why would we get just one-way tickets? I'd heard people at work talking about round-trip tickets, and I remembered seeing other people checking in saying round-trip as well.

I leaned in close to Ruth while she was checking her text messages. "Why do we only have a one-way ticket?" I whispered.

Ruth put her phone down, looked around us, then leaned toward me to whisper. "We're not coming back on a plane," she said, then leaned back to her own seat.

Huh? Not coming back on a plane? I sat there turning that over in my head. There were buses, trains, or rental cars to drive back, I supposed. Ruth glanced at me out the corner of her eyes. She could tell I was working that over in my head. My pursed lips and drawn brows were big clues that more questions were about to fly.

She leaned back towards me to whisper. "Once I have been somewhere one time, I can get us back where we came from. I've never been to Utah, so I'd have no idea where to deliver us," she said, then straightened back up.

Then it all clicked in my head. Ruth was going to transport us back. I wasn't sure how to feel about that. I didn't want to take another unexpected nap.

"But what about your car?" I leaned in and whispered back to her. "Will you bring us back to the airport? Will I be asleep again?"

She grinned at that while still looking at her phone. "My husband and boys are going to pick it up. I'm not sure yet if I'll need you to take a nap or not."

I couldn't believe the amount of time it took to have everyone board one tin can. Yeah, I said tin can. I gazed out the windows overlooking the parked plane for a long time before they started letting us board. Staff busily worked to offload luggage on carts, then another cart appeared, and they began stuffing luggage back onto the plane. I was impressed with their scanning technology. Ruth explained that was how they made sure your luggage made it to the correct destination, at least most of the time.

I had no idea how they got so much luggage crammed in that lower space.

It was then that I realized I'd be sitting in this tin cylinder that looked like a hairspray can with wings for a few hours. Yeah, I'd been up in a smaller plane, but that was for a spin around a city at a few thousand feet lower than what we were about to do.

No doubt the worry on my face was echoed by my clenched hands, which were now white knuckled. Ruth, without looking up, reached over and laid one hand on top of mine. *Ahh. Calm.* I was hoping that was a trick she could teach me. Maybe I could calm myself. It was finally time to board the plane, and I realized we had first class tickets. Looking toward the rear of the plane, I was very thankful. I wasn't sure I could've made it all the way to Utah packed in like sardines.

Once I got seated, Ruth expertly showed me how to stow my carry-on and operate the seatbelts. She opened her purse, pulled out two new magazines, and handed one to me. We hadn't stopped at the news stand, so I could only raise an eyebrow in question to her for their appearance. She grinned and started thumbing through her Newsweek. I shook my head and started reading People.

Being airborne only decreased the noise in the cabin slightly. I started trying to pop my ears by yawning to release the pressure. Ruth dove into her purse again and produced gum. Damn, she thinks of everything.

We leaned in toward one another, and Ruth began. "Tell me what's happened to you in the last six months. You don't have to tell me, of course. I'm just curious what led to your heightened emotions a few months back."

I leaned back from her as if I had been stung. I narrowed my eyes at her.

"It is a long trip," she added.

What did I have to lose? Dignity, privacy, sanity. But I stood to gain even more, because this was my aunt, my closest living relative. Well, closest until we find Emily.

SAM 106

I took a deep breath and let it out slowly as I started to explain what my life had been like for the past several months. *Just get it over with*, I told myself. Leaning toward her, I started to explain.

I didn't have many friends, other than co-workers. Of those, I'm probably closest to Beth, who was an education major like me. We'd had a few of the same classes, but she was a year ahead. Unlike me, Beth wasn't a poor, starving college student. Her parents were footing the bill for her entire college experience. The only reason she even worked was because her parents refused to pay for her sorority's extracurricular activities. Beth belonged to Delta Omega Psi Delta, and she often talked me into accompanying her to the DOPD sponsored activities. These were harmless events for the most part, and any free time not spent studying, I could count on Beth having planned our campus life. She had a car, which was a plus, seeing that I only had my bicycle. Beth always looked out for me if I had to make any trips farther than work or school.

Fall is my favorite time of year. It always has been, and

this last fall was pivotal. One night in mid-October, Beth and I were walking and talking at the track, when a group of jocks rolled onto the track as well. I'd dressed in sweats and a t-shirt with my hair pulled back in a ponytail. Beth had her curly, platinum-blonde hair pulled back in a ponytail as well, but she was still comfortable enough to show her tan legs off in a pair of shorts and new Nikes. My Nikes were well loved, very scuffed, and broken in. Living on a tight budget, you learn to make sure your clothes and shoes last as long as possible.

The group of jocks were all dressed in varying combinations of our outfits. We kept walking around the track as they started stretching in the infield. The low buzz of their joking with one another was carried to us on the breeze, and you could tell the truly cooler nights were near.

On our first lap after the jocks arrived, they entered the track almost as we were even with them. We paused only slightly to let them get ahead of us. *Hmm…preplanned?* I wondered without saying anything aloud.

It was obvious when two of them turned to face us, showing off their jogging backwards skills. After a few yards of jogging backwards and grinning for all they were worth, they turned and sprinted to catch up to their group. When they were about fifty yards ahead of us, Beth and I glanced at each other and rolled our eyes.

We'd stopped talking when we walked upon them as they entered the track ahead of us. Knowing that they'd be watching and could probably hear our conversation, we waited until they made the turn before we started talking again. Beth had been giving me the details of one of her recent dates, and I was avidly listening to each detail. I hadn't dated much. My emotional hang-ups had left me sometimes withdrawn and many times shy, so I lived vicariously through

Beth and her active social life. Group activities with her sorority sisters were fine, but a one-on-one date was a hard step for me to take.

We could hear the jocks pressing up behind us, so we moved to the outer lanes to let them pass. The same two backward-jogging guys performed the maneuver again. I thought they were probably looking at Beth, so I glanced at her. She simply kept her chin level to the ground and never broke her stride. It kept going through my mind how nice it must be to be so confident. We discontinued our discussion until they were again far enough ahead not to overhear.

On their second lap around, one of the two jocks turned to jog backwards just as I stumbled over my own two feet. We bumped into each other and ended up rolling on the ground. After determining neither of us were maimed, we laughed. The guy, Jeff, kept apologizing for knocking me down. He kept insisting he'd caused the incident, regardless of my protests. He was six foot two, with blond hair, deep-blue eyes, and a California tan, and he was on the baseball team. After he introduced himself, he asked to make up for the collision by taking me for coffee at Starbucks. I'd wrinkled my nose and declined, thinking it would be too much of a good thing. I loved my job and my java, but returning there with a guy? Not with this guy. Not right then.

He helped me to my feet and, after reassuring himself that I was okay, turned and sprinted to catch up with his group. When he was gone, Beth told me how she'd met him previously at a sorority-fraternity mixer. She went on to say that one of her sorority sisters had dated him, so she knew a little about him from her as well. He was a decent guy who treated his date well, when he wasn't busy with baseball practices or games. He was a physical education major with aspirations of landing a pro baseball contract after college.

She stopped talking about him as his group jogged past us again.

Jeff gracefully slowed his jog to stay even with me. Grinning, he asked again if I was okay, then asked if he could call me. I thought I could handle that, so I agreed. He grinned then jogged to catch up with his group. It was only after he was gone that I realized he hadn't gotten my number. I turned to mention it to Beth and found her smiling from ear to ear.

"It is about time," she drew out slowly. "I thought you'd never want to date anyone."

"I didn't agree to a date," I pointed out. "I just agreed to let him call me. But he didn't ask for my number. What should I do?"

"Let me handle it," Beth said sprinting ahead of me.

Ugh. I was going to be embarrassed if she ran right up there and tackled him to give him my number. But she didn't even make it to his group before breaking away from the track and heading for the car. Once there, she dug around for a second then sprinted back to join me.

I'd kept walking, almost mortified at first, then slowed down some so that by the time Beth returned I was even with her. In her hand Beth had a folded piece of paper and an ink pen. While jogging, she slipped both items into my pocket without saying a word, but the grin on her face remained.

I was busy looking at her and watching the guys come around the last turn in the track, again gaining on us. Suddenly, I was nervous. My hands grew clammy and my chest tight. If Jeff stopped again, I didn't know if I'd be able to breathe.

Sure enough, he stopped. He didn't turn around, jogging backwards this time. He just stopped jogging all together and started walking beside me. Beth, saint that she was, picked up her pace, pulling ahead of us and giving us privacy.

We talked about classes the next lap around the track. When we got back to the parking area, the rest of his group stood waiting. Sly grins all around. He introduced me to a few of the guys. They were anxious to leave as they'd gotten their run in and were simply waiting on him, the driver. They started to leave, my embarrassment creeping up on me again. Twice now he was leaving without getting my phone number. Maybe he didn't really want to talk to me. I kept standing, watching them walk away.

When the group was halfway to the parking area, Jeff turned and sprinted back to me, finally asking for my number. I was prepared, and I was smitten.

Over the next few months, in between classes, games, and his marathon practices, we dated. Christmas holidays had me unsure of what to expect. I'd never dated anyone beyond one date. Jeff was going home for the holiday break, and I was staying at school. I didn't have family to go visit nor any to come visit me. We went out before he left, and he gave me a stuffed bear wearing a baseball uniform sporting his number. I baked him a batch of double chocolate chip cookies with walnuts, which was his favorite.

As Christmas goes, it had been one of the better holidays I could remember since my parents had passed away. I worked as many days as I could during the break to make a few extra dollars. My free time I spent going to the library, reading, and going back to the library. When Jeff returned a few days before the new semester began, we picked up right where we'd left off.

Jeff lived in the dorms, but he came to my apartment almost every day, except when he had baseball or fraternity activities. He was attending school on a baseball scholarship, and his parents covered the bill for extra activities. He had a car and spending money, and we had a lot of dates, until spring training began.

We'd been taking things slow, mainly my doing. While I was 21 and very inexperienced, I wasn't unaware of the way my body reacted to his. Make out sessions on my couch would get steamy, but then I'd have to break it off and send him home. As soon as he was out the door, I'd blow off steam, sometimes with calisthenics but many times just screaming in frustration while taking a cold shower. I wanted more, but I had ideals in my mind.

My plan was to be a teacher, and to me, that meant acting a certain way. Teachers who slept around were less likely to be offered good jobs or ever find tenure, at least the ones I knew of. Not to mention living in the same town, where it would be very easy for everyone to know your business. Jeff and I had discussed this several times, and he said he understood, but we were still both frustrated.

Spring break only increased the tension when I went home with him to meet his family. Jeff was originally from Alabama, and his family had a condo on the beach near Ft. Morgan. The invitation had been extended for me to join them. They wanted to meet me, but I wasn't sure about meeting them. We'd been dating since the beginning of the fall semester. Nothing serious, or at least I didn't think so.

Since I was a starving college student, with barely enough funds to cover rent, we made the ten-hour trip in his car. My foster parents always said, "You really don't know someone until you live together." I think that needs to be extended to, "You really don't know someone until you travel with them!"

I hated the way he drove. Two hours into the trip and not even out of Arkansas, he was one of the rudest drivers I'd been around. Halfway through Mississippi we had our first argument over rest areas versus truck stops. By the time we reached his parents' condo, we weren't speaking. His parents picked up on the tension as soon as we arrived.

Besides his parents, Jeff's brother, Gary, was staying the week. Gary looked a lot like Jeff but was bulkier and very immature for his age. Just my opinion. His father looked very much like Jeff, but his straight, blond hair was thinning. His mother, almost as tall as me, was wider by several inches. She was, however, very carefree and loving to her men. She was very personable and friendly when she showed me to my room. *Touchy-feely* was the term that came to my mind. She acted like she wanted us to be friends, but I was leery. I wasn't sure I wanted to get to know these people all of a sudden, but I smiled and decided to make the best of it.

The first full day as I walked on the beach, Jeff made the effort to walk with me and hold my hand. I'd never been to the beach before and was mesmerized by the white sand and the sound of the water rolling in to lap at our feet. Well, that and holding his hand. It was obvious he was trying to make up for the car trip. That evening, after the family meal and bonfire, when everyone had retired back to the condo, we walked in the moonlight. When we returned to his family's beachfront view, it all went downhill fast.

We started out playing in the shallow water, then lying on the sand. I was laying on my back with Jeff to my side, bodies touching down our length. He kissed me gently with almost butterfly kisses. He went from my lips down my jaw line to my ear, and I gasped. When he moved from my ear down the side of my neck, I felt myself starting to relax. He came back to my lips, and we both let our hands explore the others arms and back. I wrapped my arms around his neck loosely, and his hands traveled down my sides, to my waist and back up to cup me gently, causing me to moan out loud. I couldn't think of anything except the sensation.

I was wearing a two piece, and it took very little effort for Jeff to put his thumb under the lower edge of my top and then rub. The more I arched up, the more he raised the lower edge of my top to reveal more of me. When my breast was fully exposed, and the air hit me, two things happened at once. I knew my nipple clenched tight, and sound returned.

I could hear the waves hitting the beach, and I became aware of where we were. I was startled. "Jeff," I whispered. "We have to stop. Your parents could walk out here any minute. I can't do this here, this close to them."

Jeff had moved his lips back to my jaw. When he reached my ear, he whispered, "Let's jump in the water. We can move far enough out that no one would know. We can leave our clothes here."

I shoved against his shoulders and started trying to arrange my top back over myself at the same time. "No! I won't do it. I can't."

I could tell him the truth, or I could tell him what I wanted him to know. Lying to him was one thing, but I knew deep down my fears of abandonment, intimacy, and losing control were the real problems. Hell, just the fear of not knowing what things felt like kept me pushing him away.

"You know how I feel about this. We might be hundreds of miles away from school, but I still won't take that chance. I have to be able to hold my head up and look at a lot of teenagers in the eye next semester."

He rolled over on his back, throwing an arm over his eyes and almost hissing. "What the hell does that mean?"

"You know how hard it is for a woman to get a job teaching if everyone knows she sleeps around. It's not that way for men. It's a double standard. You'd get hired in a New York minute regardless of what rumors went around about you. I've only got myself, Jeff, and I have to be careful.

You're lined up for draft choices when we graduate. I'm not trying to be a prude, okay. I was really, really enjoying myself." I was sitting up now and sighed as I wrapped my arms around my knees. "We both know when you get drafted, you're moving. Your family lives here, and who knows where you'll end up. I don't think either of us wants to talk about marriage right now."

I glanced over my shoulder to find he was still on his back, face covered. "Don't get me wrong, I really like you, but I don't think both of us strongly liking each other should be the basis for where I think this was going right now." I turned and looked down at him. The glow from the windows of his parent's condo was just barely enough to be able to make out his form but not his features. He still had his arm slung over his eyes, hands in fists, and breathing deeply.

"Fine," he said, rolling over and jumping to his feet. He never turned back to look at me but started walking away up the shore line into the farther recesses of the night.

I sat there for what seemed like forever before I gathered my sandals and went back in the house to find my own bed. Jeff's parents were sitting in front of the TV watching the evening news. I didn't say anything, just crept down the hall to my room, closed the door, and left the light off. I changed clothes and crawled in my bed, frustrated beyond belief. I wanted to cry but felt too drained by the encounter.

My refusal to lose my clothes with Jeff got me the silent treatment for the rest of the week, for the most part. We did have some yelling matches in between, and I discovered he was very good at slamming doors. His family tried to act like nothing was wrong. I spent my days walking the beach and swimming. Evenings were family meals and more beach life. Jeff and his brother started going clubbing halfway through the week, while I was left to fend for myself. The trip back home was even worse with the deathly silence. I was glad I had my fully charged iPod shuffle, fully charged, before we hit the road.

It was during that ill-fated week, that the sleep walking started. The first night, I went to bed mad at Jeff over our fight. I know, not bad right? Except I awoke on the beach next to where there had been a bonfire the night before. His mother said that everyone got up and no one could find me. The doors to the condo were all still locked, …with locks that could only be set while you were inside. Locked. Huh?

This was repeated the next night as well. I'd never been known to sleep walk. I'd lived on my own since I started college, and without roommates, how would you know if you walked in your sleep? Here was Jeff's seemingly normal family telling me I was outside of the house each morning. The funny thing about it was that I'd wake up in the places that I'd formed a good memory. The bonfire his family and neighbors would have practically every night on the beach, and the shore where I found starfish and sand dollars. Never once did they find me in Jeff's car nor near his room. The nights I spent on the beach asleep, I'd been lucky that no one else bothered me.

Once we returned home, things didn't improve. Getting back into classes and work seemed to take my mind off our problems. I figured that we'd just go our separate ways. I'd lick my wounds, learn from the experience, and move on. A week after we returned, Jeff showed up at my apartment. I'd been washing dishes when he knocked on the door. I was shocked to find him standing there, hands in his pockets, looking sheepish with a smile.

"Hi, Sam," he said, "I miss you." Ducking his chin into his chest, I thought he looked embarrassed.

As well he should be. The thought whipped across my mind.

"Can I come in? I want to say I'm sorry for last week and see you."

I stood there for several moments, staring at him. When I didn't move, he looked up and gave me a dazzling smile, cocking his head to the side. "I really do miss you," he whispered.

I narrowed my eyes at him just slightly. *Should I, or shouldn't I? Should I, or shouldn't I?*

Oh, to hell with it. "Sure, come on in. I was just washing dishes." I held the door while he walked in. He didn't offer to touch me, keeping his hands in his pockets. He moved to the middle of the room and just stood, kind of rocking back and forth.

I rolled my eyes to myself and walked around him back to the kitchen. He followed, leaning against the counter opposite of the sink. I returned to washing my dishes. He cleared his throat after a span of dead silence and then started randomly talking about his friends and their spring breaks. I listened, nodding my head occasionally to show I was listening while I dried dishes, but I really didn't hear what he was saying. I was rehashing in my head what had happened on our trip.

At some point I must've stopped drying and was staring off into nothingness. I didn't hear him move, but suddenly he was at my back, wrapping his arms around my waist and pulling me back against him. I stiffened at first as he put his lips near my ear.

"You haven't heard me, have you, Sam?"

"Um, sorry, I must have just zoned out. What did you say?"

"I asked if you can ever forgive me, but I think you were already zoned out," he whispered softly in my ear.

I wasn't sure I wanted to forgive and forget. But he was my first real boyfriend, and I missed the companionship. I bent my head and was looking at his arms wrapped around me, and a tingle ran from the top of my spine to my knees. Having him that close, with his breath warm against my ear, was making my resolve weaken. I took a deep breath and laid my dishtowel on top of the stack of dishes I'd been drying. I wrapped my arms over the top of his, hugging only his forearms.

"I've missed you, too. I'm sorry about everything that happened as well. If you still want to see me, I guess we can try to date again," I said, leaning my head to the side to glance at him out of the corner of my eye.

He turned his head slightly and kissed me on the cheek, still holding me tightly against him.

Okay, this wasn't so bad. He wanted to kiss and make up. Try to work things out. I could handle that. He released me and moved a step toward the living room, holding his hand out to me.

"You can finish those later. Let's just watch some TV, okay?" He was smiling again.

"Sure," was all I could say, sighing. After all, it was Friday night, and I could put the dishes away after he went home.

We walked hand in hand to the couch. I had basic cable included with my apartment, so I was sure we could probably find an old movie. Well, old to the public, but probably new to me. Affording cable as part of my rent was one thing; making it to the movies was something else.

Jeff found an old Robin Williams comedy, and we sat side by side, holding hands. Halfway through the movie, I remembered I had some microwave popcorn I could make. I left him sitting on the couch while I marched off to the kitchen to whip up the treat. I hoped it was the buttered kind. If we weren't at the movies, at least we could pretend.

I dumped the results into a mixing bowl, glad I hadn't burned it this time. When I returned to the living room, Jeff had sprawled on my couch, making himself at home and leaving me nowhere to sit. I grabbed the few throw pillows I had and sat on the floor in front of the couch, making sure I sat where he could reach the popcorn too.

Towards the end of the movie, when the bowl was empty, Jeff hung his hand over my shoulder. He'd occasionally turn his hand on its side, extend his thumb upward, and stroke the side of my cheek. It was pleasant enough after the initial shock of it, so I just smiled and kept watching the show. The movie was hitting its high points for the ending when Jeff leaned in and kissed my left cheek. Then he moved his hand down my right arm, stroking up and down softly. When I sighed, he started kissing my ear gently. I closed my eyes, leaning my head to the side, allowing him easier access.

He sat up quickly, putting his legs on either side of me. He grasped my upper arms then started lifting and turning me toward him at the same time. I never fully stood up, and he was easing me toward him where he sat on the couch. When I was within inches of his face, he reached out and moved my knees, one at time, to either side of him so that I was straddling his lap, facing him. He sighed then smiled.

I was lost on sensations at that point, riding that wave of warmth you only get while someone strokes your ear with a very soft tongue, and I wanted to kiss him very badly. I wrapped my arms around his neck and leaned in as far as I could, while I stood on my knees on my couch. We kissed, and my sense of reasoning left. Tongues danced while his hands slowly stroked my back up and down. At some point, without realizing it, I'd gotten as close to him as I could while on my knees and discovered I had him straining his neck backwards.

I'm not terribly tall but, on my knees, I was standing taller than him. I need to change angles or whatever, but I just couldn't think. I sat back, more on my heels which brought my lower anatomy in direct contact with the front of his fly. The old, thin, baggy sweats I was wearing left nothing to the imagination as I felt the shape of him against my sensitive flesh. Suddenly, I couldn't get enough. I needed more.

Pressing into him, trying to get closer as we kissed, I raised myself slightly against his chest, causing the lower contact to lessen. With a mind of its own, my body instinctively sought his as I sat back down, stirring up fires that I couldn't seem to resist. A moan escaped from my lips, as Jeff nipped at my earlobe then soothed it with his tongue. His lips slipped down to my neck, causing me to arch my back and rub myself against him repeatedly.

"Oh my God!" was all I could think, then I realized it had escaped from my lips, but I didn't care. Tightness started in my upper thighs and lower stomach and kept building until it settled into one huge sensation somewhere south of my waist.

Jeff seemed to know what his body was doing to mine, because his hands moved my hips to a rhythm, grating my body against his as his lips nipped and licked at my neck.

I grabbed his face between my hands and kissed him fiercely, grinding myself into him, needing him to stop this exquisite torture. . . and then the world shattered into a trillion different pieces. It seemed like everything stopped, even my breathing, until I went limp against him. Jeff gave a dirty sounding chuckle, wrapping his arms around me and holding me close. My heart was beating against my ribs so hard I thought I'd be bruised if I looked.

"Was that what I think it was?" I asked breathlessly when I could form words.

"Mm-hmm," Jeff murmured, and started nibbling on my neck again.

The reality of the situation hit me hard. I'd had an orgasm and didn't know what was happening until it was all over. I stiffened just slightly. I was suddenly embarrassed. I'd kept my contact with him going because I liked it. My body really liked it, and three hours ago I was convinced I was alone again. I hadn't had time to think if this is what I really wanted. Sure, my body had definite ideas of its own, apparently, but I couldn't wrap my brain around it.

"My parents are nowhere around," he whispered in my ear, followed by his tongue swirling around the outer edges of the same ear.

I'd still been breathing deeply before he whispered to me and was trying to focus on what he said, when his hands moved lower over my stomach. It wasn't until I felt him run his fingers under the band of my sweats that what he said, and what I was feeling, shocked me into motion.

I jumped up so fast it caused me to roll off him and onto the floor in front of the couch. He looked down and glared at me as I was readjusting my T-shirt and shaking my head no. "No, Jeff!" I glared right back. "Just because I let you back into my house and am willing to make up doesn't mean I've changed my mind."

"What do you mean?" he gaped at me. "You just dry humped me and got off. What about me? I just get stiffed here?"

"I'm sorry, Jeff. I don't know what happened. I didn't know what I was doing," I stammered from the floor, as I felt my face burning bright. I covered my face with my hands and shook my head. Was that really considered having sex?

"I'm sorry, but you need to go," I whispered.

"You don't get it, do you?" he ground out, flashing white teeth in a forced smile. "I have so many girls who want me. They don't turn me down when they come to my room. Hell, they don't turn me down in the back seat of my car. You think denying me really hurts me? Hell, I can get laid within the next hour, but I really wanted you. Fuck you, I don't need this, you, or your morals for a job you don't even have yet." He was struggling to stand up, his face going crimson.

I looked up, still shaking my head. He looked at me and then started kicking the front of my couch and coffee table. He stomped to my bedroom door and started punching the closed door.

I reached my limit. Not only was I a little scared of him, now I was getting mad, too. I scrambled to my feet and opened up my front door, took three steps back, then started yelling for him to get out.

The building manager had already been called by a neighbor, I guess. He arrived just as Jeff turned and took a step toward me. Jeff stopped when he saw the man, turned, and stormed out. After I reassured the manager I was fine, and he left, I locked my door.

I sat on my couch and stared at the door I'd just locked. I was mortified because my apartment manager had seen the end of that scene. I was alone again. Sure, I was lonely, but I'd lived in foster care for most of my life. I wasn't going to be pressured into something I wasn't ready to do. I let the tears flow and sat up all night, crying. Not for the loss of him, but for the loneliness. For having lost my adoptive parents. For not having been rescued. For having no other real family that I could turn to at that moment.

Of course, I omitted the sleepwalking and my intimate awakenings, but I gave Ruth the overview of dating Jeff and our breakup. She listened, intently nodding where appropriate and asking questions when I was too vague. We only paused when the stewardess delivered refreshments.

We still had lots of time floating through the air as I tried to think of what to tell her next. When the stewardess left each of us a fresh cup of coffee and peanuts, I figured *"What the hell,"* and went ahead and told Ruth of the sleepwalking incidents. How I'd fall asleep on my couch watching TV, then find myself the next morning on my bed, still fully clothed. That made her sit up straighter. I even thought she was going to spill her coffee for a second. She glanced all around us then nailed me with a gimlet eye.

"I mean, it was real embarrassing sitting in that doctor's office in that damn paper gown," I added.

What was she narrowing in on me for now? It had been embarrassing, but why did I feel like I suddenly had to defend myself? "You did ask for my heightened emotions, didn't you? I thought it was funny and was running out of my life story, so I just threw it in. I didn't mean to make you mad," I finished, ducking my head.

Hell, I couldn't tell if she'd even taken a breath, just that she had a narrowed looked. I glanced back up as she eased back into her seat. Leaning her head back against the head-rest, she closed her eyes, exhaling at the same time. What the hell had I said to put her over the edge?

"How many times?" she asked without opening her eyes.

"Enough that I was close to losing my job over it," I replied, taking the opportunity to mirror her seating position. This didn't sound like it was going to be good.

"Tell me all about each one of those, and don't leave anything out," she said, turning to me with an intense look.

So, I told her all of it, from waking on the beach to the early morning store opening. She shook her head a few times, but only slightly. I don't think she intended for me to notice, but I had, and it was really starting to worry me.

"So, that's why I ended up at the doctor. Things were back to normal not even a week after I started that journal, so I never went back." I felt like I was suddenly on the defensive.

"The journal helped you, dear, but what helped you more is that your emotions came back to an even keel," she said, starting to grin again. The mischievous look came back to her eyes as she leaned in close to my ear and whispered, "I hate to tell you this, but you weren't sleepwalking."

I jerked away a few inches so I could look her fully in her face. "What's that supposed to mean?"

Get me trapped over a state I couldn't even see, and now she wants to play pop quiz again. Ruth picked up her magazine, flipping through it with that look still on her face. I darted my eyes around the cabin then focused back on Ruth.

She seemed to be thinking of something very entertaining as she turned each page without really reading it. She thumbed through that magazine three times, with me staring at her, before I finally broke.

"Fine, tell me," I almost hissed it through my teeth. "You're dying to tell me, so you might as well get it over with."

She grinned harder then, and I thought she was going to have a sore jaw if she held it any longer. Ruth leaned over toward me again as if to whisper. I met her over the arm rest, turning my ear so I could hear what she wanted to share.

"You've already been doing your own jumping, my dear," she said, and straightened back up.

I jerked back looking at her. "Jumping? What do you mean *jumping*?"

"I mean you've been doing your own time traveling," she

said very low. "You've apparently been doing it in your sleep."

"I don't know what you're talking about," I began. "I just know that I went to sleep in one location and woke up in another. I know that's sleepwalking." I was frowning hard at her now, lips pursed tightly.

"Call it what you want. I've only heard of a few others that can do that—travel while they're asleep. It's a rare talent, but a talent you apparently have. And you did this before you even had your jewels." She stopped and cocked her head to the side a little, still smiling. "It just shocks me to think what you can do with a little training, especially now that you're wearing your stones."

I wasn't smiling. I still had my brows furrowed together. I could feel the muscles straining in my forehead. I slowly turned my head to face foreword and reached up with one hand to try to massage those brows back to a relaxed state. *Jumping*, I thought. She's calling it jumping. Could that explain how I ended up in locations with locked doors? I exhaled loudly and put my head back against the headrest with my eyes closed.

Was any of this real anymore? How much more bizarre were these new discoveries going to be? Would I really get to meet my sister? I wondered what she could be like. If we were truly identical twins, would we be identical in everything? I sat there becoming tenser by the minute. I'd forgotten the fear of flying and replaced it with the dread of the unknown before we landed. Ruth must have sensed my unease, because the next minute I felt her hand on top of mine. The calm that she could give me eased my shoulders and the deep frown lines. As I felt myself start to relax, I felt the tug of darkness that I was learning she could send me to. Great. Psychic time-out. I was out like a light.

EMILY 101

*A*s I normally do when I'm on the graveyard shift, I slept all day. I hated that term, mostly because I really don't want to start thinking about what all it implies. I looked back at my bed from the bathroom door and appreciated the silence. My apartment was high enough that I didn't hear the street noises. My old apartment had been closer to the streets, and I never slept. This high up, not only do I not hear cars, but I feel safe enough to really sleep.

I'd have to be on the clock soon, so I needed to get it in gear. Taking a deep breath and stretching at the same time helped clear my sleep-muddled brain. I glanced around my room, and my attention was drawn to the photo frames I had on top of my bureau. I missed my family terribly, but I wouldn't be able to contact them just yet. I knew they were truly hurt that I'd ceased communication with them. It was just another case of adding insult to injury given the disappointments I'd given them since I graduated high school. But, until I felt they'd be safe, I couldn't call them. I loved them, and that meant I had to keep them safe.

Sighing deeply, I headed to the shower. Breakfast would have to wait. Well, maybe not a true breakfast, since this time of day everyone else would be getting ready for dinner, but that was just part of the job. I loved my job, though I did wish the hours and pay were better. It wasn't every day you could help people *and* carry a gun to legally use when needed.

The water was heated to near scalding and the mirrors already steamed up by the time I crawled under the jets. Compared to a year ago, it really wouldn't take me long to shower. My hair had been much longer, but now it was short, almost to the point of being boyish. I didn't care. I liked my new look. It was wash and go hair; a few swipes with my brush, some hair gel, and I was set. It would dry in whatever fashion I put it in, and I didn't have to worry about perps yanking my ponytail when making arrests.

My partner, Mickey, thought it was sad that I'd cut my unruly, dirty-blonde, shoulder-length hair. He was older and not particularly happy with women on the force, but he didn't verbalize it—much. You could just see by the look in his eyes and the small shake of his head when he saw me do something very unladylike. He would draw his lips to a thin line and say, "Kid, how are you ever going to find a husband if you keep this up?" I knew he cared, and some of my behaviors bothered him, so I tried hard not to shock him.

When I got out of the shower I glanced in my bedroom and realized I was really pushing it tonight. If I didn't get moving, I'd be late, and Mickey wouldn't be happy. I wiped the mirror and saw my face, nearly jumping backwards. I'd torn my contact lens last night when I was cleaning it. I rarely take that contact out since it was the kind you could sleep in.

Having one blue eye and the other a deep green had been a curse growing up. Mom had grown tired of being called to school every day when I was in grade school because I'd beaten the shit out of whoever made fun of my eyes that day. To keep her job and her sanity, my mom got me a contact lens to match my blue eye when I was nine, and I'd been wearing one contact ever since.

My parents had brown eyes. When I was old enough to chart eye color in middle school, I figured out my eye color didn't equate with theirs, and they let me know I'd been adopted at birth. They told me that they knew nothing about my real family, other than my mother had died immediately after my birth, which didn't help to explain my different eye colors.

Once I'd gotten over the shock of truly seeing myself again, I quickly put the new contact in place, then looked at myself in the mirror again. "She was right," I said to my reflection. "Who are you?" I looked at both my hands, then back at the mirror again, and thought, *"What are you?"*

I suddenly remembered the room of an old Native American woman in Sherman, Texas. I hadn't thought about her in a long time. I'd have to make some calls to check on Sally, but that would have to wait.

I glanced at the clock again. Damn, I was really going to be late. I rushed to the closet to start dressing. It was the beginning of summer here in Utah, but unlike back home in Texas, the air was still breathable. Pollution notwithstanding, you could still wear long pants and not die from heat exhaustion. I didn't even mind my uniform, because temperatures could still drop to the 50s some nights, which was my shift.

I decided that breakfast would have to wait until Mickey and I were on patrol. Being late and eating would only make that worse.

Salt Lake City has two precincts, Liberty (east) and

Pioneer (west). I was assigned Liberty, which was closer to my apartment and the downtown area. I'd meet up with Mickey and we'd patrol the parks and around the hospitals on the east side of the city. As long as we stayed busy, the night would go by fast.

Even as I hurriedly dressed, my eyes were drawn to the bureau again and a picture of Kevin and m in a group the evening I'd graduated from the Police Academy. If fate had turned out, I would've been Mrs. Kevin Alexander. But things never turn out the way we want them to. At least I found out what an ass he really was before I'd said, "I do."

We'd met when I worked dispatch for the Vegas Police Department. He was five years older and a seasoned patrolman, even then. We worked the same shift and would clock out at the same time. Soon, I was told by some coworkers in my department that Officer Alexander intentionally clocked out at the same time I did so he could see me. I couldn't help but smile when I saw him after that. If I reached the time clock before him, I found myself stalling to make sure I saw him.

Kevin was very attractive, with dark-gray eyes. He was tall, standing six foot three. Broad shoulders, narrow hips, and a head of dark-brown hair trimmed very short. You could tell that, given any length, it'd be curly.

We eventually started talking, and soon after he began trying to convince me that joining the police force was the better career choice, because working dispatch was a dead end. I was still contemplating that career move when he was offered a position in his hometown of Salt Lake City. Even though we'd only been dating a short time when he moved back home, I was suddenly lonely. We took turns jumping on a plane once a month to visit each another. On one of his trips to see me, he talked me into joining him in Salt Lake City.

I had considered a move to Salt Lake the year before, when that thing from Texas found me again in Vegas. I say that thing, because that was all I could think of to call it. It was evil, and that's all I could say about it. I'd been raised in a very Christian home, taught not to seek evil, but I never understood what that meant until I was in college.

EMILY 102

$\mathcal{J}$'d graduated high school a year early and was accepted to Baylor University, receiving an academic scholarship. I was participating in Rush week activities when I discovered the evil among us.

Hazing was illegal, but somehow most of these organizations still found ways to bend those rules, walking on the fringe of breaking that law. One of the pledge meetings was held at the ill-fated Waco compound that had burned several years before. It was more than that; it was the Mount Carmel compound.

That ill-fated night, I rode with a group of other potential pledges, and we were more than a little confused over the location. The girl riding shotgun was named Kitty. Her name made me giggle. I was sitting in the back seat, grinning to myself, as Kitty shared some gossip on the current sorority members.

"I heard that the current President, Connie, is obsessed with the occult," she said in her deep Mississippi drawl. "She has this thing about karma, or that's what I heard." She waved her hand as if shrugging off that idea. "She wanted us all to come out here for this meeting, to see if we could feel the evil that she thinks is still at Waco."

I was glancing around the back seat at the other would-be pledges, and they were all nodding their heads, as if agreeing to what Kitty was saying. I raised my eyebrows then sat back to listen and wait on whatever so-called evil they were going to introduce us to. If this was their idea of something fun, or a necessary part of pledging, I was gravely skeptical about my future with this group.

We arrived after sundown that Saturday evening, driving through the normally locked gates to find several other cars present. Connie was standing in the middle of a large group of bright-eyed freshmen, while one of the sorority members was handing out candles. Another girl lit them as we joined the group.

"We are going to walk across the area where the David-ians lived and later died. If any of you get scared, please feel free to return here to the parking area. There are other sisters here who will stay with you until we finish walking the area," Connie announced. She then turned, leading us across the field, giving us the history of the events that had taken place so many years ago.

I held my candle and glanced from face to face as we followed behind her. Some of the faces that glanced back at me showed real fear. The night sounds that Connie tried to talk over didn't go unnoticed. When a clap of thunder sounded to the west, a girl toward the back of the group gasped and started crying. A sorority sister stepped away from the front of the group and then walked back to the now-distraught pledge. We never stopped walking, and Connie never stopped talking. I overheard the sorority sister whisper to the crying pledge. I glanced back over my shoulder to see the two were now heading back the way we came. I wasn't really afraid of the dark, but I didn't want to be remembered as a chicken that couldn't walk through this little adventure.

Being that it was September in Texas, you might think the weather would've been nice, but it wasn't. It was still hot and humid, and a storm was building to the west. The thunder increased as we walked while Connie continued to talk. She switched from explaining the events that happened here to explaining some of the history of the sorority. The more she rambled, the more bored I became, and my attention started to wander. I started to really pay attention to the night noises.

When the wind picked up, we attempted to shield our candles by cupping a hand to block the breath of air that was trying to extinguish our flames. I could smell the promise of rain, as lightning joined the thunder. I remembered being a child and my mother teaching me to count the seconds between a lightning strike and the clap of thunder. I smiled at the memory. On the next strike I started counting. *One Mississippi, two Mississippi...*

Connie paused long enough to really notice the rain was on its way before turning to begin leading everyone to the safety of the cars. I'd hoped we'd reach the cars before the bottom fell out of the storm, drenching us all. The next lightning strike lit the sky more than it had before, and then I caught movement out of the corner of my eye.

The lightning only lasted a fraction of a second, but that was enough time for me to realize someone was about fifty yards to my right. I glanced back at others in our group to see if anyone else noticed, but they were all intent on playing follow the leader. I turned my face in the direction where I'd seen the man—or woman, or whoever it was—but the flickering candles didn't emit enough light for me to see more than three feet past the edge of the group. I squinted harder.

Surely it was just another sorority sister planning on scaring the daylights out of us when the time came.

I glanced back at Connie as she led us to the cars and wondered how much of a scare she was planning on inflicting on us. I decided I really didn't like this chick. One crying pledge for the night was enough. I really didn't want to ride all the way back to campus with a car full of sobbing coeds.

I waited to see if I could detect any difference in Connie's voice. Maybe she'd say a magic word, then our "shadow" would jump out, making everyone scatter in fear. Connie carried on lecturing us on the responsibilities of pledges, should we decide this was the sorority for us. Personally, I'd already made my decision: This wasn't my cup of tea.

I could see a faint flicker of light and knew the parking area was just ahead. The wind blew even harder, and the seconds between the lightning strike and the thunder decreased. I strained my eyes hard to look at where I figured our shadow would be, but I couldn't see anything. The hair on the back of my neck continued to stand on end, like my body could sense something was wrong, but my eyes couldn't see what it was.

We all took a collective sigh of relief when we could see the cars. Some of the girls started extinguishing their candles. The girls at the front of the group kept their candles lit, and in the dim light, my eyes adjusted, allowing me to see the shadow close to our group.

I leaned to the girl on my right and whispered, "Do you see anyone out there?"

She whipped her head around to look in the direction I was indicating, then shook her head no. When she started walking faster, I knew I'd scared her.

I continued to look for the shadow while we walked, but I slowed my pace. Those who'd been behind me started walking around me to keep up with the main group. Finally, I just stopped. The girls who passed me were glancing over their shoulders at me, and I could hear them faintly whispering about me. I paid them little notice, as I had no desire to listen to the screaming and crying that I expected any minute.

I stood still through lightning, thunder, and another brief glimpse of the shadow, only to find it was no longer walking. It stood facing me. Goosebumps started up my arms, and every hair on my body stood at attention. "*To hell with this,*" was my only thought as I started walking toward the shadow. If enough of the girls still watching me could see what I was walking toward, if they could see what was supposed to scare us, maybe we'd avoid it all together.

The closer I got to the figure, I found it was harder to distinguish the shadow from the real darkness. I felt like I was less than ten yards from the shadow, when lightning struck again. I stopped dead. There was nothing in front of me now. I'd heard nothing before the clap of thunder, but now I could hear the group tromping on the dry, dead grass. I'd heard nothing in front of me or to the side where I knew our shadow had been. My heart began to race, my pulse throbbing in my ears, and I heard less and less of the sounds around me, making reality hazy. I slowly turned around, squinting, trying to focus on the dark to see if anyone was still there. With my chest tight and my heart racing, I didn't hear anything, so I shrieked when that Mississippi voice addressed me.

"What are you looking at?" Kitty asked in her cheerful southern drawl.

I'd grabbed her wrist and drew back a fist so quickly that we were now both completely startled. I lowered my fist, but kept a hold of her arm, gasping for air.

"I thought we were being followed and they were going

to jump out and scare us, but apparently it was nothing. I just didn't want the girl who was crying earlier to be any more upset."

I panted a few more seconds then stood up straight. I could see the rest of the group standing in front of the cars now, and they were all quiet as they looked back toward us. I don't know who, but someone decided the darkness was a little much and had turned on the headlights. While Kitty and I weren't in the direct beam of light, we could see each other more clearly now. Kitty glanced at her arm where I was still holding tight, then back to my face, frowning. I released my grasp.

"I'm sorry, Kitty. I guess I over-reacted when you walked up on me."

What else could I say? I glanced over my shoulders since there was more light now. The electricity in the air had increased, and there was a smell of rain. I knew we needed to leave, but I just couldn't without having surveyed where we'd just been walking. I turned my back on Kitty, slowly scanning as far as the light from the headlights would let me. Still, there was no one there.

When I came back around, Connie was walking towards us shaking her head. "You girls okay?" she asked.

I nodded at Kitty, motioning for her to go ahead of me to the group. "Let's just go home," I said.

When we were in step with Connie, I asked, "Is there anyone with the group following us out there?" I motioned to the darkness with my head as I asked.

Connie frowned a little, shaking her head. "Now why would someone do that?" she asked coyly.

"Oh, I don't know. I got the impression you wanted to see who would scare easily. It would only make sense for you to plant someone to scare us somehow," I said with the flattest tone of voice I could muster. I wanted to keep my face blank, but my wide eyes likely prevented that.

"You're being paranoid, I think," Connie whispered as we reached the group. "Now, ladies, I appreciate you all coming out tonight. Our next meeting is Monday night, and I hope you'll all consider pledging with us. Have a safe trip back, and may God bless you all." She finished her little speech, looking directly at me with one arched brow. That look really puzzled me, but no one else seemed to pay attention as they returned to their vehicles.

I'd waited until my car was loaded, standing at the back door, before I turned and looked out where we'd been walking. A bolt of lightning struck just as I placed a foot inside the car and glanced back toward the compound area. Then I saw the shadow, standing and staring at me. I know it was still there, staring at me, because the hair stood on end again. I quickly glanced inside the car to see if anyone else saw the shadow, but their expression showed no fear. When I turned back to the shadow, it was again gone. I jumped into the car, slamming the door. I didn't know what had just happened, but I sure as hell knew I wanted away from here.

EMILY 103

*L*ife went on as usual after we returned to campus. Sunday was filled with study groups, and on Monday classes started. I didn't go to the next sorority meeting that night. A few of the girls were headed out to the meeting as I was returning from the library around dusk. Some of them I recognized, while others looked only vaguely familiar. Kitty was in the group.

"Aren't you coming?" she asked.

"No, I think I'm sitting this one out," I replied.

Half of the group had stopped with Kitty to talk to me, while the others glanced over their shoulders and kept going. I could hear the whispers and giggles. They probably thought I was really out there now. Not many kids who graduate high school early and begin higher education do so without gaining a reputation of being overachieving nerds. The sorority adventure Saturday night would provide more ideas about my personality. Kitty tried to talk me into going, but finally accepted my decision.

As I watched them go, I could hear the thunder rolling in again from the west. Saturday night's storm-front had continued, and we were receiving some much-needed rain. As this wave of storms began to bear down on campus, the hair on my neck started to rise. I turned in a slow circle, scanning all around. Security lights were just coming on across the campus. Closer to the buildings and trees, shadows fell as the lights flickered on at the top of their poles. I could barely see other students walking toward the center of campus, where most activities took place.

Our dorm was on the edge of campus, with a multitude of parking lots beyond that. Night-class students who commuted were heading to their assigned classrooms from those parking areas. Turning back, I started off to my own room. An hour or so later, the storm had passed but had knocked out the power to the majority of the campus. It hadn't been a particularly violent storm, but either a transformer had been hit by lightning or someone hit a light pole while driving in the downpour. Either way, it was dark.

I had a book light and was using that to study with since the power went out. Hours of reading by book light made me tired of reading. I rose and stood by my window, peering down into the courtyard. I hadn't realized how dark the area was without artificial lighting. I looked up at the sky and could see distant stars beginning to creep back out.

The storm front was almost fully past us now but not yet enough to allow the stars to brighten our area. When I looked back down to the courtyard, movement caught my eye. Thinking it was students returning to the dorm, I squinted to see if it was my roommate. Headlights were shining from the parking lot across the street, but not directly where I was looking. At the far edge of the headlight's glare, I saw a shadowy figure. It was looking up at me, and I knew immediately it wasn't another person.

I could feel its gaze pouring into mine. Not to say that it

had eyes; I couldn't make any out from this distance. I was frozen to the spot, feeling true terror begin to take over, my heart in my throat, almost choking me. The shadow seemed to grow in size, as if it were rising to my window. I couldn't move, and that scared the shit out me.

Suddenly, my door opened, the power came back on at the same time, and I stumbled away from the window, gasping. I would've screamed, but I didn't have enough air to make my voice work. I fell against my bed, then looked up to see my roommate standing in the doorway, frowning at me.

"What the hell happened to you, girl?" she asked, coming in and closing the door.

Vanessa Black was my assigned roommate. She was Native American, Cherokee to be exact, and so pretty it hurt to look at her at times. She was two years older, wasn't bothered by my overachieving nerd status, and treated me like a younger sister. She'd shown me around campus, and while she told me she wasn't sorority material, she'd been supportive of my participation in rush week activities. I sat blinking at her, my mouth slightly open. She giggled and started unloading her book bag on her desk.

"Girl, you look like you've just seen a ghost," she said.

I closed my mouth quickly, staring at her back. What would she think? "What if I said I think I did?" I asked.

She whipped around and homed in on me with her dark brown eyes. "What did you say?" she asked in a sharp voice.

"I said, what if I did see a, uh, ghost," I was still shaky.

She saw immediately that I was scared and was at my side within seconds. "Tell me what you saw."

I told her. I told her everything, starting with Saturday night. "It was the same. Whatever that was outside just now was the same thing I saw Saturday night. It's like it followed me."

"Wow." Vanessa was wide eyed now, too.

I wasn't sure she'd even believe me, but I had to tell someone. Vanessa looked at me seriously, got up from my bed, and walked to the window. She stared down into the courtyard for a few minutes, then drew the shades closed, but she didn't move. She stayed with her hand on the shade cord, staring at the closed shade, but I knew she wasn't looking at them. Slowly, she turned around and stared at me.

"You don't believe me, do you?"

"Yeah, I do." She sighed deeply, then went to sit on her bed facing me. "I believe you. Not everyone would, but I do. I was raised with this kind of stuff."

"What do you mean 'raised with this kind of stuff?'" I asked.

"I spent a lot of time with my grandmother when I was growing up. My grandmother believes in the old ways, the old beliefs." She gazed down to her hands in her lap where she'd been twisting the ring on her finger.

I'd noticed the ring before but hadn't scrutinized it. It was the color of a deep ruby stone, but not an actual ruby. As she watched herself turning the ring, I looked at it closer too. It looked very old and Native American.

"I usually don't talk about my family to anyone outside of the tribe, but I think you need some help. Would you be willing to meet my grandmother?" She glanced up, giving me narrowed eyes now.

"Do you think that's necessary?"

"Yeah, I think it is. You've seen an *udiyvli-asgaya*, and now he's following you."

"A what?"

"A shadow man. It would translate to a devil or a ghost, maybe closer to a demon, but we don't have a word for demon."

"Okay…What do you mean he's following me?"

"Devils sometimes pick someone and attach to them. I think that's what's happened to you. I don't know as much as my grandmother does. I never wanted to learn it. So, I know just enough to know it's dangerous. I wanted to get out, get an education, get away…" She trailed off then looked away from me, as if she was almost embarrassed. "We need to see my grandmother. She can tell us more about what's going on. I wished to hell those girls had stayed away from that old compound."

It was my turn to be distracted then. I twisted my hands, squeezing them together. Was this really necessary? Did I want to learn more about what was going on and what it meant?

"Will it get worse? This thing following me?" I asked.

"I'm not sure, but I do know we can't get rid of it on our own. We need help," Vanessa said, nodding.

"Okay, now you're starting to worry me. So, we go see your grandmother, and she'll tell me how to get rid of this ooodly-whatda."

"It's pronounced ooh-dee-yuh-lee ah-sss-gah-yaw."

"So, when can we go?"

"It's about a three-hour drive, so it'll have to be on the weekend."

"Okay, I'll go. I'll meet your grandmother."

The next morning the dorm was alive, and the hallways hummed like a hive of bees. Everyone was excitedly talking in half-hushed voices when we stepped out of our room. Looking in both directions, at everyone in the hallway not going anywhere, we were puzzled. I looked at Vanessa, and she shrugged her shoulders. "I don't know, I've never seen a party like this before."

One of the resident attendants was pushing her way

through the hall with a clipboard. She was apparently taking roll. When she got to us, she checked our names off, then Vanessa put a hand on her arm. "Hey, Regina, what's going on?"

The look on Regina's face was frustration and fear all rolled together. She took a deep breath and leaned in close to Vanessa to whisper, but I still heard her.

"A female body was found next to the courtyard this morning." She looked around us to see who was near before she continued. "They can't identify her yet, and since it was right outside our dorm, they think it might be one of us. The RAs are going floor by floor, taking roll. So far, all of mine are accounted for. Get comfortable. No one is leaving until they clear the crime scene." She was shaking her head as her eyes filled with tears.

Vanessa nodded while she patted the poor girl on the shoulder. Regina turned in the opposite direction to continue her task. I was in shock, *A body in our courtyard!* Our courtyard that we could see from my window! I grabbed the doorknob, putting my shoulder into it to get the door open as quickly as I could. I left the door open and Vanessa behind as I rushed to our window to peer out. At exactly the spot I'd seen the shadow last night, there was a barricade and a tent. Apparently, they'd been at it a while, and with as many people that were standing around, I was shocked we hadn't heard anything before now.

I heard the door close and knew that Vanessa was walking up behind me.

"You don't think…" I began, and let it trail off.

"Do I think what?"

"Do you think that the shadow thing I saw last night has anything to do with this?"

"I don't know. I really don't know."

She was standing beside me now, looking down to the courtyard below. We stood there for a long time, wondering what or who was under that tent as my anxiety was skyrocketing. There was a lot of activity in the courtyard, but we couldn't hear any of the sounds.

After we tired of standing by the window, we took turns keeping watch. I worked on a paper due next week while she stood watch. Vanessa surfed the net on her laptop while I watched. She wasn't able to find any details on any of the media websites, but we could see reporters just behind the police tape. So, we waited.

At 10 a.m., Vanessa saw a gurney wheeled to the tent. "I know that guy with the gurney. His name is Ben. He's in my law history classes. I'll see him tomorrow. Maybe he can give us some insider information."

I'd joined her at the window as she pointed him out. It didn't take long after that for the gurney to make its return trip to the CSI team van. A shiver ran up my body as we watched them wheel the gurney through the courtyard, and I felt sick when an arm fell out from underneath the sheet covering the body. You couldn't tell much, except that it was a small hand, much smaller than the CSI member's who tucked it back under the sheet. It was smaller, like a girl's, and the skin was dark, but not that of black or Asian skin. The skin seemed to be darkened, as if from burning, appearing almost withered.

I had the sudden urge to be sick and ran from the window to our bathroom. I stood in front of the sink, running cold water to splash on my face. Vanessa, looking numb, went back and sat on her bed. I'm certain I was paler than she was, but she wasn't looking her best either. The cold water helped calm my stomach, then I went to lie down on my bed. We said nothing to each other, lost in our thoughts.

About an hour later, a white sheet of paper was slid under our door. I let Vanessa retrieve it. "It says we're to attend a mandatory meeting in the downstairs common room, at 1 p.m. Imagine that."

She laid the notice on her desk, then went to stand at the window. I rolled over and hugged my pillow tight, watching the wall. What had happened, and to whom? We were about to find out.

At 1 p.m. the entire population of the dormitory converged on the downstairs common room. Several of the sofas had been pushed to the walls, providing seating for a lucky few, while the rest of us took seats on the floor. I sat on the far right of the room, with my knees up in front of me and arms wrapped around them. I prayed the whole time we waited in silence that I didn't know who was under that sheet.

Finally, the house mother came to the front of the room and stood between the two large screen TVs. A police officer stood with her. She was visibly upset, with puffy eyes and tear stains on her cheeks.

"I know you have many questions. The police are here to take any information you may have, if you saw something." She paused then pushed on, her face mirroring her emotions. "We believe the victim is Kitty. She's the only one unaccounted for during the roll call, but an autopsy is needed to identify the body." Her shoulders started to droop, and we could see she was at her limit. "This is Officer Taylor, and he has a few words now."

Officer Taylor informed us that CSI would be in the building for the next few days, continuing their investigation. He asked anyone with any information to come forward, then gave advice on how we should protect ourselves in the coming days. After dark, travel in groups when possible and avoid dark alleys. He didn't have any ideas on how Kitty was killed.

As the rest of the girls started filing out of the common room, I stayed on the floor. I'd seen Kitty on my way into the building, and she'd been on her way to that sorority meeting. It was my civic duty to tell what I'd seen. Not what I'd seen from my dorm room—who'd believe *that*?—but I'd admit to having talked to her. The rest of the girls who'd been with her stayed, too. This was one of the longest days of my life.

Wednesday, after all our classes, Vanessa and I drove to Wendy's for a bite to eat. Eating cafeteria food 24/7 could suck, and I needed to get off campus, so the outing was a breath of fresh air, at least until Vanessa was driving us back. Never taking her eyes off the road, she turned her signal light to turn into the parking lot for our dorm when she said, "I talked to Ben today." She didn't say it very loud; it was almost like she didn't want to mention it at all.

"Was he able to tell you anything about what happened?" We'd learned late Tuesday night that dental records confirmed the body was Kitty. We'd all cried.

"He didn't really want to talk about it, but I told him my roommate knew the victim. He waited until class was over and all the other students were gone to give me some details." Vanessa had parked the car by now but hadn't killed the motor. She leaned back against the seat staring ahead through the windshield, still gripping the steering wheel.

"Em, this is some bad shit." She sighed heavily then shook her head, kind of to herself. "Ben says the body looked like all the fluids had been drained out, even the eyes. Her hair was gone. He said the burns were like nothing they've ever seen." She took a visible swallow, and I feared she might be getting sick thinking about it. She was holding the steering wheel so tightly her knuckles were white. Then she shook herself like a wet dog.

I didn't know what to say. I was numb, in shock, and afraid all over again. It took a few minutes before I realized Vanessa was still talking.

"You okay, Em?" she was asking.

From the look on her face, I could tell she'd asked it a couple of times before it registered with me. I nodded.

She put her hand on my shoulder. "Let's get in before it gets any darker. I don't like being out this late." She grabbed her bag and made sure her can of pepper spray was in hand as we walked back to our rooms.

While Vanessa jumped right into reading, I couldn't get settled. I went from my desk to my bed and back to the desk, reading or trying to read. At least I tried to put on a good front. I ended up wandering to the window, looking out at the night. It was a star-filled night, and you could see into the distance across campus. I lost track of time as I gazed at the stars. I glanced down and found that dark shadowy figure in the exact place I'd seen it Monday night. The exact spot where Kitty was found. The spot where so many students had placed flowers in her memory. It was there. I didn't feel like it could get to me right then, but I could sense it looking at me. The shadow lifted a hand and pointed up at me. That scared me into gasping as I stumbled back from the window.

Vanessa was with me instantly. All I could do was point to the window. Vanessa stepped around me, and scanned the campus just has I had. "What was it, Em? Did you see something?"

"I saw it again," I whispered. "It was in the exact same spot as Monday, where they found Kitty."

I covered my mouth and realized that wasn't helpful when

you were trying to breathe while scared shitless. Shifting, I just wrapped my arms around myself instead.

"What's happening, Vanessa? Why is this thing following me? It was pointing at me!" I was getting a little louder now and maybe slightly hysterical.

Vanessa reached me in a few strides and grabbed me by both shoulders. "It's gone now." She stood there looking at me. "We have to see my grandmother Saturday."

One student a night went missing the rest of that week. Kitty was the only one found. I shuddered to think what happened to them. I couldn't wait for Saturday. I stayed away from the window the rest of the week, especially after dark.

The following Saturday we made the three-hour trip to Sherman, which was almost to Oklahoma. Vanessa drove, so I paid for the gas. Like the majority of Texas, Sherman was flat. The fall had scenery in various shades of brown, the product of a very dry summer

Vanessa had called earlier in the week to let her parents know we were coming. Her grandmother lived with her parents. She explained on the trip that her father had worked his way up through the Sherman Police Department then attended law school. He was currently in the private sector and doing very well for the family. Her grandmother came to live with them when they bought a larger house on the western edge of the city.

"Grandmother likes to stay busy so she can feel she's still useful. She's not exactly accustomed to living the way my parents do now, so she stays behind the scenes. She insists on cooking and cleaning. My mother is Anglo, as my grand-mother would say. She and my grandmother weren't the best of friends in the beginning, but now they're very close. Anything my grandmother wants or wants to do is fine by my mother," she explained.

We arrived at Vanessa's parent's house shortly before noon. Her parents greeted me warmly, excited to meet any of Vanessa's friends, as she'd never brought anyone home. The aroma of food cooking made my stomach emit noises I couldn't cover up. We all laughed about it, and Vanessa decided it was time to find her grandmother, who'd been absent from the welcoming committee.

"She has to be somewhere close to the kitchen. She always cooks a large lunch on weekends, because my father's home," she said as she led me through the enormous house.

The kitchen was toward the rear of the house. We passed through a formal sitting area, dining room, then made our way through the butler's pantry before we entered a restaurant-quality kitchen. Steam rolled over a large stove, but no one was present to watch. Vanessa shook her head but kept heading through the kitchen.

While she told her parents we were coming, she hadn't explained the purpose of the visit. Her grandmother, since moving to the upscale Sherman community, didn't like meeting new people, especially not Anglos, as Vanessa had also explained in the car.

We exited the kitchen and kept heading for the far side of the house, apparently the mother-in-law wing of the residence. Vanessa motioned me to pause behind her as she knocked on a door that was covered in what looked like an old Native American blanket. The colors and patterns were vibrant. When no one answered, Vanessa shook her head then opened the door anyway.

"*Enisi*? Are you in here?" she called as she opened the door.

I stayed where she'd indicated, letting her go into the room by herself. I heard a low voice that replied, but it wasn't in English. The soft voice had a singsong quality to it, but it was strong, with a commanding presence. Vanessa talked to her in the same language, but I couldn't see her from the door. What I *could* see from my designated point was a room filled not with posh decorations like the rest of the house but Native American artifacts.

The walls looked like someone had taken an old wooden barn apart then reconstructed it here in this million-dollar estate. I had to smile, thinking of what it took to convince someone to pull this interior off. I took a step closer to the door as Vanessa talked with her grandmother so I could see more of this intriguing room.

I looked up at the ceiling and found that it was covered in old canvas strips. It was rather fascinating to think who came up with this idea, but with the old wood it really worked. The canvas hung—or I should say drooped—every four feet or so. Old, rounded, possibly pine poles were tacked up, running across the ceiling. The canvas drooped on either side of the poles and gave an effect of being outside in a tent-like structure.

As I gazed further into the room, I appreciated that I'd entered without being invited. I only realized this as I found myself looking at Vanessa's back, behind the open door. She stopped talking then turned to me, smiling.

"It's okay, come in and meet my *enisi*," she said.

I walked closer to Vanessa and looked to where she was indicating with her hand. There was a little woman that looked almost withered. Years of working outdoors had played a large role in the darkened skin that looked almost like soft, worn leather. The wise eyes that looked at me were set a little farther apart than you usually see, and it made me stare at her. She wasn't paying attention to my rude behavior, because she was narrowing her eyes to give me what amounted to the stank eye.

She was sitting in an old rocking chair, and as she watched me, she raised her right hand to start rubbing a long, beaded necklace, all the while muttering under her breath. I realized how rude I was and shook myself out of it. I nodded to her while smiling, extending my hand while Vanessa told her who I was.

"*Enisi*, this is Emily Hunter. Emily, this is my grandmother, Sally Black."

Her grandmother replied, her voice rising just slightly. Vanessa reached out to me then lowered my hand with her own, frowning. She spoke back to her grandmother in the same language, but it was almost anger filled this time. Her grandmother responded in the same tones as her mutterings, never getting loud, but it was starting to get a little unnerving. I'd lowered my hand to my side, but I wasn't smiling anymore. I was busy glancing between the two as they took turns speaking.

"My grandmother means no offense, but she's afraid to shake your hand," she told me, a frown creasing her brows.

"What did I do?" I asked.

"You didn't do anything," she started. "She thinks you're an *atsasgili*, a...uh, witch."

My jaw dropped just slightly, then turned to a grin quickly. I thought it was funny. "A what?" I asked, still amused.

"You say it ah-jaw-sss-gee-lee. I told you she still believes in the old ways and all the old tales. So, you'll just have to ignore her for the most part. She doesn't mean anything by it."

I turned my attention back to the little form sitting in the rocking chair, still rubbing her beads and murmuring. I nodded to her, grinning. I was going to have to hear more about this. While I'd been raised in Texas, I'd never been this close to truly old-school Native Americans.

"She taught me when I was small. She can understand English, she just chooses not to speak it unless she's out of the house," Vanessa explained.

I nodded my understanding, glancing at Vanessa out of the corner of my eyes but still watching her grandmother. Sally just nodded back then started to smile.

"I'm glad to meet you," I said.

"Is good to meet you," she replied.

"Grandmother, Emily needs your help."

Sally looked at me then widened her eyes, more in question than anything else. She rattled off what sounded like questions to Vanessa, but the only word I recognized was the word Vanessa had just used for *witch*. Vanessa nodded and replied to her.

"Tell me," Sally said, pointing toward me.

Vanessa grabbed an old-fashioned, wooden ladder-back chair, dragging it in front of her grandmother's chair. She indicated for me to sit as she turned back to grab another chair. I sat down slowly. I don't know why, but I really didn't want to give her grandmother a start if she was truly afraid of me. I sat down, and the wise, old brown eyes narrowed in on me. I told her of the experience I'd had.

When I told of the sorority, Sally would frown and glance at Vanessa as if she didn't understand what kind of club I was talking about. Honestly, I wished I didn't know either. I finished by telling her of the courtyard apparition. She nodded while she rocked, looking down at the beads she was rubbing. I looked at Vanessa, and she shrugged back, indicating she had no idea what her grandmother was doing.

Sally might've looked withered, but when she hopped out of her rocking chair all of the sudden, she was anything but.

She was the quickest eighty-five-year-old I'd ever seen. She crossed between our chairs, heading to the opposite side of the enormous room to what must be her closet. She entered the enclosure but left the light off.

We turned to watch, but we could only hear objects scooting across the floor. A few minutes later something must've fallen, because we then heard a large crashing noise. Vanessa and I both jumped to our feet, and Vanessa was halfway across the room when her grandmother reemerged carrying a small wooden box. She looked up at Vanessa, almost shocked that her granddaughter was running toward her.

"*Ayule*, child, you worry too much," she said, shaking her head and smiling up at Vanessa.

I hoped that Vanessa's 5'9" mother's genes carried over to her daughter. I really didn't want to think of Vanessa at this age, barely reaching five feet.

Sally walked back around Vanessa, still shaking her head and chuckling under her breath. She went back to her rocking chair and sat down, placing the box on her lap. She opened the box's hinged lid, but it was facing her, so I could only see the top of the lid. It had many of the same symbols that were woven into the blankets and rugs hanging in her room. She searched around in the box then came out with a long string of ruby-red beads. She closed the box, laying the beads on top of it.

"You must go to the *atsasgili* in your own family," she said, looking directly at me.

I frowned, turning to Vanessa.

"Witch. She means you must find the witch in your family," Vanessa said, shaking her head. "*Enisi*, Emily was adopted. She doesn't know her true family."

Sally raised both of her eyebrows in shock, *tsk*-ing under

her breath. She scooted to the front of her chair then held out a hand toward me. I just looked at her hand. Vanessa had said she wouldn't shake my hand because she was afraid of me, but now she wanted to touch me? I looked over my shoulder, but Vanessa had come to stand beside me, so, shifting, I had to look up now.

As if seeing the question on my face, Vanessa frowned and started asking Sally something in their native tongue. Sally drew her hand back then looked up at Vanessa for a second. She nodded her head, said something, then leaned forward again, extending her hand to me, palm up, as if she wanted something.

"She says she thought you'd been raised with witches. That's why she wouldn't shake your hand before. She says she can see now you truly have no training," Vanessa paused, frowning down at me. "I'm sorry about this Em, really. I had no idea she'd be pulling any of this kind of stuff. But she wants to kind of read your palm, feel your essences. It's okay, she won't hurt you."

I frowned slightly but was a little curious what this little old woman could do. I'd never been around anything mystical before last Saturday night. While that experience had me scared, this little woman had me intrigued. I placed my right hand into her upturned open one. I'd placed my hand, palm down, onto her open palm. Her touch was light but steady.

Using both of her hands, she then turned my palm over so she could observe it. Her brows drew together, and she started murmuring to herself again while she slightly rubbed the palm of my hand with one of her forefingers. She'd would glance up at me occasionally while she continued to stroke and mumble. Each time, she'd just grin then turn back to my hand.

This went on for several minutes. I'd look back to Vanessa, and she'd shrug while bugging her eyes slightly. When her grandmother finished, she patted my palm with her own, retrieved the beads from her lap, then placed them in my hand. She curled my fingers over the beads, patting the closed hand, then leaned back.

"You're only half a person now, *ayule*, and I think it will be many years before you're whole. I cannot take this *tsvs-gino* from you," she said, and I looked up at Vanessa.

"Devil, Em. She says it's a devil."

I looked back to Sally, who was nodding.

"Yes, dee-vil. My grandmother called it a *vardoe*. I cannot make it go away. Only your own kind can do that. You need this necklace. Red symbolizes success, and I am praying you are successful in keeping him from you. So be it, as I wish. But you are not safe here, *ayule*, not until you are whole. You will be safer with this necklace. And salt. You will need much salt. Salt wards off dee-mons and dee-vils. Place salt in doorways and windowsills to keep it from entering your home."

This was puzzling. I'm not whole, and I need salt? I looked to Vanessa, and she shrugged again while releasing a huge sigh.

"What about Vanessa? She'll need a necklace, too, won't she?"

"No, *ayule*, Nessa is safe. This *vardoe* follows you. Nessa knows how to be safe after dark. She has her ring."

It was then I noticed the beads on Sally's necklace matched that in Vanessa's ring.

"*Enisi*, is there anything else?" Vanessa asked.

"Yes, *ayule*. Lunch. We need to eat." Rising from her chair, she placed the wooden box in the seat, stepped forward, patted me on the shoulder, then turned, leaving us standing in her room. Vanessa and I both shrugged to each other then followed her out.

For the most part, I think the beads helped. At least it helped me think I was safe. I no longer sensed an evil presence, and the disappearances on campus ended, unsolved. However, I still worried about going home to my adoptive family for fear this thing would follow me.

A few other times that semester and the following spring semester, I caught glimpses of what I thought was the shadow man—devil, demon…whatever the hell it was. It was enough to keep me unnerved and fearful to be out after dark. Other girls in our dorm laughed behind my back. I kept my ruby beads with me at all times and, when it was dusk, wore them openly on top of my clothes.

When my first full year of college was nearly complete, Vanessa informed me she was transferring to Dallas the following semester. Her father had gotten her an internship at a law practice there. She was a pre-law student, so it was right up her alley.

She was moving home for the summer, and that left me wondering where to go. If I went home, I ran the chance of the shadow thing following me there, and I didn't want to put anyone else in danger. I researched as much as I could about demons, devils, and witches. Yeah, witches. I couldn't figure out what Sally had meant about witches in my biological family.

My parents told me my adoption was closed, so I never bothered to look. My parents were great. I had no complaints about them, and as far as I was concerned, they were my parents. No question.

Instead of heading home at the end of the spring semester, I decided to travel and see some of the world, by bus. I think I wanted to see if whatever was following me would continue to do so, as a kind of test before I decided if it would be safe to return home.

I packed my books and school things then shipped them back home to my parents' address. I closed out my bank account into traveler's checks. With my money, two bags of clothes, and my laptop, I set out on a bus toward the west.

I didn't tell my parents about my plans. I just left. Somewhere along the way, Kansas City I think, I lost my cell phone, but that was okay. I'd let my family know where I was once I stopped.

When I got to Vegas to switch buses, my purse was stolen. Save $250 I'd hidden in my computer case, I lost all my money and my ID. While at the police department to report the robbery, I saw they had job openings in the dispatch department. I wasn't going home anytime soon, and I sure as hell wasn't going to ask my parents for money. I reported my missing purse, which was found the next day. My money was gone, but my driver's license had been left. Claiming the purse, I then applied for a job, all in the same day.

Since what was stolen was strictly traveler's checks, I was able to replace those. I enjoyed the lights of Vegas during the evenings, but only from the small hotel room I'd rented. It was off the beaten path, but I wasn't concerned. It was clean and had lots of security.

My first purchase after renting the room was a bag of salt. I know housekeeping must've thought I was nuts. It made me feel safer, so screw opinions.

Here, I was just another girl, not the overachieving nerd. No one knew anything about me.

I made a few friends and we'd go out partying—often. I was still underage, but because a few of the girls were dating officers, no one questioned my age. We drank and played slots at the casinos, and I felt I fit in.

I went through a short goth period, wearing all black, including the scary makeup. I even dyed my hair jet black, but I didn't really care for the look. When it grew out, I returned to my natural dirty blonde.

When some of my friends started piercing more than just ear lobes, I joined the crowd too. I got the cartilage pierced on one ear, but the pain involved with that caused me to stop with just the one. Instead of putting in a stud, I got a band, covered in tiny diamonds, that wrapped around the outer edge of my ear. I was proud of having bought my first real piece of jewelry. I never took it off.

The longer I was in Vegas, the more often I left my red beads at home. I'd gotten a low-rent apartment after my first paycheck and never looked back.

Still, I didn't reveal my true address to my family. If I mailed them anything, I made sure it didn't have a return address. When I called them, it was with a prepaid calling card so they couldn't trace it. I knew it was wrong to keep things from them, but in my mind, I was keeping them safe.

EMILY 104

*T*he photos on the dresser had taken me down memory lane, but I returned to the present in time to finish getting ready and jump on the tram to work, knowing Mickey would be pissed I was late again. Before locking my door, I made sure my small line of salt was still intact across my threshold before heading to the train station, always watching to make sure I wasn't followed.

Working nights had given me the fear at first that the shadow might have followed me to Salt Lake City, but so far, I hadn't seen the shadow. I began calling it a shadow man because it fit better in my brain; telling myself I had a devil or demon following me put me over the edge. I now wondered if the salt on the threshold was still needed since I hadn't seen the shadow man, but I kept it in place just the same.

There weren't many people at the train station when I arrived and fewer on the car I jumped into. I leaned back in my stiff plastic seat, closed my eyes, and returned to my thoughts of the recent past and how I ended up here. My breakup with Kevin had been almost two months ago, yet it felt like a lifetime ago.

After I moved in with Kevin, engagement ring on my hand, he finally convinced me to apply to the police academy. He'd taken it upon himself to make sure I got in without any hitches. I was just over twenty at the time. Normally you had to be at least twenty-one to be accepted, but Kevin was close to several higher-ups, and they'd made an exception.

Attending the academy during the day, I worked dispatch in the evenings, but only part time. Kevin said he'd support us during my time at the academy, but I didn't want to rely on him completely. Moving in together had been an adjustment for us both. I'd enjoyed being my own boss in Vegas, so I wanted my own spending money.

Kevin never knew that I had a string of salt under his front door mat, but what he didn't know didn't hurt him. He didn't clean anyway, so no one knew but me. Since we weren't on the ground level of his building, I didn't worry with salt in the window sills. It was *Salt* Lake City, after all.

After I'd graduated from the academy, I was assigned to my current station, while Kevin worked out of Pioneer, the west side station. It was strange at first, both of us working on the same schedule. I was in the probationary period, so I was allowed to work days most of the time. Kevin had moved up to a plain clothes detective and would smile whenever I entered a room, proud as a peacock.

It was after my probationary period that I cut my hair, and Kevin's smile soon disappeared. I hadn't told him of my decision to cut it. Just showed up one afternoon with it short. He was angrier than I'd ever seen him, and we argued over it—a lot. I didn't understand. After all, it was just hair.

Around the same time, I was reassigned to the evening shift. Kevin and I started seeing less and less of each other, except passing one another into or out of our apartment. I tried to keep the same sleeping patterns on the weekends, and

Kevin was none too pleased with that. Our interactions decreased, and we had sex even less than that. I could feel us drifting apart, and it weighed heavy on my heart most days, like someone was sitting on my chest.

Then, one night during my shift, Mickey and I had to assist in an emergency delivery in the back of a cab. I was smaller than the rest of the crew, so I was in the car when this lady delivered. It was like playing catcher in baseball; she pitched, and I caught. After the ambulance arrived taking mother and child to the hospital, Mickey insisted that I go home and change. My uniform was soaked with bloody mucus membrane and amniotic fluid. When I started to get chilled, I agreed. He dropped me off in front of my building, waiting while I ran up to change.

As soon as I opened the door to our apartment, the hair on the back of my neck stood up, and I knew something was wrong. There were empty beer bottles and a pizza box on the coffee table, while the stereo was softly playing the romantic station Kevin liked when he got frisky. Dread knotted in the pit of my stomach, cinching tighter with every step I took. I noiselessly walked into the kitchen and found it much like I'd left it. I turned and saw the bedroom door was closed and felt my chest tighten. I walked over, placed my hand on the door, and took a deep, cleansing breath, as if I was breaking in on a crime scene.

I threw the door open to find the bed was empty, but it was a mess, the smell of sweat and sex hitting my olfactory system. I stood there, trying to breathe deeply and calm my heart rate, but I was seeing red now. I felt like my entire body was vibrating with rage.

Only then did I hear the shower running. Taking a deep breath then exhaling slowly, I braced myself, heading for the bathroom. Repeating the breathing exercise as I placed my hand on the doorknob, I gently opened the door.

The bathroom was steamy from the shower and the sex Kevin and this woman were engaged in—in our shower. I stood there, frozen, watching them through the fogged glass. Kevin was taking this woman from behind, while she braced her arms on the tiled wall. The slightly foggy glass left nothing to the imagination, leaving me standing there with my lips compressed so tight I thought my face muscles would crack. I narrowed my eyes at the pair, trying to think of what to do, then I realized I had my hand on the butt of my revolver, and I was vibrating again.

I took a couple of quick breaths then made myself release the gun. I reached over and flipped the switch for the exhaust fan, since Kevin had never quite gotten in the habit of using this appliance. The noise made him freeze against the woman, whipping his face toward me. The woman did the same.

"I don't know how many times I've told you, but it really is better for the bathroom if you use the exhaust fan," I said. Then I turned around and left.

I was numb when I made it to the car where Mickey sat waiting for me. He frowned when he saw I was still wearing my wet uniform. I was no longer cold, but I was still vibrating. I sat in the passenger seat for a few minutes, staring out the front window then casually opened my door, leaned over, and threw up until I was empty. My throat hurt, my head was pounding, and my heart was broken. I closed the door and told him to just drive.

I shivered at the memory, coming back to myself on the tram as the conductor announced my stop. I exited and made my way to the station. My recollections this night had me in a sour mood. I was hoping our combined moods (mine plus

Mickey's) wouldn't feed off each other or this would be a long night.

I entered the near-empty squad room to find Mickey giving me the evil eye. *So much for not getting crossways with Mickey.*

Mickey Parish, a twenty-year veteran on the force, had been my partner since I'd graduated the academy. He was a few inches shorter than I was and solidly built. His wife adored him, as he did her. They had two grown children. One was older than me, and the other had just started college. He said his wife was having a difficult time with the empty nest, and he hoped to take her to Vegas soon for some fun. He always said this with a wink just to ensure I knew what he meant. Honestly, I was glad he was comfortable telling me about his personal life. Not many men his age would, given my age. After only a week on patrol together, Mickey and I had become best buds.

Given how it happened, Mickey knew all the dirty details of my breakup. He has some strong opinions about pre-marital relations, but he never talked down to me because of it. He made his point through stories, not lectures, which I appreciated.

After my breakup, he and his wife, Lucy, would invite me to their house for home-cooked meals. I think Lucy felt sorry for me, enough so that she didn't mind us talking shop while we ate. They're a great couple, and I thought their kids were lucky to have them. They'd gone the extra mile to make sure their kids got into the best colleges and weren't lacking funds to survive the college years. Their oldest son, an attorney, had been married for only a year. I could tell Lucy was ready for grandkids by the way she talked about her new daughter-in-law.

But until those grandkids arrived, Lucy needed a hobby. I

became that hobby. Lucy was totally in my corner when she learned about my breakup. Mickey took me home with him the morning of the breakup and made me spend the night in one of the boy's rooms. The next day, Lucy had insisted on helping me move.

Almost immediately I'd learned that Kevin had a thing for taking prospective law enforcement talent and building their career. He'd just elected two new rookies this time. I knew the woman's name, and I hoped that, once her training was completed, she'd be assigned to the west side precinct and I'd never see her again. So far, so good.

This evening, Mickey didn't seem to be pissed at all for my being late. He was actually smiling by the time I made it to his desk and sat down. It was a sudden switch, causing me to wonder what he was up to.

"Sorry I'm late. I don't have an excuse other than I just got wrapped up in my own thoughts," I said, ducking my head.

"Don't worry about it. There's plenty of crime for us. You being a few minutes late won't matter that much."

He got up from his desk and started donning his gear. Since I kept my gear in the women's locker room, I told him I'd meet him outside by the car. He just nodded, still smiling. I could tell tonight was going to be interesting. I was just hoping it wouldn't be as strange as the previous night. Nothing had been that strange in a very long time.

Last night, the weirdness began not long into the shift. A woman called in a missing child report, and we were tasked with making the initial contact. In the middle of the 911 call, the caller changed the story from missing child to that of a runaway, which makes a big difference in the kind of police support sent. When a police officer hears "missing child" under the age of thirteen, thoughts turn to a kidnapping, and large numbers of police are involved. A runaway fifteen-year-old girl with an eighteen-year-old boyfriend, who left a note, will only receive one team to take the report.

When we arrived at the home of the caller, I surveyed the front yard of the house and decided I would've run away too. No one had bothered to cut down the overgrown weeds, likely left from the previous summer. Now the weeds were brown and matted in places by the garbage strewn around the yard. The aura of the yard made me dread entering the residence.

Mickey could tell I wasn't pleased. He stood perfectly still, knowing I'd notice, causing me to look at him. He shook his head, as if to tell me to can my opinions. I nodded back. He was right, I had no right to make rash judgments about the report before we had all the facts. I nodded again as he knocked on the door. I covered his back.

We were greeted by an overweight bulldog of a woman with rolls of fat around her middle, which were silhouetted from the lights in the house. She wore a thin, light-colored, extra-large, men's-style wife beater shirt, which showed us everything that she had—or didn't have—on. Her fleshy, saggy breasts could be seen clearly, and I found myself staring while Mickey averted his eyes over her shoulder. He introduced us, asking if we could enter. As much as I didn't want to stand here eye to eye with this woman's chest, I really didn't want to go into that house. I could smell it from where I stood.

She eventually backed up, letting us enter. Mickey stood aside then gestured for me to go first. We both stood against one wall of what could only be described as a living room. It was stuffed with furniture, a television, and junk everywhere. There were stacks piled high on some of the furniture, with the occasionally clear cushion where a person had sat. The coffee tables were covered in empty food containers and potato chip bags. I'd want out of here too.

Mrs. Hogue offered us a seat, while she sat in the recliner directly in line with the TV, which was blaring a late-night show. She turned it off as soon as she sat down. Mickey nodded me toward the couch, while he remained standing. I sighed, walked over, then sat on the front edge of the couch, fearing what was hidden under the piles next to me. I took out my note pad, opened it, rested it on my lap then glanced up at Mickey for him to start the questions.

Mickey was an excellent investigator, and I was glad he was my partner. I felt like I always learned so much from him. This was no different. He had a calming effect on the mother, as his demeanor was always one of understanding.

However, I could tell he wasn't impressed with her mothering skills. Her main complaint was that, since her daughter had been gone for three days, she had no one to cook her dinner. I kept my head down and continued taking notes.

Sometime during the interview, I thought I heard rustling noises behind her chair. Turning to look at her, I found she was looking at Mickey, and he was frowning. I raised my eyebrows to him to see if he'd heard what I was hearing, but he kept his attention on the mother. I decided it was in my head, returning to taking the copious notes that Mickey had taught me were necessary for a good official report.

Deep in thought on how to describe the mother's demeanor, I suddenly felt a sharp pain shoot through the back of my Achilles tendon. I jumped straight up, thinking I'd been bitten by a snake, and ran across the room to stand by Mickey.

"What's wrong, Em?"

He had his hand on the butt of his gun and took a step away from the wall, taking a better stance to survey the room.

"Something bit me," I started, breathlessly. I leaned down and ran my fingers over the back of my leg, coming away with a little blood.

I knelt, rolled down my sock, and found two small puncture wounds on either side of my leg, behind my ankle and just above the top of my shoe.

"It looks like a snake bite. Damn!" I felt like I was going to be sick.

"Ma'am," Mickey said, turning to the mother, "what kind of snake do you have in here?"

"Oh, it's not a snake," she looked up at us with a shocked look on her face. Then her face changed as she shook her head. "It's my daughter's damn pet."

"Pet? What kind of pet has a bite that looks like that of a snake?" Mickey never took his hand off his gun but steadily watched the room to see if anything else would jump out to bite us.

"It's a ferret," she said, in a matter-of-fact tone. "I hate that damn thing. It's always eating the crotch out of my panties." With that, she got out of her chair and walked to the kitchen, leaving us to gape after her.

"Did I hear that right?" I asked Mickey.

"I hope to hell we didn't," was all he said.

A few minutes later Mrs. Hogue returned with some paper towels and a bottle of rubbing alcohol, which she handed to me before sitting back down in her chair. She just sat back and blinked at us.

I poured the alcohol over the wounds, gritting my teeth. It would have to do. Mickey'd had enough. He pulled out his ticket pad and then proceeded to give the woman a ticket, since she was unable to provide proof of current vaccinations for the ferret.

I was barely listening at that point. My fingers tingled but

I chalked it up to the adrenaline of the situation. I wanted to get out of here and go get as many shots as I could. Tetanus would be good, but tequila would be better.

When we got back to the car, I was still rubbing my lower leg, and Mickey got the giggles. He never said a word. He just burst into laughter. At first, I was mad, but his laughter was contagious, and I laughed with him until my sides hurt. This story was going to get a lot of mileage.

I reached down one more time to rub my ankle, wishing it would just stop hurting. My fingers started tingling again as I rubbed. The tingle turned my attention away from the immediate pain, focusing on the new sensation. I'd vaguely felt the same strange humming or buzzing I'd had the night I walked in on Kevin, but this was different. Was this an allergic reaction to being bitten by a ferret? Are ferrets venomous?

Mickey had called in our situation and reported he was taking me immediately to the ER. In between focusing on my pain and the tingle, I hadn't realized we were at the ER until Mickey killed the engine and got out. I was afraid the bite would really hurt when I tried to walk, but it didn't. We made our way into the ER, registered, then sat waiting for my turn.

I was stunned by the number of people in the ER who were there for non-emergencies. Emergency rooms have become after-hours care centers for the population who were unable or unwilling to go to a doctor during normal business hours. While I didn't feel I was technically an emergency, it was department policy to be checked out immediately if you were injured on the job. Since we worked the graveyard shift and no regular clinics were open at this hour, this was the only choice we had.

An hour or so later, it was finally my turn. Mickey stayed in the waiting area, reading a Field and Stream magazine. Triage and vitals were taken by the nurse, then I described what happened before I was escorted to an exam area. The nurse instructed me to hop up on the exam table and remove my shoe and sock and informed me that the doctor would be in shortly. I just wanted to get the shot and go home. Why did health care have to be this complicated?

I hopped up on the table and drew up my injured leg to remove my shoe before rolling off my sock. I looked down to where I thought the bite mark would be, but it wasn't there. I leaned down to inspect both sides of my leg. Still, there was nothing anywhere. Was I losing it? Was it the other leg? I pulled up my other leg and jerked down that sock. *WTF?* I knew I was bitten; there was still blood on my sock. I had been bitten, so where were the bite marks now? God, they were going to think I was a total head case when they came to examine me.

I jerked my socks on as fast as I could, replaced my shoes, and jumped off the table. There wasn't any pain! I leaned over, pinching my skin all around the blood on my sock, and that didn't hurt either. I swung the door open to find the nurse returning, frowning when she saw me.

"Going somewhere?" she asked.

"Yeah, we got a call, and I have to go." What else could I say? All I had was a slightly bloody sock and no wound. What would they say to that?

I pushed past her, walked to the waiting area, then motioned to Mickey for us to leave. He glanced at my feet as we walked to the parking area.

"I guess they do good work here. I thought I was going to have to carry you out of that house, and now look at you. You're walking like you always do. Doesn't it hurt?"

I gave him my tough girl face. "Nah, I'll tough it out." I shrugged and kept walking. I really didn't want to think about this right now, and I sure as hell didn't want to tell Mickey what had happened, when I didn't understand it myself.

We headed to the car, where Mickey reported us back on duty then started to drive us away, but we didn't get very far.

We received a domestic violence call taking place in front of this very hospital, of all places. Mickey only had to drive to the front of the hospital, where we parked then walked to the front entrance. There was an extremely tall woman sitting on the bench by the front door. She was bent over, holding the side of her head.

She had long, curly, golden blonde hair that would make you think of the curls that Shirley Temple had as a kid, but much longer and fuller. She didn't appear to be crying, even as she sat with her elbows on her knees. She did seem confused when we approached and identified ourselves, then she straightened.

Damn, she was tall even sitting down. I felt the hair on the back of my neck stand up, goosebumps shooting across my arms, so I rushed to her side. Mickey stayed a few feet behind me, talking on the mobile com unit that hung from the shoulder his uniform.

"Ma'am, are you okay?" I asked, knowing she wasn't, because she looked like hell.

The left side of her face had the bright colors of fresh bruising. One eye was so swollen her eyelashes were barely visible. Her lip was busted and swollen, and a small trickle of blood oozed from her nose. She looked at me with her good eye. That eye was the strangest blue color I'd ever seen on anyone. It was the kind of blue that made you think of the ocean around tropical islands, clear and bright. Not that I'd ever been to one, but my computer screensaver of a tropical beach came to mind.

The woman tried to smile, causing her to wince with the pain. "I think I'll live."

"Are you hurt anywhere else?" I asked, assessing her status.

"No, it's just my face." She grimaced as she said this, leading me to believe it hurt when she talked.

"Who did this? Where did they go?" I asked, my eyes darting around our area.

"He, uh, we had a fight. He knocked me around a little then he ran off toward the parking deck."

"I'm on it," Mickey said. Turning, with his gun drawn, he ran toward the parking deck, still talking into his radio as he went.

"Ma'am, what can I do to help? I know you're hurt, and you need to go to the ER."

"No, no doctors." She managed to say, shaking her head no at the same time. She looked fearful.

I knelt in front of her. "Ma'am, you really need to be seen by medical personnel," I said, placing my hand on her lower arm resting in her lap.

"No, I'll be okay."

She put one hand on top of mine then squeezed. I got a little shock, like electricity from that squeeze, and jerked slightly. I tried to rise to my feet and back away at the same time, but she held my hand so tightly against her arm that I couldn't move. My heart started to accelerate when I realized she had my right hand, my gun hand. How stupid had I been to do that? I knew better than to put myself at a disadvantage.

"Ma'am, you need to let go," I said calmly.

"Officer Hunter," she stated.

I tried to tug again.

"How do you know my name?"

"It's on your name badge."

Duh. Now I felt stupid and trapped.

"I'm not going to hurt you. Please, just sit down beside me," she asked, her bright blue eye pleading with me.

I felt that I needed to protect her, but with the energy she was throwing off, it made me think I might be the one in need of protection. I'd have to think my way out of this one.

On my com link, I heard Mickey saying he'd found nothing on his first-floor sweep. He'd called for backup to assist in the search. It was a seven-story parking deck, after all.

I sat down beside her, my hand still held under hers, and she tried to smile again. Her lip split just slightly more, causing a small trickle of blood to start flowing. I instinctively reached my left hand up and wiped my thumb under the cut. As soon as my skin made contact with hers, I froze. I didn't freeze because I was scared. Well, I was, but it was because I literally couldn't move. I looked up into her one good eye and saw laughter in it.

"What do you feel right now, officer?" she asked quietly.

I shook my head, because I had no words for what I was feeling. Thoughts of racing away from her screamed in one part of my brain, while another part told me I could fix her. What the hell was that?

"You want to fix my face, don't you?" she asked, again in a whisper.

My heart was racing. Still holding my hand, she placed her other hand on my shoulder, and I instantly felt calmer. This was going way beyond creepy now. My training told me to get the hell away from her, but another part of me was happy to be there with her holding onto me.

"What are you?" I whispered back.

"Don't fight it," she said. "Lay your thumb across my lip, Emily."

"Why?"

"Because you can make this all go away. Trust me."

"I don't know that I can trust any of this right now, lady."

"Aurora. My name is Aurora. Just put your thumb across my lower lip, then tell me what you feel."

I don't know why, but I did what she asked. I slowly extended my thumb across her lower lip as she asked. When I pressed my thumb to her lip, I felt the electricity again. I felt a tingling in my hand as I held it to her lip. It felt like energy flowing back to her, instead of into me. I wanted to jerk my hand back, but the part of me that wanted to fix her face kept me glued to the task.

I even closed my eyes, concentrated on her lip. I knew her face was one of those you would see on marble carvings or paintings from ancient times. It had to be. I just felt it. When I opened my eyes, she was still staring at me, the brow over the uninjured eye arched, as if in question.

"Can I move my hand now?" I whispered.

"Yes."

When I lowered my hand, the lip was healed. No swelling, no split, no bruising. I gaped while she smiled.

"What just happened?" I asked.

"You fixed my lip. I thought it was pretty obvious."

She was laughing at me. I could tell it in her voice, and it had me leaning toward being pissed off. That thought was gone as soon as she squeezed my shoulder ever so slightly.

"Who and what are you?" I asked again. I felt confused, curious, and scared all at the same time, but calm.

"It doesn't matter right now, Emily. What matters is that I'm going to let go of your other hand, then you're going to place it on my bruised cheek. I want you to cover as much of that side of my face as you can. I am willing you not to run, so just know that you can't."

She smiled at me with her newly restored lower lip working like it was supposed to. She had a dazzling smile. I stared back at her, taking in all the features of her face. I nodded then I turned my gaze to her eye. She loosened her grip gradually, finally releasing me totally. I first rubbed the back of my wrist where it had been held, but we never broke the gaze.

I raised my right hand, spreading my fingers to cover as much of that side of her face as I could. My hands weren't small, but she was a good seven inches taller than me, and she was proportionate to her stature. She closed her one good eye, leaning her face into my palm. She reached out and took my left hand, holding it between hers.

"Think about it, Emily. All you have to do is think about what you want to do," she said.

I could feel the power again, hers against the skin of my palm, my own forcing it back. I knew her face had to be one that could launch a million ships, and I wanted to see for myself. I closed my eyes again, thought about how her skin would feel soft, how her high cheek bones would fill out the skin, and the swollen eye that would be unmarred as she would be able to look at me with both eyes. I saw it in my mind and felt the power in my hand.

I realized I'd been holding my breath and I let it out on a sigh. Damn, I was suddenly tired. What the hell was going on? I opened my eyes again to find her smiling at me for all she was worth. I jerked my hands away and was astounded to see how right my instincts had been. She was beautiful, and she was smiling at me like I'd just invented electricity.

"Who are you?" I wanted to know.

"The question, Emily, is who are you?"

"Right this minute, I don't know."

"Well, you can call me the ghost of Christmas future."

"What the hell does that mean? How did I fix your face? Hell, who hit you in the first place?"

She shook her head but continued smiling. She had a dimple that had been hidden by the swollen mess of her face. "You will be okay, Emily. I promise you." She said this as she was rising off the bench.

"Wait a minute! Where do you think you're going? You can't just leave."

"Oh, yes, I can, officer. Your partner will be back any minute, and he'd never understand what you did to fix this. Trust me on that one. But I will see you again, very soon."

She reached back down to where I was sitting, placing her hand on my shoulder. I glanced at that hand, then she rubbed her thumb down the side of my neck, and the world went black.

I'd only been out of it a few minutes, and when I came to, Mickey was walking around the corner of the building. As soon as he saw I was alone, his hand went to the butt of his gun, and he started surveying the area.

"Where'd she go?"

"I…I don't know. I told her she had to go to the ER, and she refused, saying she'd be alright. I don't know if she hit me or what, because the next thing I knew, you were walking around the corner of the building, and she's gone." We both stared at each other for a long moment.

"How's the head?"

"I'll live," I said, while rubbing the back of my head. I knew I hadn't been hit, but I had to make it look real.

EMILY 105

*W*e'd returned to the squad room at the end of our shift to complete the final reports for the night. Mickey contacted dispatch to track down the phone number and time of the call for our hospital victim. He'd returned scratching his head. According to dispatch, they didn't take a call, nor did they send us out on a call. We stared at each other. Just when I thought things couldn't get any stranger.

After last night, I was so hoping tonight would be normal as I crawled into the patrol car with Mickey. He liked to drive, so I let him. Yeah, it bothered me to let him drive all the time, but it was Mickey, and after last night's call or non-call, I didn't want to have to concentrate on driving. Not with my mind a million miles away. We're supposed to respond to accidents, not make them.

Around three in the morning, Mickey announced it was time for lunch, and I didn't argue. I'd skipped eating before work, and the doughnut I'd washed down with stale squad room coffee was wearing off, and it hadn't settled right with me anyway. My stomach didn't feel right. It wasn't anything specific I could point to…just not right. Luckily, Mickey's choice tonight was one of my favorites, a mom-and-pop diner that was open 24/7, the kind you could order from the entire menu all day or night.

The waitress took our order, and since we were regulars, she knew we'd have the usual. Mickey had been in a good mood when we left the squad room. It wasn't that he was in a bad mood now, but he'd said little while we were on patrol. He just drove in silence. It wasn't until after the waitress brought us fresh coffee that he opened up.

"Well, Lucy got her wish come true," he began, a large grin on his face.

"Really? Which one would that be, Mic?"

"She willed a grandchild to be on its way."

"Well, congratulations, Grandpa!"

"Thanks. I think I'm going to need all the well wishes I can get. Since the kids came and told us this morning, I've not had a moment's peace. Hell, I barely got four hours of sleep this afternoon." His voice sounded peeved, but the smile and shine in his eyes told a different story.

"I know you'll be great grandparents. Tell Lucy I said so."

"Yeah, I will, just as soon as she slows down enough to listen. The moment they said baby, her momma hormones kicked in. She was a planning fool when I snuck out to come to work."

I reached over and patted his forearm. "It will all work out."

I was happy for the whole Parish family, especially Lucy. At least now I'd be off the hook. She could finally close the chapter on the "Emily Hunter Life Remodel." That little project was over. I grinned just thinking about it.

Around 5:30 in the morning, when commuters started to stir, we had a fender bender to work. That was the extent of our night. Mickey dealt with most of that, because I really wasn't feeling well at all. The food I'd ordered had been good going down, but it wasn't sitting well now. I felt clammy and nauseated.

By the time we walked into the station, I had my shirt unbuttoned and untucked. I knew this wasn't going to end well. I'd left Mickey to finish up the paperwork and tried to use the ladies' room near the squad room, but unfortunately, the night shift meant maintenance used the time to make needed repairs. As there weren't many women on the force, there weren't many choices now, so I had to make my way down to the public lobby to use that restroom. My stomach was cramping badly, and I was surprised I'd made it this far.

I normally locked my weapons in my desk while we were in the station, but time was a luxury I didn't have, as my mind was more focused on finding the ladies room. I'd been sick in front of Mickey only one other time since we'd been partners, and I didn't want to repeat the process. I'd seen enough to know that being a woman already had a mark of weakness against me. Showing more, just by being sick, was something I didn't want to do any more than I had to. Right now, I had to, and I didn't like it.

After my stomach was empty, I sat on the floor in the stall. I knew the cleaning staff always finished this area first, so it was somewhat safe to sit on. I felt weak but needed to rinse my mouth and clean my face before I left the restroom. I just wanted to go home.

I heard the outer door of the restroom open then close. I knew I wasn't alone, but I didn't really care. Surely, I could face one citizen. I heard a stall door close then listened as someone took care of their business. When I felt I had enough strength for my legs not to wobble, I stumbled to the bank of sinks.

I looked at myself in the mirror. My hair was a mess, but I didn't care. Resting my elbows on the edge of the sink, I sagged over it while the water ran cold in front of me. I cupped my hands under the water and brought a little of it to my mouth. I swished it around to get the taste out of my mouth then spit it out again. I was repeating this process with my eyes closed when I heard the other occupant flush then open the stall door. I kept my eyes closed and splashed water on my face.

While the other person in the room didn't make any noise walking to the sinks, I knew she was there. I could feel her presence. She'd not come to stand right beside me, but I knew without looking up there was just the one sink between us.

"I'm sorry, but are you okay?" she asked.

"I'll be fine, thanks," I said, then started rubbing the back of my neck with water.

I heard her running water. She washing her hands, and when she got a paper towel, I thought I was home free, since she was leaving. But I was wrong. I looked down at the floor and saw her feet near mine.

"I'm sorry," she began. "I really don't mean to bother you, but are you sure you're going to be okay? I could go get you a soda if you need it."

I was actually feeling much better by this point and raised my head to look in the mirror. I looked at my eyes first, then glanced in the mirror to look at her image. I froze. I was looking at picture of myself from a year ago. She was looking down at me, my back, not in the mirror to actually see my face. I jerked up abruptly, spinning to face her. At the same time, my hand was going to the butt of my gun. When she saw my face, her mouth dropped open.

We each took a step backwards, slipping on a wet spot in sync and losing our footing, then we both sat down hard on the tiled floor. I wasn't sure which shock was greater: having my spine jarred from the fall or the fact that I was looking at someone who looked just like me. The only exception was this person had two green eyes.

The door to the restroom opened, then another lady entered. She saw my doppleganger sitting on the floor first, raised an eyebrow, then came into full view of me also sitting on the floor. She smiled, walked farther into the room, and came to stand in front of the sinks halfway between the two of us.

She looked from one to the other, started shaking her head, then turned to the mirrors. She pulled out her lipstick, started applying the color to her very full bottom lip, paused, then said, "Girls, I'm sure there is a really good reason that you're both ass-planted on the floor, but really, you both need to get up."

We both looked at each other again then back to her. More correctly, she looked back to her. I was too busy taking in this apparition in front of me. The lady by the sink washed her hands then walked between us to the paper towels. When she turned back around, she looked at each of us again, smiling and still shaking her head. She walked up to me first and extended her hand down towards me.

I took her hand with my left hand, leaving my right hand on the gun. For some reason, I didn't want to let it go. After I was on my feet, she continued to hold my hand. I noticed this was more of a handshake pose and just stared down at our hands. I also became aware that I started to not worry about my gun. I suddenly felt safe, and that confused me. I whipped my head up, looking her in the eyes.

"Emily," she started, "I'm so very glad to finally meet

you. I wasn't expecting to find you so quickly and definitely not in the ladies' room, but regardless, I'm so happy to be here."

She'd stopped shaking my hand while she was talking. I could only stare at her. The lady behind her was scrabbling to her feet. The woman in front of me released my hand, turning quickly to offer her assistance as well. When my double was on her feet, she started smiling wide as well.

Was I missing something or what? The older woman put an arm around my double's waist, then just stood there.

"Oh, my name is Ruth. I'm your Aunt. And this is Sam, your sister."

I'm not sure which was more confusing. The fact that two women caught me in the restroom at work then proceeded to tell me we were related or the fact that one of these relations could be my twin if not for the eye color. I slowly took a step backwards, looking from one to the other.

"Is this a joke?" was all I could choke out.

"Sam, please, take out your contact," Ruth said.

Sam turned to the counter, set her backpack down then retrieved a contact lens case from within. She leaned over, took one contact out, placed it in the container, and then turned around. If my hair had been longer, I would've been looking in a mirror. Her eyes were identical to mine, only in reverse. Our eyes mirrored each other, and the hair on my whole body went on point.

I backed up until I bumped into the wall.

"What do you want?"

I was suspicious as hell. Why today, of all days, did this fall in my lap? As if I didn't have enough problems, now my long-lost family wanted to have a reunion!

The older lady said, "Emily, we just want to talk. We just

flew into town last night. I've been searching for both you and Sam. I found Sam first, then she came with me to find you."

She took a tentative step toward me, and my hand went to my gun again by instinct. She threw her hands up, palms open toward me, as if she was showing she was unarmed. She stopped moving forward when she realized how nervous she was making me.

"Honest, we're not here to harm you, we just want to talk. Have you ever wondered about your real family, Emily? Or is it Em? Your mom, Linda, used to write to me and send me your school pictures. She labeled them as Em. Do you still go by Em?" She leaned her head slightly to one side still smiling.

"What do you mean my mom wrote to you?"

"Em, um, can I call you Em?"

I nodded, and she continued lowering her hands at the same time.

"Em, I'm very tired. I've been on the road for over a week now. You look like you've had a long night. Can we go somewhere and grab a cup of coffee?"

"I have to go back to the squad room. I was only in this restroom because ours was being cleaned." I paused. Why the hell was I sharing that? I guess I could at least listen to what they had to say. "Can you wait for me in the lobby? There's a coffee shop down the street. We can go there."

What else was I going to do? I have a sister! I'd traveled almost halfway across the country to keep my family safe, and a family I never knew existed was standing in front of me; now I had more to keep safe.

We agreed that they'd go ahead to the coffee shop, and I'd meet them in half an hour. I was numb as I went back to the squad room. I changed clothes as quickly as I could and headed out to meet them. What the hell was about to happen? Suddenly, I felt my life was about to take a new direction.

When I arrived at the coffee shop, I couldn't see them and thought they'd decided not to meet before I found them at the back of the shop, in the farthest corner from the door. They sat in the booth, facing each other, but when the older lady saw me, she smiled then switched to the other side of the booth as I walked toward them. She even gave me the seat with the view to the door. It was as if she knew I needed to sit where I could see what was going on in the rest of the room. Since college, I'd never wanted to sit with my back to a room again.

When I sat down, I looked closely at each of them. Ruth sat smiling at me. My twin just stared. I wasn't certain if she was frowning at me or was just as uncertain of this meeting as I was. They'd already ordered their coffee, the waitress returning just after I sat down. I was somewhat of a regular here. Mickey and I often came here many mornings after our shift.

"Officer, what will it be?" she asked, coffeepot in one hand.

"Just coffee today, Tess," I said, without looking away from my twin.

Tess glanced around the table, checking coffee levels. She glanced at faces after she finished inspecting their cups, then her mouth dropped open. She switched her look to me, then back to the Sam. *My sister's name was Sam, huh?*

Tess closed her mouth, then and started grinning too. "I'll be right back with your cup, Officer."

When she was out of ear shot, Ruth took control of the situation.

"I'm glad you came. I mean *we're* glad you came. I think

Sam here is in a little bit of shock, and she knew we were looking for you. Must be the difference between theory and reality," she said, then took a sip of her coffee.

Sam's coffee looked like it hadn't been touched. She sat with her hands clasping each other on the table. At the mention of her name, she shook out of her trance. She glanced at Ruth sideways, and one corner of her mouth rose. She turned back to me then dropped her eyes to the table.

"To tell you the truth, even with knowing that I had a twin, I just can't get over it. We look so much alike," she said.

It was obvious she talked with her hands. Even while they were on the table, she turned them over one another. I could see scrapes on her palms, and it made me frown. I wanted to touch her hands. I don't know why, but I felt compelled. Ruth noticed my expression.

"Emily, what's wrong? I know you have questions, but there's something you don't like?" Ruth said. The last wasn't exactly a question but rather a statement, like she could read my face.

"How did you hurt your hand?" I asked, pointing at the injured palm.

Sam turned both hands over, then I could see they were both scraped. "Matching set, I guess," she said, glancing at both palms then to Ruth.

Ruth grinned bigger.

"Both knees match, too. Ruth took me, umm, hiking a few days ago. Let's just say I'm accident prone and wasn't dressed for the occasion." She looked back up to me then turned both palms flat on the table on either side of her coffee cup, blushing. I guess she was embarrassed over having fallen down.

"You want to touch her, Emily," Ruth said.

I jerked my gaze. "How did you know that?" I asked, almost in a whisper.

"Sam, hold your hand out for Emily."

Sam glanced at Ruth, who was nodding her head slowly as if to say, *"It's okay."* Sam cautiously slid her left hand across the table to me. When her hand was halfway across the table, she turned her palm up, then paused, looking at her hand then back up to me. I reached out and placed my right hand on top of hers before I even thought about it.

I was watching her face when we made contact. The pupils of her eyes contracted then flared as the tingle at the base of my spine tightened. I knew my pupils matched hers. I became more aware of the room in an instant. I looked down and jerked my hand up, hovering over where she held hers.

"Ruth," Sam started, "does this always happen like this?"

"It's okay, Sam, its normal."

"Do you mind telling me exactly *what* is normal?" I asked.

"The two of you are making contact for the first time in twenty-two years. You spent the first 9 months in the womb side by side, then you were separated. It's just a reconnection, a reestablishment of your bond," Ruth explained, like she was explaining why the sun comes up every day—because it just does.

I felt unexpectedly drawn to Sam, suddenly wanting to protect her. I felt sad that she'd fallen and hurt herself, then I felt the tingle at the base of my spine spread to my shoulders, making me sit up taller. I took a breath then laid my hand back on top of hers. I stared as I felt the tingle move from my shoulder toward my hand. I knew what the end result was going to be, and I wasn't sure how they were going to take it, but I couldn't stop myself. I let it flow from the palm of my hand into hers. When the exchange hit her palm, I felt her tense. Sam wanted to jerk her hand away, but Ruth grabbed her wrist, holding it in place. Sam had a wild-eyed look, turning to stare at Ruth.

"Just breathe, Sam," Ruth whispered.

It only lasted for a few seconds, then I released her hand, pulling mine into my lap. The tingling was still there but less intense. We all looked at Sam's palm, where we found the scrapes had disappeared. Sam was stunned. In the space of two heartbeats, her surprise turned to a small giggle, then she started smiling. Ruth released her hand, then Sam withdrew it from the middle of the table, running her fingers over the now unmarred palm. She kept smiling as she smoothed over it a few times then looked back up at me, turning slightly in the booth to face Ruth. I knew she was watching the room more than looking at Ruth, then she slid her right hand across the table towards me.

"Can you do this one, too?" she asked quietly.

Okay, my personal circus act didn't bother them. Ruth knew what I was doing. She'd stopped Sam from jerking her hand back the first time. I slowly extended my hand to the top of Sam's, letting the tingle flow again, never taking my eyes off Ruth. Again, it only took a few seconds, and as I pulled my hand back to my lap, Tess walked up with my coffee. Sam shifted back in her seat to face the table. She'd put her hands in her lap, and I knew she was smoothing both palms together to feel the lack of scrapes. Tess took their breakfast orders and left us again.

"Okay," I started, "you don't seem the least bit surprised by what just happened. You even look like you know something about it. You want to tell me what the hell kind of freak I am?"

"Freak? You think that makes you a freak?" Sam asked, aghast, shaking her head.

"Sam, let me." Ruth leaned back in the booth, crossing her arms over herself almost in a hug. "Emily, I'll tell you as I told Sam; this isn't really a conversation we want to have in public. I know you have questions, and yes, I know what just happened. You healed your sister. You want to touch her, and you want to protect her. You can't help it. The bond has been re-established, and you're old enough now to realize it. You want to help her, but you don't know why. If you'd been raised together, it would've just been an automatic response. Neither of you would've questioned it. She probably would've just come to you as soon as she'd been hurt. That is, if you were still children, but you're grown now. What I can say is that I am sorry you were separated," she said, exhaling with the last sentence.

She glanced around, sat up straighter, then looked me dead in the eye. "Emily, you're in danger, but I think you already knew that. Let's eat then find someplace else to finish our discussion." She reached, almost instinctively, to rearrange her coffee cup and saucer on the table.

Tess was heading our way with another pot of coffee. How did she know Tess was coming our way? I glanced back between the Ruth and Sam.

I knew from experience that if someone tells me I'm in danger to listen to what my gut tells me. I could always listen to what she needed to tell me, then if I didn't like what I heard, I could run again. I could start over, but looking across the table at a sister I never knew I had, I found I didn't really want to be separated from her. I wanted to know more about her. I had to know more about her and Ruth before I'd make up my mind.

"Okay, after breakfast we can go back to my apartment. It's not far. We can take the train. The station's just down the street. But make no mistake, Ruth, I'm not afraid to do what I have to do to protect myself," I said, narrowing my eyes at my newly found aunt.

SAM 107

 $\mathcal{I}$ sat there staring, not believing that my sister—my twin—was sitting across the table from me. Emily's short haircut looked good on her, but I wasn't so sure I'd be comfortable with that style. She looked tougher than I ever thought I would or could be. Hell, she even had a diamond-covered band as an earring, in the cartilage. Just the thought of getting one of those made me flinch. She might've had a whole family growing up, but she seemed older than our age.

I watched her give a cold, hard look to Ruth, and at first I thought she was going to tell her to just go to hell. The way she'd said that she'd always protect herself had an edge to it. One that you could almost cut the tension with that had been building between the three of us. Ruth just smiled, nodding calmly.

Minutes later Tess brought our breakfast, and we ate in near silence. Before I could finish my pancakes, Ruth stood up at the end of the table. She looked back and forth between the two of us and nodded with a calculating look, her lips pursed.

"Listen, girls, I need to run a quick errand. Emily, will you take Sam back to your apartment with you? If you give me your address, I'll meet you there."

Emily looked calmly from Ruth to me then back again. "Sure. Let me write down the address," she said, reaching for a napkin from the dispenser.

Ruth grabbed a pen out of her purse and was at the ready when Emily looked back up. After Emily jotted down the address, she handed it and the pen back to Ruth. Ruth's face was blank, and I couldn't read her expression. It looked cold and weary. She watched Emily for a few heartbeats, then she put the napkin with the address in her purse, turning to me.

"Sam, I know I said I'd keep you safe, and I will, but Emily is going to take care of you right now. You good with that?" she asked, raising her eyebrows in question.

"Sure. But I think I can take care of myself. I'm not a child, and I'm a lot tougher than I look," I replied, with my brows drawing in. I wished these two would stop looking at me like I was a child. It was really irritating.

"We have much to discuss, ladies. I've saved this conversation so both of you could hear it at the same time." She looked around the café casually, but I knew she was really wondering who was near enough to hear. "I'll meet you both at the apartment in about an hour," she said, then turned on her heels without looking back at either of us.

We both watched Ruth until she was out of sight then automatically looked at one another. This was odd. I broke off the gaze first and went back to my pancakes. I needed something to fill the silence that suddenly felt awkward. I focused on my pancakes, trying not to look up, but I could see Emily's hands across the table slowly turning her coffee cup around in a circle.

After the fourth spin of the cup, she cleared her throat. "I know this is bizarre for the both of us. Tell me, were you adopted, too?" she asked, then placed her hands, palm side down, on either side of the cup.

I glanced up. She had a very calm expression on her face. "I probably know more about you right now, Emily," I started.

"Em. Call me Em. Everyone else does," she said, with a twitch at the corner of her mouth. She looked like she wanted to smile but didn't pull it off. She could cut off her expressions the same way Ruth could. I knew she must make a good cop. The thought made me smile. She had a career already, and I was floundering to finish college.

"Okay, Em. Yes, I was adopted too. Apparently, Ruth arranged both our adoptions. She said they kept in contact with both our adoptive families, but for some reason my family up and moved to Arkansas and didn't let Ruth know. Ruth said our mom came from Arkansas. Or at least that's where she lived until she moved to Texas."

I'd stopped eating, and suddenly found I wasn't hungry anymore. For the last few days, I'd just gone with the flow of the situation, the stories Ruth told me, and I hadn't thought about the real details of why our mother had left Arkansas or why she'd chosen Texas. While I recounted the highlights of Ruth's stories to Em, I didn't want to tell her how Ruth found me or what had happened since she'd approached me in Hashtags. That would have to wait.

Tess returned to give us our check. After we settled up the tab, I followed Emily out of the café. We walked in silence down the sidewalk toward the train station, then we rode in silence to the exit for her apartment. Her apartment wasn't far from the station, and we continued to walk in silence all the way to the front door of her high rise.

Em seemed to tense before we even reached the building.

On the street in front of the building, she'd looked all around, not caring that she was making it obvious to all who passed. She kept her sharp eyes on the people passing, while she slowly turned a complete circle. She'd obviously done this many times before.

The apartment building itself was a cookie cutter building that you'd find in almost every city. Dark tiled flooring led the way to a narrow hall where the stairwell and elevator were located, just opposite rows of mailboxes. Emily used an access key card to swipe her entry into the building, repeating the process again to call the elevator. When we reached her apartment door, she opened it with an old-fashioned key.

Shoving through the entry, Emily held the door open for me. As I walked in, I noticed what looked to be a line of salt in front of the threshold. I decided that was none of my business, and just looked around the room. The room was tidy, and given that she had a real job, I could see she could afford a few more household items than I could. Nothing was fancy, just plain and simple.

The apartment had an open floor plan, where the living room, dining area and kitchen area all flowed together. The living room furniture was dark, the fabric in solid colors. She had a pub-style table in the dining room. I walked to the middle of the living room then slowly turned, taking it all in. Emily strode to the kitchen, placed her keys and bag on the bar, then turned to look at me with her hands on her hips. She shook her head but had a blank look on her face.

"I really don't know what else to tell you, Sam," she started. "Ruth apparently kept up with my adoptive mother. I just wish I'd known about it. You think you know someone," she said, shaking her head again, then dropping her gaze to the floor. "Make yourself at home. Since Ruth will be here shortly, I really need to shower and change before we continue our family tree conversation. I've already been sick this morning then stunned by our little reunion. There's a coffee pot and grinder on the counter. Beans are in the freezer. I have a feeling you know how to use those," she said with a grin. Without any other preamble, she walked to her bedroom and closed the door.

EMILY 106

I looked at the bedside table and saw that it was now 10 a.m., which meant I'd been sitting on the edge of my bed with my head down, elbows on my knees, for the last fifteen minutes. I had to stretch to uncurl my back muscles. I also needed to get in the shower since Ruth would be here soon, but the dread of what I felt was coming had me tense. I shook my head to myself, hardly believing what had happened in the last three hours. A twin sister, an aunt, and apparently a whole lot of secrets. I hate secrets.

I suddenly remembered Sally telling me that I wasn't whole but that one day I would be. I wondered if this was what she meant, that she knew that I was a twin. Then I thought of the rest of Sally's conversation. I had to find the witch in my family to help me get rid of the demon that had followed me from Texas. The idea of evil around me was one thing, but thinking that my twin would now be near it too made the hair on the back of my neck stand up.

While Sam gives the impression she can take care of herself, and she'd had a tougher upbringing than I'd had, I wondered if she'd encountered anything like the thing that had been following me.

I gathered my clothes then headed to the shower, appreciating that the hot water was a God send. I was rarely sick, but when I was, I wanted to be clean as soon as I got over it. As I stood under the water, head bent, letting the beat of the water work on the tense muscle in my neck, I turned my hands over repeatedly, inspecting them.

Sally had refused to shake my hand until she learned I'd been adopted, then she'd said I had to find the witch in my family. Did she refuse to shake my hand because she thought I was a witch? The hot water couldn't keep the goose bumps from shooting across my skin. Is this what Ruth and Sam were going to tell me? And just when I thought these last few days couldn't get any stranger.

SAM 108

$\mathcal{I}$'d made a full pot of coffee and found cups before Emily reappeared. I was sitting at her dining table sipping my coffee, and Emily looked intense when she entered the room. I cocked my head to the side, trying to figure out what could've happened during her shower. She mirrored my head tilt and smiled, but it didn't reach her eyes. Yeah, something was up. I could just sense it.

Em went to the kitchen and poured herself some coffee before she came back to sit at the table. "You said you had a matching set," Emily said.

"Matching set? Set of what?" I asked, confused.

"Your scrapes, you said your knees matched your hands."

"Oh, yeah," I began. "I do—or did, I mean. I forgot all about my knees since the reminders on my hands are gone now. Thanks, by the way."

"You're welcome. Do you know how I fixed those?"

"Um, no, I don't. That was the first time I've seen that." I'd better shut up. I didn't want her upset and have her deciding to kick us out before I got to know her.

"But you've seen other things like this, I take it?"

"What is this, an interrogation?"

"Yeah, I think it is. I'm a cop, remember?"

I was trying to think of just how to respond to her last question when there was a knock on her door. Saved by the frickin bell. Thank you, Jesus, Ruth had arrived. Emily, however, wasn't so happy.

"Did you answer the buzzer for the front door?" She pegged me with a hard glare.

"What buzzer?" I replied, looking around for what she could mean.

"Oh, this is not going to be good," Emily muttered as she walked to the kitchen first, pulled a revolver out of a drawer, then made her way to the front door. She stood to the far side of the door as the knock came again.

"Who is it?" Emily asked.

"It's me, Ruth. I think you're expecting me, remember?" Ruth's voice was slightly muffled by the door, but I could tell from experience her brand of smart ass was shining bright.

Emily lowered her gun from where she'd been pointing it up at the ceiling and shook her head. She stepped back to the door, unfastened, unbolted, then unlocked the door. Yeah, she's a little safety conscious.

opened the door a crack then peered outside to see Ruth standing there. Her smart-ass comment was reflected by the smart-ass expression on her face.

"Aren't you going to let me in?"

I took a deep breath then stepped back, opening the door as wide as I could before saying, "I'd like to know how you got here without being buzzed in." I still had my gun in my right hand and motioned Ruth inside with it.

She raised an eyebrow at me, then glanced back into the hallway and said, "You better be glad I'm going in first." Ruth shook her head as she stepped into my apartment. "You care to put that thing away?"

I stepped into the living room, tucked the gun in the back of my jeans, and raised both hands. "Feel better now?"

It was then that I heard the voice in the hallway. "Well, she might not, but I know I do."

And then she came through my door. The Shirley Temple-looking domestic violence call from the other night. I gasped, grabbed my gun, and got into a two fisted stance. I was holding my breath, looking down the barrel when Ruth walked straight up to me, put her hand on top of the gun, and forced me to lower it.

"It's alright Emily, she's with me," she said.

Then she placed her other hand on my bare forearm, making me feel immediately calmer. Almost as calm as I'd been when I'd fixed Shirley's face. When I remembered that, I whipped my gaze back up to Shirley. She had an eyebrow raised, grinning. She raised both hands, shrugged while walking into the room, closed the door, then headed to my kitchen.

"God, that coffee smells good. Is there any left?" Shirley said, and just kept walking.

Sam had kept her seat at the table, and while she looked calm, she had a frown on her face, looking puzzled. I looked back at Ruth, then she nodded and took my gun away from me.

Took my own damn gun! And I let her! Oookay...

"I promise you're safe. You're both safe," she said. Ruth tossed my gun in her purse then headed for the kitchen. "Aurora, don't drain that pot. I need some more coffee too."

I looked at Sam. She shrugged her shoulders while shaking her head then returned to drinking her coffee. I went back to the dining table got my cup of coffee then moved to the chair where I could see both the kitchen and the front door. Yeah, I was still paranoid.

Ruth and Aurora whispered while they were preparing their coffee. This was so not going to be a good chat. I could just feel it. I looked down at my cup, twirling it around on the table as I usually did when I was nervous. I didn't hear them walk toward us or sit down, but it made me jerk backwards when I realized they were there. I glanced quickly at Sam, and she was rubbing the middle of her brows, shaking her head again.

"Is there something I'm missing here?" I asked.

Ruth and Shirley—or Aurora, I suppose I should call her —raised eyebrows at me while they sipped their coffee.

"What do you mean?" Ruth asked.

"This woman," I pointed across the table at Aurora, "had the hell beat out of her night before last, and now she waltzes in here like your BFF. Something's going on here, and I'm not sure I understand or like it. Someone needs to start explaining, now. Sam's given me a few background details, but I know something else is going on."

Ruth took a breath, holding it for a second as if in deep thought, then let it go. "First things first, let's have some introductions. Sam, Emily, I want you to meet my oldest, dearest friend, Aurora Orvalho. Aurora, you've met Emily, obviously, and this is Sam," she said, indicating with her hand.

Aurora gave a small nod to each of us, maintaining the shit-eating grin on her face.

"Okay, so enough with the formalities. I was once told by an old Cherokee lady that I was only half a person. That one day I'd be whole. Is this what she was referring to?" I asked, waving my hand slowly toward Sam, then back at myself, repeatedly.

Ruth cocked her head to the side in thought then finally said, "Maybe. I haven't been around any tribes lately. They tend to steer clear of us."

That got my attention.

"Why would they steer clear of us?" I asked, looking Ruth right in the eye. But as soon as I said it, the rest of my visit with Sally Black came back to me again.

"What else did this ancient share with you?" Aurora asked, jumping in the mix.

I hadn't noticed her attire when she'd first come into the

room, but she had on a linen jacket that wasn't one bit wrinkled. I hated wearing linen. It always looked like I'd worn it to bed within an hour of putting it on. Aurora rose out of her chair, removed her blue jacket and hung it on the back of her seat. She sat back down waiting for my answer.

She raised both her eyebrows, then raised her hand to motion for me to continue talking. I barely noticed the motion of her hand because my eyes were too distracted by the tattoos on her upper arms. She was amazing with her golden hair barely sweeping the top of her shoulders. She was wearing a linen tank top that matched the jacket and jeans. She looked like a foreign model, but not quite as skinny as runway models. And then there were those tattoos.

The tattoos were like arm bands, about an inch wide in an intricate weave of black and green. Wide circles on the outer edges with a loop running through the middle, it had straight pieces that would peak on the top in a sharp angle between the loops, to descend angling to the lower side of the band. It was mirrored top and bottom in points.

I was entranced by the dazzling colors. Here and in Vegas I'd seen my share of tats, but none with these vibrant colors. Even the color of fresh tats didn't come close to these. I was beginning to wonder what kind of ink had been used when Aurora waved her hand in front of my face.

"Hello, are you with us?"

Shit, now I was embarrassed, and my face burned with the evidence. "Yeah," I said, pointing to her artwork, "I was just taken with your tats."

She glanced down at either arm, folding them across her perfect chest then shrugged. "Yeah, I've enjoyed them over the years. But you didn't answer my question."

I just stared back at her, trying to remember what she'd asked.

"Please, pay attention," she started, then I realized that she had an accent. I hadn't heard it the other night, but it was definitely here now. "I asked about your encounter with one of the ancients of the native tribes."

I frowned at her. What an odd way to phrase a question. I was sure she hadn't talked like this the other night. "She was the grandmother of my roommate in college."

"And did you visit with this elder often?"

What the hell was this? I didn't know it was my turn to be interrogated.

"It's okay, Aurora, I have a few questions I want to ask, too."

I turned now to look at Ruth. "And those questions would be what?"

"Why did you run away, Emily? Your family has been worried sick," Ruth replied with a look of concern.

"I thought you said *you* were my family." I said loudly, deciding there was no better time than now to try and turn the tables.

"You know what I mean," Ruth said, narrowing her eyes at me. "But let me save us all some time. The world isn't exactly as either of you expected it to be or knew it to be, and I think you're both realizing that."

Suddenly Sam spoke, "Why is there a line of salt in front of your door?"

We all looked at Sam as she looked from me to Ruth then Aurora before returning to eyeing me.

"I know it's a little rude, but hey, everyone's asking questions," Sam said as she shrugged her shoulders then leaned back in her seat.

Aurora and Ruth both looked at me with raised eyebrows.

"Oh, I've got to hear this one," Aurora mumbled, before she took a sip of her coffee.

"The old Cherokee lady, Sally. She told me salt would protect me," I said. The looks on their faces left me feeling a little embarrassed.

"Protect you from what?" Ruth said, placing her forearms on the table, leaning forward.

"Well, she said it was a demon."

Holy shit! That got their attention, because Aurora stood up so fast I thought she would knock over her chair, then she started scanning the room. She walked to the door and checked out my trail of salt, then she walked to the windows to check there, too. Ruth was frowning hard as she stared at me. She glanced at Sam, who was quiet now, with bugged eyes.

Ruth finally spoke, "I think you better start from the beginning, Emily, and don't leave anything out."

"Is this what you meant by saying we're in danger?" Sam asked.

"No, not exactly," Ruth said, leaning back in her chair.

Aurora came back to the table and sat down, ramrod straight in her chair. She tucked her hair somewhat behind her ears then crossed her arms again. "Why not the windows, too?" she asked.

I looked around the table at the three of them staring back at me, then I told them about that rush week my first year of college. I told them about the trip to the compound and about what I saw while I was there. Sam looked a little frightened, but she didn't say anything. Aurora and Ruth kept stealing glances at one another, both hard in thought. I stood up while telling about Sally and Vanessa then pulled my string of beads out of the drawer where I kept my gun. I brought it back to the table and laid it in the middle while I repeated what I remembered about my visit to Sherman, Texas. I could tell Aurora wanted to pick the beads, and she actually made the motion to reach her hand out but stopped herself. The beads just lay there. Ruth watched me, nodding occasionally.

"So why not the windowsills?" It was Sam now asking.

"I just felt like I wouldn't need to place a barrier on the windows when I'm this high up. I've not seen this thing since I moved here. I even stopped carrying the beads. I just figured that since this is Salt Lake City, maybe I was protected just by that." Shrugging my shoulders as I finished, I felt a little relief. Not since Vanessa had moved to Dallas had I discussed this with anyone else. I glanced up to see Aurora and Ruth staring at each other, both still frowning slightly.

I turned back to Ruth and gave her my narrowed cop eyes. "This isn't the danger you were talking about, is it?"

Ruth took a sip of coffee, put her cup on the table, then opened her hand toward the middle of the table. The beads slid across the table and into her hand, almost too fast for my eyes to keep up. My mouth dropped open as I scooted my chair back, trying to get away from the table and, at the same time, my hands reaching to my back for my gun. Then I remembered I didn't have it. Shit.

Ruth held the beads in one hand while she smoothed over them with the other. She concentrated on them as if they could reveal some truth only she could see. I glanced at Sam, and she was calm as a cucumber. Aurora was watching the beads in Ruth's hands. She wasn't exactly happy with them.

"Emily, this demon isn't the danger I was talking about. Please sit back down." She indicated my chair. "I'll give you your gun back later. What I'm about to tell you will turn your world upside down. Sam," she said, nodding at the end of the table where my twin sat quietly, "you've been with me for almost a week, and I know you've seen things happen which, to you, have little to no explanation. Em, having just met you and seeing what you can already do, I know you suspect things are on the opposite side of normal."

Ruth got up and took a few steps toward the kitchen. At first, I thought she was going for more coffee, but she turned and paced, pausing behind Aurora's chair. "We've all been told bedtime stories. We've heard ghost stories, fables, and fairytales." She paused then took a deep breath. "It's all true, girls. All of it." She just stopped, putting her hands on her hips, looking at both of us.

SAM 109

 looked at Emily. We were frowning at each other, and I knew from the look on Emily's face that she was experiencing the same disbelief I'd had a few short days ago. Emily seemed to be absorbing all of this, so I decided it was time to speed things up and get more answers.

"Ruth, the other day when I asked if the Boogeyman was real, you just replied, 'That depends on what your idea of the Boogeyman is.'" I even used air quotes. "So, what does that mean? What about Emily's demon or devil or whatever it is."

"To some degree, all the Boogeymen are or have been real. Some creatures have died out, while some are very much still part of the world. Not everyone can see or sense them, but they're there." She paused, but the goose bumps were already starting to cover my arms. "I've already told Sam, and now I'll tell you, too, Emily; witches are real. Not in the sense of the most popular tales or even the stories you were told. But I'm real, and so are you. We are direct descendants of the Goddess Aurora." She paused, looking between the two of us.

EMILY 108

I could see the look on Sam's face, and I can only guess that my expression matched hers. We turned at the same time and looked at the golden-haired beauty across the table from us. Aurora gave us her dazzling smile. "Please. You think I look that old?"

Well no, she looked like she might be thirty, but that was it.

Ruth continued, "Ladies, we are the real deal. We have powers, or talents, that would blow the socks off the world if they knew. We've lived in regular society for thousands of years. Sam, the only reason I didn't tell you all of this is simply because it's too much to take all at once. Like taking a semester of Eastern History, but you get it all in one day. There's just no way to absorb it all. So, I've been telling you a little bit at a time. I wanted you and Emily together to hear the majority of it." She was talking with her hands now. "A witch is the most recognizable term in this day, so we've just accepted that word to describe us. Of course, we try to keep a balance in the world, using our powers. To help mankind, if you want to look at it that way." She started pacing again, rubbing her temples at the same time.

"Aurora, I told you that Koresh guy should've been stopped when they first realized he was possessed. We should've never agreed to let the wizards clean up that mess." She was getting pissed. I've seen lots of people get pissed, and she was winding up for a big rant.

Aurora locked gazes with Ruth then said, "I know, but 'I told you so' will not help now. Focus, Ruth. I need you to focus and get all the information out. We have places to go and things to do. You know that. Get this done, now."

Dropping her head, Ruth sighed and went back to her seat. "Emily, I'm sorry, it seems you picked up the *vardoe*. We'll take care of that just as soon as we can."

"You mean it's still there? Out there right now?"

"No, not out there right now. Well, not in this state, at any rate. Old Sally was right, salt does ward them off, but as soon as you move far enough away from here the *vardoe* will latch back on to you. That will be our first order of business before we go home."

I glanced up. "When are you planning to leave? Didn't you say you just got here last night? Where are you staying?" What the hell was wrong with me? Was I really going to try to be Suzy Homemaker and make sure they were all comfortable?

"Aurora and I are actually going to dash home tonight then come back for the two of you in the morning," she said, with the straightest look on her face.

Yeah, go home tonight and be back in the morning. I looked at Sam and frowned. "I thought Sam said you lived in Arkansas?"

"She's right. We do."

Now I was puzzled. I looked at Ruth then at Sam again.

Sam just quirked one side of her mouth, raised an eyebrow at Ruth, and nodded. I turned back to glance at Ruth, but she was gone. Just gone. I was startled then looked in turn at Sam's and Aurora's faces, but they weren't concerned. Ruth walked out of my kitchen with another cup of coffee then sat back down again.

"What the hell was that?" My heart rate was increasing, and I could hear the blood pounding in my ears.

It was Sam who broke the silence.

"Near as I can tell, Ruth can apparently go wherever she wants, whenever she wants, as long as she's been there before. No airplanes, no car." She held her hands, palm side up, in front of her like she didn't know what else to say, then turned toward Aurora and frowned.

"I'm not sure about Aurora, as I just met her here, with you. But by the way she's been acting, I'd say she's in the same boat."

Aurora gave a slight nod of her head in Sam's direction, as if to agree with Sam's assessment. "Yes, I would be in that same boat girls, just as you both are." She broke out her dazzling smile again, first to Sam and then to me before she looked at Ruth, shaking her head.

"So, you plan to leave Sam here with me and come back for her in the morning?" I asked.

"I'm coming back for *both* of you in the morning," Ruth said. It was clear by her voice that she meant business and there was no room for discussion. It was my turn to get pissed now, I guess.

"I can't just leave. I live here. Who do you think you are, coming in here and thinking I'm just going to up and walk out on the life I've built here?" I could feel the heat start to rise up my neck and onto my face. I was appalled that this woman, whom I'd just met, thought I was going to happily let her disrupt my life. I'd worked hard on my life here.

The longer I sat there thinking about it, looking between the three of them, I was suddenly aware of that vibration deep down inside of me that had surfaced the night I walked in on Kevin and that woman. I placed my hands, palms down, on the table and closed my eyes. I was hoping to start counting backwards from ten to buy myself some time to breathe.

"What's happening?"

Sam sounded a little excited, and I opened my eyes, still trying to catch my breath. It was then that I realized the coffee cups were vibrating too. I looked at my hands on the table, then again at the cups, and the vibration intensified. I knew that if I didn't get my breathing under control, the whole table would flip over.

Aurora stood up quickly, grabbing her cup of coffee off the table. Ruth did the same, but with her left hand, she reached across to my forearm. As soon as her skin touched mine, the world went dark.

SAM 110

*A*urora and I both reached out to keep Emily's head from hitting the table, while Ruth continued to hold her forearm. I reached her first, grabbing her shoulders, easing her down onto the table. Ruth arranged her arms so that her head could lie on them, as if she fell asleep in that position. I frowned up at Ruth.

"So that's how you do it! I knew it was something about your touch, I just wasn't sure what it was, but did you have to do it to her, too?" I wasn't feeling too charitable at the moment. I felt like I'd been attacked too, even though I knew what was happening to Emily and that it was altogether harmless.

Aurora answered me quickly, "Ruth was right, Sam. Emily needed to calm down. You saw the table and cups. If she kept going, we'd have had another quake. It's better this way. She'll wake up in a little while and be okay. You did every time, didn't you?"

So, this is what led to the quakes Ruth said I'd caused. I looked back down at my twin's sleeping face, and a thought struck me. "Why did you have to split us up?"

Ruth closed her eyes for several long moments, taking in one breath after another, then opened them to stare back at me. "Trust me a little while longer, Sam, please? Emily needs to hear all of this too, and I really don't want to explain it twice. She'll be awake soon."

Ruth looked around the room then nodded to herself. She reached over, put both arms around Emily's shoulders, then told me to step back. The next thing I knew, Ruth had Emily stretched out on the couch. She looked peaceful, and the movement didn't even wake her up.

I went over and sat down in the floor in front of her sleeping body and just watched her sleeping face. I don't know why; I just did it. As I grasped that I was staring at her face, I realized I'd even moved. Ruth stood, patted me on the shoulder, then went to the kitchen.

I could hear her opening the refrigerator then the cabinet doors. Aurora followed Ruth but just stood leaning against the cabinet. She was tall enough she could lean her butt against the top of the counter. She said nothing. Just watched Ruth. I turned back and watched my sister.

I looked at my own hands then at hers, where Ruth had placed them across her stomach. I looked back at my hands, and I felt a tingle start in the tips of my fingers, like the tingle that passed between us back at the diner. I glanced toward the kitchen and saw that Ruth and Aurora were reading something on the countertop, not paying any attention to me.

Reaching up, I placed my hand on top of Emily's. At first, nothing happened. The tingle was there but remained unchanged. Then the tingle felt like it began to move. I looked at my other hand in my lap because it tingled too. I opened it, flexed it, then closed it. I looked at Emily's face as her eyes twitched under her eyelids, like she was dreaming. I wanted to know her better, but her being asleep was just a waste of time to me. I frowned, and in that same moment, I flexed my free hand in a fist, quickly, without thinking. The tingling in my right arm flashed toward my fingers. I felt the power of it cross from my hand into Emily's, then her eyes shot open. She breathed a few quick breaths when she saw my face, then the excited look softened. She started to say something, but I put my hand over her mouth. I wanted to see what Ruth would say. I didn't like being knocked out like this, and I'm sure Emily didn't like it either.

Emily looked at me, confused. I shook my head, indicating the kitchen. She looked toward the kitchen and was able to see Ruth and Aurora bent over the counter, reading. She looked back at me, then I nodded, taking my hand off her mouth. I stood and gave her a hand in sitting up. Once she was vertical, I sat down beside her, with our legs touching. I don't know why, but I put my hand out to her again, and she took it. It was the eeriest feeling, like the touch was electrified. We both realized it, glancing at our hands.

Emily leaned in toward me and whispered, "What the hell happened?"

"I'm not exactly sure what you'd call it, but best I can tell, Ruth has the ability to send us off for a nap whenever she likes," I whispered back. Emily leaned back to looked at me. All I could do was shrug.

She leaned back into me, "So she's done this to you, too?"

"Let's just say you need a few more of those to match my number of naps," I said, nodding my head back at her.

"Why are we whispering?"

"I don't think Ruth expected you to be awake so soon. I think I, uh, kind of caused it."

"And the whispering?"

"I'm kind of curious what they'll think when they see you awake. I'm also kind of afraid of their reaction. I just touched your hand, and it was that tingling, like at the diner, and then you woke up." I took a breath and shook my head. "I'm not sure that I buy into all of this, at least that I can do any of it. I saw what you did, and I've seen Ruth disappear, but I'm just not sure what that means about me. You were pretty panicked before Ruth touched your arm. Did you realize you were making the table vibrate?"

Emily thought about that with her brows drawn. She was looking at the floor now, but I don't know if she was really seeing it. Slowly, she shook her head no, then looked at me.

Sitting next to Emily, I could see past her into the kitchen. I saw Aurora glance over her shoulder, then do a double take. She never said a word, just broke into another one of those grins then turned back to the counter. When she moved, I could see a big book open on the counter, and I knew I hadn't seen it before. Then I saw that damn purse of Ruth's. It hit me: Why I hadn't looked in that purse when I'd had the chance? Something is very peculiar about that damn bag. I decided my next mission was going to be to find out what the hell was up with it.

Emily squeezed my hand, causing me to look back up to her, then our eyes met. That was all it took.

"Is it just me or is Aurora a little strange too?"

I know neither of us said this out loud, and I knew it wasn't my thought. I searched Emily's face. Could we both do this? So, I decided to think back.

"I think there's something odd about her, too. If you can hear me, nod."

Emily's eyes widened, just a little, and a smile crept upon her face. She took a few seconds then nodded back to me.

"I wouldn't have believed it if we hadn't just done this. Telepathy, too. I wonder if Ruth knows?" she thought back to me.

I was shocked but, at this point, not too shocked.

"Ruth thinks I've been time jumping as well. I had some sleepwalking issues a few months ago, but I'm not sure I want to really believe that it's part of the whole jumping thing. When we left my apartment a couple of days ago, she touched my arm, then I woke almost one hundred miles away." I was frowning thinking about it.

Emily looked at me, a little puzzled. *"Sam, what's so odd about waking up one hundred miles away?"*

"It should've taken us around two hours to get there, Emily. My guess is that it was under forty-five minutes."

That raised her eyebrows, and she looked a little stunned, then we both turned, looking toward the kitchen. We'd both pursed lips, looking at the ladies hovering over that book. Ruth suddenly stood up very straight, almost rigid, and cautiously turned in our direction. She locked eyes with me first then Emily. Looking back to me, she narrowed her eyes and was about to say something when Aurora put her hand on Ruth's arm.

"Leave it alone, Ruth," Aurora said, without turning to look at us.

Em and I let go of each other's hands, and Emily gave Ruth a flash of her grin. Ruth shook her head then turned back to the book on the counter.

"Did they bring that big book in after I was out?"

"Uh, no. I have a feeling Ruth got it out of her magical purse." I whispered.

Emily whipped her gaze back around to me, then grabbed my hand. *"What the hell does that mean?"* she thought at me.

I looked at our hands then back at the kitchen. *"Well, it's kind of hard to explain. Things just appear when that purse is around, and she doesn't leave it unattended very often. Oh, hell, I don't know. Just forget I mentioned it."*

"What else isn't she telling us, Sam? Do you believe she's a witch?"

"Em, I've seen things in the last few days I've no other explanation for. Things that make you think we're not in Kansas anymore."

Emily looked at me, grinning. Letting go of my hand, she stood quickly, grabbed a paper weight off the coffee table, then reared back to throw it as hard as she could toward the two women in the kitchen. At the exact same time, Ruth and Aurora swung around as if they'd sensed something coming. As the paper weight left Emily's hand, Ruth raised her palm but never flinched, even as the paper weight hit an invisible wall, bounced backwards, then fell to the floor.

"Why the hell did you do that?" Ruth asked Emily, staring at her, hands on her hips.

"I just want to understand this. You are the real deal, aren't you?" Emily asked.

"Did you think I was Mary Poppins?" Ruth asked, giving Emily the evil eye. "How do you think we got to your front door earlier? How do you think you fixed Sam's hand? It's not just me in this blood line, dear. You're in this just as much as I am, whether you like it or not."

"Ruth, what aren't you telling us? If you say we're in danger, then we need to know what kind of danger you mean. We need you to come clean here. You need to give us everything. We're not children, and apparently not one hundred percent normal, either. I think we get that now." She paused, turning around looking to me. She pointed to me then looked back to Ruth. "Did you know we can read each other's thoughts?"

That stopped Ruth dead in her tracks. She opened her mouth to say something but closed it, then opened it again as if she was going to say what she was thinking. Then she closed it again. She turned back to the kitchen counter and grabbed her purse, jerking it along with her to the other end of the kitchen, then began to rummage through it. We all just watched her. Aurora seemed a little startled too, and she watched Ruth as intently as we did. Ruth would dig in her purse, stop, close her eyes, take a deep breath, and then start digging again. I took a couple of steps to stand beside Emily, neither of us knowing what to do except watch.

Ruth finally brought out a very large bottle of vodka from her purse. She stopped, took another deep breath, then closed her eyes. She looked like she was concentrating hard. She opened her eyes, put her hand back in the purse, then brought out a large bottle of Coke, this just confirming what I already thought about that damn purse.

"Aurora, do you know what's going on?" I asked.

"Looks like Ruth decided she needs a drink." Aurora had crossed her arms, leaning against the counter, watching Ruth. She shook her head then reached out for the book. She didn't touch it but left her hand hovering above the book. Then it was gone. Once the book had disappeared, she looked at Emily. "Glasses?" she asked.

"To the right of the sink," Emily told her.

Aurora moved to the cabinet, brought out four glasses, and went to the freezer for ice.

"If you just *poofed* that book, why did you have to get glasses out of my cabinet?" Emily asked her.

"Oh, some things you just need to do the old-fashioned human way." She continued to put ice in all the glasses as Ruth stood staring at the sink. She didn't move. Aurora shook her head then proceeded to fill all the glasses. The last glass I could see, she put more vodka in than coke. I figured that one was for Ruth. Ruth looked shocked and wasn't getting better from what I could see.

Aurora turned, handing us each a glass before nodding to the table. We took the glasses then followed her to the dining table. Aurora brought Ruth's glass with her, placing it in the same spot Ruth had sat in earlier. Emily took her place where she could see the whole room.

"I don't think my empty stomach can take this. What do you girls like, hmm? Chicken sandwiches, burgers and fries?" Aurora asked.

Emily and I looked at each other then said in unison that chicken sandwiches would work. We didn't even have a chance to blink before Aurora slid her hand above the table, like Vanna White turning a letter, and suddenly we all had Wendy's fast food sitting before us.

"Isn't it stealing if you don't pay for it?" Emily asked.

Aurora pegged her with narrowed eyes, closed her eyes for a few seconds, then sat down.

"Prayers?" Emily asked.

"No, I created a credit card receipt for the drive through, just to save your morals." Aurora said, again with the narrowed eyes.

Emily held up her hands as if to say, "Okay I give up."

"I still want to know who beat the hell out of you and why," Emily asked.

"You can pay anyone to do pretty much anything these days. It was nothing, really," Aurora said, as she snagged a French-fry, popping it in her mouth.

"Yeah, but why would you want someone to hit you?"

Emily wasn't going to let it go. Imagine that.

Aurora turned to Emily but didn't smile. "Ruth sent me to find you. I knew you'd look something like Susan after Ruth sent me a text telling me that Sam looked like her. But I had to make sure. Your crew cut didn't help, and I didn't want Ruth flying out here until I was sure I'd found you." She put her hands on her hips, shrugged, then continued. "I guess I wanted to see if you knew about any of your powers yet. Call it a test." She stopped, that shit-eating grin making another appearance, then added, "I guess you figured out you passed, huh?"

Emily glared at her.

"Aurora, we're sorry Ruth's upset, but what did we do?" I finally asked, looking to the golden goddess on my left. It was time to change the subject.

Aurora glanced back to the kitchen, shook her head, then started arranging her food. Ruth remained frozen where she'd fished the refreshments out of her bag. Over her shoulder, Aurora called to Ruth. "Ruth! Come eat, then we can talk about this." Then she simply continued preparing to eat.

Ruth finally let a loud sigh leak through her lips. She looked down at the counter, shaking her head. Emily and I continued to watch Ruth while Aurora dug into her food. She'd been nice enough to have gotten us all plain drinks, as well.

Aurora looked around at both of us, her mouth full of food. She shook her head then turned to look at Ruth. Rolling her eyes back in her head was her only sign of exasperation before she *poofed* to Ruth's side, then *poofed* right back to the table with Ruth. She guided Ruth to her chair and sat her down, then she returned to her own food.

It was when Ruth looked up at us that we could tell she'd been crying. Like the flip of a switch, she suddenly snapped out of it. Emily and I were both opening our mouths to speak when she raised her hand towards us.

"Just give me a minute. I'll be okay," she said breathlessly. She raised her right hand up in the direction of the kitchen, then suddenly her purse was there. "Just give me a second. Really," she said again, searching the depths of her bag then pulling out some tissues. She dabbed her tears then her nose before she turned back to us and smiled. Reaching over, she squeezed Aurora's forearm then reached for her glass. The mixed drink. She raised it up, as if toasting. "To Susan."

We raised our drinks and toasted in the air as well, but not before Ruth had turned up her drink, draining it. We bugged our eyes. Aurora kept eating.

Ruth seemed to come to some resolve with herself. She'd polished off her drink quickly, then turned to the other drink Aurora had furnished with our impromptu meal. As suddenly as Ruth's issues had come on, she was now back to herself. She settled back in her chair then started reliving the experience of taking me on my first ever cross-country air travel. She was mainly addressing herself to Aurora. Emily and I looked at each other before we proceeded to dig into our food as well. If they could act like nothing was wrong, so could we.

With the meal out of the way, Aurora flashed her arm again, and just like that, the remnants of the meal were gone. I could see Emily was stunned, as her mouth hung slightly open. I'd seen more of this than she had.

EMILY 109

"*I* know you both probably have questions about your mother, and I'll answer those in good time." She took a deep cleansing breath before she decided how she wanted to proceed.

At this point I figured it didn't really matter. It was going to be a long afternoon.

"Girls—ladies, I mean—when your mother passed away so suddenly after you were born, we were all shocked. Even the medical staff was at a loss for words. Given the suddenness of it, an autopsy was required." She looked at the table then, like she didn't want to meet our eyes.

I didn't know about Sam, but I was okay. It was sad to hear it, but I had the parents who raised me. I had a feeling that this would cause Sam more emotional distress than me at the moment, so I avoided glancing in her direction.

Ruth gave us each a look before she continued. "The autopsy found nothing, and everyone was more confused. Mother and I were both there. We held you both that first day. We never left you alone. Mother and I were convinced that having found no medical reason for Susan's death, there were greater forces at play." She leaned forward and placed her face in her hands, bracing her elbows on the table. "I'm even more convinced of it now. It reaffirms that we did the right thing by hiding the two of you."

She stopped and took another deep breath. We all waited, thinking she was going to continue, but the silence grew. This was not productive, not in my book. She had to get on with her big reveal. I was beginning to get agitated the longer we sat there waiting. Secrets. I hate secrets.

I looked at Aurora, but she quickly averted her eyes back to watching Ruth.

"Ruth, just say what you need to say," I said, reaching out to place a hand on her forearm. "Please? You said it yourself. We're not children anymore. That ship has sailed. We're grown, and we need to know what's going on and what secrets have been kept from us."

I looked back to Sam, who was deep in thought herself. She arose slowly then walked around to Ruth, kneeling down beside her, placing her hand on Ruth's arm. "Ruth, I've been with you for three days now. You asked me to trust you, and I have." Sam was looking intensely at Ruth. "Now you need to trust Em and me. You need to tell us all of it. What we don't understand, we will eventually. You know I'll ask a lot of questions, but we'll be okay. I promise you. Trust us with the truth."

Ruth raised her head again then turned her hands to hold each of ours. She looked between the two of us then finally looked at Aurora, who spoke. "Ruth, it's time. You've held on to this story, and your speculations, far too long. It's time to tell it all." From the way Aurora spoke, she seemed to know the story in its entirety.

Ruth nodded back to Aurora and began. "I think your mother died of black magic." She squeezed our hands quickly then added, "I know lots of questions are forming, girls, but let me try to get this all out first."

I nodded back to her. Sam mirrored my agreement as well.

"What you girls just did convinces me even further that black magic was the cause of your mother's death.

I glanced to Sam as she straightened up, staring back at me. Her eyes were a little wide now. "What exactly did we do, Ruth?" Sam asked, as she moved her hand to place it on Ruth's shoulder.

"Telepathy isn't part of my family's talent." She said it like we'd understand what she meant. She looked between both of our confused faces, then Aurora took over.

"What your Aunt is trying to say, ladies, is that bloodlines have different sets of skills." She paused when I raised my hand.

"What do you mean by bloodlines?"

"Ruth explained to me it's kind of like a caste, witches are in one bloodline and wizards in another. Only women can be witches, while only men can be wizards, and they can't mix," Sam said, shrugging. "Go on, Aurora."

"Skills can be traced back through your ancestors. Not all of the skills a mother has will manifest in each daughter, but for the most part, you don't add to your skills if it wasn't there to start with." She was shaking her head slowly when she finished, then looked back to Ruth.

Sam asked the obvious. "Well, if telepathy isn't part of our family, Ruth, then where did it come from?" She turned then slowly walked back to her chair, never taking her eyes off Ruth.

"I said it's not a part of *my* family's talent, Sam. I didn't say it wasn't a part of *your* family's."

That confused both of us.

"Just say it, Ruth. You're confusing us again." I'd drawn myself up straighter in the chair.

"I'm saying it had to have come from your father."

We were both stunned again.

"But Sam told me you didn't know who our father was," I said, then glanced back to Sam to make sure I'd understood her earlier.

Sam nodded then added, "Ruth said our mother never told her about our father, that she never wanted to talk about what happened during her trip. I distinctly remembering you telling me that, Ruth."

"That's exactly right. We didn't know. Still don't. We knew she was happy she was going to have the two of you, but she didn't want to tell us who your father was. She acted scared for a while when she came home, like she was afraid of something or someone."

Sam was getting anxious now, leaning on her elbows while talking with her hands again. "You told me that our bloodline is passed from mother to daughter. If that's the case, how could our father pass us the ability for telepathy?"

"Our bloodline is of witches. Witches pass skills from mother to daughter. I remember when my mother sat me down to tell me all of this at your age. I couldn't wrap my brain around it, but it's taken years of seeing it to believe. It's like your brain has to be rewired in order to really believe and comprehend." She wrapped her arms around herself like she was suddenly cold. "There are other bloodlines, and there are other beings that possess different skills than we have. As for your father, we have two possibilities to choose from, and I'm petrified to say either out loud."

She paused, then sat up in her chair, a little straighter. "Ladies, your father is either a wizard or a faerie."

I busted up laughing. Honestly, I had no idea what to do

at that moment besides that reaction. Seventy-two hours ago, I was doing battle with a ferret, and now I'm finding out that I'm half witch and half wizard or faerie. *Right!*

Sam put her hand on my forearm. I thought she was upset until I heard her thoughts. *"Em, let's hear this out. I'm confused too, but we really need to hear all of this."*

I didn't think back to her, just pulled my arm out of her reach. I truly didn't want anyone else in my head right now. I wasn't even sure if I wanted to be in my head.

"Sorry, I, um…you have to admit this is all a little fairy-tale-ish. Granted, knowing a demon has been following me around for the last five years did take some getting used to. Playing the electric company with my hands for the past few days was kind of buffered by what old Sally told me some time back too." I put my face in my hands, took a deep breath, then rubbed my face while I exhaled deeply. "But really, wizards and fairies?"

"I said earlier it's all real. All the legends and fairytales are real. The only thing I can ask of you right now is to please try to keep an open mind. I have lots more to explain."

I met her eyes, and it felt like I could see to the bottom of her soul. There was pain in her eyes over the loss of my mother, I was sure. There was a sparkle of intense joy, and I could only imagine what that was, but there was also a hint of fear. The fear caught my attention.

"I'm sorry. I'll try harder." Was that what I was supposed to say? I wasn't sure I wanted to know more, but in for a penny, in for a pound, right? *Shit.*

Aurora stood then started pacing like a drill sergeant. Hands folded behind her back, she took measured strides, with her head down. She was thinking and talking at the same time. "Ruth suspected for a while that someone would be coming to look for Susan. If he knew she was pregnant when she left Europe, Ruth figured your father might come to claim you. She came to me, briefed me about the situation, and asked for my help. We decided hiding your birth was safest."

Did she just say she helped Ruth hide us? That upped her age by twenty years, but she didn't look a day over thirty!

Ruth drew my attention back by gesturing. "I knew we'd have to locate you—I mean, reunite you—when you came of age. As the history of human civilization goes, as you know very well, Sam, there are evils that befall all beings. It doesn't have to be a mass murder or a crack dealer, but our culture has had its share as well. Some of the evils that have been recorded in human history can be attributed to our culture's influence."

She took a breath but kept going. "Not to give you a history lesson, but in the mid-1920s the faerie population immigrated, I guess you could say. They just appeared one day. Now, they have two sides in their society. The Unseelie Court, which thrives in negativity and evil, made their first appearance in Washington, DC. They say the capital is a place where the movers and shakers gathered, and greed followed. They caused the stock market to crash in 1929 then fed on the despair that followed.

"Their opposite side, the Seelie court, moved in to keep an eye on the Unseelie side of things. So, both groups have battled for souls on the hill ever since. We've all seen an upstanding citizen go to Congress, then that man or woman becomes corrupt. It's the Fae, plain and simple. Everyone has speculations about JFK's assassination."

She reached for her drink, popped the lid off, then held out her hand. Her bottle of vodka appeared, and she took the lid off then poured a slug in her cup, using the straw to stir.

"Marilyn Monroe got mixed up with some of the Fae. Those of us on this side of the supernatural think her death was an affair gone wrong. Fairies don't like to share; know that first. Speculation was that when she sang to JFK for his birthday, her Fae boyfriend got jealous, and they fought from that night until her death in August. We think the Seelie stepped in to cover it up, making it look like a suicide. But still, they couldn't calm the Unseelie down. The Unseelie who'd been her lover was hot to even the score. To his thinking, JFK stole Monroe from him. JFK's family being Irish didn't help the matter either. The Seelies worked for months and thought it was finally smoothed over. They couldn't have known the Unseelies would follow the president to Texas, and we all know the rest of that story." She took a long pull of her drink from that straw then started shaking her head and waved her hand in the air like a bug was flying in her face. "Forget about that. Sorry, I digressed for a minute. Anyway, it's not common for fairies to mate with witches. When a witch is around a faerie, we've found that some of our powers are muted. For some reason, their powers can weaken ours, almost like they absorb them. Which makes me think it's unlikely your father is Fae. But that doesn't mean it's impossible."

Sam was taken by this new history Ruth had just revealed. What history buff wouldn't be? I could see her wheels turning to ask more questions, but Ruth waved her off before she could voice any of them.

"You can get more history facts later. We have some added difficulties here," she added, then handed her phone to Aurora as she spoke. Aurora took it, looked at the phone then Ruth, and raised a brow.

"It's time to make the call."

Aurora nodded, then started dialing the phone. We sat there in our own thoughts. The air conditioner kicked on, and the sudden rush of air made me jump.

"Slade, it's me. We need your assistance in a big way. Can you come?" She nodded, said "uh-huh" a few times, and ended the call.

No sooner did she hand the phone back to Ruth than a man suddenly appeared in my kitchen entry way. I jumped to my feet, reaching toward my back for my gun, only to remember that Ruth had taken it.

Both Ruth and Aurora rose to greet the man standing there. And what a sight he was. He was like a Greek god. At least six foot four, with broad shoulders that ran to a very narrow waist and hips, this man was built for action. I let my eyes wander back up to feast on the gorgeous face. Damn. He was hot, with a golden tan and hair slightly darker than Aurora's. It would probably be shoulder length if he hadn't tied it in a tight ponytail. He stood there, smiling, then opened his arms wide. Ruth and Aurora took turns hugging this hunk. When their greetings were satisfied, Ruth turned back to us at the table.

This man just looked at Sam, and his jaw dropped.

"Susan? Is that really you?" He gaped, almost taking a step toward Sam, then I caught his eye, and he jerked like he'd grabbed an electric wire.

Ruth stepped forward toward the table. "Slade, this is Samantha and Emily. They're Susan's daughters. Ladies, this is Slade."

"Her daughters? You told us they died in childbirth." He looked thunderstruck, gaping at Ruth.

"I did, Slade. I lied. I had to hide them, and when I tell you why, you'll understand."

We all stood there as Ruth recapped the whole story. As she told about how she tracked down both Sam and me, I was a little stunned and glanced toward Sam. She was giving me the same curious look that said we'd have to talk later. Slade nodded a lot, various emotions playing across his face as Ruth retold what we knew up to this moment. Then she threw in, "Who did you send to Texas during that Koresh mess?"

Slade thought about it a few minutes, looking off in the distance to help his recall. "Oh, you mean the compound raid and all of that?" He waved a hand like he was fighting off a pesky gnat. "I let the southern rep delegate that. I was busy trying to make peace with the Unseelies. There was a lot of nasty business with the FBI during that year. Why do you ask?"

I could hear he had an accent like Aurora's. I looked from one to the other, wondering if they were related, but their facial features were distinctly different. This man had brown eyes, so it really was only a resemblance.

"Well, our Emily paid an unfortunate visit to that site a few years ago and picked up an unwanted travel mate. Can you get rid of it?"

"Of course, I'll take care of it personally," he said, glancing at Sam then me, smiling as he said it. "Are you available tonight? We'll have to do this after dark, you know."

"Ruth, you said only women were witches," Sam said, her eyes wide.

"I did, but I also told you all fairytales are real. Slade isn't a witch. He's a wizard, and wizards are different than and separate from witches," Ruth explained. "Like Aurora and me, Slade is on the consul. We've worked together for years, and we need his assistance for your *vardoe*."

"If I may…" Slade stepped forward toward us now. "I may have to bring in an associate."

"If you trust him, Slade, then we will, too. But we have bigger problems than just *vardoes*," Aurora said.

know Aurora and Ruth trusted Slade and his associates,

but I didn't know anyone, and I hoped Aurora didn't think we'd follow her instincts as our own. Ruth nodded in agreement with Aurora. "I think Slade will need full disclosure. Let's all get comfortable."

Everyone was sitting around my dining table again, but with only four dining chairs available, I stood beside Sam's chair. My eyes felt grainy and were burning. I'd really need to take my contact out soon. Everything felt surreal at this point. My vision felt fuzzy around the edges, but I didn't want to miss anything.

"Emily looks like she's about to fall asleep where she stands," Aurora observed.

Everyone turned to look at me. I blushed and tried to widen my eyes to keep them from sticking together. I felt if I blinked too much at some point they wouldn't reopen.

"Really, Em, we've kept you up well past your bedtime, I'm sure," Ruth said, reaching to place her hand on my shoulder, but I dodged away from her. I really didn't need her help with another nap.

"If we're going to play tonight, I'm going to have to get some sleep. But I'm afraid I'll miss something," I said, again trying to keep my eyes wider than normal.

"I'm a little ragged too," Sam jumped in. "Maybe a nap would do us both good." She smiled at me. "If you don't mind, could I crash, too?"

I frowned at her. Why did this seem odd? I only had the one bed. It was big enough, but I hadn't shared a bed with anyone since my breakup with Kevin. But this was different; this was my sister asking to share space with me.

Ruth nodded, "We need some prep time. I need to pop back to my house for a few hours and check on the situation at home. Don will be wondering where I've gotten to anyway. He and the boys should be home by now."

Ruth looked tired too. She held out her hand, and her purse was suddenly there. "I think the girls could use some alone time, short as it may be. Slade, can you meet us here around six-thirty tonight? I'm sure you were in the middle of something when we called, and I hate to waste your whole afternoon." Ruth paused then looked back at Aurora. Aurora nodded once distinctly.

"Aurora will stay here while I'm gone. We can all go to my house after we visit the compound in Texas tonight. I'll have to prepare my family for your sudden appearance, ladies, but it will all work out," she finished, smiling but still looking tired.

Sam stood and took a step closer to me. I had my arms folded in front of me, and she crossed her arms in a similar manner. She'd gotten close enough to me that by the time she crossed her arms, our elbows touched, apparently on purpose as she mentally spoke to me. *"This way we won't miss anything that we both need to hear."*

I thought back to her, *"I was hoping that was your plan. I'm about to fall asleep where I stand."* Sam just smiled without turning to face me.

"I think we'll be okay. We don't need a babysitter, Aurora. I think we can manage. We're just going to sleep," Sam said, with a lift of her chin, staring down the woman.

"Oh, I'm sure you will. But Ruth wants me to stay, so I stay. Besides, there's generally something good on TV." Aurora was already up, scoping out the remote control.

"I keep the remote in the coffee table," I said, pointing. "But I only have basic service."

"Oh, that's okay, I'm sure I can find lots." Aurora didn't even look back to us as she went to take command of the media situation. She found the remote quickly enough and turned on my TV. Within seconds, she was surfing all the premium channels and finally settled on Underworld.

"I don't think I want to know how you just did that," I said, shaking my head.

Aurora settled herself lengthwise on my couch, ignoring us. "I love how Hollywood comes up with this stuff. If they only really knew!" And, with that statement, she tuned us out.

Ruth turned back to Slade. "In a few hours, then?"

"Of course."

He bowed at the waist to Ruth then turned, making a half bow to us, and *poof!* he was gone.

Ruth walked over to both of us, glancing between each of us, like she was memorizing our faces. But if what she and Slade said was true, she was really seeing our mother. When she was apparently satisfied with what she saw, she nodded her head. "I'll be right back." Then she was gone too.

Sam turned in Aurora's direction, but she was absorbed in the bloodbath on the TV screen, stretching her back muscles as she yawned. I led the way to my bedroom, and Sam followed. I changed into my pair of Kevin's old boxers and an oversized T-shirt while Sam used the bathroom. She came out of the bathroom, glancing around the room.

"I, um...I can lie on the floor with a blanket," she stated.

"No, there's plenty of room," I said, turning to look at the bed. "Isn't it funny how women can pile up in bed, like a sleep over, and it's just sleep. You mention it in front of men, and it's their wet dream," I mumbled, then froze. Shit, I was really tired if I was being tacky in front of people I'd just met.

"And they've been that way for centuries," Aurora called from the living room.

"Uh, forget that last bit. I'm punch drunk, I think. Just get in the bed, and let's try to sleep."

After she took her shoes off, Sam crawled on the other

side of the bed to lie on top of the covers. I was flexing my shoulders, trying to ease some of the tension, and she turned on her side to watch me. When I was satisfied with my slightly relieved muscles, she smiled then put a hand on the bed between our two pillows. I glanced at her hand, then back to her face. I put my hand over the top of hers, and she closed her eyes.

"What caused you so much distress that you caused quakes here?" Sam thought to me.

I thought about that for a few minutes, then thought back to her. *"I was engaged. I came home to change clothes one night and caught him with another rookie...in our shower."* I relived that memory in my head, then her eyes flew open, and her mouth made an *O*. I frowned before I caught her next thought.

"I saw it! I just saw what you remembered!"

It was my turn to make the shocked face and be embarrassed, as I'd recalled Kevin's last performance.

"It's okay, I'm not shocked over that. What shocked me was that I could see what you recalled." Sam thought to me.

I tried to ease that look off my face then closed my eyes, my hand still on top of Sam's.

"Can I show you what happened to me? I've not told anyone else. I was too embarrassed to tell Ruth when she asked why I'd gotten upset and caused my quakes."

I thought about it a second then nodded my head. I thought she was still watching me, but I thought back *"Okay"* just in case.

She went back a little farther than I did, as she thought about a guy. Okay, a cute guy. I saw little snippets of dates, Christmas, and Valentine's Day. Then I saw the beach and felt her anger at him during the trip. When she thought of their encounter on the beach, my eyes shot open, looking at her.

She was still lying there, eyes closed, a little frown on her face. Shit, she was still a virgin. I closed my eyes again, then tried to keep up with her memories.

I felt like I should've blushed when she showed me her first 'experience' in her living room. The pain of finding out who and what Jeff really was made me sad for her then. Yeah, I felt bad for me, too, but I'd lived my pain and moved on. Someone had hurt my sister, and shockingly, I wasn't too happy about it.

We opened our eyes simultaneously, then a small tear traced down the side of her nose. That's how tears fell when you were laying on your side. I reached over for the pillow-case, then gently used the corner to wipe away the tear. I leaned over, and for the first time in my life, I hugged my sister. She was stunned for a moment but hugged me back.

"You two are thinking way too hard in there. You really need to go to sleep." Aurora's voiced trailed off from the living room over the sounds of her movie.

"What the hell? Are you a dorm mom now, too?" I yelled back.

She just laughed.

We separated, and I lay on my back. Sam turned to mirror me. I don't know how I'd turned into a pod person in the last eight hours. I closed my eyes then smiled to myself. I have a sister! I also have an aunt and, apparently, a dorm mother. I exhaled loudly, then sank deeper into the mattress. I was still holding Sam's hand, but I finally went to sleep.

ϑ

SAM 111

J hadn't meant to sleep as long as I did, but when I woke up, Emily was already out of bed, and the door was closed. I stretched while gaining my bearings, then glanced around the room. For someone that looked just like me, our tastes were completely opposite. Not that it's a bad thing, just different. I saw some pictures on her dresser and wandered over to look at them.

There was one of Emily with her parents when she was about six. We looked just alike even then. I shook my head, then gazed at the assortment of photos showing Emily at different ages. It was difficult to pick her out of the Academy group portrait, since everyone was wearing identical hats. There was a picture of a very deep kiss between her and a man...I'd guess to be her ex-fiancé. I realized I'd picked up the picture only after I was sitting it back down. I was a bad guest going through her personal items.

I put my shoes on after I washed my face and was ready to join my family. *Wow, I never thought I'd say that again.* Aurora was asleep on the couch, and Emily had her laptop on the dining table. She was again sitting where she could see the entire room, her back to the wall. I glanced around to see who else was there but found it just the three of us. Emily watched me cross the room to where I took ownership of my chair from earlier.

"What time is it?" I asked.

"5:30. It's not time for everyone to meet yet. I made some more coffee, if you want a cup," Emily offered, before taking a sip of her own.

"I'll pass for now."

"So, we're going to Texas tonight. I haven't been back there for a few years. It seems strange to go and not see my family," Emily said as she looked into her coffee.

I wondered if she could see anything in it. Would I be able to?

"You and Ruth are all the family I have now, so I guess I consider you lucky in a way. When did you figure out you were adopted?" I asked.

Emily thought for a few seconds, then said, "Around the time I realized my eye color didn't fit in with the rest of my family. That along with my hair color. Everyone else had dark hair, and I was a near blonde. I guess I was in grade school when they sat me down and told me. I'd started asking pointed questions about our differences."

I nodded my head, thinking what that would've been like. My own adoptive mother waited until after my father had passed away and we'd moved to Arkansas before she told me. "And this thing we're taking back to Texas tonight, what's that like?" I wanted to know what I should be expecting.

"It's hard to explain. It feels like evil, and your skin crawls. That's the best way I can explain it. That, and don't get separated from anyone. I'd hate to think I lost anyone else because of it."

Emily was giving me a very pointed stare, like she disapproved of me going with them.

"What?" I finally asked, when she continued to stare and the silence grew thick.

"It's not you, Sam. I was just thinking. I was wondering how exactly we're all getting to Texas tonight. I was thinking about it when I woke up, and I guess I'm a little nervous." Emily confessed.

I shrugged, glancing to the couch where Aurora was napping. Or, at least, I hoped she was napping. "I guess they'll take us with them. I've never really been awake when Ruth took me to other places." I looked at my hands in my lap and kept talking, but my voice was lower now. "I guess my sleepwalking was really jumping. I just don't remember any of it." I glanced back up to her and tried to give her a reassuring smile, but I think I failed. "So, I don't know what to tell you to expect, because I don't really know myself." Again, I shrugged. I hoped she believed me.

Emily kept her eyes on my every move while I spoke, just nodding then frowning. She put her coffee back on the table, typed more into her laptop, then turned her computer around, showing me an aerial shot of where we'd be going this evening. She slid the laptop to me, then left her seat, taking her coffee cup with her.

"Emily, can I use this to check my email?" I didn't want to be rude and just assume that I could use her personal items.

"Sure. I need more coffee. Help yourself."

Emily went about tidying her little kitchen while I checked my email and Googled a few things. Hell, I even Googled Aurora Orvalho and came up with nothing. I ended up playing solitaire on the computer while Emily went on with her kitchen cleaning. I think neither of us knew what to say right then and were nervous of what was to come.

Just before 6:00 p.m., Aurora stretched and reanimated herself from her slumber. She glanced around the room, stuck her nose in the air and, after taking a deep breath, broke into a smile. "Coffee is ambrosia to my senses," she said, heading to the kitchen. Her very large feet were bare, and I could see the tattoos covering them. They somewhat matched the tattoos on her upper arms. It made me wonder where exactly she originated from.

ɔ

EMILY 110

*A*t exactly 6:00 p.m., my apartment suddenly felt too crowded. Two men appeared side by side, just outside of my kitchen entrance, and Ruth popped up in front of the TV. I wasn't as jumpy this time. At least this time I knew Slade was coming. He'd politely asked to bring an associate, so while I'd cleaned my kitchen, I rehearsed in my head how not to jump when they showed up. I think I only flinched this time.

Slade strode forward to help Ruth. She was carrying not only her purse but also bags of what appeared to be groceries. Aurora went to help her as well. I went to join Sam at the table. I didn't even question the arrival of the food this time. I just went with it. I was getting better at this. At least I hoped I was.

The man who'd arrived with Slade stood back, eyeing my apartment with frank approval. He was around five foot nine with short, wavy black hair. He looked like one of those perpetually happy people who smiled all the time, and his eyes would be laughing at you regardless of what you did. He placed his hands behind his back and rocked back and forth on his heels, watching the three elders of our group managing groceries. Bags of groceries landed on my table, then the three proceeded to unload the contents, but I kept my eyes on the new guy. Something about him intrigued me just a bit. He was cute, with a dimple in his chin and jade green eyes, but it wasn't *that* kind of intrigue.

Everyone continued with removing food from the bags, and the stranger finally cleared his throat. Slade whipped around, and his face started to blush.

"Oh, I'm so sorry. How rude of me. Ladies, may I present Ken Tribedeaux." Slade held his arm out toward Ken as if he was presenting a prize bull at the county fair. "Ken, the ladies," he said, turning then repeating the motion with the other arm toward the rest of the room.

Ruth walked up first, holding out her hand. "Ken, it's very nice to finally meet you. I'm Ruth."

Ken smiled even wider now. "Ruth, I'm charmed. You're even lovelier than the accounts I've had of you."

It was my turn to raise my eyebrows, because Ken had an amazing English accent. Not broken English, but very proper English. I glanced at Sam, and she was smiling too. I guess she was intrigued as well. When I looked back, Ken was rising from apparently having kissed Ruth's hand. Wow, I really was impressed. Ruth stepped back, and I noticed her smile touched her eyes this time. Then she made introductions to the rest of us.

Aurora, last but not least, skipped up and gave Ken a very large bear hug. He kissed her soundly on the lips, then they both burst out laughing. Breathless from their encounter, they broke their embrace then came to the table, holding hands. Ken glanced around the table and very quickly started checking the seating space. He snapped the fingers on his free hand, and my table was suddenly crowded with the addition of two chairs. Matching chairs, I might add. What the hell, if you can't beat 'em, join 'em. I just smiled because I was done asking where things came from.

"I take it you know each other," Sam said, looking back and forth between the two.

"Ken and I go way back. We've had several assignments together," Aurora said, still smiling as she dropped his hand then took her seat.

"I'll call this meeting to order," Ruth said, standing to the left of Aurora. "Before we leave here tonight, girls, you need to know that your lives will never be the same again." She made sure to make eye contact with both of us. We in turn glanced sideways toward one another.

"I think we've got that so far, Ruth. But there are a few things I don't understand. Like what you meant when you said 'assignments' or Slade's handling the compound. What aren't you telling us?" Emily asked, her hands folded together on the table, leaning in just slightly.

Ruth walked to her own seat and sat down. She nodded, more to herself than to us, and pursed her lips, working them back and forth like she was arguing with herself.

"It's harder to explain this part. But you remember I said I believe your mother died because of black magic, right?" She eyed us both before she continued. We both nodded. "Each family of the supernatural community can lose their lineage. Meaning they can't pass their supernatural abilities on to the next generation."

Sam cocked her head sideways, puzzled, but Ruth kept on.

"For instance, our family would've lost our lineage if the two of you'd died at birth. I don't have daughters, so I would've been the end of the line. But we have both of you now, so we keep our lineage." Ruth waved her hand over the table, and the food she brought in was assembled as a beautiful meal in front of each of us, but she never stopped talking.

"Sometimes, families who are unable to pass on their lineage, for whatever reason, become angry, and resentment builds because they feel they were slighted. So, while it's possible for the lineage to skip a generation, it's unusual, and as a bloodline nears extinction...Oh, how do I describe this?" Ruth's voice trailed off, and she stared at Aurora as if asking for help.

Aurora nodded, then finished for Ruth. "It's like they cross over to the dark side." She said, grinning.

Ruth frowned, shaking her head at Aurora and rolled her eyes to the ceiling. "Oh, grow up, Ro! But, yes, to steal from the movies, they turn to the dark side. They try to get back in the inner circle, but it never happens." She emphasized inner circle. She could see I had a question forming but held her hand up, as to ask me to wait.

Ruth got up then began to pace in earnest. Kitchen, living room, circle. Kitchen, living room, circle. She stopped behind Aurora again. "Members of the supernatural world can sense each other's powers. Yes, you'll be able to as well, after you've had some training. Now, when a bloodline has become extinct, it means the leader of that line has no one to succeed them, no one in the next generation to train. In our family, for example, if I were an only child and only had male children, and then my boys had daughters, my granddaughters wouldn't be able to take my place leading our family. What powers that might have passed to them would be muted. If they practiced those powers, that would only be black magic." Ruth paused for a breath.

Sam and I frowned at each other again. The more Ruth

explained, the more puzzled we became. Ruth waved her hand toward both of us, like she was erasing something.

"Some time back, a witch who was the last of her line was able to sense a spark in a distant relative. This witch tried to enhance the spark of that relative by developing curses and using black magic. It's not normal magic like we use. We don't wave wands or chant spells. Black magic witches use curses and spells. The only reason they can do that is because their bloodline was once full-blooded witches."

She looked very serious now. "I think your mother ran into the Black Magic Witches while she was overseas, but I don't have proof of that right now." She paused and reached for her drink. Grasping it in both hands and holding it close to her chin, she again paced from the kitchen to the dining table, deep in thought. I turned and looked at Sam, one eyebrow arched as if to ask if she was buying this story so far.

She shrugged, taking a sip of her own drink.

If we're going to have any kind of relationship as siblings, Sam needed to start learning to find her own voice. I knew she had one. I looked around the table. The men were watching Ruth with blank faces, giving nothing away.

I jumped when Ruth started talking again.

"All magical groups answer to a sort of council. There's a hierarchy, similar to human society. Each magical group has its own ruling group, and from within that ruling group, representatives are selected to sit as a Peer to the Realm. My grandmother told me they used to call our witches council the Witches Brew." She stopped then grinned at us. "Yeah, I know what you're thinking. I thought the same thing. Granny said the term Witches Brew started out long ago, because it was overheard by some of the puritans on the east coast, then everyone took it to mean black magic spells being cooked up.

It gave all witches a bad name." She shrugged, sat her glass back on the table, then started pacing again.

"I'm the current representative from the Brew to the Peer of the Realm. All Realm members sit on the consul, and they hear disputes from each group that couldn't be resolved by their own Kaste." She swept her hands out to indicate the men and Aurora. "Of course, I mean all of us here."

They all met our eyes and grinned, nodding agreement to what she was saying, then Ruth continued. "By being on the Realm, we're also automatically entrusted to be investigators, peacemakers, or enforcers. We don't know when we'll be dispatched or to where. The Sovvern makes the decision on whom to send."

Sam and I both turned to look at Aurora, sitting across the table from us. With her arms still crossed, she just smirked, but Ruth went on. "We just receive a message with a *w* on it. The *w* represents the will of the consul. That means the consul has decreed an action or creature be dealt with, and the Sovvern will dispatch one or many of us."

At this point, she was facing us while pacing. "Now, I've received a dispatch and must report to a meeting with other representatives in the next month. I don't know who else has been chosen or what else I'll be doing, yet." Ruth continued, "I've told you this much so I can explain that I'm about to lose my seat on the Brew. If I lose that seat, which our family has held for years, I'll also lose my seat as a Peer."

That made Sam and I sit up, and we both started trying to ask questions at the same time. Ruth raised both hands, palms out to calm us both. I pointed to Sam so she could go first.

"Why would you be losing your seat?"

"Each witch family is guaranteed a seat on the Brew, as long as there is another generation to take over as head of the branch. I've filled the role since my mother passed away.

Since I don't have daughters, the seat would pass to my sister. As Susan is deceased, the seat goes to the two of you, but you were both hidden at birth. My mother and I discussed it at the time, and we reported that you both died when Susan died. We had her cremated so no one would be able to verify that you weren't in the box with her."

Sam and I started to protest again, being shocked at this news on top of the rest. Again, Ruth raised both hands to quiet us.

"I know, I know, it was wrong of us, but we wanted you protected. Remember, bloodlines with no other descendants lose their seat with the Brew, and we wanted everyone to believe that. Some families become desperate when faced with the loss of their seat, and they resort to stealing newborns of other bloodlines, even though that won't help them. They kind of go a little crazy to keep their seat on the brew and become very creative to maintain it. But back to us. I have until the next equinox to present the two of you to the consul to maintain our seat."

Sam and I exchanged a shared look of surprise.

"Ruth, where exactly is this seat you keep talking about," Sam ventured to ask.

"Not only that, but when's the next equinox?" I added.

"The Equinox happens around the 20th & 21st of March, and then again September 22nd and 23rd. You'll learn to remember those," Ruth started pacing again. "While the equinox doesn't take two whole days, it's tradition that the consul does take two days to perform its business." Ruth stopped by Slade's chair, took a deep breath, then let it go just as slowly. "Where? Now that's a little more difficult to describe. You've heard of the Aurora Borealis, right?"

I drew my eyebrows together in confusion, then looked across the table to the Aurora in the room. Sam took the bull by the horns and asked, "Am I wrong to suddenly think that's a *where* and not a *what*?"

"You'd be correct. Educated types believe that it's just a phenomenon of geomagnetic storms. In a way, that's correct. Kind of. I like to think of the borealis as our magical smog," she said, with a huge grin, apparently happy with her analogy.

"Magical smog?" I asked. "You want to come again?"

Aurora jumped in. "Oh, it's magnetic alright. You could say the consul meetings are always very charged, at least emotionally. When you get that many heads of groups together someone has to show off. And don't forget the consul meets to settle disputes and make rulings. It never fails that magic flies," she said, leaning back, her curls shaking all around her head. "That, added to the expression of our essence, just builds in the atmosphere. It's beautiful, but no one knows how electrified it really is." Aurora emphasized electrified by widening her eyes as if shocked while she said it.

Ruth nodded in agreement. She looked at us like a proud professor who'd just had Einstein's theory of relativity explained by her top pupil, but I was still lost.

"Ruth, I understood that the borealis was over Alaska. Are you saying we have to go to Alaska?" Sam asked, still with her eyebrows knitted together.

I knew I'd have a headache working before long.

Ruth held the back of the chair she was standing behind, letting her shoulders sag just a bit. "Yes, and no," she said, again on a long sigh.

"And that would mean what?" I asked.

"It means Alaska is generally where the Northern Lights are seen. There's a similar effect called the Aurora Australis. Those same lights are seen in Antarctica, South America and Australia. They're the same thing. It's the same effect, but each just represents the portal that we use to meet. It's called the Realm of Lights. It's the realm we have to enter to meet."

Sam's frown got bigger. I continued to stare at her, her eyebrow quirked and her lips drawn in a very narrow line. I knew what pressure I had to put on my mouth to make that expression, so I knew she was just as confused as I was.

"Are you saying you just go to another…what, realm or world?" I asked.

"More or less, but remember, we are witches, and we can travel where most can't," Ruth said, shrugging her shoulders and finally pulling the chair out to sit back down.

"We. You keep saying *we*. Who exactly are you referring to?" I asked.

"Oh, Emily, dear," Ruth said, shaking her head, "Sam and I have already been doing a little traveling, and you will, too."

Sam bugged her eyes then shook her head, too. "I know we've gotten to a couple of places in record time, but I distinctly remember waking up and just being there. I've no idea what you are talking about now," she demanded.

"Oh, Sam, did you not tell me about your round of sleep-walking?" Ruth met her eyes with a questioning look.

"Yeah, but I told you that stopped when my stress level went down." Sam just wasn't ready to buy into this, not just yet.

"Did you not say you woke up in places that were locked, and nobody ever figured out how you got in there, right?" Ruth would have made a good prosecuting attorney, I was thinking. She could give you one of those looks that made you think your grandmother was standing there ready to twist your ear if you told a big one.

"Well, yeah, but that doesn't mean anything, does it?" Sam first glanced to me as if looking for support, but I had none. Then she looked to Aurora, who reached over and patted Sam's hand.

"It's okay, I've never heard of anyone taking all of this at face value," Aurora said, in that sympathetic tone of voice you use with children.

"Listen, Aurora and I've done our homework in trying to find you both. It's been a little harder to find you than we first thought. We're facing a deadline, and I need you both to come home with me when we finish tonight." Ruth was now standing between Sam and Aurora, but she was looking directly at me. Ruth continued. "Emily, I knew you'd be the hardest to convince. That's why I tracked down Sam first, while Aurora came here to find you."

Aurora grinned at me from across the table when her name was mentioned. I narrowed my eyes at her, but she just grinned that much harder.

Ruth looked at both of us and pleaded, "Don't blame Aurora. She did what I asked. She had to know that you were in fact Emily. Susan was a teenager the last time Aurora saw her, so she had no idea really who to look for. She didn't see your mother as an adult to know that you both look identical to her."

Slade stood by his chair and snapped his fingers. The remains of the dinner they'd eaten while Ruth talked were instantly gone. The food in front of Sam and me was the only thing left.

"Ruth, we must leave soon. Ken and I made a stop by there before we came here so I'd know where we're going. This way, we can all go together, so long as each of you hold one of our hands."

"Oh, you know I always love to hold Ken's hand." Aurora leaned into Ken's shoulder, and then they both burst into laughter again. I wasn't sure I wanted to know the inside story of these two, but it did make me wonder.

"There are just a few problems, people," I started, "the first of which would be called my job." I crossed my arms over my chest and leaned back in my chair. "I know that Sam has school to return to, so how are we going to pick up and relocate without jobs or careers?" I looked around the table. "You all look respectable and upstanding, like you have good jobs. Sam and I don't have that, and I've worked damned hard to get where I am right now."

"You'll have time to pursue other interests after you've had some training." Ruth crossed her arms, mirroring my stubborn look. "But, really, you won't need a job. Just something that makes it look like you have a job, if you really need."

Well, now, that's confusing, too. I glared at her. "What do you mean, 'if we really need?' Of course we really need to. The bills don't pay themselves."

Aurora jumped up from her chair, patting her hands together as she shrugged her shoulders like a five-year-old anticipating playing with a puppy. "Oh, please, please can I take her? Can I take her?"

"I'm not going anywhere with you," I flung back with a look of disgust.

Aurora's face fell into the oh-so-disappointed, childlike, pouty-lip look, but you could see the laughter was still in her eyes.

"Ro, please don't bait her." Ruth sighed. "Emily, we have more to show you after our trip. I've already sent your captain a letter explaining that you request a leave of absence due to a family emergency. I've read your employee handbook and learned you get time for something like this," she said, waving her hand like she was explaining to other people in the room.

"I don't think the department is going to appreciate me saying I have a family emergency because I come from a long line of witches, do you?" I was starting to get a little steamed. I didn't appreciate my life being turned upside down. Those are my choices and mistakes to make, not hers.

Ruth turned and gazed at Sam, sitting quietly. "Sam, do you trust me?"

"I trust you, Ruth...I think. But Emily does have a point," Sam said quietly. She glanced at me then back to her hands. "What else are we going to have to do, Ruth? How are we going to prove who we are, if that is what this is all about?"

Ruth stood taller, bracing herself as she considered what she was going to say. "We'll have to submit your DNA to be verified, but those are just mouth swabs. It will take a few weeks for that to come back. So, during that time, we"—she gestured with her hands, indicating the others around the table—"will have the privilege of training you how to use your new talents. But, I have to say, I think this mind link the two of you have going on is working quite well already." She smiled, happy that something was working better than she expected.

I nodded, "That's all well and good, Ruth, but September? Do you really expect us to be with you that long? What about my job, and Sam finishing school?"

"Ladies, give me one week. Please. That's all I'll ask. Just one week to discover what you didn't know you possess. One week to live up to your potential. If you decide after a week that you really need a job or to finish your degree, I'll leave you both alone," she finished, shoulders sagging slightly.

Sam looked at me then back to the table. Damn, now I felt guilty. I turned and looked at my living room and kitchen. I'd gotten really comfortable living here. I turned back to look at Sam as she fidgeted with her fingernails. I thought about not seeing her again, and a knot formed in my stomach. It was really not something I wanted to think about right now.

I reached a hand toward Sam, and she looked at my hand for a few moments before looking up to my eyes. I could tell she was having problems with this idea now, too. She finally placed her hand in mine, and I felt that connection click into place again, then I forgot everyone else in the room.

"What do you really think?" I thought to her.

"Emily, I want to get to know you, I really do, but I don't want you to have to give up your job for it. I can't ask you to give up what you've worked so hard for," she thought back.

She tried to sound convincing, but I could sense that she, too, was saddened by the thought of our separation. I took a deep breath and turned to Ruth. "One week. I'll give you one week, then I have to come back."

Ruth nodded and smiled as she dropped her gaze to the floor at her feet.

EMILY 111

They allowed me to pack a couple of bags before we left. Ken, Slade, and Aurora gathered in the kitchen to discuss the night's work, while Ruth talked on her phone. Sam kept her seat and watched everyone go about their business. Remembering Texas like I did, I didn't think Arkansas weather would be much different this time of year, so I packed the majority of my summer clothes, a pair of sneakers, and a pair of hiking boots. As I was zipping my bag, Ruth came in the bedroom and handed me my gun, butt first.

"You can bring this, but I don't know that you'll need it."

I just nodded, taking it from her hand, then added it to my toiletries bag. I'd hoped I'd be home soon. My haircut required frequent trims, and it was getting a little long for my preference right now. With everything packed, I rolled the bags to the living room, left them by the door, and then turned to face the crowd.

Slade walked to where I stood then glanced around at everyone else. "If you'd all come near now and take a hand, we need one of the girls with each of us. Ruth and Aurora are more or less just tagging along. Our main focus will be to make sure the girls get there."

I felt nervous, "What do I need to expect here, guys?" I needed someone to help calm me a little. I'd been through training for many types of situations, but I wasn't sure that anything I'd learned would help me with what was about to happen.

"Ah, yes," Ken started, then he looked to Aurora. "That would be a good question. Ro, can you help us describe that which is about to take place?"

I heard Ken, but I was looking at Sam with questions in my mind. She came to me and put her hand on my forearm. "Emily, I don't really know. We're going to have to trust them on this one."

Aurora stepped forward. "If I might," she said, extending an open hand to me. I narrowed one eye at her, took a breath, and nodded. She placed that hand on my stomach then looked down at me from her Amazonian height. "You'll feel a pull, here in the middle of your body. Just a slight tug that makes you want to take a step forward with it. When you feel it, don't fight it. Take the step. Close your eyes if you want. We'll guide the rest." She dropped her hand, taking a step back, still watching my face.

"Close enough for now, Ro. Thanks," Ruth said. "She'll get the feel of it." She paused, looked at Sam, and added, "You'll both get the feel of it." She turned, giving each of us her reassuring smile.

"Okay, let's do this," I said, reaching for Ken's hand.

His hand was larger than mine and slightly calloused. That made me wonder what else this handsome man did in his life. Sam took the last step to hold Slade's hand. Aurora stood to the other side of Ken and held his hand playfully, as if she were a smitten sixteen-year-old.

Ruth walked to my luggage, waved her hand above it, and it disappeared. She nodded to Slade as she walked to his other side. Before Slade took her hand, he snapped his fingers, and my apartment was suddenly thrown into the darkness. I think my retinas were in shock as he said, "On the count of three, Ken."

This was only replied to by Aurora giggling, then the start of the count began. When Aurora said 'three,' I felt that tug she referred to and the overwhelming desire to step forward. I took a deep breath and did just that. There wasn't enough time for me to realize there was a difference, but the sounds of night and the dry heat of the great outdoors were the first thing I noticed. I'd my eyes shut tightly, and still had them shut when Aurora was suddenly in my ear, whispering, "You can open your eyes now."

I did, and I found Sam, Ruth, and Slade standing at the exact same distance that they'd been standing in my apartment. The sun had set, and while not completely dark, the faint haze of the sinking sun was just disappearing on the horizon. Landing here, I suddenly remembered from the news that Texas was in near-drought conditions—that and the feeling of standing in front of an open oven.

We were standing in the middle of an old country road that I remembered too vividly. The entrance to the old compound was directly in front of us. There was a house behind us, off to the left. I could tell someone was home by the cars in the driveway and the glow of the television light coming through the huge picture window in the front.

I turned back to the road which led into the compound. There was a house to the right of the road, but there were no cars parked at the house, nor were any lights on. I only hoped no one was living here. The sense of evil, of what happened there, seemed to wrap around me like a second skin, causing the hair on the back of my neck to stand up. Instead of having let go of Ken's hand, I only now realized we were still joined. I was holding his hand so tightly I was sure that with proper lighting I'd see my knuckles were white. I stared at our hands, and he smiled.

"It's okay, love, just stay with me," squeezing my hand back. I took a deep breath and felt it catch in my throat.

Sam came to stand beside me. "What now?" she whispered.

"Now we jump to the next horizon. We only need Emily for this. Ladies, if you'll stay here with Sam, we'll be right back," Slade said.

I looked at Sam. I knew my heart was pounding loudly.

Sam glanced over her shoulder to Ruth, then back to me. She put her hand on top of mine and thought to me, *"I'll go with you if you want."*

I smiled back at her, trying to hide my fear and hoping it worked as I thought back to her, *"I'll be okay."*

She nodded, took her hand off mine, then walked back to stand with Ruth. Ruth wrapped her arm over Sam's shoulders, squeezing her with a sidewise hug, nodded once more to Slade, and then I suddenly felt that tug and urge to step forward.

I followed it with my eyes open this time. I felt like I was in an old Star Trek or Star Wars episode, but only for the moment it took my brain to make that comparison. Streaks of light rushed toward me as I felt that tug move me along with Slade and Ken. I felt like I was driving the Millennium Falcon as it hit warp speed, but only for a second. Everything suddenly stood still, but my knees were wobbly to the point I was glad I was still holding Ken's hand. He just smiled sweetly. I looked back and could barely make out the figures standing on the road. I took another breath and was about to exhale, when the urge to take a step tugged at me and the light show started. At the end of that session, we were farther away from the original compound, closer to a line of trees.

By the time I exhaled, I'd stumbled forward with the landing. Ken stumbled forward with me for a step as Slade reached to steady me with both his hands, but I recovered quickly. I was glad I wasn't feeling queasy.

"Thanks, I think I'm okay now," I whispered.

Slade stepped as close to me as he could without crawling on my back. "As soon as we release your hands, you'll feel the demon return. I can feel him out there already, but I've kept you blocked from it," he whispered, close enough that I could feel his breath on my ear.

I shivered from the feel and nodded.

"What about Sam? Is she safe?" I whispered back.

"She has your aunt to shield her right now, and all is well. We're going to bind the demon to that tree," he said, extending his hand to indicate an old, weathered tree that still had a fair amount of leaves on it. In the dark, it just looked like a dark blob.

Again I nodded, unsure what I should be saying. I glanced around us and hoped that no one else would ever come near this tree.

"What do you need me to do?" I whispered on an exhale.

It was Ken this time that said, "Just stand there and look pretty, love. We'll do the rest." He released my hand, taking a few steps back.

I was turning to look where he'd stepped when Slade backed away, releasing my elbow as well. The hair on my body stood on point all at once, and the queasy feeling returned. I figured it was just fear playing with my nerves.

I turned slowly to see if anything was coming toward us, because I had a sense that whatever had been following me all these years was suddenly coming up from behind me, closer than I ever wanted to think about. Instinctively, I dropped both hands to either side of my body and stood as rigid as I'd seen Ruth stand earlier today. "I feel it," I said.

Slade and Ken moved to flank me on either side and slightly forward, as if they could stop what was coming for me before it would make contact. Within seconds, they turned to face each other, and a sense of dread swarmed over me. As if mirror images of each other, both men slightly bent their knees, like they were waiting to pounce. I caught a sense of movement coming toward me, but all I could see was darkness. How do you see a shadow in the darkness? You don't.

In unison, Ken and Slade threw their arms straight up, and lightning flew from their fingers and wrapped around something above me. It gave me the feeling of being in the middle of a tornado. I couldn't see much except the small, swirling tornado wrapped in electricity, reminding me of the Tasmanian devil cartoon character. I took a step backward toward the trees as a gurgling noise was released from the thing wrapped in bands of light.

"Move backwards, then come up behind me," Slade said, as calmly as he would in the middle of the opera.

I didn't question him and moved as quickly as I could. The men started walking sideways toward the old tree, forcing the demon trapped between them to move along as well but keeping it in front of them. Within inches of the tree, both men threw their arms forward toward the tree, and the bands of lightning wrapped themselves around the tree, demon included.

The bands continued to wrap around the tree, and around the demon, pulling it closer and tighter to the tree. The moaning sound started to increase in pitch, like nails on a chalkboard, causing me to put my hands over my ears. When the lightning finished wrapping itself around the tree, the tree started shaking. The light and the demon were suddenly sucked into the trunk of the tree. The tree shook harder, causing several older upper branches to fall to the ground, then the ground started to shake too, rolling outward from the tree. When all signs of the demon had faded, there was a loud *pop* at the base of the tree, and all was silent.

Both men stood up straight, but their shoulders sagged like they'd just wrestled a bear. Ken shook his head as he walked toward me. I kept looking from one man to the other then back to the tree.

"Now what?" I whispered. Only then did I realize how tense my body was. If I'd brought my gun, it would've been in my hand. I longed for it to be in my hand. Something solid I knew I could defend myself with.

My eyes must've been saucer sized as the men walked to me, but it was Slade who did the talking. "We're done. We bound the demon to the tree. Our work is done."

"You're done? You mean that's all it took?" I asked.

"Well, that and some intense thoughts toward Mother Earth to keep the damn thing in its place this time," Ken said, grinning at me.

"Can I do that?" I asked, raising my eyebrows. "Talk to Mother Earth, that is?"

"We're not entirely sure yet what all you can do, my dear. At the least, you should be able to call the light show. The rest, we'll have to wait and see," Slade explained.

Both men extended their hands to me, then we turned in the direction from which we'd come. The sense of dread was gone, and the hairs on my body were lying at peace.

"Think about that spot in the road, where we left the others," Ken said gaily beside me.

Holding the men's hands, I closed my eyes and pictured

my sister and the two others standing in the middle of the road. That tug started again, and as I leaned in its direction, I knew to step, then the only thing I felt was a sudden whoosh of air on my face.

I heard Sam exclaiming before I opened my eyes. When I did open them, I found the three women standing in front of us. At least I didn't stumble this time.

I took a steadying breath, "That was…different," I said, looking between the three women.

Aurora was grinning, making her teeth glow in the darkness. I thought it must be the moon reflecting from her teeth. It was then that I remembered that there'd been little illumination from the sky before we left, and now it was clear and bright, and I could hear the symphony of night bugs singing their songs.

Ruth touched my shoulder, and I turned to face her. "Let's go home, ladies. I left a pie cooling, and Don was finishing up some cookies. I bet he has a pot of coffee ready, as well."

Ruth turned to the men then and smiled. "Thank you, Slade. You too, Ken. We wouldn't have been able to do this without your help."

Both men nodded, but Ken went a step further, bending at the waist in a low bow. "Of course, my lady," he said, as he returned to being fully upright.

"Now, Don thinks I drove back to Branson to pick you two up. I left my car out of sight, not far from my house," she explained, but then she noticed Sam's and my expressions.

Sam broke in first. "How do you keep it hidden?"

"Years of practice, dear. No need to worry, Aurora's been with me enough times to know the location where I hide my car."

Slade stepped forward and brought out his cell phone,

checking the time. "Ruth, Ken and I will bow out tonight, but we'll meet you around ten in the morning."

Before any of us could respond, both men disappeared. Sam and I gaped at each other then turned back to our elders. Aurora was still grinning. She reached out, grabbing my forearm, as I saw Ruth do the same to Sam.

SAM 112

With a tug, a step, and a light show, we were in the middle of a humid forest, the sounds of insects humming all around. I gasped as Ruth let go of my arm. Aurora and Emily were already standing beside Ruth's car, but Emily was standing with her feet slightly apart, resting her hands on the roof of the car, head hanging down. From the look on Aurora's face, she was enjoying the show.

"Emily, will you be okay?" Ruth called out to her.

She nodded, and you could hear her take a breath. "I think I've had a little too much traveling tonight," Emily replied, under her arm.

"Do we need to call the ambulance?" Aurora asked, dead pan, but you could tell she really wanted to laugh...and taunt.

"Go to hell," Emily said, shaking her head. Then she let go of the side of the car to stand straight.

Aurora laughed out loud, and the rest of the night sounds quieted.

"Please, everyone, get in the car," Ruth said, pointing her key fob at the car. The lights blinked, and the car started all at the same time. "It's too muggy to keep standing out here. Let's find a cool room."

"Why the key fob? I thought you'd use your powers to just start the car," I asked, sliding to the driver's side backseat of the car.

Ruth was leading the way. "Habit," was her only reply.

We drove less than five minutes when Ruth put on her turn signal. I wasn't sure why she bothered with the blinker when we were on a dirt-packed county road, but I kept it to myself. The driveway was about a half mile long and made for smoother riding than the county road we'd just left. There were woods on either side of the drive for the majority of the way, but it broke into a wide, open space where the house sat.

We'd ridden in silence since we got in the car, and I jumped when Ruth said, "Don has so many lights turned on, I wouldn't be surprised if they could see us from the space shuttle."

Fortunately, she was talking to herself, and the only person who saw me flinch was Em. She put her hand on my shoulder, and I eased back in my seat. But Ruth was right; the farmhouse and its wrap-around porches were all lit up. The landscape lighting edged the yard, leading to the side of the house, where you could see a very large barn.

The barn had a security light mounted high, near the roof. It illuminated a good portion of the front of the barn, with light spilling back toward the house. The circular drive had two trucks parked on it. Ruth pulled up behind the last truck, put the car in park, then flipped on the overhead light before she started arranging her hair and makeup. I caught her eye in the mirror, and she winked.

Aurora turned all the way around with her arm across the back of the seat, and of course she had that shit-eating grin in place again. She looked from one of us to the other and back again, her grin only getting wider. Emily tensed as soon as Aurora had started to turn around. The second sweep of Aurora's baby blues in Emily's direction prompted Emily to flip her off. Aurora arched an eyebrow then turned back in her seat, laughing while she shook her head.

Ruth put her hand on the door, took a deep breath, and called back to us, "Girls, your bags are in the luggage hold. If you don't feel like bringing them in, I'll have one of the boys come back out and get them."

With that, she was out the door quicker than Emily and I could turn to see that indeed our luggage was back there. Aurora crawled out of the passenger side then waited for Ruth to join her in front of the house. We unfolded ourselves from the backseat, went immediately to the back of the car to get our luggage, then rolled our bags around to join Aurora and Ruth.

Ruth smiled as we approached and turned to start up the steps. The front door opened, and three dogs ran out to greet us. Well, they came to greet Ruth. They circled her as she tried to walk up the steps, bending to place a hand on one then another as they jumped around her. Aurora shook her head but seemed to have proceeded farther along than we were. The commotion from the pets distracted us from the mammoth man who was now standing on the porch, holding the door open.

If I hadn't known better, I would've sworn he was the Marlboro Man. *Damn!* He had dark, curly hair, trimmed close to his head. You could tell he wore a hat of some kind. He had salt and pepper sideburns and the stubble of a beard which was probably just past a five o'clock shadow. He was tanned from spending many days outside as a farmer. He had crinkly laugh lines around eyes that were ice blue, and he was smiling as hard as he could. He wasn't watching us but his wife as she climbed the stairs.

Ruth was laughing at her puppies and slightly breathless when she straightened up at the top of the stairs. She stopped laughing when she saw him. It was like two magnets were suddenly aware of each other.

I glanced to Emily and found she'd broken into a grin, which only made me break into one as well. As nervous as I'd been about entering Ruth's domain, I suddenly felt like I was home.

Aurora stepped forward and caught the door as Don moved forward to wrap himself around his wife. Don was at least six feet tall. He leaned in a little and put his head to the side of Ruth's, then they seemed to be whispering.

I felt a little awkward, and apparently Aurora did too, because she was looking off into the darkness of the yard, toward us, then into the house. She smiled into the house, then turned back to us. "Come on, ladies. I smell coffee and dessert."

That broke up the happy reunion in front of us, but Ruth was beaming even more than she had over the last three days. For the first time, she almost looked embarrassed.

We entered the door ahead of Ruth and Don to find ourselves in a large family room that was open to the rafters of the second floor. Everything was tongue-and-grooved solid wood. The walls were lighter, but the floors were a dark-stained, dense-grained wood. The furniture was overstuffed leather placed in front of a large, open fireplace. The opposite wall opened into a massive kitchen, with a large dining room beyond that. We made our way to the middle of the room, turning to take in the view. The furnishings were sturdy but far from plain. While the furnishings weren't lavish, they were items built to last. Years of use were evident from the scuff marks on the floors and the coffee table. This furniture wasn't just for show.

When we heard the door close behind us, we turned to face our aunt and her husband. Well, I guess that makes him our uncle. New concept. Ruth was still smiling, holding Don's hand as she came to join us in the middle of the room.

"Boys," she called past us.

Three men came filing out of the kitchen, they too as lovely as Don.

"Girls, these are my boys, your cousins," she said, releasing Don's hand as she went to the first one in line. He was six feet tall like his father, and a complete mirror image. He leaned down, embraced his mother, then kissed her on the cheek with a big grin. "Girls, this is Seth."

Seth then turned to walk toward us, his hand outstretched, as Ruth turned to the man behind him.

"And this is Scott," she said, receiving a bear hug and another kiss.

Scott spun her around before he released her, causing her to giggle. He was only a few inches taller than Ruth. Turning to us, grinning, I could see the mix of his mother and father, but with Ruth's brown eyes. He, too, came with his hand extended to shake ours. Emily and I extended our own hands then introduced ourselves.

We barely heard Ruth talking to the last of the men, as we were giving these men our full attention. When Seth and Scott moved to the side, the last of the Oaks brothers came forward, and we were stunned. I know my mouth probably hung open, and glancing, I saw Emily had the same expression.

The man standing beside Ruth could've been a triplet to us twins. With Emily's shorter haircut, it was a very near duplicate of her features; the exception was that this man stood at least 6'3". Ruth beamed back at us, and I know she said something, but we'd missed it, listening to the voices of her older sons.

"I'm sorry," Emily started, "but we didn't catch what you said, Ruth."

Her smile expanded, "I said this is Nathan, my youngest."

They came forward together as Emily and I glanced at each other. Nathan extended his hand to Emily first, and I thought she slightly flinched as their hands met, but I couldn't be sure. When he turned his hand to me, I knew for sure she'd flinched, because I did. There was a slight electric charge, like static electricity. I tried hard not to change my expression as we exchanged 'happy to meet you' greetings.

"I thought that Nate looked a little like your mom for a long time, ladies, but now that I've seen the three of you together, I find it damn eerie," Don boomed behind us, shaking his head and laughing.

Aurora broke the little reunion up. "Guys, I don't know about you, but I want desert."

I was wondering where she puts it all. Damn!

EMILY 112

*A*fter the delicious dessert and fresh coffee, I was dead tired and very grateful to be taken to my room. Since Seth and Scott no longer lived at home, Sam and I were given their old rooms. The only other bedroom upstairs belonged to Nathan—I mean, Nate. It seems that Ruth referred to him as Nathan, while Don called him Nate, but he answered to both. It had been well after midnight when we finally made our way to our bedrooms. Having been working the graveyard shift, I was used to staying up late, but without my full day of sleep, I felt a little punch drunk.

Don and the boys told stories about breaking horses and working cattle to Aurora, who apparently knew all the animals by their names as well. I was entertained but glazed over by the time I laid my head down that night.

Normally, six hours of sleep could have me on the rebound and good to go, but today's activities had taken their toll on me. I slept until nine the following morning. I felt refreshed but awoke disoriented in this new bedroom. I lay on my side, facing the door, and it took a few minutes for reality to shift into place. It had been a little over twenty-four hours since I met my sister and aunt, yet here I was, a world away from my own life.

What the hell am I doing here? was my first panicked thought, but the feeling eased when I thought of having fixed my sister's scrapes in the café. I'd given Ruth my word that I'd give her a week, and I resolved to get started.

Sitting up, I threw my feet over the side of the bed and listened to the world outside. I could hear farm noises, and that surprised me a little. I knew they raised horses, but the sounds of chickens and either goats or sheep surprised me. Not in a bad way, because hearing it did make me smile. It'd been a long time since I'd petted a farm animal, and I wondered how long it had been for Sam, if ever. Deciding to make the best of this week, I got in gear to join the world.

True to their word, Slade and Ken drove up in a Jeep Cherokee at 10 a.m. on the dot. Scott and Seth were back as well, but they were already out helping Don with the stock. All the men wore jeans, t-shirts, and hats as they left the house. It seemed that Don was cutting hay, and his sons were ready for the work.

While we ate breakfast and drank coffee, Ruth explained that she had to insist on a few things. First, we had to submit to DNA testing, to prove we were related to her. Next, she wanted us to practice our powers and learn more of what we could do, or at least what she thought we could do. So, our first assignment of the day was a trip into town with Ruth to see her family doctor.

She'd called ahead, making the appointment prior to our arrival. I started to get irritated at her certainty that we'd both be here today, but I'd let it go…for now. Sam seemed comfortable with it all, but she'd been with Ruth for a couple days longer than I had. It was Tuesday now, and I paused to remember that Monday had been the Fourth of July, a holiday. How had Ruth made an appointment for the doctor on a federal holiday?

As that thought crossed my mind, I narrowed my eyes at Ruth, standing with her back to me by the sink. Sam must have sensed my dark thoughts, then reached to place her hand on my arm. I didn't look at her but continued to stare at Ruth.

Sam must've read my thoughts. She thought back to me, *"Em, I thought about it, too. She must've known we'd all be here today and made arrangements last week. I don't like it either, but we're together now. I'll stay if you will."*

I thought about it again, wondering what difference it made, and let it go. I nodded then went back to my coffee. Just because I accepted it didn't mean I liked it.

With the trip to the doctor's office out of the way, we proceeded to the nearest cell phone store. Ruth wanted us to have phones similar to hers, which appeared to be the top of the line, but she wanted us to get what we wanted. I took the plain-Jane, black version of Ruth's phone, while Sam selected a cranberry-colored model. We were set.

SAM 113

With the doctor visit and shopping completed, Ruth decided all her guests should take part in our training. Aurora was the lead of our troop outing, and since she seemed to know where she was going, I felt safe. We walked to what I imagined was the middle of Ruth and Don's farm. Our first lesson would deal with jumping, as Ken told us, and he even used his air quotes when he said "jumping."

"I understand that you've done a bit of this in your sleep, Sam, so I know you'll be a natural." Ken said.

"Did you also hear that I'm not an outdoorsy kind of girl?" I asked, giving him the eye.

"Yes, as a matter of fact, I did hear that. But I can't help you with that now, can I, love? We'll stop over there by that pond," he said, pointing another hundred yards away.

We'd walked single file from the barn, with Aurora in the lead. Ken was immediately behind her, and I'd been placed in the middle of the line. I looked back over my shoulder at Emily to see how she was faring in bringing up the rear, and she was smirking, as if she was enjoying the entertainment.

I stumbled and tripped a few times on the trek, but Emily always jumped to catch me before I actually took the dive. It was almost like she knew I was about to take a dive even before I did it, and she was right there at the right time. That made me smile regardless of the surroundings. Someone was looking out for me.

When we reached the pond, Emily scooped up some rocks and started skipping them across the water. We watched as her last rock skipped farther than the rest. Ken shook his head, drew his arm back, then slung his arm forward, just as Emily had. But Ken hadn't picked up a rock. The next thing I knew, a boulder landed in the water. We could feel the splash from twenty yards away. Damn. I was impressed.

Emily slowly turned back to us, narrowing her eyes at Ken. "Show off," she teased.

"Alright, then," Ken started. "Who's first? Your auntie's waiting back in the barn. All you have to do is clear your mind and think about that spot in the barn, the one near the back wall, by the stack of hay."

Aurora stood to the side of the pond, arms wrapped around herself and staring out across the pond. Without any warning, she disappeared. We all looked at each other, then Ken waved off in her direction, "Typical Ro. Just ignore her."

As if that would explain anything.

Ken did a few stretches then went to demonstrate how we should stand. He stood, clasping his hands behind his back, head bowed and eyes closed, like he was praying. We stood, looking at him, and after a few seconds, he opened one eye to peek at me. When he saw I was still there, he opened his other eye and frowned.

"Ladies, cooperation, please! We have to work on this. Don and the boys will be back any time, and they cannot be any part of this."

He was right. Don and the boys—which seemed odd to say since they were older than we were—had gone to work in the hay fields. Ruth expected them back at any minute.

"Fine, I'll try," Emily said, with a little sag to her shoulders, almost like she was defeated.

"Marvelous. That's the team spirit."

Ken was just too damned perky for me sometimes.

EMILY 113

I stepped forward, closer to Ken, then turned back to see Sam giving me a skeptical look. I shook my head.

"I know. I have doubts too," I said out loud.

To myself I was thinking, "*I have lots and lots of doubts.*" But I had jumped last night with Slade and Ken, so I knew what to expect. Kind of.

"Focus, Emily. You need to focus and see in your mind what you remember of the barn. Picture the back wall where the fresh hay is stacked. Remember the sweet smell of the hay," Ken said. He stood to my side, eyes closed and chin extended toward the sun with a semi-pleased look on his sweet, British face.

I closed my eyes and tried to picture what he was suggesting, but the tug I'd felt last night wasn't there. I squeezed my eyelids tighter and still felt nothing. I could feel my shoulders becoming tense by the second. "I'm not feeling it, Ken. I can't feel that pull," I said, then took a deep breath, eyes still closed.

Ken placed his hand on my shoulder. "Exhale slowly, Emily dear. That will help you calm your nerves."

I nodded, eyes still closed, and tried to exhale as slowly as I could, forcing the muscles in my neck to try and relax. The air was peaceful around us, and I could hear all the sounds. I could also hear Sam fidgeting a few feet away. I gave up and opened my eyes but had to let them adjust to the sudden onslaught of light. I couldn't help but grimace at the difference.

"I'm sorry, Ken. I just can't figure it out." I was shaking my head while I looked at him.

He had his arms folded over his chest, and it was his turn to shake his head, giving me the once-over.

"How about you, Miss Sam? Want to see if you can sense the tug? Hmm?" Ken asked, turning to look at Sam.

"I don't know," Sam replied, shaking her head as if not completely sure of herself.

Right there with ya, sis, I thought.

Sam stepped closer to Ken, planted her feet, then shut her eyes too. Again, Ken described the interior of the barn, including the smells that go along with it.

Suddenly I heard the dry grass crackle behind me, like something landed. I turned to find Aurora standing behind me with a cookie in each hand. She smirked at me but continued munching on one. I shook my head. How could she eat all the time and look like she does? It wasn't fair. If I ate like she did, I'd be as big as the barn they wanted us to jump to.

"I don't think they have motivation," Aurora mumbled around the cookie in her mouth.

That statement alone pissed me off, and I turned to face her again. I could hear Sam suck in a breath, and knew that she agreed with my attitude. Aurora had an apologetic look on her face and started waving us down.

"I mean no offense, honestly. I just mean that, while you want to learn, you have no true motive to move," she said. Then her apologetic look turned very calculating as she started to get an evil grin on her face. She looked past me to Sam then back. "I think we need a goal or two."

She disappeared from right in front of my eyes and was suddenly standing right beside me. She grabbed my arm, then I felt the tug and saw the light show, and suddenly I was back in the barn with Ruth. From her seat on a bale of hay, Ruth was startled for only a second before she started frowning.

"What are you playing at, Ro?" she said, almost whispering.

"Me? I'm not playing at all, dear."

Then she jumped us back to the pond.

Sam was sputtering, trying to ask questions, but before she could, Aurora let go of my arm and grabbed Sam's. Then they were gone. I looked at Ken, but he had a perturbed look on his face. Not a good sign.

"What is she doing, Ken?" I asked as I strode over to stand in front of him.

"I wish I knew. Aurora does have a strange sense of humor at times, so there is no telling what she—" He wasn't able to finish that statement before Aurora was back. Without Sam.

I caught the gleam in her eye as she finished chewing the last of her cookie, grinning. I took a step toward her, but she disappeared again. I whipped all the way around, looking for her. When I'd decided we were alone again, I went back to Ken.

"What is she playing here, Ken?" My voice had taken on my no-nonsense officer tone.

"I only wish I knew," he said on a sigh.

Again, I heard the crackle of grass then a sudden gasp that

had me whirling about to see Sam standing there with Aurora. I was about to nail Aurora with a few expletives, but she held up both hands to me.

"You've both been there and back now. You both felt the tug and pull of the jump. You can both do it." She folded both arms and gave me her dazzling smile. "Go ahead, try it now, both of you."

As if that's going to make us able to jump.

Sam, who'd taken a step away from Aurora, moved cautiously to stand by me. But neither of us ever took our eyes off the golden goddess.

"Oh, for heaven's sake, Aurora, I just don't understand your way of thinking sometimes. There was no need to scare them," Ken rebuked her, coming to stand to the other side of Sam.

"Oh, I've not scared them, Ken," she said, narrowing her eyes toward him. "Not yet," she said, as she turned her gaze at me. "Ladies, you're going to have to be able to think on your feet, make quick decisions, and make sure you land somewhere safely, out of the line of fire."

"What the hell is that supposed to mean?" Sam demanded.

"I mean that one day you might find yourself in a situation that is life or death," Aurora defended that statement, not by meeting our eyes but by dropping her head to gaze at the dry grass at our feet.

"What would either of you do to protect the other, hmm?" she said, looking back to us again.

I was starting not to trust that look. Sam opened her mouth and started to take a step forward, but I grabbed her belt loop, holding her back. The motion startled her, and she turned toward me, a puzzled look on her face.

When I turned my attention back to Aurora, she was

rubbing both hands over her face as she turned to walk away from us. She was mumbling, "Think, think, think, think," as she headed in the opposite direction. She stopped, dropped her arms, then called out, "Ken, go back to the barn and wait for us." It wasn't a question.

Something in her voice commanded your attention even with her back to us. Ken opened his mouth to speak, then decided against it. Finally, he said, "As you wish, my lady," bowing his head and jumping at the same time.

"That's rude," Sam whispered.

I couldn't argue with her. There was a good twenty yards between us and Aurora, which was fine by me. Aurora casually turned to face us, but there was no smile now. Her face was blank as she stared from one to the other. As if in slow motion, she extended her right arm, raised it to face level, then snapped her fingers.

Holy shit! There were at least fifteen adult crocodiles lying between us and Aurora. They seemed just as startled to be here as we were to see them. Sam and I jumped backwards in unison, which caused all the crocs to jerk their heads toward us. My heart rate went from nothing to heart-attack mode in the space of a second.

"She won't let us get hurt, Emily," Sam stated, with an amount of confidence I didn't realize she held. We were out of our element, and what's worse is Sam hated the elements we were in.

"Don't be so sure of that, little lady," Aurora called back to us.

The sound drew the croc's attention back to Aurora, and that made me smile just a bit, but it quickly faded. Aurora was taken aback only for a second as the crocs looked at her. She looked at her new pets then at us, smiled, and jumped again. I looked around as quickly as I could without making any sudden moves.

"Now what?" I wondered aloud as quietly as I could.

The reptiles in front of us jerked back to look at us again. The largest of the group inched forward from the back of the party. His tail alone was about six feet long. He slowly started through the group, nudging his snout between others standing in his way. One by one, they'd part, and he would edge forward. Those behind him then started to make their way as well—right toward us!

I hadn't taken my hand off Sam's belt loop, and as I started edging my way backwards, I pulled her with me. Too soon, I heard the soft sounds of my foot squishing in mud and realized we were trapped between the crocs and the pond. *Hell's bells!* I could feel the vibration of fear begin to ripple out of Sam as I pulled her closer. I knew it wouldn't take the big croc in front of us very long to reach us.

"It won't do us any good to scream. We're too far out," I said, almost to myself.

I was estimating our chances as a few of the crocs on the sides decided to go for a swim, slipping into the water. Once they were buoyant, they started sliding toward us; all that was visible were their eyes, the tips of their noses, and the motion of their tails in the water. I could only hear my heart pounding in my throat by this time.

Sam had grabbed my lower arm and was trying to get me to let loose of her belt loop. It was only when she slapped at my hand that I realized she'd been talking to me.

"What?" I asked, "What did you say?"

"I said she'll be back. She won't let them get us. Relax," she said, as she slapped at my hand again. "And let go."

I glanced back at her where my hand was still gripping, then I let loose of her loop as two things happened at once. I heard the slithering sound of the largest croc and whipped around in time to see Aurora pop back behind the group of reptiles. I was about to scream at her for leaving us here when she drew up a pistol and leveled it at me. I realized quickly that it was my pistol! Suddenly I was so pissed I was about to plow through the reptiles that separated us just so I could wrap my hands around her throat.

"Go ahead," I called to her, "pull the trigger! Do it!"

Not taking my eyes off the gun, I watched her finger tighten on the trigger as I prepared to lift my foot and take my first step toward her. As I was about to take off at a run toward Aurora, I felt Sam's arms wrap around me just as I heard the sound of the gun. I felt the pull, saw the bright lights, and we were in the barn.

I broke free of Sam's arms as soon as our feet touched the barn floor, and she let out of whoosh of air. I stumbled forward a few feet then turned on her. Ruth came up off the bale of hay where she was sitting, clapping her hands. Slade remained seated but nodded his head in agreement as he joined her cheering. I thought Ken was going to break out in dance. I was pissed.

As soon as I found my footing, I started toward Ruth. "Do you know what that crazy bitch just put us through?" I yelled, not caring who might hear.

Ruth's look of pride took a quick detour. The smile left her face. "What do you mean?"

"I mean, your bitch buddy just nearly made croc kabobs out of us, and then the bitch shot at me!" I screamed.

Ruth's eyes went round, the whites showing. The men had stopped their cheering and moved to either side of Ruth.

Sam reached out again, placing a hand on my shoulder to stop me. "I did it, Emily. I really did it. I got both of us here," she said, disbelief in her voice.

For the moment, I forgot about being shot at and set up as croc kibble. We were where we were supposed to be. I hadn't had time to concentrate on the jump. I hadn't really felt the tug, it was just over and done with, and here we were. Some of my anger eased as I watched the expression on Sam's face, marveling at what she'd just done. My shoulders sagged from relief. I'd been shot at before, but never by someone had I known. My anger and the adrenaline rush suddenly left me. I smiled at the look of disbelief on Sam's face.

"Not only did you do it," I began, "You brought me with you. Not to mention saving my life." I glanced over my shoulder to Ruth and the guys then shook my head.

When I turned back to Sam, Aurora was standing behind her, with the gun pointed at the barn roof, but she was at ease —something I suddenly wasn't.

I grabbed for Sam before I thought about it and slung her behind me. "You freaking bitch," I roared, and then started toward her like a streak of lightning.

Poof. She was gone, and I had to come up short. I whipped around to look at Sam and Ruth. Ruth squinted one eye, then looked up at the hayloft over my head. "Out with it, Ro. What the hell have you been doing?" Ruth said, very calmly.

I moved around where I could see up to the loft as well. Aurora stood there, leaning over the rail, smiling down on us all. "Well, I really didn't feel like hanging out in the field all day, waiting for them to get around to jumping, so I gave them some incentives." She was still grinning as she shrugged.

"You shot at my nieces?" Ruth asked, again very calmly.

Aurora shrugged again. "Guilty, but in my defense, they're just blanks." Her shit-eating grin was back, and she was gone again. I spun to find her in front of Sam, warming up for a bear hug.

"You did it, kiddo! You did it!" She was almost dancing around, she was so proud. "How does it feel? It's been so long since I first jumped that I've forgotten what the first time feels like." She danced around then hugged Ken, who in turned bopped around with her.

"You shot at us…with blanks?" I asked, trying to reach a calm place.

Aurora nodded and hooked elbows with Ken to swing around in a reel. They stopped, breathless. "I've never had the honor to be with someone when they had their first time, you virgins," she giggled.

Sam went still, and her face went blank. The only way I knew she was put off by the comment was the flush of red that started low on her cheeks and on her lower neck. For her sake, I prayed no one else saw it.

"Ro, couldn't you think of some other way to be creative?" Ruth asked, pegging her friend with a gimlet eye.

"Well, not off the top of my head. I thought the crocs would scare them into the jump, and when that didn't happen, I thought about our young officer here. However, she chose to Dirty Harry up on us, and it was Sam who figured out the real alternative." She bowed in Sam's direction.

"You shot at me…with blanks." I couldn't get over it. I was stunned speechless, and my anger still simmered on the back burner.

Ruth started toward us, and I could tell by the look on her face she was trying to figure out the quickest route to end this standoff. She took the high ground. She walked over to Sam and hugged her tightly.

"I know your mother would've been proud." She turned

while hugging Sam to look at me over Sam's shoulder. "Both of you," she added.

She reached for Sam's shoulders, then held her away from her for a few seconds, then hugged her again, closing her eyes. I wasn't sure what the new emotions on her face were about, but I didn't ask, either.

"How about you, Em? Are you going to try again?" Aurora asked from across the barn, holding Ken's hand.

I shook my head. "I think I've had all the jumping excitement I can stand for one day," I said, then turned for the door. Over my shoulder I added, "Enough crocs, too."

As I cleared the door, I heard Ruth ask, "And what did you do with your new pets, Ro? I better not have anything in my pond that wasn't there to start with."

I just kept walking.

SAM 114

*S*eeing Emily walk out of the barn saddened me just a bit. Ruth had her arm draped over my shoulder, holding me to her side, still in a half hug. She leaned her head close to mine and whispered, "It's okay, Sam. Let her cool off for a bit." She leaned forward to look me in the eyes then smiled again.

"Do you think you can do it again?" Ken asked as he walked toward us.

Slade followed him while saying, "Congratulations, young lady. Nicely done."

Aurora made her way over to one of the horse stalls and started stroking the neck of an appaloosa. The horse leaned into her hand, shoving her shoulder with its head. She'd stroke and whisper then glance back at us, the mischievous spark still in her eyes. She winked at me before she turned her back on us completely.

I turned back to those standing around me. "I don't know if I can do it again," I said.

I thought about what had happened, and it really wasn't

so different than when everyone jumped last night. The pull at the center of your body, the flash of lights like a million stars strobing toward you all at once; all of that was the same. The only difference was that I'd wanted to be somewhere safe, pronto. I knew Ruth was waiting on us to jump casually. I hadn't thought that Aurora would really hurt us or let us be hurt until I saw the gun leveled at Emily. That terrified me, and apparently set my mind to be where Ruth was, because I knew she would never attempt to hurt us. I smiled back at everyone and shrugged. "I don't know," I said, looking up to Ruth.

It was Ken who wanted to try more. "Oh, love, could you try to…oh, I don't know…jump to your room?"

I turned and looked at this man. He was decidedly handsome, but he wasn't my type. I smiled at that and admitted to myself that we'd never be anything more than friends.

"Let's see," I said, and started thinking about the room I'd left this morning.

I felt a tug, the need to take a step, and before I realized it, the lights whizzed by, then Ruth and I stood in my bedroom. I kind of stumbled as I came out of the landing, finding Ruth's arm still around my shoulder.

I hadn't thought to turn loose of her before I started thinking about my room. Ruth was in the middle of letting out a gasp which turned into her giggling slightly as she hugged my shoulder.

"That's my girl," she said, and the next thing I knew, we were back in the barn with me stumbling, again.

"She was marvelous," Ruth announced, grinning from ear to ear.

"But I didn't bring us back here," I exclaimed, looking out the barn door toward the house. I was beginning to worry about Emily.

"No, I brought us back," Ruth said, squeezing me one last time, then letting me go. She took a few steps toward Aurora, now leaning against the stall, the horse almost nipping at her curls. She pushed off from the stall, grinning, and walked toward our little group.

"No harm, no foul," Aurora said, looking at me with both of her hands raised in mock surrender.

I took a deep breath then let it out. "No harm," I replied. My worry for Emily had my brows drawing together. I'm sure Ruth saw it too.

"There will be more time for practicing later. I think we need to start cooking for my men," Ruth announced, pulling her phone out to check the time. "They won't stay out much longer in this heat, and I need to mess up a kitchen. Ro, you want to give a hand?"

"You know I'm always up for messing up a kitchen, Ruth. Slade, will you and Ken be joining us?" she asked, as she ran her arm under Ken's to link their elbows again.

"Ken is going to stay on a few days. I have a few things to take care of. I'll be back in a few days, unless you need my help again. If you do, just give me a call," Slade said. He took a step forward then leaned into Aurora, kissing her on the cheek.

Aurora closed her eyes and exhaled deeply. "You always smell yummy," she said.

Ruth was still shaking her head over Aurora's behavior when Slade pecked her on the cheek. He turned to me, made a deep bow, then *poof!* He was gone. I didn't know if I'd ever get used to this type of appearance and disappearance.

Ruth turned to me then. "Go check on her."

I nodded, thought about my room, and was suddenly there. I didn't stumble as much this time, but I did let out the breath I'd been unconsciously holding, letting my shoulders ease back to a normal stance.

Seconds after landing, I took another deep breath, smoothed my hair back to tame my ponytail, then went to find Emily. I figured she'd be in her room, but I was wrong. I checked the rest of the upstairs before starting down the stairs. I found her in the living room.

I guess in all the excitement and exhaustion of last night, I hadn't realized an upright piano stood on the far wall. Emily was standing to one side of the piano, picking up photos, staring at them, then putting them back where she'd found them. I cleared my throat as I started across the room, as I didn't want to startle her anymore today. She glanced at me briefly, gave me a shy smile, then turned back to the picture in her hands.

"If I hadn't seen you and knew I had a twin, I think I would've been shocked at how much we look like her," she said flatly, holding up the picture.

"Wow," I said, looking over her shoulder. "I think I agree."

We were silent as she picked up more pictures to show to me. There was no need to talk now. We both felt a sense of loss looking at near mirror images of ourselves. It was one thing to see Nathan and know we really did belong in this family, but seeing our mother near our own age was staggering.

I became aware of the sounds in the kitchen almost immediately. I could tell by the sing-song voices that Ken and Aurora were teasing each other, and the giggling that followed was contagious. I felt myself smiling, too. I sensed Ruth behind us before I ever turned to see her, leaning against the doorway, watching us. I gave her a quick smile and could tell she sensed the same loss we did. Her smile was not as bright as it had been in the barn, but she was trying.

I turned, glancing at the array of pictures on the piano, when Ruth cleared her throat.

"Sam, do you think you can run an errand for me?" she asked, as she started across the room.

Emily and I both turned toward her. I frowned as I looked out the window toward Ruth's car. Sure, I held a valid driver's license, but that didn't mean I wanted to drive Ruth's car anywhere. I turned to her, puzzled, and said, "I guess if you really need me to."

I didn't recognize my voice as I said it. I hoped they didn't sense my dread.

Ruth shook her head and chuckled. "No, I didn't mean for you to drive anywhere. I wouldn't ask you to drive around somewhere you've not been before." She stepped toward the window, looked out at her car before she turned, leaning back against the window casing, folding her arms under her chest.

"I was thinking Emily might be interested in a few new rings," she said, raising one perfect eyebrow at me.

I glanced at Emily and knew the intention of Ruth's suggestion was completely lost on her.

"You do remember the place, right?" she went on.

"Um, yeah, I remember it okay," I said, ducking my head. "Do you really think I can get us there and back?" I asked, glancing back up to her.

"Oh, ye of little faith," Ruth said, smiling again. "Go ahead and take her. Flashlights are in the barn. You might want to change your clothes first, then grab a few bottles of water to take with you. You'll have to wait until dark; the park is still open now. Oh, and I'll find you a knife."

I glanced at Emily. Her puzzlement was evident.

"I don't need any new jewelry," Emily said, leaning her head to one side, looking at Ruth then to me.

"I think you'll like these. Come on, let's get our hiking supplies."

EMILY 114

*A*s nightfall grew around us, Ken and Aurora offered to go with us. I wanted the company because I knew Sam didn't like the great outdoors, but Ruth vetoed the idea, wanting us to go alone. It was a family place, therefore more important that we go alone.

Ruth gave us a backpack then directed us where to find flashlights in the barn. Before we left, she produced a penknife and handed it to Sam. I was a little confused by that, but I was carrying my gun at the small of my back, so I decided to let it go.

Ruth gave me the keys to her car, giving us directions to the spot where she hides her car when she jumps. I was mindful of her instructions, anxious of what we'd find, but I was interested none the less. My anxiety stemmed from my inability to jump by myself, at least not yet.

After we parked in Ruth's hiding spot, Sam gathered all the hiking equipment then came to me where I sat in the driver's seat. Without any preamble, Sam grabbed my wrist, and I felt the sudden tug, then damn, here came the lights. Instantly, we were standing in the forest.

I think it would've been smarter if we'd gotten the flash-lights out before we left the car, as I now found my retinas adjusting to the sudden difference in the lighting. I swayed a few seconds like I had vertigo, before Sam let go of my wrist.

"A little warning would be helpful," I snapped at her.

"What?" she called back, raising her voice, as the sound of a waterfall splashing was drowning out all sound.

I shook my head, meaning to just ignore my qualms.

She shrugged, "Sorry. I really do like this place."

Sam took the backpack, pulled out the flashlight, and then fished out the penknife next. She handed me the flashlight to hold then held her own hand in front of the beam. Looking at her hand while raising her voice, Sam explained that, as Ruth told her, this magic only works with blood of direct family members. She opened the penknife, put her hand in front of the light beam, then pricked her finger as she smiled tightly. She squeezed a drop of blood, then turned to smear the blood on the rock.

"Trust me. This is cool, but you have to do it too," she explained loudly.

I was eyeing her like she'd grown a third eye in the middle of her forehead. *What the hell*, I thought before I stepped toward her, and we traded flashlight for knife. Sam continued to grin, and I hated that she knew more than me. I pricked my finger, and it hurt like hell. Like a bee sting that grew in pain. Mirroring what Sam had done, I smeared the blood on the face of this mammoth rock.

Within seconds of smearing my blood on top of Sam's, the deafening sounds of the waterfall decreased. I grabbed the flashlight from Sam then started throwing light all around us. I really needed to see where we were and what surrounded us.

To the right was nothing but forest. To the left was the base of what appeared to be a mountain that went straight up.

I shined the light up that rock face and couldn't see the top. Damn! With my hearing returning, I turned to Sam. She was standing with her hands in her back pockets, rocking back on her heels.

"Come on. It's this way," she said, taking the flashlight back.

I hadn't thought to point the light ahead of us, where there was apparently a cave. What must've been the waterfall was now just a mere trickle, landing in front of the cave and running down boulders to what looked like the head of a creek. I guess I'd been standing in awe of my surroundings when Sam turned around, grabbing my wrist to drag me along.

"Come on, Em, we can come back later. I'll bring you during the daytime, and we can play tourist."

"Where are we?" was all I could whisper, but I got no answer.

I wasn't sure why I felt I needed to whisper. I just did. I followed Sam into the cave, descending into the earth. The coolness of the air wrapped around me the farther we went. I was glad I had on my hiking boots and jeans, but I wished I had a jacket. I thought about seeing Ken pull dining chairs out of thin air at my apartment and suddenly wished I knew how to make things I needed materialize. A jacket would be top on that list.

As we entered a large, cavernous room, Sam said, "Just stay right there and trust me," as she switched off the flashlight.

By sound alone, I knew she was walking away from me. When the sound of her steps stopped, the walls started glowing with an increasing intensity that shocked me. I could see Sam standing at the wall, with her hand on the rocks. But those weren't rocks, they were diamonds. *That* made me smile.

"Told you you'd like it," Sam smirked.

"Like it, yeah, but what the hell is it?"

"Ruth said it was our family's heritage. That our family has used this cave and these diamonds for generations. She'll have to give you more details. I'm still fresh here too."

"But why are we here?" I asked, puzzled.

"Um, to get some diamonds. I thought that was obvious."

She held out her hand, displaying the jewelry she was wearing.

"Ruth brought me here the day she found me. We took some of these stones to a jeweler Ruth knows, and these were made for me. They somehow boost our powers, I think. Hey! Maybe that's why you couldn't jump on your own."

Sam looked like she'd made some big discovery and was proud of herself. "I've had mine for a few days now. Other than the day I put them on, I haven't really noticed any difference," Sam said, with a frown.

"So, we just pick up a few of these stones and have more jewelry made?" I was turning and looking at the glowing walls as I made my way to where Sam stood. I put my hand on the wall too, and the intensity of the lumens was almost blinding. I let go to cover my eyes.

"Here, I'll take my hand off, then you put your hand back on. It's something you need to really feel, too," Sam explained.

With both our hands off the wall, we fell into almost pitch dark. I reached out immediately, placing mine back. Now the light was at the level Sam's touch created alone. She was right. I could feel power from these precious stones, and it warmed my hand. I stood there and played. I put both hands on the wall, then alternated between hands, hands and fingers, then just fingers, as we both watched and felt the change in the light source.

Sam walked around the large space, looking at one stone then another, sometimes putting a finger out but never her full hand on them.

"You were right, Sam, this is incredible."

"Apparently this is why we never need a job again," she said almost sadly.

I looked all around me at this astounding display of the earth's riches. There was no way to estimate the worth of this deposit. To think we were inheriting this was mind blowing. I could only guess how long this room had been used. Maybe Ruth could tell us more, but given the size of the room, you could tell how much had been already taken out.

The thought that I was suddenly rich made me smile. Not because I didn't have to work if I didn't need to, but because I suddenly didn't have to worry, at least not about money. There are always going to be other worries. One of those was standing in the room with me. I don't know why, but I suddenly felt very responsible for someone else.

ʔ

SAM 115

A few days into our visit at Ruth's, Ken was still working on Emily's jewelry, and we learned why Ken's hands were calloused. He could apparently take tools and make anything, not by magic but by hand. While my rings and other jewelry only took a few hours at the jewelry store, Ken was starting from scratch, without the pre-molded gold in stock.

Luckily, Don had an area set up, out by the barn, where he could shoe his horses. Ken, being Mr. Resourceful, adapted many of the tools Don had to melt down some old gold, which Ruth said she found around the house. We didn't ask, and she didn't tell us anything different. We were learning to just roll with it and to go on faith without too many questions. I wasn't sure if this was real progress or not.

Aurora would come and go. More often than not, she wouldn't stay any length of time. The frostiness that had started between Aurora and Emily was still there. When Aurora did show up, Emily would create a chore in the barn and then stay there until she sensed that Aurora was gone. I asked her about it one day, but she just smiled and shrugged her shoulders. Maybe she had some sixth sense that she wasn't truly aware of yet, like pets that can sense earthquakes. Hell, who knows.

Once Ken finished his handiwork, Emily was able to replace her current cartilage ring with a new, shinier version. He'd crafted a pinky toe ring, ankle bracelet, and a pinky finger ring as well. I think I liked them even better than my own.

The metal in the rings looked like golden threads, woven together so tightly they appeared solid. No wonder it had taken this long. The links in her bracelet seemed to be held together with magic, because I couldn't tell how they were really banded together. Emily was absolutely in love with them as much as I was.

I tried to not let my envy show, but I think Ken sensed it. While Emily was still fingering the last few items before she put them on, Ken walked up to me, extending his hand while feigning a frown. "Here, my dear, let me have a look-see."

He examined my ring then my bracelet. He made small *mmm* noises as he turned from one piece to the other.

"Yes, these are nice, but given who you are, these shall have to be replaced."

When I started smiling, he did, too. You just couldn't beat Ken.

"Ken, where are you from?"

I couldn't help asking, because I suddenly realized that all conversations had focused on Em and me.

"Over the big pond, my girl," he said, dropping my wrist and turning again to watch Em with her new sparklies.

Something about the way he said that made me sad for him. I knew he was out of our league as far as dating material, but it didn't stop my wondering about other possibilities for him. He'd been so generous to us since the moment he walked into our lives. I hadn't stopped to wonder if maybe he was giving up some of his own life to be with us for the last few days. I'd have to try to get more information, because there were questions I couldn't let go of, not in the long run.

I noticed Emily put the final ring in place, and I gave her my full attention. I was wondering if her experience would be similar to the one I'd had.

EMILY 115

Ken was giving Sam's jewels a little attention as I was putting on my last ring. They were gorgeous. The workmanship was out of this world. Even Aurora looked impressed.

Ruth looked like an expectant grandparent as she stood just a few feet away from me, biting her lower lip. I couldn't even begin to guess what that could be about. I heard Sam take in a small gasp of air, like she was about to be dunked under water, and I turned quickly toward her.

"What is everyone so up in arms about?" I asked, looking from one to the other.

"I'm sorry. I just remember how my jewels affected me when I first donned them," Sam said, exhaling. "I got a little excited is all."

Excited? She's getting excited over me putting on some bling? To each their own, I thought as I slid the last ring in place.

Then it happened. I felt breathless by the electricity surging through my body. I blinked wide once, then glanced down at my body. For a split second, I thought I saw a suit of armor, the kind you see on a knight. Then it was gone.

"Uh, what the hell was that?" I asked, breathlessly.

"That's what I was waiting to see," Sam giggled. "I wondered if it would do the same to you, and by the look on your face, I'm guessing it did."

"Tell us what you saw, Emily," Ruth jumped in, putting a hand on my shoulder at the same time. She looked so proud.

"Did you see it, too?" I asked, puzzled and looking at my arms, legs, and feet before looking her in the eyes.

"No, only the wearer sees a glimpse of your protection. So, tell us, what was it?" Ruth asked.

"Mine was like chainmail. A suit of armor," Sam threw in.

"It was armor but solid, not chainmail," I said.

"It's different for different people," Ruth added.

"What does it mean exactly?" I asked, still looking at my jewelry as well as my body.

"The only thing my mother could ever tell me was that it means you're more protected now. I've never really seen a difference, but I wouldn't like to press my luck by not having it," Ruth said.

"By not having what?"

We all jumped, turning to the voice and finding Nate standing there, hands in his pockets. He had a questioning look on his face as he stared down his mother.

"How long have you been standing there?" Ruth asked quietly.

"Long enough to finally get a few answers," Nathan replied.

There was a ripple in the air you could feel. A visible shudder passed over Ruth as she turned to face Nathan. "I don't know what you're talking about, Nathan," Ruth said, raising her chin slightly like a child caught with her hand in the cookie jar.

Nate beamed at his mother. Shockingly, it was the same smile as the one I shared with Sam. Genes: what odd things they were. "Mom, I've watched you disappear for years now," he said, shrugging, "I just never knew how to ask what was going on before now. You've found them now," he said, indicating us with a tilt of his head, "and there are more people popping in and out of here now than when grandma passed away."

He kept grinning, and I was wondering how long it would take for Ruth to give in. He obviously knew more than he was supposed to know. To me, in a way, it was a relief that someone else knew. Someone normal. As if this family could have normal.

Ruth looked like the air had been knocked out of her body. Her shoulders were slumped and eyes cast down to the ground. Aurora walked up to her and placed a hand on her shoulder as she whispered in her ear. Ruth nodded a couple of times but didn't look up immediately.

Sam and I were glancing at each other while Ken crossed his arms over his chest, watching everyone from the sidelines. He looked like he was struggling to make a decision.

"I think I shall take my leave now. It appears you have much family business to attend to, my dear," he announced, shaking his head. He turned, extending his hand toward Nathan. "Be gentle with her, ol' chap. Mums are never what they seem, and yours is an extraordinary specimen."

Nathan met his hand for a firm shake, nodding his head. He never took his eyes off his mother, but he did jump a little when Ken was suddenly gone without having released his hand from their handshake.

"Geez, that's hard to get used to. I've watched you pop in

and out of here so many times I didn't think being close to it would startle me. Guess I was wrong," he said, running his hand through his hair. His face was full of mischief as he took the last few steps to his mother then wrapped his arms around her.

"It's alright, Mom. I've kept your secret for a few years now, and I don't plan on talking about it now," he said, hugging her.

Ruth seemed to come back to life more as each second passed, then she slowly started to hug him back.

"I'm just afraid that I've put your life in danger now," she said, ever so low, but not so low that we couldn't hear. "You weren't ever supposed to know. Your father doesn't even know."

"I know he doesn't know. I know Scott and Seth don't know either," he said, rocking back and forth as he held her.

"I may be the baby of the family, but I've known how to watch everything that goes on and keep it to myself." He was turning in a circle, still rocking slightly so he could see us. "You, too, huh?" he asked, looking between us.

We looked at each other then back to Ruth, as if asking permission to admit our own parts in this family tradition. But we didn't have to respond, because Ruth leaned away from Nathan, looking up at him.

"For our family, it's only the women who have these gifts, Nathan," she said, then glanced back to us. "The girls are only just learning their talents."

Nathan's grin grew as he glanced at us. then back to his mother. "I've got your back, Mom, and theirs, too."

"What about my back?" Aurora chimed in. She stood with her hands clasped low behind her back, swaying slightly back and forth, like a child.

"I seriously doubt that you need anyone watching your back," Nathan chuckled.

Aurora stuck her bottom lip out in a mock pout but broke out into a big grin. "Damn, I'm glad that's over. Can we eat now?"

We all glared at her.

"What? Can't a girl be hungry?"

EMILY 116

I'd been jogging daily since our return from the cave. Sam would accompany me at least part of the way, doing her brisk walk. When she started to fall behind, I'd double back to join her for that last part of our trek.

We were learning more about each other, like most new friends do. I found that we each shared information openly but held back those things that might cause embarrassment. We found that we'd handled situations similarly, and more often than not, we found we'd had similar events happening to us, like learning to ride a bicycle or having difficulties with geometry. Who'd have thought we'd have had so much in common, despite growing up apart?

It was Wednesday, July 13th, one week from the day Ruth and Sam walked into my life, and I had a decision to make. Was I ready to give up being a cop? Truthfully, I wasn't sure. Our week together was nice, but I missed my own space and my own schedule. When we weren't practicing jumping, we were helping out on the farm. Actually, Sam was the only one practicing jumping, because I'd yet to make that step on my own. I began to cringe when it was my turn to attempt to jump.

Ken, who returned the day after Nathan's revelation, was our usual instructor, and I appreciated his help immensely. I refused to participate if Aurora was involved. She'd started giving daily side lessons to Sam after most of the training had taken place. I don't know where they jumped in these private lessons, and I didn't care.

Ken was being ever so patient with me during our lessons. He would end up jumping with me or by starting the lesson with me jumping with him. I just couldn't get the feel for it by myself. I don't know if it was an inability to be motivated, or maybe I just didn't have the genetic makeup to do it by myself. I convinced myself that if I didn't have this talent, I could live with it. I could still heal minor injuries, and that talent was put to near daily use because Sam truly was a klutz.

It was during one of these healing rounds that Ruth found us in the bathroom we were sharing. Today's misadventure found Sam turning her ankle, and with her newfound, expert jumping skills, she brought us both back to the bathroom.

"I thought I heard someone up here," Ruth said, coming in the door.

It was open already, so we couldn't complain about the lack of privacy. Assuming her normal stance of hands on her hips, looking down at us, Ruth shook her head in dismay.

"Sam was intent on keeping up while I jogged. I didn't know she was running to catch up until I heard her plow the dirt." I was shaking my head too.

Sam grimaced as she glanced up at both of us. "Give it a rest, okay?"

"Why didn't you let Emily fix it where you were?" asked Ruth.

"I thought I could just repair scrapes," I said vaguely, as I looked first at Sam's foot propped up on the side of the tub then back to Ruth.

"We didn't think about it, I guess. I just opted to come back here to clean up first," Sam said, hissing as she found a nice raw spot that was oozing a little bit of blood.

"Emily, it's not just scrapes and bruises you can heal. You know that," Ruth started, but paused as I gave her the evil eye.

I guess Aurora had shared with her about the bruises I'd healed for her that night in front of the hospital, because I sure hadn't.

Ruth must have sensed my immediate flare of irritation, because she put her hands up, almost as if surrendering, but she continued. "You can take care of whatever you set your mind to. You just haven't tested it on anything else—I mean any*one* else."

Ruth smiled, and I glanced to see Sam eyeing me with a look of appreciation.

"Please Em, could you try?" she asked, pausing in her wound cleaning to poke her bottom lip out in a pout of pleading. "Please?"

"What the hell," I said. "I can't seem to do anything else magical. Practice makes perfect, or at least that was what I was told when I learned to shoot a gun. If nothing else, I can take you to target practice."

Sam's bottom lip stuck out further. Now it was my turn to surrender. I sat on the edge of the tub by her now-angry, swelling ankle then rubbed my hands together, closing my eyes. I normally just used one hand for her usual, everyday scrapes, but this time I placed a hand on each side of her ankle, then I started concentrating.

Opening my eyes, I met Sam's gaze. I stared and felt the

tingle on my shoulders begin to move, inch by inch, down both arms and toward my hands. I kept my eyes locked to hers and watched as the tingle crossed from my hands into her body. The pupils of her eyes flared at what must have been the initial crossing, and it made her gasp. I heard Ruth move closer, but I didn't glance to be sure.

I felt heat flow from my hands to her ankle, and her pupils would contract to pinpoints then flare with each surge of heat. The little gasps added to the effects. I dropped my sense of self, or at least that was how I saw it, and thought to her at the same time, *"Sam, if I'm hurting you, tell me now."*

She shook her head. "It's not pain coming across. I don't how to describe it really, it's just a different sensation. It's stronger than what you normally use to fix my scrapes. But it's not bad."

Ruth turned and leaned against the counter. That much I could tell out of my periphery. Normally she didn't stay during these little sessions, but she seemed to be prepared to stay for the duration.

She cleared her throat. "Em, have you thought about what you're going to do now?" Ruth asked cautiously.

"I think I'm fixing my sister's injuries," I replied, as I moved from her ankle to her skinned knees.

"Oh, I don't mean this," she said, waving her hand at Sam's lower extremities. "I mean your job and apartment."

I suddenly lost concentration and looked up at her. No, I hadn't thought about it much. I had thought about it a lot. Sam froze as she watched me. I could feel her tense under my hands. My hands that were no longer in the process of healing her injuries. I'd lost my concentration and, with it, the healing energy that was my only claim to fame. I sighed then looked back at Sam's knees.

"Yeah, that," I said, pausing. "I've been thinking about it a lot."

Again I paused. For some reason, I thought Sam had stopped breathing, waiting for me to finish. I glanced up at her, and found her eyes wide, almost in a state of panic. I reached up and grabbed her upper arm. "Breathe, Sam. I'm staying. I'm staying with you. I can't leave you. Who'd take care of all of this?" I said, smiling and waving back at her knees and ankle.

〴

SAM 116

I let out the breath I'd been holding when Emily smiled and pointed back to my injuries. I felt so relieved I threw my arms around her neck. I wouldn't let myself cry, not in front of her and Ruth, so I started to laugh instead. Better that than the alternative, and I was happy.

Emily hugged me back and laughed with me. I heard Ruth let out her breath as well, and we turned to look at her. She was watching us, with tears in her eyes too, smiling as she nodded her head.

"I'm glad, Emily. I can't tell you how happy I am to hear it. Aurora won't have to wipe your memories now," she said, cocking her head to the side and smiling bigger.

Wipe memories? Could someone really do that? Seeing my sudden questioning look, Ruth rolled her eyes toward the ceiling then turned to walk back out.

"You'll need to go back and take care of your belongings there, Em. We have space in the barn you can use for storage for a few weeks," she said, heading for the stairs. She stopped at the top of those stairs then turned back to look at me and

Emily. "I really am happy," she said, suddenly very seriously, before she turned quickly and descended the stairs.

Emily was suddenly blank faced, and turned to me, "What do you think that was all about?"

I shrugged, "I'm sure it has to do with our mother. Not to mention finding out Nathan has been spying on her for years."

I was happy as my heart soared. My sister had chosen to stay with us, with me. "But hey, think you can finish here first? I'm sure there are lots of things we can help with before you head back to Salt Lake," I said, nodding to my knees and holding up the palms of my hands to remind her of the work she was doing.

"Yeah, I think I can finish. The question is do you think you can take us back to my apartment?"

"Really? You really want me to take you back?" I said, stunned.

I hadn't thought about how she'd get back there and never thought she'd ask for my help.

"Well, I definitely can't get there myself without a car or a plane. Besides, your way is definitely quicker."

As it turned out, Ken accompanied us back to Salt Lake City. Ruth was okay with me taking Emily to finish her business, but she was concerned about how we'd handle the packing and moving on our own. Once we were back in Emily's apartment, Ken and I sat and drank coffee while Emily made the trip downtown to say her farewells to the station and her co-workers. We figured it would be personal and she'd want the time alone.

With her resignation out of the way, she then made plans for all of us to have dinner with her now ex-partner and his wife. She said that would wrap up the evening, and we could return to Ruth's immediately after. Ken bowed out of dinner, but with just a snap of his fingers in each room, he cleared out Emily's belongings then took his leave of us.

Having dinner with Mickey and Lucy Parish was a sweet but sad affair. They were apparently quite attached to Emily, but in seeing me they understood her resignation from the force and her desire to live with me. Lucy talked the entire evening of their soon-to-arrive grandchild, while Mickey stoically nodded and grinned where he was supposed to.

I could tell parting with them was hard on Emily, but she held up like a champ. We were away from their house before she let the tears flow as we walked in silence back to the train station. Once in the stairwell and out of view, I took us back to my room in Ruth's house.

"You know we'll need to find somewhere bigger to live, right?" I asked after we landed. "My apartment's just a one bedroom, too."

"I hadn't given it any thought really," she said, nodding and heading toward the door, when she stopped suddenly. "We better pop back to Ruth's car and bring it home. Everyone thought we were going shopping. We still have to keep up that act, you know."

I popped us back to pick up the car, and we returned as we'd originally left, by automobile.

Nate met us at the door. "Hey, I've been thinking. This fall, I'll finish my masters, you'll be finishing your final year, and now Emily is moving in with you. Why don't we get a house and share expenses?"

Ruth moved in behind him, clapping her hands as she did. "Bravo, Mr. Educated! I think you have a great idea." She turned immediately and started for the kitchen, calling as she went, "Don, let's buy a house near the college. These three are moving in together."

We all glanced around to each other as Don called back to her, "Sounds great, honey. When can they move?"

We all laughed. I guess Don was ready to have his house —and his wife— back to himself.

SAM 117

A couple of weeks passed, and Emily grew more confident with her choice to stay with us. I was happier than I'd been in as long as I could remember. We started our days helping with the animals close to the house and barn.

Don and Nathan would leave for the larger stock items midmorning and would return closer to late afternoon or early evening, depending on how involved the work was that they were doing. It was now part of Nathan's duties to keep Don away from the house when we needed him to.

Ruth finally gave in to the fact that his knowing her true family history was handy. All we had to do was let Nate know what our goal for the day was going to be. It gave us the time needed for practicing jumps and any other items they could think of to try.

Apparently on the list of other items was 'calling' objects. This was supposed to mean that we could call items to us, out of thin air. Practicing that ability wasn't productive.

Another skill we should've acquired was shielding. Ruth described this as being able to protect ourselves from other creatures' abilities or keep them from sensing our powers. This was even more tedious, because how did you figure that one out? Sure, you can think about an object, and theoretically it should pop into your hand, but shielding? Yeah, right.

Most evenings were spent in the family room with Ruth, pulling out old pictures to give us a sense of a mother we'd never know. Then there were grandparents, great grandparents, and countless generations that came before us. We heard old stories that could be told around the rest of her family. Other stories could only to be told without their presence. Well, that is, for the most part. Nathan got to be present for some of those big secrets.

The nights the whole family was together, Don would nod and drink his coffee as Ruth spun the tales. The crinkles of smile lines around his eyes always emphasized their color and twinkle as he watched his wife.

Our newfound cousins were entertaining as well. Seth and Scott, the two oldest, were seriously dating some young ladies from the next town over. They didn't always make it through story time because of plans they had with dates. I was sure they'd heard these stories before and weren't missing much.

It was just a little unsettling, if I wasn't thinking about Nathan, to suddenly see a taller, male version of myself and Emily. The more we were around him, the more at ease I was with this guy who could help us pass for triplets. Well, except for his height, that is.

Most days, after dinner and story time, Aurora popped back into our lives. She was kind of like a mentor to me. Em tried to stay clear of her. I think it became a challenge for Aurora to either piss Emily off as much as she could or win her over. I was hoping she was working so hard at trying to win her over that it ended up just pissing Emily off. A girl could hope.

Aurora was fun, and I enjoyed spending time with her. She wasn't like many people I'd met. Her mannerisms, not to mention the way she sometimes put sentences together, were a little odd. Many evenings we'd leave the house for what we said was a walk. When we were out of sight of the house, Aurora would have me take her hand, then we'd jump to some of the greatest sunsets around the world. Some were even sunrises.

We talked of books and world events, as well as men. Well, mostly men. I was in awe to be around her in public. She was a magnet for men, no doubt. She'd smile and wink more often than not.

Half the time, I wasn't sure where we'd jumped, and I didn't ask. I just knew we were in different countries because of the use of different languages and how differently people dressed. Aurora, of course, had been to these places before, because how else could she jump to those locations? Not just those locations, but specifically closets, storage sheds, or wine cellars that was always unoccupied when we landed. Regardless of where we landed, she could speak their language fluently.

When time permitted, we did a little shopping from street vendors. I was collecting little trinkets, thinking towards gifts for my friends and former co-workers. Now that I had a little bit of money, I could be more carefree and shower a few gifts on the few friends I had back home. If I ever got back home…

It was still several weeks before classes would start, and I'd need to get back to pay my rent soon or give notice, depending on how soon Ruth thought she could purchase a house for the three of us.

*

EMILY 117

*A*s Sam spent more time practicing her jumps with Aurora in the evenings, I spent more time helping Don and Nathan with the chores around the barn. It was rather calming to spend time currying horses and gathering eggs. Even mucking stables was something I found enjoyable. There was a great peace to the farm. It hit me one afternoon that this was the most at peace I'd been since even before I'd graduated from high school.

I'd talked to my adoptive parents a couple of times now, and even with those calls, I didn't get the sense of belonging that I did here. I felt like my life had slid into place. Sam and I were relaxed around each other but still weary of each other at the same time. We'd both been solitary creatures, and the habit was a hard one to break. Well, at least for me it was.

Sam was spending some quality bonding time with Aurora. I was happy for her, I really was. My relationship with Aurora had gotten off to a bad start from meeting her outside of the hospital in Salt Lake, and then there was the time she'd nearly made croc kabobs of us. So, I wasn't expecting the blow up.

SAM 118

I'd taken a shower after lunch while Emily helped Ruth clean the kitchen. With the whole family present, good old-fashioned washing and drying of dishes always took place. With more people in the house now, we all took turns. I had my turn yesterday, and tomorrow would be Nate's, with Don's turn coming last. Apparently, sharing was something this family did well, at least as far as normal family activities were concerned. For the magical family activities, sharing was a definite no-no. In all activities, no one seemed the least bit concerned about the sudden appearances of Aurora, Ken or Slade.

Shower-taking around the farm could sometimes become a twice daily affair for some of us, because the work could get very dirty. My daily number of showers depended on how bad I looked after I took a tumble or had a run-in with mucking stalls. Today had been one of those days.

I was still nervous around some of the more high-strung horses, which in turn had me falling all over myself to stay out of their way. Everyone was used to my spills now, and while today's fall didn't have me taking a direct hit in one of the stall 'bombshells,' it was bad enough that I wanted to shower before lunch. But everyone assured me that I was clean enough to eat before showering, so I'd postponed the activity.

The bathroom sat at the head of the stairs, with Nate's room on the left and ours on the right. After blow drying my hair as best as I could, I headed to my room to sort some of mine and Emily's laundry.

When I opened my door, I froze. Propped up against my headboard, with my journal in her lap, Aurora looked up to me with a blank look on her face. My journal. My most intimate thoughts and feelings since the week of finals were being read by someone else. Even freshly clothed, I felt naked. I stomped over to the bed and snatched my journal out of her hands. I guess I hadn't heard her pop into my room over the blow dryer.

I took a deep, enraged breath. "What the hell do you think you are doing?" I'd intended it to be quiet, but it came out almost a shriek.

Still, she just gave me this blank look, infuriating me even more. "Is there something wrong?" she asked, furrowing her brows. There was no guilt in her voice.

"Wrong? How can you ask? How could you, Aurora?" I was still shrieking.

"Was there something wrong with reading this?" she batted her eyes at me, still not understanding my anger.

I heard feet rushing up the stairs toward us, but I didn't turn around, because I knew who it would be.

"What's going on?" Ruth asked, almost hesitantly.

I could feel her over my shoulder.

"I was just reading," Aurora stated flatly, as I started going off.

"She was reading my journal. That's what she was doing," I emphasized *that* with as much sarcasm as I could throw in.

"I am thinking now, by your reaction, that was a bad thing," Aurora said, her voice dropping just a level below her normal cadence. A slight shade of pink started on her high cheekbones, and she dropped her gaze to the floor.

"Ro, really," Ruth said, and you could hear disapproval in the tone of her voice.

"I'm sorry," Aurora breathed out on a whisper, still looking at the floor.

I was still so mad I was shaking. I hadn't been this mad since my breakup with Jeff. A burning started at the base of my spine then began inching outward, down my legs and up my back. My vision started to narrow and go blurry around the edges, but the burn wasn't blurred in the least.

Since I'd learned what I was capable of, I became more aware of this sensation than ever before. I was out of breath, then suddenly I felt hands on my shoulders. Realizing it was Emily, I let her gently pull me backwards.

"Oh, Sam, I'm so sorry. Aurora wasn't raised as we were. She doesn't understand boundaries like we do. She truly didn't realize she was infringing." Ruth was shaking her head, with a look of understanding, loss, and pity all rolled into one gaze.

The subject in question raised her eyes up to me, but not her chin, like a child caught. "I am sorry," Ro started in the whisper, but her voice got stronger. "I never thought that, as friends, it would be wrong to read what you'd written."

Emily put her right arm over my shoulder, wrapped around my upper torso, and the motion pulled me back toward her until our bodies were touching. She was close enough to whisper in my ear as she leaned in. "It's okay. Let it go. You've got to calm down, Sam."

When I didn't respond, Emily tried again in her normal voice. "I think Ruth and Don like their house the way it is."

That caught my attention. She'd made contact to help calm me down. Was I that close to causing an event? I thought about it a second and felt the burning energy that wanted somewhere to go. Yeah, I guess Em was right. I was about to let loose something that shouldn't be indoors.

I looked back at Aurora, still sitting on my bed. The look of innocence was gone. The look was totally mischievous now.

"Why did you tell him no?" she asked, in a clear voice.

"Aurora!" Ruth half yelled.

I felt as if she'd punched me in the stomach, knocking all the breath out of me. How could she ask? How could she be asking me questions about what she'd read in front of everyone? I'd managed to hold the burn back, but now I felt like ice water had been thrown in my face.

I shook my head and tried to break free of Emily's grasp. I had to get out of this room, away from all of them. When we met, I'd shown Emily what had happened with Jeff, but I'd felt compelled to share with her, my sister. I was just getting to know Aurora over these past few weeks, but I didn't feel close enough for show and tell with her. Now I felt betrayed. A single tear slid down my cheek as I realized it was a bad idea to be here. I broke out of Emily's hold and backed toward the door, grabbing my shoes as I went.

"Sam, it's going to be okay," Emily said, turning to watch me, but not reaching out to stop me because Ruth had grabbed her wrist.

"Sam, Don and the guys are all still out in the yard. Don't

do anything we'll all regret," Ruth said in a sad voice. The tone of it made me think she was feeling sorry for me.

"I don't need pity from any of you," I said. I trotted down the stairs as fast as I could, stopping on the last stair to put on my shoes. I needed a wide, open space badly, if only for a walk. I hit the front door and kept going.

SAM 119

*L*uckily, all the men were in the yard between the house and the barn. I didn't look back as I headed down the driveway for our usual daily walking route. I wrapped my arms around myself while I walked, and though it was hot outside, my insides felt like ice.

I'd trusted Aurora, but going through my journal was wrong. As I took my walk down the dirt country road, I tried to focus on calming down. I noticed the gathering clouds, but I didn't remember the weatherman calling for storms today. There weren't any hints of thunder yet, so I decided I could probably walk the normal route before a storm could cause problems, if it got bad.

I started trying to focus on my breathing. In through my nose, then a slow exhale through my mouth. Repeat. The blood was beginning to pound a little less in my ears, and I could hear the sounds of the summer forest return around me. Several more yards and I dropped my arms, no longer hugging myself.

I recalled my breakup with Jeff and how stupid it all seemed now. Not that I'd get back together with him. I know the road to hell is paved with good intentions, so what was my intent? What had I been saving myself for? It no longer mattered if I ever got a job teaching, so what did it matter if anyone found that I'd slept with someone?

Emily had so much more life experienced than I did. She was a cop and had lived with her boyfriend-slash-ex-fiancé. I bet no one ever questioned her, and it sure as hell didn't hurt her career. If nothing else, that living arrangement had improved her career.

I shook my head to myself, in total disbelief of my life and how prudish I must've appeared to everyone around me. Had I really been so blind to living my life out loud? I knew I'd built a bubble around my heart and myself since the passing of my adoptive parents. I'd created inner walls to keep anyone from getting close enough to hurt me. But now, here was Emily, and even without thinking, I'd let her inside. Honestly, to some degree I'd let Ruth and her whole family in as well.

So, where do Aurora and Ken fall inside my walls? I liked Ken, and I even trusted him, but he wasn't close to me. Aurora was my problem. I'd let her in, and she'd betrayed me. As I tossed around that betrayal in my head, I suddenly wondered if she'd really betrayed me. Ruth told me Aurora hadn't been raised as we were, and guessing from the occasional accent that bled through her speech, she'd grown up in another culture. But what culture doesn't respect boundaries and privacy?

All of this puzzled me, and what was worse, it made me want to know more about her, even while being irritated at her. I realized I wasn't really pissed now, I was just irritated, and I could live with irritated.

Maybe Aurora truly hadn't meant anything by her invasion. She hadn't dug through my personal belongings to find the journal. I'd left it on the nightstand. Maybe, for Aurora, just picking it up and reading it was a natural response.

I began deep breathing again, and I could think more clearly. I could smell the pine needles, and that fresh turpentine smell that made me think 'clean,' which gave me a chance to smile. No, Aurora hadn't meant to hurt me. If she'd had those sorts of intentions, she could've done a lot worse during our jumps. Maybe I'd overreacted, but that meant I'd have to apologize for my outburst. Shit.

I walked a few more yards then realized I was to our usual turning point. Half my walk was over, and I was feeling better. This situation was salvageable. Ro and I would work this out. I knew I'd have to talk to her about it, and just as this situation called for honesty, I knew it was time to be honest with myself, as well.

Turning back toward the house, I contemplated jumping to my room but decided against it. I was sure the men had seen me leave by the front door, and it wouldn't work to be seen coming down the stairs. I'd have to walk back the same way I came, and I knew it was for the best, because it would give me time to think of what I'd say to Ro and where I should start. I broke my stride, slowing down, thinking of how to begin my apology. I crammed my hands into my pockets, hunching my shoulders. Defeated stance? Yep.

I kicked a few rocks along the way, watching my tracks in the dirt as I backtracked to the house. I wasn't watching where I was going, intent on following my tracks. I suddenly stopped short when I saw several more shoe prints in the middle of the road. One set walked a complete circle around my previous set of footprints. *Maybe one of the guys followed me*, I thought, looking all around the road, but I didn't see anyone. I looked back to the tracks in the dirt and found more tracks to the right side of the road, like a group of people had been standing there.

I heard a faint popping sound and whipped around to the other side of the road where I'd heard the sound. There was a man standing there, a man I didn't know. He was just a little taller than me, with stringy brown hair down to his chin. His skin had a grey cast to it, and it made me think of a cancer patient I'd once seen on TV. He looked strung out, and then I wondered if I'd stumbled upon a drug dealer.

I began to slightly back up as a slow grin started to form across his face. I glanced behind me as I was about to break into a run and found similar, darker face just inches from mine. I jerked to a halt. He looked strung out, too, with the glassy look of someone who'd recently had their fix.

"Oh, shit," I let escape.

He had a blank look on his face, which quickly changed into a wide, open-mouthed smile. As I began to back away from him, he reached and grabbed my wrist.

"Hey, what do you—"

I couldn't finish my question, because I was speechless at the final reveal of his open mouth—an open mouth full of razor-sharp, pointed teeth. I tried to pull my wrist free of his grasp, but he was much stronger than I was.

"Let go!" I screamed.

"Hold her, Dominic. Don't let her get away. We've waited too long for this," said the man I'd seen first. He was closer now, from the sound of his voice.

I leaned backward, digging my feet into the dirt, struggling to get my wrist free. I felt hands on my shoulders, pushing me forward.

Dominic was trying to grab my other wrist, but I couldn't let that happen, and I wiggled between the two men. Then I felt a piercing sting on my shoulder.

The first man was biting me! I gritted my teeth to keep from being sick. His head rubbed against my ear, and I could smell his hair. It was the sickening smell of sweat that hadn't seen soap and water for several days. The pain became so intense that I started to scream. Someone would surely hear me.

I didn't think I was that far from the house, but that didn't matter. I only had time to register that this is going to hurt before Dominic slammed his fist into my jaw, and everything went black.

❡

EMILY 118

I knew Sam wasn't in a great frame of mind when she'd left, and I didn't blame her. I'd made peace with my decision to give up my life in Salt Lake. I'd rebuilt my life a couple of times now, and moving to Arkansas wouldn't really be that bad. I had family here, and we'd have a lot of time to get to know each other. Not having to work for a living is a new concept, but I think I'll manage to adapt. Right now, I'm not so sure Sam is in the same peaceful frame of mind.

Ruth had held me back when Sam ran down the stairs. "She needs a little time to herself, Em. She'll be okay, just give her some breathing room."

She'd turned then on Aurora, who was biting her lower lip.

"I really did screw things up this time, didn't I?"

Ruth shook her head, exhaling. "Emily, can you finish up the dishes? I think I need to have a chat with my dear friend now."

I nodded my head and turned to go, but not before I glanced at Ro from the top of the stairs, and I was satisfied that she was adequately abashed by her behavior. I'd gladly take care of the dishes; Ruth's tone when she said 'dear friend' wasn't at all friendly, and I knew I didn't want to be on the receiving end of that tone. The fact that Ro was made me smile.

But Sam had been gone too long. Her usual walk was normally completed in forty-five minutes. She'd been gone now twice that long, and I was getting a little nervous about it. The knot forming in my stomach was reminding me of that sixth sense I always had as a cop. Something was wrong, I could just feel it.

I grabbed my phone and dialed her cell, only to hear it ringing on the kitchen counter. I walked through the kitchen, glanced at Sam's phone on the counter, and shook my head as I stepped out onto the wraparound porch.

I walked slowly around the house a couple of times, trying to convince myself that there was nothing wrong. But the slower I got in my walking, the greater the sense of dread. Enough of this! I stopped pacing the porch and went to find Ruth.

She was in her office with Aurora, and they had that invitation from the consul sitting on the desk between them. They both turned with questioning looks as I stood in the doorway.

"Sam's not back, she didn't take her phone, and I'm starting to feel funny about it," I said, running my hands up and down my arms like I was cold, but I wasn't.

Ruth and Aurora both looked at the grandmother clock on the wall.

Aurora was the first to suddenly stand, grabbing the desktop with both hands. "Oh Ruth, can you not feel it?" she asked.

Ruth turned pale as she sat in her chair, frozen, looking at me. "We were so busy discussing the consul's invitation that I guess I lost track of time. I didn't even feel the electricity in the air," Ruth said, rising slowly from her chair. She moved stiffly as if she had been in a car wreck.

"What is it? Are you saying I'm not the only one feeling freaky now?" I asked, but I was past the anxious feeling now, heading into full-blown panic mode.

"Aurora, call Slade and Ken and ask them to get here. Em and I are going to drive the loop and see if we can find her."

Ruth was suddenly in full motion, grabbing her car keys and cell phone off the desk, and we were out the door.

"Tell me what's going on, Ruth," I insisted while we were heading to the car.

Mid-summer in Arkansas can be a mixed bag of weather at best. This summer, the sweltering heat was making national headlines, and the inside of Ruth's car was proof the stories were true. If walking outdoors felt like an oven, getting in a car that had been sitting in the sun was like walking into a volcano. Sweat was running down my body now, and Ruth was breathless by the time she threw the car in reverse.

"My best guess is faeries. I can feel them now," she said, looking over her shoulder as she turned the car around.

Not a good day. Definitely not good. "You said 'them.' How can you tell it's more than one, and what do they want?" I asked.

"Emily, I'm not sure how to explain the difference of feeling one verses a thousand right now. I just know they've been very close and used their powers to shield themselves from us. They've dropped it now, and I can only guess they want us to know they've been here, and that's what we're feeling. What's worse is I'm afraid they have your sister."

She glanced sideways at me. I guess for my reaction, but she kept the car heading straight. I was instantly numb. *No, this can't be happening.* We'd just found each other, and now some faeries have taken her? My chest grew tight. The vibration that hums through my body, which I now know is part of my powers, started in my shoulders and was working its way out.

"She could've jumped back to your house when she realized she was in danger," I said very low, almost to myself.

"No, not with faeries around. If they were too close before she realized she was in trouble, she might not have been able to jump. If they shielded themselves this well, I'm sure she had no idea what was about to happen. Even if she had, they mute some of our powers. Running back to the house would've been the only real option."

My mind was still racing with thoughts of loss as Ruth turned the bend in the road. Since it was a rural country road, dirt and gravel were typical in this area. This section of the road looked like several cars or four wheelers had been doing donuts in the road or had some kind of wreck. Ruth slowed the car down to a creep and eased through this section, which was no longer than two car lengths.

"This is where they found her," she said, breathlessly. She drove past the section slowly and stopped. She didn't turn the car off but put it in park then started looking around the roadside.

"How do you fight fairies? Did you tell us that already?" I asked, my hand on the door handle as I looked into the woods on my side of the car.

"If your skills are strong enough, you can do a few things with the elements. If not, always bring backup," she replied, then reached into the glove box and brought out a pistol.

"Lead can slow them down, but steel is better," she said, checking the clip. She looked up at me and narrowed her eyes. The gold flecks in her brown eyes were sizzling. I could see anger and fear all rolled together.

"This is why we kept you both hidden. I hope you understand now why it was so important," she said, nodding to my door. "Ease out on your side, and follow me."

I nodded and did what she asked. We walked cautiously to the spot where the dirt was the most broken up by tracks. We studied the forest on either side of us as we walked, and Ruth kept the gun pointed at the ground. I could feel the hair on my body stand as we moved closer to the exact spot where my sister had been stolen. There were footprints in the dusty road, and it was plain to see that she'd put up a struggle.

I walked around the area, looking at the tracks, but could neither find where they started nor where they went. It was like everything landed right here and then was gone. The humming in my shoulders was increasing, and it felt like I was going to have muscle spasms.

Ruth stood in the middle of the road and closed her eyes while lifting her face to the sky. I let her have her peace for a few seconds, holding back my questions.

"They jumped. They all jumped to this location and then left again. Someone's been following me, I can sense it now," Ruth said.

"If only one has been following you, how did this many get here without knowing where they were going?" I asked, indicating with my hands the sets of tracks on the ground.

"Different flavor of powers," she said, shrugging and looking around the roadsides again. "We'll go back and meet up with Aurora. Maybe Slade and Ken have made it here by now."

"How do we find her, Ruth?" I asked.

"I'm not sure right now. Let's see if the others have any ideas."

"No," I said firmly. "I can't wait. She can't wait on us."

Ruth had already started for the car but stopped, turning quickly to face me, eyes flashing her anger again. "And what do you think you can do?" she asked, in a tone I hadn't heard from her before.

I didn't know what I was going to do about it. I had my jewelry now, but that hadn't seemed to boost my ability to jump or do any other kind of magic, save for healing minor injuries. I didn't even think about my limitations, I just thought about the barn, and suddenly I was there.

It happened so fast that I stumbled at first, as if I'd landed hard, grabbing for a post to keep from falling. The only times I'd jumped successfully were with other people, and this stunned me. I'd have been happier if it'd been under different circumstances, but I couldn't afford the time to congratulate myself. I looked around to make sure no one else was there. If the others were on the porch, I'd make sure they didn't see me in the barn. I needed to be alone, away from everyone right now.

I walked to the stack of hay at the back of the barn, then sat down on a bale, resting my elbows on my knees and holding my face in my hands. I closed my eyes and prayed. I was scared, so I knew Sam had to be, too. I let the tension that had been building in my shoulders ease slightly and took a few deep, cleansing breaths, exhaling slowly.

One.

Two.

Three.

I counted, thinking the words and spelling them to myself at the same time, to allow more time for the calming process work. I could still feel the essence of evil on the air, of magic that'd been used. I could breathe it. I was able to taste different elements of it, which made me think different people, or I guess I should say different species. Maybe this was what Ruth meant by knowing it was more than one.

Suddenly, I had a sense of at least twenty different flavors and had a rough idea of what Sam had seen. I closed my eyes tighter and thought about Sam, how it felt for us to touch or talk to each other without saying a word. I thought of her trip to the beach and the way she saw the ocean lapping on the shore, of her breakup with her boyfriend. Then there was something else. I stiffened, not realizing what it was. I was puzzled.

I saw the ladies' restroom at the Salt Lake City Police station, and I was sitting on the floor in my uniform. I watched Ruth walk in between us, then I realized I was seeing this from Sam's memory of our first meeting, but I didn't think she'd ever shared that with me. I frowned, trying to recall when she could've presented this to me. I relaxed a bit more, then I could see us walking to my apartment that first day. Next I was holding the door open for Ruth and Aurora. Again, it was from Sam's point of view, not mine.

I thought to myself, *Sam I wish you could hear me right now, the way we mentally communicate.* I sighed heavily with that thought and then jerked, startled, when a thought came back to me.

"I was wondering how long it would take you to try this. Please tell me you're safe."

I got a sense of fear from her, then tried to reassure her. *"I'm okay. Are you?"*

I was afraid if I moved or opened my eyes, I'd lose contact with her, so I tried to breathe slowly so I could hear above the blood pounding in my ears.

"I'm scared, Em. These are some freaky bastards. I've never seen anyone like them before. They were just there on

the road and grabbed me. I kept trying to fight them off, but one of them hit me, and then it all went dark."

As she thought to me, I could see her memories from the road. Damn, they were ugly! "Sam, do you know where you are? Can you see anything?" My hostage negotiation training was kicking in, but I needed to know where she was.

"My powers won't really work, Em. I tried jumping at first, and when that didn't work, I started thinking to you, but it's like the thought couldn't travel far. I'd almost given up hope until you came looking just now. I think I'm in a barn or an outbuilding of some kind. The floor is dirt, and I smell cut lumber. I don't know how we got here or how far away I am. There are no windows, just the door, and I tried it already. It's bolted from the outside."

As she recounted what she'd seen, I suddenly realized I could see what she was seeing. Not as a memory, but as it was happening. Under different circumstances, I'm not sure I wanted this ability, but for now I was thankful as Sam walked me through her captivity space.

"I can see light under the door, and what I guess is someone walking by it every once in a while. I guess they're guarding it, huh?" Sam thought to me.

I shuddered to myself. "Yeah, that'd be my guess. Can you move? I mean, did they tie you up or anything? Are you hurt?"

Sam took a few seconds to answer, but I wasn't panicked, because I could see her looking around the space where she was being held. "Yeah, I'm tied up, or at least my hands are. While I was fighting to get away, one of them bit me. It hurts like hell, but I'm okay. My jaw hurts from being hit, but I'll live."

I had to get to her. I was trying to think of how to get her out when my phone started vibrating. "Sam, can you see or *hear what I see and hear where I am?"* The phone kept vibrating.

"No, I can only feel you when you're in my head. It's different than the other times we talk like this. Now it's just one sided."

I could sense her frowning, trying to figure it out. *"Listen, my phone is ringing. I'm sure it's Ruth. I'll be right back."* When I felt her nod, I opened my eyes and the phone at the same time.

"What the hell do you think you're doing?" Ruth yelled as soon as I had the phone next to my ear.

"I've talked to her, Ruth. I mean I've found her. Kind of." I was whispering, because if Ruth was at the house or outside of the house, chances were that she'd hear me talking.

"Tell me," she said, her anger deflating and her voice evening out.

I told her about the link Sam and I had and what Sam was seeing now. She was very quiet while I informed her what Sam had shared with me. "Are you still there, Ruth?"

Her answer sounded as if it came from the inside a tin can. "Yeah, we're here. Where are you, Emily? You need to work with us on this. I can feel your wheels turning on how you can save her, but don't do anything rash. You damn well better not be planning to play the lone ranger here."

I didn't answer.

"I can sense that you're still in the county, Em. Come back to the house, and let's figure something out," Ruth said.

I could hear male voices whispering in the background and what I was sure was Aurora answering them.

"Ruth, I have to get her back. A month ago, I wouldn't have walked across the street to meet you people, but now..." I let that thought trail off, then I stood up from the bale of hay and started pacing. "I've got the feeling they aren't patient people, Ruth. They bit her already and punched her in the face. I don't know what the biting is supposed to mean, but I won't let them hurt her again," I said, exhaling.

I'd walked so far away from my bale of hay that I suddenly noticed I was in the doorway that led out of the barn to the house. I could see movement in the big windows behind the dining table. Ruth was standing there with her back to me.

"Emily! Don't do this. Not alone. You've not had enough training yet."

I could see her talking with her hands, and the rest of the crew standing around looking at the phone on the table. I took a deep breath and Ruth froze, arms in mid-air as if she'd thrown them up like a white flag, but she froze because something hit her. It didn't take me long to figure out what happened, because I'd seen this in my apartment the day we met. She knew I was looking at her and whipped around to stare at me through the windows. The shock on her face was quickly replaced by anger. I could see Slade and Ken start moving toward the back-porch door.

"Emily, please, come in and let's do this together," Aurora said, moving to stand beside Ruth.

"Look, there's no time. I'll signal you or something," I said.

I dropped the phone to the ground. Shock spread across Ruth's face as Ken and Slade walked towards the barn to retrieve me. I reached to the side of the doorway then grabbed the flashlight that was kept in case of power outages. I looked again at the house to see Aurora and Ruth disappear at the same time. They were jumping to me. I closed my eyes as quickly as I could, then pictured the inside of Sam's prison. Then I jumped.

SAM 120

I would've screamed if I didn't have a gag in my mouth when Emily landed in front of me, facing the door. She stumbled but righted herself quickly, turning to look at me. She flipped on a flashlight, and I felt like my retinas exploded. I hated being blinded! I tried to tell her to get the light out of my face, but it was difficult with the gag still in my mouth. She must have sensed it, because she dropped the light, moving to start untying me, gag first. I was relived to be able to breathe freely again.

While Emily unbound my wrists, she began thinking to me. *"These people who took you are faeries. At least that's what Ruth thinks they are."*

She came around to look me in the eyes and began to run her hands over my wrists to see if I was injured. I jerked my hands back. I'd had enough handling for one day. *"I don't care if they're the flying monkeys from the Wizard of Oz! I hate them! And I'm sorry, but I don't want to be touched right now. Nothing personal, I feel like I've been pawed enough."* I rubbed my wrists. They were chaffed but not raw. I'd live.

"Where's the bite?" Emily asked.

I reached over my left shoulder and found that it was still oozing slightly and very tender. Emily moved behind me again, pulled my collar down, then brought the flashlight up so she could see. She gasped, and I knew it wasn't pretty.

"These faeries must have some nasty pointed teeth. This looks like a shark bite." She released the shirt, moved in front of me, and covered the light beam with her hand. In the dim glow, she looked me over again for more injuries, but she didn't touch me.

"Em, those are the scariest things I've ever seen. Aurora was right: Hollywood really has no idea what's truly out here. I'm okay. Turn the light off. I don't want them to catch you in here, too."

Emily turned the light off and crept to the door. My eyes had grown accustomed to the lack of light, and I could see movement and shapes but not details. I could see Emily as she went from one side of the door to the other. She didn't touch it but looked all around, then she walked the perimeter of the space. I was happy to just sit, able to breathe now that the gag was gone and my hands were untied. I regretted wearing shorts today because, even as hot as it was, I didn't like being exposed to the creepy crawlies that lived in dark spaces like this.

I watched Emily's every step as she walked the wall opposite the door. Before now, I hadn't paid much attention to the back wall, but now I could see huge gaps between the wall boards, making it much less sturdy than the other three.

"I didn't realize you could see through those until now," I thought to Emily.

"You probably couldn't see it because it's darker on the other side. There's no direct sunlight. From what I can see, it looks like a shed added on to this building," Emily thought back to me.

I watched Emily squat down. She looked first through one board and then another. She'd stand then turn at different angles to get a better look.

"You started that conversation, Sam, so maybe since we're here together, talking to each other this way, we aren't as affected as when we are on different sides of it."

I thought about it for a minute, nodded, then realized she had her back turned, and it was dark. *"Yeah, it seems to work. But now what? What are we going to do?"*

Emily came to stand next to me, frowning down at me in the shadows. I don't think she'd thought this through completely.

"Tell me you have a plan, Emily. Please, please tell me."

Emily turned from me and switched the flashlight on but kept her hand over it to diffuse the light. She walked the walls again, but this time she cast as little light as possible while she looked up the walls.

On the right hand wall, she found a wooden support from the floor to the ceiling. Six feet off the ground from this support was a stack of lumber. Someone appreciated their woodworking, because the stack was sorted by size and color. There was a ladder attached to the wall at one end of the stack. The wood of the wall and the ladder were the same dark gray color and dried out. No wonder I hadn't seen it.

Emily climbed up the ladder to the stack of lumber. Quietly, she slid a piece of lumber to the side, and then another. It didn't take long for her to find a piece to serve her purpose, but what that purpose was, she hadn't yet shared. We were going to need to make a more conscious effort to let each other in.

She looked back at me and flashed the light quickly then left it off to get my attention. *"Let me hand this to you. I want to make as little noise as we can for the moment."*

I walked over, received the stick of lumber, and was inspecting it. It was roughly three feet long and a good two by two inches, like a post you might see on a railing. I felt along its edge and found it was smooth, like someone had sanded it before they stacked it, which meant less of a chance of getting splinters.

Emily crawled back down the ladder soundlessly. I was impressed, but after all, she'd been a cop. I'm sure there was a class in creeping. She must've taken it. Emily went back to the door then got down on all fours to look under it. A few seconds went by, and I could tell from the shadow that wandered around outside that the guard was still there.

Emily moved closer to the shadow and looked under the door again. She crawled back away from the door before she stood and walked over to me. She took the piece of lumber from me, and even in the dark I could tell she was grinning.

"Sam, I want you to sit back where they put you. When I get in place on the side of the door, I want you to start moaning as loud as you can. Then I want you to fall off your seat and hit the ground as hard as you can and as loud as you can. Make your back face the door. When the guard comes in to check on you, I'll hit him. Or her or whatever the hell it is. We could try to jump, but Ruth said they're likely to have muted our powers, and I'd hate for us to get separated. We'll have to run for it. I wish now I'd kept the damn cell phone. If we can get far enough ahead of them, we can try to jump."

I listened, carefully nodding. *"Em, where's your gun?"* I asked. While I didn't want that man—thing, whatever—near me again, I was willing to try if it'd get us out of here. We'd have the advantage with extra weaponry.

Emily's mouth fell open just slightly, her eyes widened. She was shocked, or so it seemed. *"I, um, forgot it,"* she said, running both hands through her hair and over her face, exhaling loudly. *"Sam, I just didn't think about it. Hell, I even threw my phone down. What was I thinking?"*

I held my hand out and thought of Emily's gun, calling it out of thin air. When it materialized, I attempted to hand it over, but she shook her head, backing away.

"No, you keep it with you. If this plan goes wrong, you'll need it. I'm hoping to keep this soundless, and that," she thought to me, pointing to the gun in my hand, *"will draw attention."*

I'd never shot a gun before. The cool metal felt weird in my hand. Not knowing what to do with it, I tucked it in the waistband of my shorts then pulled my shirt out, effectively covering it. The sleek metal gave me a brief moment of shivering, but I gave myself a mental head smack to get focused, reminding myself that I wanted to get the hell out of here.

With the plan set, Emily moved to the side of the door, where we both could see the shadows under the door. She nodded. I started moaning loudly, then I flung myself to the ground with dramatic effect. It worked!

We could hear them talking. It wouldn't be good if more than one came into the room. From the next noise we'd heard, whatever they were using to hold the door closed was removed. With my back to the door, I could only tell that there was an increase of light in the room.

They called to me in some language I couldn't place, but I remained frozen on the ground. I prayed there were no creepy crawlies around as I heard them take a few tentative steps inside. Their strange language calling to me grew louder as they entered the building. I just hoped and prayed Em could get us out of here.

*)

EMILY 119

I flattened myself against the wall as they came through the door. Yes, two faeries came in, and the man in the lead was over six feet tall. I guessed that the other was a female, only by the slight appearance of breasts, but I couldn't be sure. Regardless, I still had to take both of them out. Sam was doing well on the floor, not moving, but I could sense her terror.

The faeries had put enough space between themselves, and by the time the first one was about to lean over Sam, the second was only halfway into room. I stayed in the shadows and quietly made my way to the nearest faerie.

Holding the stick of lumber like a baseball bat, I drew it back as I advanced. When I was within striking distance, I let it fly, catching the faerie at the base of the skull, where it made a sickening thud. The faerie made an "ugh" sound as its knees buckled.

As this faerie went down in slow motion, the bastard standing over Sam turned to look over his shoulder. I took a quick step closer, pivoted on my left foot, and swung myself around 180 degrees to strike him under the chin with the lumber. He dodged at the last second, causing me to stumble and fall, landing on my side. Before I could right myself, he lunged in my direction, growling distinctly.

"Shit! Sam, use the gun! Use the gun now!" I screamed mentally as he descended to wrap his paw around my ankle.

I let him come closer, leaning over me before I drew my other leg back and kicked him in the jewels. As he doubled over, moaning, holding himself, I scrambled away, circling toward Sam as she was leveling the gun.

The faerie turned stiffly towards us, breathing through his nose. My kick had landed maximum damage, but my pride faded quickly because apparently it wasn't enough, as he straightened to his full height, baring his teeth. He took one tight step toward us, like he wasn't sure he could make a full step, and Sam squeezed the trigger of my gun. The sound was deafening, but the shock registered in his eyes.

I was waiting to see the blood spurt out of his chest, and apparently he was too, as he clamped his hands over what should've been a wound, looking down so he could watch it, too. No blood even seeped through his fingers.

I grabbed the gun from Sam, pulled off two more shots straight into the kill zone of his heart, and still nothing happened. *"Em, did you ever change Ro's blanks?"*

"DAMN!"

Mr. Faerie realized at the same time I did that my gun was literally useless, and he lunged for us again. Dropping for a quick sweep with my leg, I was able to snag his ankles and took him down, arms flaying wildly. Landing on top of me, his sheer size knocked the wind out of me, then I heard a *thud*, and he went loose limbed on top of me, dead weight.

Quickly, Sam was pulling him off of me with one hand as she held on to the piece of wood I'd used to knock out the first faerie. Unlike the first faerie, he'd went down with an "oof" sound. Luckily, both were closed injuries. No blood was visible.

Sam kept her grip on my bat, and we started toward the door. I peaked in the direction of the house and saw the other faeries gathering, I supposed to discuss the gun shots, but we didn't have time to stop and explain.

Clearing the opposite side of the building at a dead run, I don't know why, but I'd come to the conclusion that we should run east. It was opposite of the sun, and I could use that as a guide, but it was more cloudy than sunny and growing darker by the second.

It'd been nearly two o'clock when Ruth and I'd left the house looking for Sam, so I guessed it was now around three o'clock, but with the treetops and clouds blocking most of the sun, I couldn't really tell. The fact that they knew we were running put us with even fewer chances for a successful escape. They were after us!

I heard a cry from the shed, and I think my heart skipped a few beats. We were in the trees when I heard more sounds of distress, probably upon discovering the two that I downed, but we didn't have time to worry now. We were on the move.

We ran as fast as we could. Sam tripped a couple of times and would've fallen if I hadn't grabbed her by the elbow. We were equal in our strides, and I was surprised to see that she could keep up. I'd been staying in shape for my job, but I hadn't figured Sam to be doing the same voluntarily. However, I knew we wouldn't last long.

Tree branches and briers were constantly slapping at us. The bigger snags, we tore free from and kept moving. A couple of times we had to stop because the briers and underbrush were so thick that we couldn't go any farther.

We switched directions several times, but not back in the direction from where we'd left the shed. We could hear yelling in the distance, and I knew it wasn't going to be a happy reunion if the faeries caught us. Minutes later, when we came to a small clearing in the undergrowth, we stopped to catch our breath.

"Sam," I wheezed, "I don't think we're going to be able to outrun them."

She was panting too. "I know. So, what, we stand and fight?"

I nodded, still trying to catch my breath. "I won't go down without one."

Sam nodded.

We came to stand back to back. Slowly we made a circular path in the pine needles, watching all directions, listening to the fury heading toward us.

You could tell few had ever been to this part of the woods. The needles from the trees were springy under our feet as we eased our way around, watching as they neared us. I was still sucking air in, and it was burning my throat.

They all broke free of the tree line at the same time. We were circled, realizing it'd been a trap all along. *So much for running*, I thought with a grim bit of dissatisfaction. The surprised look on their faces was enough to tell me that they hadn't expected to see two of us.

Whereas we'd been standing back to back in a slight crouch before they barreled out of the woods, we now both stood straight, realizing what we faced. Our shoulders touched, and I dropped my hand to my side, reaching to find Sam's hand. When we clasped our hands together, I felt like we became a tuning fork that had caught the vibration of energy in the air being thrown off from this pack.

Whoever said faeries were small, enchanting creatures was dead wrong. This wasn't a Disney affair. What encircled us were tall, gaunt men and women, none of them less than six feet tall. We were the shortest on the playing field, and I felt like they loomed over us.

"What should we do?" Sam thought to me.

"You're asking me? I thought running was a good idea when we first started this," I thought back.

"Will Ruth and Slade be able to find us?" Sam thought.

"I don't think this group is going to wait for spectators."

I'd barely finished my thought when the apparent leader stepped forward. He held his hands up, as if to calm the group. If they'd been running after us, I wanted to know why none of them were winded. My chest still burned trying to get enough air. I had to fight to hear, as blood was pumping through my head so hard it was all I could hear.

As for their leader, or whatever they called him, he was shorter than the rest but still taller than us. He took a tentative step, still with his hands out, trying to calm the group. He glanced about the ring of gruesomeness surrounding us then slowly brought his eyes to mine.

Sam couldn't see him, so I thought my description of his movements to her, followed by, *"Just be ready."*

His eyes were an eerie, pale blue, almost white and glassy-looking. His lank, straight brown hair fell halfway between his ears and shoulders. He nodded in my direction as if to ask permission, but permission to what, I didn't know, so I just cocked an eyebrow back. He broke into a slow smile. As his smile widened, his appearance changed. The dark circles that had been under his eyes seeped away. His mousy brown hair seemed to plump up. The dark highlights on his cheekbones seemed to fade away as his coloring improved. The narrowed face seemed to broaden, and in a matter of a few seconds, he went from looking like a strung-out goth to a Zeus-like god. When I realized both of my eyebrows had risen, he decided to finally talk.

"Ladies, we had no idea there would be such a treat when we started this hunt, but lo, two for the price of one. Look how fair they stand, my brethren. I can taste their resolve. What tasty morsels. Pity Slade won't be able to save you."

His voice had an almost singsong quality, and his followers, while I won't say they spoke, sounded as if they were chanting something. They appeared to think what he'd said was funny because their looks were clearly of amusement.

He quickly raised his hand away from his body, and the sounds stopped, as did the looks of amusement. His other hand, he flung in our direction, a deadly look on his face.

I only had enough time to think *"We're hit,"* but Sam squeezed my hand and turned the two of us so that she was now facing the leader. She did it so quickly that I was almost dizzy with the motion. Whatever he thought he was flinging at us struck the shield that Sam had suddenly erected. Whatever he flung struck the shield with such force it made it shimmer, but I could only see movement from my periphery. Looking straight ahead, you couldn't tell anything was there. I squeezed her hand back and took a breath.

"What do you want?" Sam asked, and her voice wasn't breathless.

I wondered how she could be calmer than I was. I was the one who broke up fights in alleys and chased criminals down the street. I should be the calmer one, but I'd have to ponder that later.

My view had changed to the opposite direction, but the bodies and looks on faces were the same. By my estimation, there were at least twenty of them circling us. A woman to my right smiled big enough that I could see her pointed teeth. She slowly put the tip of her tongue out, then traced along the front of her teeth. The look of disgust on my face only made her laugh.

"Moppet, we want you, of course. We were promised your mother a very long time ago. But we were robbed of the experience. Alas, here the two of you are. Not that anyone knew there were two of you, but we won't complain." He still had the singsong quality in his voice, completely contradicting his appearance.

"Now what?" Sam thought to me.

"If I knew that, we wouldn't be standing here."

The faerie leader spoke again. "I see your aunt has taught you well. Your shield is a thing of beauty, but it cannot hold us off forever. We long to taste your sweetness. I've sampled the bouquet already, and it is an impeccable vintage."

Again the group did the chanting thing, everyone looking happier by the minute.

Enough of this, I thought to myself. If we can't jump from this crazy place, surely there must be something else we can do.

"What do you mean you were promised our mother?" I figured if we were going to stall until we thought of something, we might as well put the time to good use. "Who promised you, and what exactly did they promise?"

"Come, child, let us not waste our time looking back on tragedies of the past. We cannot go back. We cannot change the past. We can simply live in the moment and move forward."

The group shifted slightly, as if they were going to walk in a ring around us. I watched as deep piles of pine needles made their stride slightly bouncy.

"I don't think we want to play today. How about we take a rain check and reschedule for tomorrow?" Sam asked.

His reply was just a laugh, but that laugh alone was enough to give me the willies. I thought to Sam, *"Can you handle a little quake?"*

"Giving or receiving?" she thought back.

"These faeries smashing all the pine needles seem like such a waste. I was thinking of a quick flash of fire, a little wind, and a lot of trembling might at least let Aurora know where we are."

"Elemental SOS. I like it, but I'll need a little space."

Without letting go of one another's hand, we each took a step forward, away from each other. In our practice sessions with Ruth, Aurora, and Ken, everyone was under the impression that if Sam and I were close to each other or, better yet, touching, we could double our strengths. Now I hoped we'd prove it.

"If you'll handle the shaking, I'll try for the flash and bang. I think we need to make a point," I thought to Sam.

"Do it," was her only reply.

"Let's switch sides again," I thought.

We slowly inched around in a circle, and I could feel a slight tremor start in Sam. I looked up to the sky. Even with the thick trees surrounding us, I couldn't see much, but I had to concentrate. I knew that if I closed my eyes, Sam would sense that she'd need to pay attention to the faeries I was facing, so I felt somewhat secure in blinding myself. I concentrated on calling the lightning I'd need to bring down to earth.

We'd never discussed this in lessons, so I'd no idea what I was doing. I'd have to make it up as I went along. I started thinking about watching Slade and Ken bind the demon to that tree.

My upper arms started tingling, along with my thighs, all of which was a new and different kind of feeling. As the tingling inched its way up my shoulders, I felt the short hairs on the back of my neck begin to rise as well. I opened my eyes and thought of the leader of this welcoming committee.

It began to grow darker, and the wind began to pick up. I glanced upward to see the clouds boiling more quickly than I'd ever seen a storm gather. It only took a few seconds more, and we were completely eclipsed from the sun. The wind was whipping Sam's ponytail back and forth, then the thunder started.

A few of our would-be captors looked nervously around and started their chanting again. Their leader suddenly laughed out loud. I let go of Sam's hand long enough for her to turn so we could face the same direction, looking at their leader, then I grabbed her hand again, our backs now to the rest of the faeries.

"You think to scare us? Children, please—" was all he got out of his mouth.

I raised my hand toward the sky quickly and brought it down as fast as I could, pointing at the leader. A bolt of lightning cracked from the heavens, hitting their leader where he stood. He shook violently as over a million volts surged through his body. I immediately smelled charred flesh. I then pointed from him to the ground at his feet. His clothes were now ablaze and his feet smoldering, causing the dry pine needles around him to spark to life as the bolt of lightning splintered to touch the ground.

The vibration from Sam increased. I felt the ground shake violently enough to cause the other faeries to grab at one another to steady themselves. Some in the group were already screaming and scattering. I glanced behind us and found that Sam had caused the ground there to split. It separated us from those who would have tried to attack us from behind.

I trailed my hand along the circle of faeries, and the splintering electrical current followed my direction, lighting the ground ablaze at their feet. Their leader was reduced to smoldering cinders inside that circle, and those too terrified to move simply stood stunned, their mouths agape.

I wanted to do more damage. I wanted to throw my arm at them all, but I wanted answers more. I glanced to either side then realized that the female who'd bared her teeth at me earlier had moved with the circle and was now standing in front of me. She was baring her teeth still and emitting a hiss from between her teeth.

"Familiarity breeds contempt" is an adage I'd always heard, and I decided she was my next target. I made a looping motion in the air, and a splintered electrical charge looped around her. She screamed, but it didn't burn her. I only wanted her held to answer questions. With the same hand I'd called down the lightning bolt from the heavens, I clenched my fist in the direction of the woman. The loop tightened, causing her to screech again.

It hit me that I hadn't made any of the movements consciously. I hadn't thought about what to do next. It was like my body knew to move to the next motion, and I had no idea how this was occurring. It just happened.

"If any more of you want to join your spokesman, I suggest you come forward now. Your friend here is going to stay with us a little while longer. She'll be released unharmed, but I do suggest you leave now. I'm tired of this game," I yelled to them.

Slowly, those who hadn't already run away started backing into the darkness of the trees. I still wanted my energy supply close at hand, so I had to retain my cloud of darkness for the moment. Maybe the cloud would be a beacon to direct our rescuers to this location. I only hoped this would be over quickly.

Sam released my hand and did a twist in either direction

to see all around. "They're gone," she said, almost in a whisper. "All of them."

I watched our guest shriek her anger at being held captive, then I glanced back to Sam.

"Ruth said they'd mute our powers, but with us touching I'm not sure that's true. Maybe the combination of our powers overrides what they can mute."

I raised my hands in front of my face to look at them. Who would've thought I could've conjured lightning and done such damage then used it to hold a hostage? I was amazed. It was also just dawning on me that I'd made my first solo jump, first to the barn and then to the shed where Sam was held. Not only did I make my first jump, but I made a jump that I shouldn't have been able to make. Ruth said we had to know where we were jumping, had to have seen it, before the actual jump could be set in motion.

Was the fact that I could communicate with Sam and see what she was seeing enough to allow me to jump there? Was this some other latent power that came from our father's side of the family? There was so much to talk about when we got back. First thing first, how were we going to get back to Ruth's house?

Not knowing exactly where we were was a definite drawback. Not having a phone was another. I lowered my hands to my hips and stood looking at my hostage. I wish I had my gun. Ruth said that could stop these creeps.

"Sam, grab on again," I said, holding out my left hand to her. When she took my hand, I held my right hand open, palm up, and thought about my gun. I closed my eyes and longed for the gun to be in my hand, then suddenly I felt something land there. No, it didn't land. It fell there. I opened my eyes to see my gun. I'd done it. I'd summoned my gun to me.

Seeing it, Sam let go of my hand then moved in front of

me, almost blocking my view of the hostage. She looked down at the gun in my hand, awe on her face, which turned into another huge grin.

"I know you want answers, Emily, but something in me wants to take your gun and just shoot her," Sam said flatly, the grin leaving her face.

"It'll be okay, Sam," I said, meeting her eyes.

There was a determination that passed behind her eyes. I'd seen the look on crime victims before, those that wanted revenge. I was just hoping she'd be okay. Hollow words if you can't back them up, and right now, I wasn't sure I could.

"If I can bring my gun, maybe I can summon my phone, too," I said, holding out my hand to her again.

She took it, but before I could think of my phone, hers was suddenly in her hand.

"I added a GPS program to mine. It should tell us where we are, then we can call Ruth," Sam said, stepping behind me again. "I just hope I can get a signal."

Our hostage was standing very still, watching our every movement. The sadistic smile she'd had earlier was now gone, replaced by fear. I leveled my gun at her again and smiled as big as I could. Sam was mumbling to herself behind me. I knew she was walking in various directions, probably to find the best signal.

"Got it," she announced triumphantly.

"Just make the call," I told her, not taking my eyes off our new friend.

"Ruth, it's me. It's Sam," she started. I could hear the relief in her voice and realized it could turn to tears just as quick. "Yes, I'm fine. Yeah, Emily's here with me."

She paused, and I glanced around briefly. Sam was rolling her eyes and making a circular motion with her left hand, like a hamster exercising on a wheel. With just one look I knew she was nearing the end of her rope. "Ruth!" Sam shouted into the phone. "Take a damn breath and listen to me." She was still shouting, but not as loud.

"Okay? Do I have your attention? We need you to come get us. We don't know where we are, and we have an, uh, extra coming back with us. I've got coordinates on my phone. Hang on a second while I read it off."

As Sam read the coordinates to Ruth, I was busy watching our 'extra' twist and turn against the electric rope that bound her. I was smiling to myself, thinking how much I really liked this new talent, when I heard Sam hang up.

"She say's we're near the old Davis homestead. Says that's probably where you found me. They'll be right here."

The last sentence held such relief for her, and I was glad she felt better. I wasn't sure what we were going to discover from our guest, and I didn't have time to ponder the thought. Sam's phone rang, and she answered it.

"No, we can't jump back to that homestead. Em kind of has this woman all tied up." She paused. "Um, it's not that simple, Ro, it's not real rope. It's kind of like a lightning bolt she wrapped her up in." She was standing beside me now, looking at our new friend. "No, she's not killing her with it. She did toast one guy with a bolt, the one who bit me. This bolt is only holding her. I'm not sure if we can even touch her."

Sam was shaking her head in puzzlement. "Ro, just please get here. Oh, wait a second, and let me ask," she said as she switched to talk to me. "Ro wants to know if you can call another bolt. She thinks they could see it now that they're at that old home place."

I thought about it for a moment while I glanced to the sky then back to our captive. Her eyes went wider, and I could tell she thought I'd call a bolt back to really do damage to her now.

"I'll try, but you'll have to hold the gun on my friend here," I said.

I let some of the tension leave my shoulders as I eased out of my two-fisted shooter's stance. I took a step backwards so I could see Sam clearly while still keeping an eye on the bound faerie just across from us. I handed her my pistol, never lowering it.

"Just keep it aimed at her. I'm not sure you'll be able to keep the phone call going, but let's pretend you can for right now."

I took several steps backward and almost fell into the crag in the ground that Sam had caused. This would have to be far enough away, and besides the crag, I wasn't willing to put much space between us right now. I wasn't sure how much space I was going to let between us for a while.

I tucked that thought away for later and then started to concentrate on the clouds. I guess since we were still in a bit of turmoil, the clouds had stayed overhead, not breaking up too much. I called on the same energy I'd used earlier as I raised my hand overhead, then willed a bolt of lightning to do as I bid. When I brought my hand down, pointing to the far right, the lightning bowed to my desire. I was lost in my own thoughts and didn't realize that Sam was still talking when she reached out to touch my shoulder. I nearly jumped out of my skin, but I didn't move the direction where my hand was pointing.

"Ro said they can be here in less than five minutes," Sam reported.

I nodded, breathing deeply. I realized I'd only used my index finger to direct the bolt, and as I stood there watching it sizzle, I wondered what else I could do. I relaxed the other fingers in my hand only slightly, then thrust my fingers out wide and stiff so I was holding my palm almost flat above the earth. As soon as I had my fingers spread out, an almost instantaneous movement, the lightning bolt splintered to match my fingers. I was amazed. One bolt came from the heavens, but as it came closer to the ground, around the height of the treetops, it shot out in four slivers. I smiled to myself. I could do more than I originally thought. I flexed one finger at a time, then watched as the corresponding splinter of lightning danced as I moved each finger.

"Show-off," Sam whispered. "You've really got her attention now."

We both glanced at our hostage. If she hadn't looked scared before, she was petrified now as she watched the lightning dance around the edge of the woods. I wasn't sure how I'd accomplished it, but the ground didn't burn where the bolt met it. Good planning or force of my will? I'd have to ask around later.

SAM 121

$\mathcal{I}$ felt a new force coming long before I saw anyone. Glancing to the left, I found Ruth strolling out of the woods. She was followed by Aurora, with Ken bringing up the rear. The look of relief on Ruth's face made me smile. If I'd ever doubted that she cared for us, the look on her face wiped those ideas away.

As Ruth and Ken walked over to stand by us, Aurora stood to the edge of the little clearing and folded her arms over her chest. She cocked her head to the side, observing our hostage. When she started squinting one eye, I wasn't sure if she was appreciating Emily's work or if she was thinking of what to say. The only other possibility was she'd seen this faerie before and was trying to recall exactly where she'd seen her. I didn't get a chance to think on this for long though, because Ruth was grabbing me for a rib-bruising hug.

"Sam, we were so worried," Ruth said breathlessly, but she didn't let me go.

Ken came around, patting me on the shoulder. I flinched, dropping my shoulder as quick as I could with Ruth's arms still around me. The tenderness of the bite wound brought me back to the reality of what we'd just been through.

Ruth pulled back, eyeing me. "Emily said you were bitten. Let's see," she said, reaching for the collar of my shirt.

I broke from her grip, backing away. "It'll be okay. You can look at it later," I told her. I didn't want any more attention right now.

I glanced past her to see Aurora striding up to the last faerie standing, arms still crossed. When she got within three feet of the faerie, she stopped. Glancing in our direction momentarily, she called out, "You did this, Em?" indicating the faerie with her chin.

"I guess I did," Emily replied flatly, as she held her palms out to inspect them. It was as if she didn't really believe she'd performed magic.

Aurora nodded, then walked all around the faerie. "Olga, it's been a long time," she addressed the faerie in a professionally distant tone.

The faerie watched every move Ro made. We could see the whites of her eyes, confirming that she was having second thoughts about having helped with my kidnapping. Just as the leader of the group changed his appearance before he talked to us, Olga now did the same. All the fairies had started out with stringy, dirty hair, but where the leader had started with a gray cast to his skin, Olga's skin was sallow. That changed, too.

Instead of the near scarecrow she'd originally appeared as, Olga was now almost as filled out and as tall as Aurora. Her hair was a little brassier in the sunlight compared to Aurora's blonde locks.

Aurora raised one open palmed hand away from her body in the direction of the faerie, then she flicked her wrist. The bands of electricity that were holding the faerie disappeared.

Olga stood stock still for a few heartbeats then dropped to her knees in front of Aurora and made a great production of bowing at Aurora's feet.

"Great one, it has been too long. I did not know the child was related to you," Olga said, her head flat on the ground at Aurora's feet.

I wasn't sure I'd heard her right and glanced sharply at Ruth. Ruth shook her head as if to say we'd talk later, so I let it go.

"Olga, we need to talk," Aurora announced. She assumed a military like stance, with her arms tucked behind her back, then strode slowly around the faerie.

"Yes, your grace, anything. I only beg your mercy," Olga replied, sounding as if she was near tears.

Emily stepped closer to me, reaching for one of the belt loops on my shorts. I frowned at her quickly, not understanding what she was doing before she thought to me, *"'Your Grace?' Is she serious?"*

I just shrugged. I had no idea what she was referring to either.

Ken stepped out and around us, as if he was acting as a shield for all of us, and I had to lean around him to keep watching the show. Aurora would take a few steps, pause, cock her head to the side, take a few more steps, and repeat the process.

"Olga, you need to tell us what your involvement has been regarding Susan White. Then I want to know why your little band of marauders has been playing hide and seek with us today."

How the hell did Ro jump from my kidnapping to our mother? What had she figured out that we missed? I glanced at Ruth to find a shocked look on her face as well.

"I do not know a Susan White, Your Grace," Olga replied.

"Oh, do stand up, Olga. You know you can't run, not now."

Olga slowly came to her feet, hands folded low in front of her body, while she kept her face averted to the ground. "As you wish, Your Grace."

"You may look upon me, Olga," Aurora told her as she raised one hand in a motion toward us. "Look upon these young ladies, Olga. You will remember another that looked as they do, but many years have passed since you last saw her." This was a statement, not a question. I read into her tone that you didn't want to piss her off.

Olga raised her gaze to us as Aurora had indicated. She visibly swallowed then nodded once before she dropped her gaze back to the ground. "Yes, Your Grace, I do remember one who looked as they do."

"Olga, tell me all that you know about her. Tell us all what the Fae had to do with Susan White."

Olga glanced quickly at us then back to Aurora. I could see more fear on her face than when she was watching Emily play with the lightning bolts. "I did not have direct involvement with this Susan White, Your Grace," she said, ducking her head to stare at the ground again.

"Ah, but you do know what happened. You know why the Fae were involved."

Emily let go of my belt loop to stand shoulder to shoulder with me. Ruth reached out for my hand, and I let her take it as a knot began tightening in my stomach.

Olga nodded slightly, acknowledging she did know.

"I think it best you start from the beginning, Olga," Aurora commanded.

Olga nodded again before she raised her eyes to us. She then stood stock still as she began her story. The only problem was she spoke in a language I didn't recognize.

Not wanting to interrupt the confession, we all remained quiet. Ruth would hang her head when Olga's voice would rise or sound bitter. Aurora would nod and ask more questions in the same language. Occasionally, she'd glance back to our group or nod toward us when she asked a question, the look on her face grim.

The exchange took almost half an hour, then Olga suddenly dropped to Aurora's feet again. I had the feeling Olga would've kissed the hem of Aurora's dress if she'd thought it would've helped her case. She seemed relieved, but from what, I didn't have a clue. Was she relieved to have cleared her conscience with a confession, or that her life was being spared? We had no clues because just as quickly as she'd dropped to the ground, she was gone. No *poof.* Just gone.

Aurora was still wearing the sun dress she'd had on when I'd found her reading my journal, which suddenly felt like something that had happened years ago. I was stunned by the events of the past few hours. If Aurora was shocked by the day's events, her expression didn't show it as she strode toward us. Emily was busily glancing all around us. I guessed she was as unsure as I was that all the faeries were truly gone.

Ruth gave my hand a squeeze, and I felt more secure standing between the two of them, with Ken as a defense in front of us.

"Well, are you going to share what that was all about?" Emily asked.

"Just as soon as we get you back home," Aurora started. "Ruth, where shall we land?"

Ruth looked around our group then nodded as she said, "Let's try for the girls' rooms first. We can see who is in, who is out, then change locations if we need to."

Aurora was nodding as she continued to walk toward us. Between one step and the next she was gone.

Ken turned back and winked at Emily. "I guess you no longer need me to assist you, my dear."

He bowed slightly in her direction and was gone as well.

Ruth released my hand, swinging around to stand in front of us. She looked tired, and it showed in her eyes, but it didn't hide the fear. "Girls, I don't know what we're about to learn. I've waited for answers for so many years." She exhaled then looked to the ground. "I've got butterflies and dread all rolled together." She held out a hand to each of us. "Let's go home."

We each took a hand, and suddenly we were back in my room. The tug at the center of my body that I normally felt when we jumped was no longer apparent to me. My journal was still sitting on my bed. Ken was standing to one side of the window, peeking at the side yard below, and he raised one finger to his lips to tell us to be quiet.

Glancing through my open door, I could see the back of Ro's dress at the top of the stairs. She'd checked out the house, and we all held our breath, waiting to see if the coast was clear. Ro disappeared from in front of our eyes, and I watched as the tension left Ken's shoulders as he let out a pensive sigh.

We all jumped when Aurora popped into the middle of the room with us. "All clear," she announced, handing a note to Ruth. "It looks like Nate and Slade took Don out for dinner. Nate knowing your secrets may turn out for the best after all, Ruth."

Ruth looked around the room at each of us. "Do I need to sit down?" she asked, giving Aurora her full attention.

"Yeah, let's all go down to the dining table and get

comfortable," she said, but she disappeared without letting anyone reply.

"Well, let's get this over with," Ruth said, taking a deep breath. As she exhaled, she popped out of the room as well.

"Girls, you go on ahead. I think I'll go out to the barn and visit the beasts. This is really your family's business, not mine," Ken said.

"But, Ken, to us you are family," I said, reaching for his hand.

"Thank you, Sam, but witch business, especially this, shouldn't be discussed in front of wizards first," he replied, holding up his hands as if in surrender. "I'll hear all about it later. Ruth needs you both right now. I fear what you're about to learn, and you both need to be with your aunt...and Aurora, of course."

Dropping his hands, he smiled kindly then disappeared.

"Well, we might as well get this over. Ken's right. Ruth needs us to support her right now," Emily said, walking to the door. "And, for some reason, I think going down there is a journey that needs to be walked."

"Fix this first?" I asked, pointing to my shoulder.

Emily only nodded as I turned to let her have greater access. Having that pain removed gave me time to think about the new pain we were about to share.

EMILY 120

*O*nce we were all seated around the table, Aurora waved her hand, then a coffee cake and steaming mugs of coffee appeared. Taking the knife that had appeared in her hand, she cut slices of cake, placing them on plates that appeared just as she'd begin to lay a piece down. She'd then pass the plate to one of us, and I began to get the impression she was stalling. I would've been irritated if I didn't already know that Aurora really liked to eat, so I let it go.

After we were all served and Aurora had taken her first bite, she took a deep breath, leaned back in her chair, then began to reveal the mystery of our beginnings.

Olga had informed Aurora that, in the months before we were conceived, a witch had approached some of the Unseelie around the capital. Many were becoming restless, as the Reagan administration wasn't giving them enough entertainment.

The witch in question was the matriarch of her own family but, sadly, was the last female in the line. She'd raised one son and wasn't happy that she'd soon face the loss of her seat on the Witches Brew. She knew other witches had stolen children, passing them off as their own. So, she hatched a plan to have her own son marry a witch, hoping the resulting child would be a daughter, which she could then claim as her heir to the family seat.

Her plans never materialized, because no other witch family wanted anything to do with her son. While handsome, he wasn't the most pleasant person to be around. She realized she'd have to steal what she truly wanted, and to do that she'd have to mask her own powers, as well as the faint residuals in her son's blood, before they could get close to any other witch.

"Not only would she need to mask the powers, but she'd need her not-so-appealing son to seem like a movie star. This was when she approached the Unseelies. She promised to give Susan to them, after she had a child."

When Ruth heard this, she shuddered visibly, but kept her composure as Aurora continued the story.

"So, the Unseelies were sent out across the country to locate a new witch who wasn't adept with her powers yet. Grandma X seemed to know many of the family names and locations, which she shared with the Unseelies. It didn't take them long to find your family," Aurora said, frowning. "The faeries, being experts at masking their powers and laying on the charm, convinced your sister to help them on an overseas mission. She truly thought she was going to help save the world, but it was just a plan to get her away from her home and family."

Grandma X's son was a member of the mission workers, and they both traveled in the group of faeries so the Unseelie could mask all the powers. Grandma X would appear from time to time and even met Susan. By the end of the summer, Susan and the son had become close. He treated her like a queen, as if she meant the world to him. Susan, being a doe-eyed girl from rural northern Arkansas, was completely taken in, and fell in love. He made her many promises, with marriage being the ultimate carrot dangled in front of her.

"Ruth, she did marry him. At least that's what Olga said. Susan and this man were apparently married in Scotland." She looked around the table at each of us as she took a deep breath and continued. "Olga only knew his first name: Joseph." She paused to let us absorb the knowledge.

Our father's name is Joseph. Nope, it didn't strike a chord with me.

"Ruth, do you know of any families with a son by the name of Joseph?" asked Aurora.

Ruth looked at the coffee cake on the table for a very long time before she shook her head. "I can't think of anyone by that name. But how would I know him if his mother is the last in his family? There are lots of families whose lines have died out, and lots of people have lost their seats. My mother was holding our seat at the time, and I can't remember her sharing any of the names back then."

Aurora told us it had been the middle of June when they'd wed. Joseph's mother would lurk around the couple, only showing herself to Susan when it was necessary. Before the end of July, the faerie entourage that had accompanied them became bored again.

A few of them caught news of the Iran-Iraq war winding down and decided to go play in that sandbox. When some of the faeries left, it caused some unrest with the whole group, and they became lax in escorting the couple. Apparently, they became so lax that they either intentionally let their guard down so Susan could sense the others' powers, or they just didn't care anymore.

Aurora thought they did it to cause a rift for their own entertainment. What better way to amuse themselves than to watch a newlywed couple fight and split up? Susan began to sense powers and wasn't sure what she was really feeling. It wasn't until Joseph's mother returned to the scene, unaware that the Fae had dropped the shields, that Susan truly knew who she'd married. Of course, there was a big blow up, and Susan tried to leave the group.

"My guess is this is why Susan moved away to have the girls. She wanted to keep them safe from her mother-in-law. Since everyone knew where Susan was from, she knew she had to hide," Aurora said quietly. She watched us all, waiting for some sign of our distress. Ruth was most disturbed by the whole story.

"Olga said Joseph's mother was so upset with the faeries for dropping their guards, allowing Susan to discover her true identity, that she recanted on the deal. Grandma X told the faeries she'd see them in hell before she'd let them have Susan," Aurora continued.

Sam and I glanced at one another as the story was winding down. Ruth continued nodding her head slightly, her lips tightly pursed, the wheels turning in her head. I wasn't sure if she was putting pieces of the puzzle together or if she was trying to remember details of our mother's return from Europe.

"No, she tried to see Susan in hell first," Ruth mumbled, almost to herself, shaking her head. She wrapped her arms around her body, looking to at me then Sam before she looked at Aurora again. "Did Olga say why they came here now?"

"Our otherness is known to the rest of the magical beings. You know they can sense when witches come into their powers. The faeries are still pissed over Joseph's mother recanting on their deal, and when word got out that Susan died, they got curious. They sent out an entourage who discovered she'd died in childbirth. Being the troublemakers that they are, they've been watching your family for a while," Aurora said.

Ruth narrowed her eyes at her best friend then nodded as she motioned for Aurora to continue.

"They've intermittently kept up with you. They've kept tabs on who was coming and going around your house," she swept a hand through the air indicating this very house. "When all the earthquakes started hitting national headlines, they started looking more closely. They knew the stories about young witches coming into their powers. They did the math, and considering the proximity to this location, they decided to take a chance." Aurora turned and looked at Sam closely then shook her head. "It kind of paid off for the faeries."

"Not if you consider their ringleader is toast right now," I said dryly, raising my eyebrows at her.

She nodded in agreement, smiling back at me with her pearly whites. "And have I mentioned how proud we are of you?" But her smile faded when she glanced back at Ruth, who sat stony faced. "What?" she asked of her friend.

"So, the faeries guessed that we'd lied about the girls—or at least about their dying at birth," Ruth said. She stood and began pacing around the table. She patted each of us lightly on the shoulder, almost absentmindedly as she paced by us. "If the fairies figured this out, could their other grandmother have, too?" She pondered out loud. "Do you think they'll tell her?"

"We can only wait and see. No good deed ever goes unnoticed," Aurora told her.

"They were pretty pissed when they left," Sam said, looking around to me. "You did give them quite a show."

"I don't regret what I did, and I kept my word. Olga is probably already back with them," I said in my defense.

"Olga won't go back to them now," Aurora pointed out. "They'll think she's betrayed them, just by having been held prisoner. If she returns to them now, she'll be an outcast. She'll have better luck joining the Seelies now."

We looked at her, confused, and she elaborated. "They won't trust her now. It's just how they are. Once you betray them, they're done with you. If she went back to them, which I know she didn't, they might even kill her. Olga is smarter than that," Aurora ended.

"Just out of curiosity, what was with all the 'Your Grace' Olga kept calling you?" Sam asked.

Aurora didn't miss a beat. "Oh, that crap," she said, with a dismissive wave of her hand. "My grandmother was something of a legend back in the day, and they considered her royalty. I suppose it gets handed down." Finishing with a shrug, she looked at Ruth.

To me, it looked like she was asking if the story sounded believable.

Ruth gave her a short nod then turned her attention back to us. "Girls, right now I don't know what all of this means. Once your DNA test comes back and I present that, along with you, to the consul, we can ask them to investigate this plot, which apparently began before Susan ever left home." Ruth finished with a long sigh, giving each of us full eye contact.

Her sadness was leaking through more now. "I know that won't bring her back, but I owe it to her to protect you. Even if that means involving the consul now, so be it."

"So, what do we do now?" I asked.

"You and your sister need to stay close to each other as much as possible. I now know that, trained or not, together the two of you can be a force to be reckoned with. I doubt the faeries will try anything again anytime soon, but if your other grandmother finds out, things might get a little hairy. She knows what your mother looked like at your age, and if she were to see you right now, there would be little doubt as to who you are. If I knew who she was, I'd take matters into my own hands and pay her a visit myself. Since we don't even know her name, we wait. No sense inviting trouble before we have to."

Aurora watched Ruth's every movement like a bird of prey. Her face didn't reveal what was going on in that brain of hers, and that worried me. Her face was completely blank.

Ruth went on, "In the next few days, I'll leave for my appointment with the other assigned consul members to see this mess out west. I hope you'll stay here, but I know you're both itching to move into your own place." She started to smile again, like her spirits were lifting. Maybe she was looking forward to an empty nest as much as Don was. "I'm sure Nathan will be more than willing to go house hunting with you. Don can take care of the finances if you do find something before I get back."

And with that, our meeting was over. We'd learned some interesting facts about our paternal side of the family, but not enough to solve the entire mystery. I'm not sure I looked forward to learning the whole truth.

ʔ

EMILY 121

A week had passed since Ruth left on her consul assignment, and we were continuing to help out around the house in her absence. Sam had grown more at ease when around the horses, and she changed clothes less often due to a reduction in accidents. It was still dirty work, but it was also a clean living.

We grew to depend on Nate more each day as he taught us the finer points of farm life. As he pointed out many times, the finer points are to stay away from farm life! Nate was convinced that, as soon as he finished his master's degree, he wouldn't step foot back on the farm to work. Managing the farm, maybe, but not hard work that caused blisters on your hands or sweat on your brow. Don, on the other hand, sang the praises of living a simpler life. He was still clueless as to the true nature of his wife's work, and on numerous occasions I caught Nate rolling his eyes behind his dad's back.

Mid-morning, a black Jeep Grand Cherokee came rolling up the driveway and parked in the circle. We were all sitting in the side yard, enjoying the cloudy sky with the wind that had picked up, promising rain.

I knew immediately who was in the car. I'd learned the talent of sensing powers—at least the ones I already knew. Aurora stepped out of the Jeep then stretched like she'd been driving for many hours. Of course, I knew it to be a lie because, like Ruth, she could jump at will. My guess was that she'd just left Ruth's side, wherever she was on assignment for the consul.

Aurora slid her sunglasses to the top of her head, attempting to hold her hair back like a band and allowing us to see her eyes as she walked to the patio area where we were relaxing.

"Good morning one and all," Aurora hailed as she got closer.

She was smiling, but somehow, I didn't think it was a genuine smile which would light her face and make her eyes sparkle. This smile was all business, and the rest of her face matched it.

Don rose from his seat, met her at the edge of the patio, and kissed her on the cheek while making small talk. "Nate, you want to give me a hand shoeing that black monster? I'm sure these ladies have lots to discuss," he said, turning to the rest of us.

How he knew that was beyond me. Maybe he did know more about Ruth's true calling than he ever let on.

"Girls, I'm sure Ro would like some coffee. It looks like she's driven all night," Don said.

"Don, you are so observant. I was just coming to see if the girls wanted to take a shopping trip with me." She smiled, but it didn't change the look I now perceived as worried.

"Come on, Ro. I'll put a fresh pot on just for you," Sam said, rising to head in the back door to the kitchen.

Aurora fell in step behind Sam, and I rose to bring up the

rear. Nate, who was following Don to the barn, patted my shoulder as he passed, adding a wink.

Once I'd closed the backdoor, Aurora let out a sigh. "Where are your phones?" she asked in a clipped tone.

Sam and I exchanged a look. I put my hand out, thought of my phone, and suddenly it was in my hand, with the message light flashing. I glanced up at Aurora, frowning as I tapped in my password.

"Your aunt sent you both the same message. When you didn't answer immediately, she sent me here to make sure you both read it. And to make sure nothing had happened," she said, then continued. "Let Sam read with you. The sooner you both read it, the sooner we can get you two packed."

Sam came over to stand by my side as I opened Ruth's message. We read in silence: *S/E. Hope all is well. In Northern CA. Troll war unresolved & I cannot leave yet. Hurricane to hit east coast. Need you to go w/ Ro to minimize impact the others will cause. Will be messy. Sending Ken soon. Mind Ro and watch each other's backs. Will join as soon as I can. Love, R.*

"Others?" Sam muttered, glancing up to Aurora, who stood with a cup of coffee already in her hand. "There's something coming in with the hurricane?"

"Children, did you really think a hurricane was nothing more than a tropical depression on steroids?" Aurora asked, lifting her eyebrows in mock surprise.

"Well yeah, but what others are we talking about?" I asked.

"Blood licking, life sucking creatures of the deep. Who else? So, hurry and pack a few things. We're heading to the east coast. Landfall is expected tomorrow morning in the Carolinas, and we need to be there before they are. Oh, and one more thing," she said, her face going serious, "they can be worse than faeries."

I looked at Sam, my brows drawn together. *"Other creatures?"* I thought to Sam. *"What could be as bad the Fae?"*

She shook her head. *"I don't know, but I'm afraid we're about to find out."*

REALM OF LIGHTS

HIERARCHY

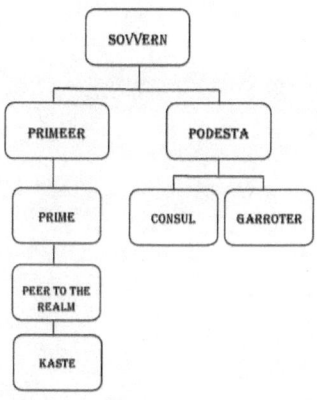